About the Author

Anne Morenn was born in London. She has lived and worked in England, Europe and Asia, and is currently based in France.

Second Chances in Brittany

Anne Morren

Second Chances in Brittany

Vanguard Press

VANGUARD PAPERBACK

© Copyright 2024
Anne Morren

The right of Anne Morren to be identified as author of
this work has been asserted by her in accordance with the
Copyright, Designs and Patents Act 1988.

All Rights Reserved

No reproduction, copy or transmission of this publication
may be made without written permission.
No paragraph of this publication may be reproduced,
copied or transmitted save with the written permission of the publisher, or in accordance with
the provisions
of the Copyright Act 1956 (as amended).

Any person who commits any unauthorised act in relation to
this publication may be liable to criminal
prosecution and civil claims for damages.

A CIP catalogue record for this title is
available from the British Library.

ISBN 978 1 80016 778 0

This is a work of fiction. Names, characters, businesses, places, events and incidents are either the product of the author's imagination or used in a fictitious manner. Any resemblance to actual persons, living or dead, or actual events is purely coincidental.

Vanguard Press is an imprint of
Pegasus Elliot Mackenzie Publishers Ltd.
www.pegasuspublishers.com

First Published in 2024

Vanguard Press
Sheraton House Castle Park
Cambridge England

Printed & Bound in Great Britain

Dedication

To my neighbour Martial Espérience for his warm welcome and constant smile.

Acknowledgements

Thank you to Vicky Gory for her encouragement and a thoroughgoing check on my punctuation.

Author's note

This story is set in 2013, when the United Kingdom was still part of the European Union, allowing free movement of people, capital, goods and services across the Channel in both directions. At that time the British had the right to live and work anywhere in Europe, and had full access to the health services of any European country. This is no longer true.

1

On the last Friday afternoon in April, Sarah Pullen sat in the first floor waiting-room of the neurosurgery department at the Clinique de la Visitation in Saint-Malo on the Channel coast of the French region of Brittany.

Her husband, James, had accompanied her, as he always did. He was becoming increasingly impatient and angry about the delay to her consultation, muttering under his breath about the lackadaisical time-keeping habits of the bloody French. Sarah didn't greatly appreciate delay; until recently she'd led a busy professional life of hard work and long hours, and she considered sitting doing nothing as the worst aspect of retirement. But whatever it entailed, this appointment was necessary.

Sarah was suffering from extremely disabling headaches. Unusually painful, they occurred first thing every morning and, although disappearing around midday, they left her exhausted, and inevitably recurred next day. Painkillers had had no effect, and relaxation techniques had had no success. James had insisted she see a doctor; he'd made the appointment and taken her to the general practitioner himself.

At the surgery James had taken over the consultation as if Sarah wasn't present. The doctor had tried to focus on Sarah's diet and pattern of exercise, but James would only accept a hospital investigation, hence this appointment for an MRI scan. Sarah knew that James would accompany her into the consultant's office here and take over that interview as well; she didn't have the habit of asserting herself in his presence. But she did hope for an opportunity to ask her own questions. The scan was intended to find tumours and other abnormalities, and whatever was found, Sarah wanted to learn how to cope with it.

She knew that her symptoms could be caused by a brain tumour, but she wasn't wholly convinced that would be the sole cause. She'd always considered that headaches were connected to stress. Undeniably there was far more tension in her life since she'd retired and moved to Brittany, and she was sure that was a contributing factor. Whatever the outcome of the scan, that stress needed to be reduced. This prolonged wait in calm surroundings had provided Sarah with a rare opportunity to review her way of life.

Sarah and James were the same age. They'd met in their first year at university in London, Sarah studying history and intending to teach, James studying economics and destined for the international finance arena.

They'd married in the August after graduating, before both started work in London. Sarah had tried hard to do everything possible to please James, but had found it difficult to keep him in a good mood. She'd fallen into the habit of avoiding arguments by deferring to his judgement and letting him have his own way.

Unfortunately, James' life hadn't turned out as he'd expected. He'd taken a junior post in a well-known firm of international financial advisors, but hadn't realised that this carried no guarantee of a career. Every year the company took on more graduates than it could ever promote, intending to employ them in lower grade positions for a few years before letting them go; only those who'd proved unusually superb would be taken on as permanent staff. After two years' work, James' contract ended summarily.

He'd been completely unprepared; he had credit-card debt and no savings. He'd immediately applied to other similar firms, with no result; they were only interested in this year's graduate cannon-fodder. In desperation he took the only job he could find at short notice, with an accountancy firm in Sheffield. Later on he'd begun working as an accounting contractor. He hadn't managed to build up capital, and now that he was retired, his only income was the state pension.

Sarah had hoped to re-join James in Sheffield by obtaining a teaching post there, but there were none advertised. However, she did find a position with a computer software company; they offered six weeks' training and then a position as a business systems analyst. Sarah took the job without imagining she'd enjoy it, but it proved unexpectedly full of interest. The company provided systems to financial institutions, and Sarah became a very successful implementation manager.

After a year she began studying in the evenings for a master's degree in business administration; on qualification she'd moved to a prestigious software organisation in London, returning to Sheffield at weekends. She'd then been head-hunted for work in Europe, which proved a success. Working long hours with no opportunity to spend her enormous salary on inessentials, she'd invested in her pension, in properties let out to rent, in stock-exchange securities and in James.

But she'd continued to defer to James at home, even when subsidising him from her earnings. When she thought about James, which she did often, her imagination always pictured the charismatic student she'd fallen in love with, the charm and the confidence he'd then displayed, his attractive personality and his winning smile.

She'd looked forward to living with her beloved James when they both retired; she'd thought of the move to Brittany as a second honeymoon. But in their years apart, James had evolved from the magnetic and captivating young man she'd adored into an embittered domestic tyrant with a hasty and irrational temper. Now retired, with both of them at home, there was no escape, and James simply refused to let her go anywhere on her own.

It had been James who'd decided to retire to France. He'd suggested Normandy; he'd seen magazine advertising of photogenic Norman farmhouses for low costs. Sarah had investigated them, and discovered reasons for the bargain prices. They all needed renovation, lacked connection to essential services, and were too far from public transport, shops and doctors. She'd begun a search for well-built, well-serviced dwellings in towns. James' only stipulation had been that they live near a cross-channel ferry terminal so that he could stay in touch with his family in Sussex.

Sarah had found the ideal residence in Brittany, in Saint-Edern, a community in the conurbation of Saint-Malo, only a short distance from the Saint-Malo ferry terminal. It was a penthouse with high ceilings taking the whole top floor of a well-designed modern block of flats. It had a superb view over the river estuary, and a private south-facing terrace opened out from its lounge. It wasn't small; it took the same space as the two three-bedroomed flats on the floor below. It was presented as a three-bedroomed apartment with a separate lounge and dining room, but Sarah had combined two bedrooms to create a huge master bedroom, and had turned the third bedroom into a spacious dressing-room. She'd removed the wall between the lounge and dining room to create a magnificently large salon, with four enormous floor-to-ceiling double windows overlooking the estuary and facing the sunset.

The block had a secure underground garage where the flat owned three parking spaces. It was near bus services to Saint-Malo centre and the outlying shopping malls. Locally there were small shops, cafés, restaurants, a choice of sandy beaches, and a large yacht harbour. Local government had organised a centre for pensioners, dispensing welcome advice but also offering leisure activities and social interaction for those no longer young. Saint-Edern was just far enough from the ferry and the famous walled town of Saint-Malo to avoid the major throngs of tourists, but was well within the catchment area of Saint-Malo's large modern hospital and local specialist medical services.

James had initially been reluctant to live in 'a mere flat', but once he'd seen the sheer size of the penthouse, and the view from the windows, he'd realised that it was spectacular enough to boast about. He could see himself entertaining there in style; the salon could host a cocktail party for sixty. After purchase and remodelling, Sarah had rented the minimum of essential furniture, and they'd moved in.

Sarah had suggested modern designer furniture, but James had insisted on antiques. They'd driven together round northern France searching for suitable pieces, and once these were in place the result had been superb. Mellow carved and polished wood and fine old leather blended well with the pieces of modern sculpture and the paintings by local artists which Sarah also acquired. The dining table expanded to seat sixteen and professional appliances installed in the kitchen would enable catered dinners.

Sarah had been intent on meeting and making friends in the local community. She and James had joined the Saint-Edern Social Club. which held a meeting every Wednesday evening and organised club expeditions to historic or picturesque places at weekends. They'd also joined a Qi Gong exercise class at the pensioners' centre, though James had soon given up, not taking kindly to Chinese philosophy and the deliberate measured pace of the exercises. But together they'd explored the footpaths around the local coastline and the villages in the Saint-Malo conurbation. For a brief period, life had seemed ideal.

But slowly the atmosphere had changed. James became almost permanently angry. He complained about the flat. He ridiculed their neighbours. He refused to eat in local restaurants. He vehemently discouraged Sarah from attempting to cook any local dishes, in particular refusing to eat the seafood for which the region was famous. He compared everything in Saint-Edern unfavourably to its equivalent in England. He seemed to regret the whole idea of living in France.

The penthouse, so expensively converted and furnished with convivial social gatherings in mind, didn't host a single party. Strangely, for a man who'd insisted on a home suitable for showing off, James didn't now want to ask either the local French or the local English into his own home, or even invite his sister to come to Saint-Edern on holiday.

In fact, James had sunk back into the solitary life he'd lived in the years while Sarah was away from home. He didn't own a computer of his own, so he'd commandeered Sarah's, and bought subscriptions to internet games; he spent hours playing them during the day, and resented being disturbed. Most evenings he spent watching movies streamed to the television. He preferred storylines involving physical violence and hand-to-hand combat and he dismissed Sarah's suggestions for different films or interesting documentaries advertised in the TV guide, so she spent the evenings trying to blank out the television by reading a book.

There was no conversation, no shared interests. The loving companion who'd suggested moving to France had morphed into a bored and unpredictable bully who lost his temper at the slightest check. Sarah had begun to wonder if he cared for her at all. He was certainly making it difficult for her to care for him.

***

At last a nurse came to take Sarah to the consultant. As always, James insisted on accompanying her. When the consultant greeted them, James immediately launched into a description of Sarah's symptoms as if she wasn't present. This was completely unnecessary, since James was simply reiterating information contained in the general practitioner's notes, which were clearly visible on the consultant's computer screen, and it annoyed the doctor by delaying his normal pre-scan procedure.

Ignoring James, the specialist spoke to Sarah, carefully explaining in clear simple French the type of MRI scan he intended to conduct. He explained the consent form as well, in good English, but Sarah was very willing to consent because she wanted the scan result. The consultant then asked his nurse to take Sarah to the scanner unit on the floor above.

James immediately rose to go with them, but the consultant forestalled him. "Non, monsieur, it is not necessary to accompany your wife. There is space in the scanner for only one head!"

James stomped into the waiting room with bad grace as the nurse ushered Sarah into the lift. In the scanner anteroom on the second floor, the nurse explained the procedure in detail, checked that Sarah wasn't wearing metal objects and dressed her in a hospital gown. In the scanner room she helped Sarah to lie down on the table of the machine while the consultant explained that the table would slide into the tube-shaped scanner, and asked Sarah to stay as still as she could for the fifteen minutes of the scan. He explained that the machine was extremely noisy, and the nurse fitted earplugs to counteract this. Sarah lay down on the table, and signalled she was ready. The process began.

It was fifteen minutes before the session was over. Despite the earplugs, the noise had left Sarah feeling shaken, but with the help of the nurse she dressed and waited in the anteroom, gratefully sipping a fruit juice. After some time, the consultant joined her. He immediately relayed the good news. There was no sign of any tumour. In fact, he couldn't see anything even mildly wrong. Sarah relaxed with relief.

The consultant apologised for not solving the problem, but added that his patients were always happier when he failed to find anything. "I'll tell your doctor I've found no obvious cause of headaches," he said, "but there are many possible causes, connected to other parts of the body, or to something you eat. Your doctor will want to consult other specialists. Meanwhile, I'll give you a prescription to alleviate the pain."

As Sarah had already discovered that painkillers had no effect on these headaches, she was quite sure that she wouldn't use the prescription. But out of politeness she folded the paper into her handbag, shook hands, and thanked the consultant warmly. The friendly nurse said her goodbyes at the lift after calling it.

When the lift arrived, in a sudden uncontrollable desire to have more time to herself, Sarah pressed the button for the ground floor instead of the first floor waiting room, and walked out into a small courtyard garden she'd briefly glimpsed as she arrived. She sat on a bench in fresh air and sunshine. The peace was broken only by a bird intermittently singing at the top of the central tree. The windows of the first floor waiting room faced the other way; she could enjoy a few more minutes beyond James' control.

She carefully reviewed what had happened. The consultant most likely to find a physical cause of headaches hadn't found one. Sarah's first thought was that the lack of a physical cause made a psychological cause or contribution more likely. She really needed to cut the stress out of her life.

Within the last four weeks, due to the headaches, her entire social life had ceased. James had told telephone callers in his ungrammatical, badly pronounced French that she was in bed and very ill. She was sure she'd heard him answer the doorbell; as no one came in, he must have turned people away. In four weeks the only other people she'd talked to were the general practitioner and today's consultant and his nurse.

This isolation wouldn't be good for anyone, and she knew that meeting two people today had lifted her spirits markedly. Clearly she needed to get out of the flat and into the company of other people. But to do that, she had to find a way to sidle past James' controlling habits without provoking his atrocious temper.

She started to deal with this question logically as if it was a problem at work. She started listing in her mind the people she would have met during a week prior to this illness, and then tried to think of a way of meeting them again. She very soon decided that the simplest people to meet would be the Qi Gong class at three o'clock on Monday afternoon. By midday the headache had usually diminished, and by three o'clock she would be in relatively normal health, tired but not in any pain.

The Qi Gong class was a friendly bunch of eight men and women with an inspirational teacher, and she'd enjoyed being part of the group. She quite liked Qi Gong as an exercise. It didn't demand much room or any special equipment, and she'd formed the habit of practising some part of the routine every evening while she was on her own in the large bathroom. It certainly kept all the muscles of the body flexible.

Sarah decided to persuade James to let her attend the class. Even if he accompanied her, she would be out of the penthouse and in the company of other people, but James probably wouldn't want to do Qi Gong himself, which would be an added bonus.

Having settled on a course of action, Sarah took the lift up to the second floor, then down again to the first so that she arrived in the waiting room from the right direction. She felt guilty at this subterfuge, but, as she'd expected, James had been watching the lift closely and was still furious at being kept out of the scanner session. "You've been up there long enough," he growled. "What were they doing, giving you a new head?"

Sarah noted that venting his anger at being side-lined by the consultant took priority over asking for the scan result. She looked at the floor to hide her opinion. "The scan takes a quarter-hour," she said, "and then the consultant had to check through all the evidence. But he's confirmed there isn't a tumour. Actually he said he couldn't see anything wrong at all."

James was suddenly alert and interested. "You're sure that's what he said? That there's nothing wrong?"

"Yes, he did. He'll report to our doctor, and he thinks I'll be asked to see a different type of specialist."

"Yes, yes, that would be on the cards. But it's really good news he didn't find anything at all." James sounded so very pleased that Sarah wondered if he really did care for her after all. "Now let's get on home, it's nearly time for dinner."

On arriving home, James poured himself a whisky, and as usual sank into his armchair in front of the television. Sarah searched the kitchen for a meal which he would accept, and tried a first course of tinned liver pâté on toast, a main course of supermarket packet beef casserole with potatoes and frozen peas, and the baker's pear tart for dessert, served with tinned cream.

At the table, James opened a new bottle of wine, poured a large glass for himself and a smaller one for Sarah. He tasted his. "Huh, it's nothing like as good as that gangling twit in the wine shop said it would be, but I suppose it'll have to do."

He then found fault with every course. The pâté was poor quality. The casserole didn't taste like beef at all. The potatoes were boiled instead of sautéed, which Sarah must know he preferred. They'd had peas yesterday; weren't there other green vegetables which could have been served instead? There wasn't enough fruit in the tart, and he would have preferred it with custard.

It was the usual level of complaint which James had produced at every meal Sarah had served for the last forty years, but she'd never been able to ignore it and still found it hurtful. After stacking and starting the dishwasher, she felt so stressed out that she said she was going to bed early. James was engrossed in watching a film streamed to the television, and merely grunted in acknowledgement.

Exhausted by the events of the day, Sarah fell asleep as soon as her head hit the pillow.

2

Probably due to her early night, Sarah woke at six o'clock on Saturday instead of at eight o'clock when the radio-alarm was set to begin. As always, she woke with a clear head and no pain.

Normally the headache arrived at about nine o'clock. Sarah's logical mind questioned whether the headache would come today at seven o'clock, an hour after waking, or time itself for nine as usual. She could only wait and see.

With at least an hour to herself, she continued her thoughts of the afternoon before, and started to analyse the stress caused by James' takeover of her life. She certainly didn't object to the move to Brittany. She wasn't wholly against antique furniture. She didn't like the car James had demanded she buy, an ostentatious SUV larger than necessary, over-engineered for town driving, not easy to park in confined spaces. But as James insisted on being the sole driver of it, she didn't feel she could object to his choice.

But James' takeover of her computer was a profound irritation. It was her old professional laptop, a fast, top-of-the-range model she'd used for all her work, in offices and in hotel rooms, as well as to keep up to date with the news and to keep in touch with her friends. It had been her constant companion. Two computer users really need a computer each, but when she'd suggested buying a second one James had absolutely refused to allow her to do so. This seemed ridiculous, given the amount he'd expected her to pay for an eighteenth century dresser or that showy car. She could easily afford a few hundred euros for a second machine. But James had been adamant that now she was retired, she didn't need a computer, and she hadn't wanted to face the almighty row which would erupt if a second machine was delivered.

But thinking through James' objection, she started to wonder whether she did need another office style computer. What she missed most was being able to search the internet, read the international news and handle emails, and nowadays people did all that from mobile phones. Of course, there wasn't much storage on a phone and it didn't have a keyboard. But what about a tablet? Judging by the hundreds of photos previous work colleagues had held on theirs, some tablets had copious storage. Some of them could have keyboard and mouse added. Even a large tablet would fit in Sarah's big leather handbag. She could go for a walk and use a tablet without James knowing about it. She might even be able to use a tablet in a different room of the penthouse without his knowledge.

All she needed was information on what to buy and where to buy it. But for that she needed internet access. Unfortunately James could see the screen of Sarah's laptop from his armchair, so he would know what she was doing if she used it to investigate tablets and eventually buy one. What she really needed was access to a different computer somewhere else.

Immediately she thought of the pensioners' centre where the Qi Gong course was held. A computer room had been set up there for teaching senior citizens to use the internet. In France it's necessary even for the elderly to become computer literate. A computer is needed to access the French government websites for paying taxes, claiming grants, checking availability of medical care, consulting a doctor, asking for a nurse, asking for a home help, applying for a passport, or updating a driving licence or an identity card.

The pensioners' centre staff were available to help the local old folk through the procedures, and when there was no formal class, the machines could be used by any member, assisted or on their own. So it was more important than Sarah had thought to return to Qi Gong class on Monday afternoon; as well as exercising and meeting friends, the pensioners' centre offered access to the internet.

She looked at her watch. It was half-past seven, an hour and a half since waking up, and the headache hadn't arrived. So it was not triggered by waking up. That meant the pain must be caused by something happening between eight and nine every day.

Taking a shower couldn't be the origin, because she took one every evening using the same shower gel with no ill-effects. Getting dressed could hardly cause a headache. So the culprit had to be breakfast. This consisted of a crispbread, a piece of fruit and a cup of coffee. Presumably she could be over-reacting to one of those? She devised a test to work out which it was. She would replace the coffee with water, and would eat nothing for a quarter-hour; if the headache didn't arrive she would eat a peach and wait a quarter-hour; if there was still no pain she would eat a crispbread. If there was no pain after that, the cause would be coffee.

***

The radio-alarm began suddenly. James woke instantly and headed for the bathroom. When she heard him move into the dressing-room Sarah got up, showered and dressed as usual. She walked into the kitchen where James was eating the substantial breakfast he always fried for himself. Pouring herself a glass of water, she said, "Would you mind if I don't have coffee today? I just don't feel like it."

She should have been prepared for the explosion. Making coffee was James' major contribution to the household, his only one apart from driving the car and buying the bread. He'd chosen the coffee machine himself, a model making both filter and expresso, with a milk-frothing device for cappuccino. He was extraordinarily proud of being able to work it. (As it was a best-selling item, Sarah was sure that six million other French residents had learned to use it as well).

James automatically objected to any change not suggested by him, and today was no different. He wouldn't hear of her cutting out coffee. He insisted that caffeine suppressed headaches. "You go and look at the ingredients on the packets of painkillers. They've all got caffeine in them. Those headaches would be even worse if you didn't have any caffeine," he said belligerently. "I won't hear any more of this nonsense. I'll make your coffee as usual and you'll drink it."

Sarah realised with utter dismay that she was quite unable to argue with James. In the whole of their life together she'd never confronted him, and now she no longer had the stamina required to fight back. She'd been badly ill for four weeks, and that had taken a toll. Completely against her will she took the mug of coffee when James gave it to her, sipped it until it was cool enough to drink, and then finished it quickly. James watched her with a belligerent expression which didn't lighten up even when she finished the mugful. The headache started as usual at nine o'clock, and James solicitously helped Sarah back to bed.

Suffocating under the waves of pain, only just hanging on to consciousness, Sarah repeated to herself what she'd discovered, over and over again, to ensure that she memorised it. She'd eaten no breakfast at all, so the trigger for the headache was coffee, coffee, coffee. The agony seemed to be worse that day, so she gave up trying to think. The pain made it impossible to sleep, so she lay in bed waiting for it to go away. It was past one o'clock before she felt well enough to think coherently, and even then she felt too drained to face James. She stayed in bed until the end of the afternoon, recuperating.

This is nonsense, she berated herself. *I've managed teams of twenty professionals in challenging environments for the last thirty years. I can't allow myself to be defeated by one man with illogical ideas. I should never have let myself become so ill. I can't confront James in my current state, so that means I have to get my health back again without letting James know I'm recovering until I'm back to normal. The first step is to stop drinking coffee, and I have to manage that without James knowing that I'm doing it.*

Sarah got out of bed in time to produce dinner, this time a simple repast of tinned soup, cold meat salad and the rest of the pear tart. She remembered that in mid-morning she'd heard James answer the telephone. "Who telephoned this morning?" she asked.

"Telephoned?" James repeated. "Those headaches are making you imagine things. No one phoned today. Next time you serve this tart, buy a tin of pears to go with it, because the baker doesn't put enough in it himself."

In the evening, Sarah sat in an armchair, mentally blocking out the sound of UK television news followed by James' American gangster film. She was extremely puzzled by her reaction to coffee. It had been a staple item of her diet for years. She began to recall every time she'd drunk coffee with no ill effect. During this exercise she remembered that when she lived on her own in foreign capitals working long hours, she'd developed a habit of making a mug of coffee in her hotel room first thing in the morning, and drinking it in intervals between showering, blow-drying her hair and dressing. She could then rush off to work without being delayed by the queues in the hotel breakfast room, buying croissants on the way to eat at her desk. This pattern gave her an idea.

When the film ended, she said to James, "I find I get a bit dizzy in the shower in the morning. I always used to have my coffee before I showered, to wake me up properly. Would you mind if I made myself coffee first thing?"

"You wouldn't know how to work the machine," James said as she'd expected.

"I could use coffee granules instead."

"That rubbish? If you insist, I'll make your coffee before I get dressed, and I'll bring it to you in the bathroom."

"Oh, James, that would be so kind of you, thank you."

***

Next morning, James headed for the kitchen in his dressing gown, and made coffee. He brought Sarah's mug to her just after she entered the bathroom. She pretended to sip it, "That's good and hot, thank you so much, James." She pretended a second sip, and James, hungry for his breakfast, left to get dressed and cook his fry-up. As soon as it was safe, Sarah tipped the coffee down the sink.

But the residual weakness from four weeks in bed still existed. James would be expecting a headache lasting all morning, and Sarah decided to fake one. That would give her three hours alone in the bedroom, since he never came in to check how she was. For at least an hour she could practice yoga floor exercises on the bed, to start building up strength and stamina. She dressed, walked into the kitchen and staged a collapse after eating her breakfast. James helped her to bed as usual.

At eleven, James followed his Sunday routine and went out to buy bread and investigate the English- language magazines in the bar-tabac. Sarah quickly left her bed, switched on her laptop and emailed Irene Ho, the Qi Gong class leader. She apologised for missing classes, said she was still unwell, and asked if she could do the exercises while sitting down, a practice followed by two disabled students during the lessons attended by James, and highly derided by him.

Irene was online and replied immediately:

'I know that you've been ill, but we would all welcome you back in class. Marie-Christine and Laure are still following the first half hour of both Class I and Class II sitting down. If you can exercise sitting down, I am sure this would help you return to your previous standard of fitness.'

Sarah deleted her email to Irene so that this reply looked like a spontaneous email from the tutor, and marked Irene's email 'unread'.

But when switching over from sending mail to reading her inbox, Sarah had intended to read the rest of her emails, expecting perhaps forty after a four-week absence. There were none at all. She stared at the screen in disbelief.

A cold feeling ran down her spine. When setting up this laptop for her personal use she hadn't bothered with full office security, assuming that it was secure because it never left her side. She'd simply used the password 'Alicia', her second name, to access the machine and her personal emails.

When she'd created a user identity for James on the laptop, he would have seen her input this far-too-obvious password more than once. She'd probably even spoken it aloud while she typed it. It would have been easy for him to remember, and it gave access to all her personal data except her bank accounts. The bank had rightly insisted on a far more secure code, regularly changed.

If her emails had been deleted, that could only have been done by James, and her own carelessness had enabled him to do it. She simply hadn't expected to be sabotaged by her own husband. Sarah closed down the laptop and went back to bed, fuming with anger at herself as well as at James, a feeling all the more intense for not being able to express it.

James returned with the bread, an apricot tart, his usual lunch of ham and cheese croissants, and a thick copy of an English newspaper from last week which he hadn't seen before. He spent the rest of the morning engrossed in its contents.

At noon, Sarah made herself a cheese sandwich and a mint tea. After his croissants, James went back to the newspaper.

"Would you mind if I used the computer?" Sarah asked meekly, swallowing her resentment at asking permission to use her own machine.

"OK," said James, "but be careful you don't make your headache worse."

"I just want to check if I have any emails."

"You won't find any. Everyone drops you like a stone once you've retired."

Sarah switched on the laptop and accessed her mail-list. "Oh, look," she said brightly, "there's an email from Irene," and as she opened it James moved at a rarely seen speed and stood behind her reading the screen. He could translate most French words singly, though he often had problems with the meaning of a whole sentence. "Irene has invited me to go back to the Qi Gong class," said Sarah, "Look, she says she's still running the classes so that the first half hour can be done sitting down. I'm sure that I'd be able to do that."

"Don't talk rubbish," said James, "You couldn't manage an exercise class in your condition."

"It's not strenuous, it's only moving slowly and controlling breathing," said Sarah.

"I still say it's too much. Tell the stupid woman to stop bothering you."

"But James, she knows I'm ill, look, she says so. She won't allow me to do too much. Laure has damaged lungs, and Marie-Christine has a spinal injury, and Irene takes very great care of them. She'll do the same for me while I'm ill."

As if those words had triggered his decision, James suddenly changed his mind. "OK, I'll let you go to Qi Gong as long as you make absolutely certain to tell that woman how very ill you are. I'll drive you there and pick you up afterwards. When is it?"

"Tomorrow, it starts at three o'clock, and finishes at five o'clock. I'll only do what comes easily. I'm truly grateful to you, James. You're being very kind to me."

For dinner, Sarah produced a starter for James of a large mushroom filled with pieces of bacon and tomato and basil, and topped with a fried egg. Then she grilled two pork chops, sautéed some potatoes and made a substantial salad with coloured leaves, cucumber, onions and herbs in a mustard dressing. She put the apricot tart into the oven to warm up and whisked an egg into milk to make custard. She worried that this meal was a little too good for a cook suffering from severe illness, but if so, James didn't notice. He complained about each course as usual while eating everything put in front of him.

After dinner Sarah said she would go to bed early. James didn't appear to notice that she spent a long time in the bathroom, quietly practising the complete set of moves and breath control that she'd learned in the first and second Qi Gong classes. She had every intention of following the whole hour of the second class on the following day. The hour of the first class was time she planned to spend in the computer room. Feeling more relaxed than at any time during the last four weeks, she fell into a refreshing sleep.

***

On Monday, Sarah used her morning to practise yoga exercises while thinking through James' deletion of her emails. She was amazed at how guilty she felt at mentally accusing him of such a thing; but there was no one else who could have done it. She realised he'd probably interfered with her phone as well, because it hadn't rung for four weeks. The phone's four-character numeric password was her year of birth, which was the same year as James' and easily guessed. She couldn't alter that password without alerting James to her suspicions, so she needed to buy herself a new phone as well as a tablet.

At noon, Sarah carefully dragged herself into the kitchen and made a sandwich. She started to pack a bag with her exercise clothes and shoes. James immediately asked if she was really sure she could cope.

"I do feel a little frail, but I want to see my friends. If you can drive me there, I won't have a problem."

James was annoyed at having promised to take her, but he did drive the car to the centre. Sarah thanked him in a thin voice and tottered into the women's changing room.

When she emerged from the changing room, James' car had disappeared. Throwing off all pretence of illness, she told Irene that she felt well enough to attend the whole hour of Class II at four o'clock. Then she borrowed the key to the computer room from the centre's office, and sat in front of a machine.

She had paper and pencil in her handbag, and jotted notes as she investigated what was on offer. After twenty minutes she set up the purchase of a tablet with its own mouse and keyboard and protective case. She also bought a large-capacity USB memory stick. She bought an internet wifi connection to a different service to that used in the penthouse, for use by the tablet. She added in a pay-as-you-go smartphone complete with its first month's subscription.

She'd thought carefully about a payment method. Although she and James had different passwords for their domestic joint accounts with the French bank, James could see all the transactions in those accounts and for both credit cards. But Sarah's rental income came through her letting business and was paid to her business account, to which James had no access. So she could pay with her business credit card.

There would be a problem with delivery, as she couldn't have the equipment delivered to the flat. But the suppliers offered the possibility of delivery to the nearest Post Office, which Sarah gratefully accepted.

She shut the computer down, locked the room, returned the key and joined the group awaiting the start of Qi Gong Class II. She was warmly welcomed by her friends. But four weeks of non-attendance and enforced inaction had left their mark, and she only just managed to keep up with the class. By the end of the hour she was extremely tired, but paradoxically felt better. The combination of exercise, chatting to friends and successfully making purchases was exhilarating.

While she was changing, she heard James' voice in the hallway, so when she left the changing room she produced a convincing impression of total exhaustion.

"I said you'd be doing too much," said James, seeing her drooping figure. "You're damned lucky I've come to fetch you. Just look at you. You certainly couldn't walk home."

"I'm afraid you're right, James," she said. "I'm really thankful to see you."

But she was interrupted by Irene, who shook James warmly by the hand while thanking him for taking such care of Sarah while she was so ill, and finished by kissing him on both cheeks. As the rest of the class realised this was Sarah's husband, they all crowded round with typical French politeness to shake James' hand or kiss him.

James was furious at being subjected to all this, especially being kissed. He didn't let rip while surrounded by the class, but spent the entire drive home complaining about the bloody Frogs and their idiotic customs, "Can't think why you want to mix with people like that." Sarah slumped in her seat only half pretending fatigue, and waited for the storm to blow over.

Once home, James downed his customary whisky before dinner, and then ate everything Sarah put on the table, doling out comments as usual. The pineapple-and-cheese first course was, "the sort of junk food served at parties, no nutritional value whatsoever." The supermarket's curried pork with rice and peas was, "absolutely tasteless. Why don't you get some decent curry sauce sent over from England?" The apricot tart was, "certainly not worth what I paid for it." His final comment was, "That wasn't much of a dinner, but I suppose I'll have to put up with rubbish every day you want to exercise yourself silly." He installed himself in front of the television for the evening.

Sarah sat watching the sunset above the cliffs on the other side of the estuary. She kept her face blank and her eyes turned away, but in a state of profound happiness, checked through her achievements to date.

Firstly, she'd identified the cause of the pain and found a way to avoid it in future. Secondly, she'd returned to her exercise class and her friends, and her morale had immediately improved as she'd hoped. Thirdly, James seemed to be assuming that she would go to Qi Gong class again, and that was wholly positive. Fourthly, she'd ordered for herself a complete new set of computing and communications equipment which would be delivered to the Post Office next day.

She was back on track to health and independence, and this time she wouldn't let anything derail her.

3

On Tuesday morning, the general practitioner telephoned. James took the call, and agreed an appointment for that afternoon. As expected, he not only drove Sarah to the surgery but accompanied her into the consultation. He produced Sarah's French medical card to allow the doctor online access to her records. He answered all the doctor's questions without giving Sarah time to reply. He insisted the problem was getting worse, and that Sarah could hardly concentrate enough to read a newspaper or follow a film (which was certainly untrue).

Sarah felt extremely guilty at taking up a busy doctor's time for no good reason, but she didn't dare provoke James' temper by publicly disagreeing with him. Her emotions were complicated by the sight of James producing her medical card. That little plastic card was personal evidence of identity. It carried her photo and a security chip full of information, and she kept it next to her passport in her handbag, which James had obviously searched.

The doctor recommended two more specialists, to check on Sarah's heart and circulation, and her digestive system and diet. He suggested dates for appointments which were both more than four weeks into the future. James demanded that Sarah be seen earlier. But the doctor had the specialists' appointment books open online, and knew that these were the earliest appointments possible. All he could do was to email the clinic secretaries to ask for earlier appointments if another patient cancelled. James had to agree to this, although he said vehemently that he wanted the whole investigation over and done with as soon as possible.

He then asked the doctor for a prescription of painkillers for Sarah, which he tucked into his pocket. He paid for the consultation, pocketing both his credit card and Sarah's medical card at the end of that action. He carefully helped Sarah out of her chair as if she was an invalid. She hadn't said a word during the whole session.

In the car, she opened her handbag and asked James for the prescription and her medical card, so that she could put them in her bag.

"It's better that I keep them," James said. "You're so bloody disorganised, you'd lose them."

Sarah furiously logged yet another wounding put-down. At work, she'd been renowned for having everything at her fingertips. She took a quick look before closing her bag; the prescription from Friday's consultant was no longer there, but at least her passport was.

French law states that everyone in a public place must carry some form of photo-identity. Sarah's passport fulfilled that requirement, but she'd preferred to produce her medical card when necessary; it was compact and more easily replaceable. If James had purloined Sarah's medical card, she needed to keep her passport where he wouldn't find it.

The thought overwhelmed her with misery. She'd hoped that when she was stronger she could persuade James to lessen his control, but now she doubted that she could. What kind of marriage did they have? What hope for their future?

***

The next day was Wednesday, and in the evening the Saint-Edern Social Club would hold its informal meeting in the function room of a restaurant a hundred metres away. Sarah had found the members to be interesting conversationalists and a good source of local knowledge, but they weren't to James' taste, and he usually dismissed them as 'the local nonentities'.

Once Sarah had staged her recovery at noon, she said she would like to go to the club meeting in the evening. James tried to talk her out of it, but she stood firm. "I want to see everyone again. You don't have to come," she said, "I'm sure I can walk a hundred metres on my own."

"Don't talk nonsense," James huffed. "If you insist on going, of course I'll come with you. But Heaven only knows what you see in that collection of old fogies."

Sarah served dinner early, and timed their arrival at the restaurant for eight o'clock. Immediately five women at a table for six invited Sarah to join them, and James had to sit three tables away. The women all knew that Sarah had been ill, and delightedly welcomed her return. James couldn't hear the conversation, but he could see Sarah's head lifting as she brightened up. He was too far away to stop it.

Sure that James must be growing angry, Sarah tried to act subdued, but Elodie and Marie-Pierre, on either side of her, had identified James' controlling nature from previous encounters. Marie-Pierre said roundly, "You're letting that man rule your life. You must stop it."

"You're quite right, but I don't know how to do that," Sarah whispered in her careful school French.

Once everyone had caught up on the gossip from their particular friends, the conversation became general and discussion turned on what to do at the weekend. Someone suggested visiting the Sunday morning educational films in the cinema. At noon there would be two short films, a historical revue of French costume from the tenth to the eighteenth century, and a documentary on the French fashion industry of the fifties and sixties.

There were other ideas for the weekend, and the club members finally split into two, those who wanted to go to the cinema and those who preferred to hire a boat to motor round the coast.

James had no intention of doing either, but Sarah was attracted by the films and signalled that she'd attend. James stalked over to where she sat. "Don't be so stupid," he growled. "You're ill. You can't go to a cinema." This was simple enough English to be understood by everyone.

Marie-Pierre laughed out loud. "Monsieur," she said in English, "to see a film, one sits in the chair. As one does here. Sarah is OK here. She is OK in the cinema."

"I drive Sarah in my car," added Elodie.

"You don't realise," James said, firmly against the whole idea, "she could be taken ill suddenly while she's there."

"In the cinema of Sunday morning," said Marie-Pierre, "there are many old and handicapped persons, so always there is a nurse."

"If Sarah is ill, I drive immediately," said Elodie. "But I prefer she takes the lunch with us, because always she has the interesting point of view."

"You're out-voted by the women, Monsieur Pullen," said Gérard Lemestre, the senior man present. "It's rare for a man to win an argument with a woman. Against six women one man has no chance at all." He spoke in English but repeated it in French. Everyone burst out laughing, especially the women. Then the members interested in motor-boating appointed someone to take charge of booking a suitable craft.

When James reached home, he erupted into a fury, accusing Sarah of stupidly endangering her health and deliberately making him look a fool in front of everyone. He stomped up and down the lounge, working himself into a rage. Sarah was in fact terrified, and instinctively dissolved into tears. That did the trick. James threw out one last insult, "You see what a mess you've made of yourself, you stupid little idiot," then sank into his armchair in front of the television, finally allowing Sarah to go to bed.

***

Next morning Sarah pretended a headache as usual, but James was still furious from the night before. He continually came into the bedroom to tell her that she was an idiot to go out when she was ill. "You deserve to be ill. You're doing nothing to help yourself." There was no way to persuade James to ease up. Sarah began to develop a genuine headache in response to the stress.

At eleven o'clock James went to the baker's. He always walked down the stairs, only using the lift to come back up to the penthouse. So today he realised that the cleaners, who were paid by the building management to clean the halls, stairs and lift every Thursday morning, had omitted to clean the stairs for the second week running. He raced back from the baker's, dumped the bread in the kitchen, shouting insults about lazy cleaners and the idle bloody French in general, grabbed papers from the filing cabinet confirming Sarah's ownership of the flat and the bank's regular maintenance payments to the building managers, took the car and drove to the other side of town to shout at the building managers' office staff.

Sarah recognised her opportunity. When she saw the car pull out of the garage into the road below, she took her largest shopping bag and ran to the Post Office in the next street. She produced her passport to confirm her identity and collected her parcel. She took it to the desk set aside for customer use, cut open the outer box with the scissors provided, tipped the plastic grommets into the plastics bin, put the outer box in the cardboard recycling bin, put all the contents into her bag with the invoice, and ran home in case James' errand didn't take him long. Dazed by excitement and the unaccustomed exercise, she took the lift upstairs, and stowed her purchases and her passport under her underclothes in the drawers of the bathroom vanity unit. There was just time to get to bed and calm down before James returned after persuading the management to send the cleaners back to finish their job properly. Sarah stayed in bed until late afternoon, as the simplest way of avoiding James while he wasn't in a good mood.

At four o'clock, there was a phone call. James answered it abruptly, but then his tone modulated into a welcome. The caller, Brian Rowley, was another Englishman, a member of the group of British expatriates with which Sarah and James had registered on taking up residence in France, and he was trying to form an English-speaking bridge club.

Brian was ringing all the local expatriates in alphabetical order; he'd already found twenty-five players before reaching P for Pullen. He envisaged a venue in Dinard, on the other side of the river, somewhere selling drinks and big enough for four or five tables of bridge. He'd organised a meeting at eleven on Saturday at his preferred hotel in Dinard to sort out the formal arrangements for a club, and invited James to attend.

James accepted immediately. He fancied himself as a bridge player, having played cards frequently. He mentioned his accountancy qualifications and experience, saying that he would be happy to serve the club in any capacity, as well as playing. Brian Rowley responded warmly, and the two men exchanged email addresses so that they could communicate about setting up the club.

At dinner time Sarah found James in an expansive mood. He said he wouldn't be surprised if he was appointed to the bridge club committee. The prospect kept him happy for the rest of the day.

The next day was the first of May, a French public holiday, and James spent all of it playing bridge on the internet, frequently claiming to have won.

***

On Saturday, James left at nine-thirty to talk with Brian in Dinard before the meeting. Sarah didn't expect him back before one o'clock. She headed for the bathroom, unwrapped her tablet and phone, put them on charge using the bathroom sockets and took all the wrappings down to the communal recycling bin in the hall so that James wouldn't realise they were hers.

The telephone initialised first. She inputted the contact numbers from her old phone, and then sent all her contacts an SMS indicating the change of phone number and her preference for receiving SMS rather than phone calls. This was necessary because she'd had to switch off the sounds indicating incoming calls and messages so that James wouldn't discover the existence of a new phone. She concealed phone and charger under her brassieres in the vanity unit.

When the tablet was fully charged, Sarah connected it to the internet using her new wifi subscription. She downloaded a copy of her usual antivirus package, plus a spreadsheet and word processor small enough to work in the tablet's limited memory, and paid for these with her business credit card.

She created a new email identity with a new supplier, and transferred her email contact list from her old email identity to the new one. From the new ID she emailed all her contacts a message in English or French as appropriate, asking them to use the new address. She explained that she'd been ill recently, and hadn't realised that problems had occurred with her previous mail provider. If a recipient hadn't had a reply to a message sent in the last four weeks would they please re-send it?

She signed on to her laptop briefly and copied all the details of her business and professional life and her properties, investments and personal banking to the USB key. The tablet read the data from the USB key as expected, and, although it worked more slowly, the tablet now functioned like the portable.

James still hadn't returned, so Sarah created another email identity using the name Irene Ho. She used a free translation service to create the description of a special Chinese massage for alleviating pain, and an invitation to a demonstration to be held at the pensioners' centre next Thursday. She sent this from the false Irene Ho to her old email. She hoped James might allow her out of the flat for this fictitious demo.

Sarah then caught up with the news sites she used to visit, and enjoyed reading for some time. She just had time to close the tablet and hide it under her panties when she heard James' key in the front door. She ran the tap loudly, before leaving the bathroom to be duly startled by the fact that James had returned.

She needn't have bothered with pretence. James was too full of his success at the bridge club to notice her. "Great group of people, some good contacts there. Got on well with all of them. Been elected treasurer. Could really make something of this." James was slurring his words, so he'd drunk some glasses. But his good mood was lasting and his grumbles over dinner not as biting as they could have been. He was even pleased that the steak Sarah served was bigger and thicker than his lunchtime one at the hotel, though he'd have preferred 'proper English mustard' to the 'Frenchified muck' of sauce Béarnaise.

After dinner, James switched on the laptop. From where she was sitting Sarah could identify the pages he accessed. He read his emails without replying to any of them, and then as she watched, he simply switched to her old mailbox. He openly entered her password, making no effort to conceal his actions. There was, of course, a new message.

James said, "Just look at that, yet another email from that wittering exercise guru of yours, Sarah. She's obviously got too much time on her hands."

Sarah translated the mail for him and said, "Isn't that kind of Irene to think of me? I'd like to see if Chinese massage can do anything for me. Do you mind if I go?"

"Go if you must," said James, "but it'll be as airy-fairy as the rest of her Chinese rubbish. I've just talked with Paul Harrier at the bridge club. He's a retired hospital consultant. His house has four bedrooms, so it's obviously worth four times as much as this piddling little flat. He's seen hundreds of elderly women with psychosomatic syndromes; he says it's obvious that's what you've got."

Sarah was so shocked that she burst into tears.

"You see," James commented, "you're over-emotional. Sooner or later those specialists will conclude you're a hysteric, and give up on you. Mark my words." He closed down the laptop and settled himself into his armchair to call up a film.

Feeling as if she'd just been consigned to a dustbin, Sarah was too furious to go to bed. How could James discuss her in such derogatory terms with a complete stranger? She watched the film without seeing it, trying to regain enough serenity to sort out the mess her life had become.

***

On Sunday Sarah was ready when Elodie arrived at half-past eleven. James was deep in a magazine, and neither greeted Elodie nor said goodbye to Sarah, but at least he didn't prevent Sarah leaving.

Sarah and Elodie joined Marie-Pierre and other social club members, and they all sat together in a block. Then Sarah recognised four of the Qi Gong class as they came in. When she waved they came to sit in the row in front of her. Sarah introduced her friends to each other, and as the chat became general, Sarah suddenly felt relaxed, happy and stress-free. She settled back to enjoy herself.

The first film started with mediaeval women's dresses, then moved through the centuries, detailing the improvements in thread spinning, fabric weaving, dye colours and dressmaking techniques until the 1850s' Second Empire. It was enthralling to watch the design of clothes slowly evolving, and amazing to realise how long it was before the inset sleeve was invented to replace separate sleeves tied on to an undergarment. The second film was a documentary on the post-war years in the great fashion houses in Paris, vividly bringing this recent period back to life. Altogether this was one of the most interesting and informative afternoons Sarah had spent in Brittany.

After the lights went up the group started to share their impressions of the films, and when Sarah expressed enjoyment of the story of the great couture houses, the woman sitting in front of her said, "You must meet my sister Gaelle. She used to work for a Paris couturier. I'll call her over," and she waved energetically across the auditorium. But when Gaelle arrived she brought her guest, an Englishwoman, Janet Rowley.

Mrs Rowley was visibly startled to be introduced to Mrs Pullen. "You can't be the wife of James Pullen, who's just become treasurer of the bridge club?"

"Certainly I'm James' wife." Sarah smiled confidently, while inwardly wondering what might come next.

"Well, I must have heard it wrong, but I was sure he said his wife was an invalid who never went out. And here you are!"

"James is such a fusser," Sarah said. "All I had was a headache, but he was annoyed that I didn't want to join the club because I don't play bridge."

"Aren't men all the same?" Mrs Rowley asked. "Though to be honest, James did strike me as rather too intent on getting his own way."

"He's a little bit like that," Sarah said with an ironic smile.

Janet Rowley grunted, "If he was my husband, I'd have a headache all the time! But the bridge club needs members, and pushy blokes are often good value on committee. I'm sure we're doing you a favour by taking him off your hands once a week."

"You are," Sarah laughed, as lightly as possible.

The social club group moved to the café where they'd reserved a table. Talk continued about the films, but Elodie and Marie-Pierre, who both understood English better than they could speak it, had followed Mrs Rowley's conversation.

"Please excuse us if we're interfering," Elodie said in French, "but we're worried that James causes you problems. He's a bully."

"The club doesn't like him," Marie-Pierre said. "We put up with him for your sake."

Elodie added, "We're worried that you're in a difficult situation because you need his money to live on."

Sarah felt a need to trust someone. "It's not like that," she said. "James has no money. I had the better job and the higher salary, and now I'm retired I'm comfortably off. But while we both worked, I didn't see James often. I didn't realise we'd grown apart. I thought a new life together in Brittany would be a romantic adventure, but it's gone wrong. I know James is difficult…" Marie-Pierre snorted, "but I feel I'm to blame for leaving him alone for so long."

"Nonsense," Elodie said indignantly. "We've seen how he treats you."

"James is using you, and you know it," Marie-Pierre said. "If you have money of your own, why don't you leave him?"

"It's not that easy," Sarah said, frowning. "I can't physically throw him out, and he wouldn't go voluntarily. If I leave, he'll follow me, and he has a frightening temper. I don't see an easy solution. I'm trying to make the best life I can without upsetting him."

"We must respect your decision," Elodie said, "but please remember that we'll both help any way we can. You only have to ask."

Sarah was nearly in tears as she kissed them goodbye.

That night, Sarah felt herself falling into despair. James would never change. He'd continue isolating her and bullying her into submission. She could cope by deceiving him, but who wants to live like that? Her health was being affected; she wasn't getting enough exercise or enough stimulation for her brain. She wondered how close she was to clinical depression and mental illness.

Making a great effort she thought of happier topics: meeting the group at the cinema, the interesting films, Elodie and Marie-Pierre. At last, she slept.

4

On Monday morning in the bathroom, Sarah risked a quick look at her tablet. Her new email ID had sixteen messages.

Her eye was caught by a mail marked URGENT from the letting agent of her three Paris flats. She risked opening that one. The agent wrote that he'd been trying to get in touch for six weeks, when one of her tenants had given four weeks' notice to quit. The tenant's deposit should have been repaid to him promptly on his leaving the flat in good order (as he had done, two weeks ago), but the agent hadn't succeeded in getting through to Sarah by phone or by email and the ex-tenant was now threatening legal action. The agent added that Monsieur Pullen had emailed that the flat would be sold, but, although the agency's sale- agreement had been sent to Monsieur Pullen for Madame Pullen's signature, it hadn't been returned. Did Madame Pullen intend to use the agency to sell the flat, or had she agreed with a different selling agent?

Sarah was consumed by fury. James had been hijacking her emails for six weeks, two weeks before she'd started having headaches, and he'd interfered in her letting business and he seemed to be trying to sell one of her flats over her head. She put the tablet away and tried to contain her anger well enough to fake a convincing headache in front of James.

Thank goodness it was the day of the Qi Gong class. Sarah fumed throughout her morning yoga exercises, and could barely hold herself in check while making herself lunch. But James was taking the day as usual. His English Sunday newspaper had arrived in the post and he was deep into the sports pages all morning and the business section during lunch. He hadn't even looked at Sarah yet.

She took her backpack into the bathroom to put her electronics in it, and then moved to the dressing room to cover them with her exercise clothes and shoes. She gently reminded James that it was time for her Qi Gong class. James put his paper aside with bad grace and stomped off to the lift. When they arrived at the leisure centre, James drove off as soon as she was on the pavement. In case she was still in sight from the car's rear mirror, Sarah walked slowly through the door and into the changing room.

Once safely out of sight, she whipped out her phone and dialled the letting agent. She asked him to email the ex-tenant's bank details to her, and to re-let the flat. She pointed out very firmly that the flat didn't belong to James, that he wasn't a shareholder in her letting company and he had no authorIty to act on her behalf. She asked the agent never to take any more instructions from her husband. The agent confirmed he did now understand, and apologised for his mistake.

When the email arrived with the ex-tenant's bank details, Sarah used her tablet to transfer money to him from her business bank account, and sent a confirming email to the agent. The agent then confirmed that he'd informed the ex-tenant of the payment, and had also re-advertised the flat on the agency's site. The immediate crisis was over.

When Qi Gong Class II started, Sarah firmly put out of her mind all thoughts unconnected with flowing movements and controlled breathing and serenity of mind. The class succeeded in being both challenging and enjoyable, a small haven of peace in a chaotic world, and the physical effort and congenial company once again made Sarah feel so much better, and so much more in control.

Driving home with a grumpy James, Sarah no longer felt guilty for deceiving him. He'd told worse lies, he'd taken worse actions, and he'd nearly landed her in legal trouble. But his actions over the flat were beyond understanding. In telling the agent not to re-let the flat he'd reduced their joint income, although he always spent most of that himself. It wouldn't have made the flat easier to sell since there's a thriving investment market in Paris properties with sitting tenants. In any case, James couldn't have sold the flat, because it was registered solely in Sarah's name; the contract of sale would have had to be signed personally by Sarah in the presence of a notary. James' actual intentions were beyond understanding.

***

Tuesday was the day of the bridge club committee meeting, held over lunch in the upper room of a restaurant that the club hoped to use for playing. During James' absence, Sarah discovered that replies to her email now numbered twenty-eight. One was from James' sister, Deborah, who with her husband ran a large and successful chain of estate agents in the south of England. Deb said she was delighted to hear from Sarah because James had said she was seriously ill and that the hospital hadn't been able to discover why. She hoped that Sarah had now recovered completely. How were things going in France?

Sarah decided not to challenge the report of her illness, but sent a cheerful reply, describing exercising, the social club, and the beautiful summer weather. She carefully mentioned that she was still waiting for more hospital appointments, because she didn't want Deb telling James that she'd said she was cured. She also omitted mentioning the bridge club in case Deb's knowledge of it made James realise that email contact had been restored.

This is becoming complicated, Sarah thought. *It's a pity to deceive Deborah. I liked her on sight. I'm sure she'd be a good friend, and she's known James for longer than I have, so in not telling her the whole truth, I'm losing an opportunity to understand him. But I don't know how close brother and sister are. I can't take the risk.*

She worked steadily through the list of her other correspondents, re-establishing casual contacts with old friends in a very satisfying way. By the time James returned she'd replaced the tablet in its drawer and was in the lounge reading a book. James wasn't interested enough in Sarah to notice how bright she seemed. He was full of news of himself. He'd scored numerous points off several committee members who had, "Not the foggiest idea of accounting practice. Where these people come from I cannot think."

The day ran its course without further incident, and Sarah went to sleep that night feeling more in control of her life. Her next big step must be to convince the doctor that she didn't need any treatment. That was a real challenge, but it must be possible.

***

The next day being Wednesday, in the evening Sarah and James walked to the social club meeting. James held on to her hand as they entered the restaurant, so that she had to sit by him, though he couldn't find seats as far from Elodie and Marie-Pierre as he'd have liked.

As the members chatted to others on their tables, James beckoned to the barman and ordered a beer. When it came he downed it in seconds, handed it back to the startled server and ordered another. Sarah was embarrassed to notice a number of members looking shocked at this behaviour. They normally ordered one drink each at the end of the meeting, and the bulk of those orders were non-alcoholic, since most members had already taken a glass of wine with their dinner.

Once the meeting began, a number of suggestions were made for the weekend. The one which found most favour was proposed by Marie-Pierre, who suggested a walk in a forest on the next Saturday to pick mushrooms.

A similar foray proposed by another member in October of the previous year hadn't met with success. The autumn colours were brilliant and the weather was fine, but they'd found very few edible fungi. But now Marie-Pierre volunteered that her son-in-law had given her the GPS references of some patches of summer cepes, which he'd twice found sprouting in the month of May. Although slightly different to the Bordeaux cepes of the autumn, they were just as tasty.

The growing areas were near one of the forest car-parks; it wouldn't be a long walk to the mushrooms, and afterwards they could stop at the nearby forest inn for a convivial salad lunch. Other members then suggested a post-prandial walk through the forest, since the car park was the starting point for a pretty five-kilometre stroll around a small lake full of wildfowl, with a good enough path for the wheelchair users to join in, and the expedition would then last a whole day.

James and Sarah had joined the mushroom-picking the previous October. James had filled their basket, but Sarah hadn't been very happy with the contents. James had bought a guide to mushrooms written in English, with pictures of each type and a note on whether they were good eating, poor eating, or poisonous. But when reading it, Sarah had found it extremely difficult to tell one type of fungus from another in the labelled pictures. She'd bought a pack of mixed wild mushrooms the previous day, and when they got home she'd made James his requested mushroom omelette with the bought ones, and threw the picked ones in the pedal bin.

Unfortunately, the next morning James had finished a packet of ground coffee, stepped on the bin-pedal to throw it away, and recognised the mushrooms he'd picked lying in a heap on top of the rubbish. James had treated the expedition as a competition, and had been extraordinarily proud of picking far more mushrooms than anyone else. To find that Sarah had thrown away his prize collection provoked a condemnation which could probably be heard on the seafront five storeys below.

So when Sarah joined the others in voting for gathering mushrooms, James decried the whole idea. "What's the bloody good of you going mushroom picking? You threw away all the ones I picked last year," he fumed.

"But I wasn't sure they were all good to eat," Sarah protested.

"That is true," Elodie said in English. "I think you had some dangerous."

"No, they were not," James said belligerently. "I checked them all in the book." His voice had risen; for a minute Sarah thought he would start shouting, but a sweet voice interrupted.

"Last year is last year, monsieur. This year, there will be cepes," Marie-Pierre said. "Not need for a book, only a cepe resembles a cepe. You come and you enjoy."

Somehow James found himself agreeing to go on the trip. As this was the end of the meeting, he ordered a double whisky, which the barman delivered with the blank face a professional wears to show disapproval.

James' agreement to join the expedition didn't prevent him berating Sarah all the way home, in the hearing of club members, several passers-by and all the neighbourhood residents. She put up with the humiliation until she found herself inside their own building, then dissolved into tears in the lift. It was the only possible defence, however much Sarah despised herself for using the tactic.

***

Thursday was the date of the fictitious Chinese massage. Sarah asked James for a lift to the pensioners' centre. She walked slowly into the women's changing room, but when she heard the car reverse out of the drive, she obtained the key to the computer room from the office, plugged her tablet into a vacant socket, connected it to the internet and accessed her mails.

There was good news. The agent had already found a tenant for the vacant flat – unsurprising considering the demand for housing in Paris – and his email attached the letting agreement requiring her signature. Sarah copied the document to her USB key, took it to the office where there was a pay-as-you-go printer- scanner, paid twenty cents, printed the agreement, signed it, and paid another twenty cents to scan it back to USB. She emailed the signed agreement to the agent using her tablet. This would serve for the interim, but she would eventually have to sign the original document, so she asked the agent to send that to the local Post Office for collection.

Sarah read the additional emails which had arrived from friends and sent off short replies, but afterwards she still had twenty minutes before James would arrive. She decided to spend them in the centre's garden. She locked the computer room, returned the key, and strolled outside to sit on a sunny bench. The light breeze was invigorating. Clumps of pale blue agapanthus were blooming spectacularly in the flower bed.

Sarah's thoughts returned to Marie-Pierre asking why she didn't simply leave James. Sarah's arguments against that had been valid. James was physically stronger. He wouldn't agree to leave himself or to let her move away. He insisted on accompanying her everywhere she went; she could never go beyond his knowledge and control.

But the bridge club and Qi Gong class had changed the situation; they provided Sarah with times when James wasn't there. She could now arrange to disappear. She'd want to take her wealth with her, but that would be easy. She simply needed a new bank where she could open an account and ask for her income to be paid into it. She could then move somewhere James wouldn't guess. Using a credit card or bank auto-teller would betray her whereabouts to the police – if James called in the police – but paying by cash would not. So all she needed was a new bank account, a large quantity of cash, and a place to stay.

James' poor French wouldn't make it easy for him to find her, and Sarah could ensure he started the search at a disadvantage. If during the last bridge club meeting of the month she took out all the cash from their joint accounts and then left, taking her laptop with her, James would have no details of her life or finances and no connection to the internet. His mobile phone fee and his credit card debt had to be paid on the last day of the month, and when they weren't, both services would cease. James would have no means of continuing to live in France; he'd have to return to England and live off his pension there. With luck she'd never see him again.

The key to everything was the new bank; Sarah needed a different address to give them. On impulse she telephoned Marie-Pierre to ask for help, and immediately struck gold. Marie-Pierre owned a four-bedroom house, letting two bedrooms to students, reserving the third for family visitors. She proposed giving Sarah a rental contract for her third bedroom, to act as proof of her address.

Marie-Pierre mentioned that her daughter-in-law owned a guesthouse in Rennes, but that wouldn't be an ideal refuge, as non-French visitors had to be reported promptly to the police. If James reported her disappearance, the local police would trace Sarah too easily.

Instead, Marie-Pierre recommended her cousin's farm in the Basque country near Biarritz. He owned six holiday cottages, and reported to a different regional police force at three-monthly intervals. Sarah was sure that James would never think of looking for her in a cottage in the Pyrenees. Marie-Pierre arranged to email the address and itinerary, and she assured Sarah that if there was no spare cottage available when she wanted one, a family friend needing urgent assistance would of course be housed in the farmhouse.

Marie Pierre then described her attic: weatherproof, large and almost empty. She suggested storing Sarah's winter clothes immediately. Elodie would be happy to move a carload across Saint-Edern. Suddenly everything fell into place. Sarah could see the possibility of moving her possessions out during successive bridge club meetings without James noticing, followed by one last move of things visible to James, such as the local paintings, the laptop, and the music centre, at the same time as she emptied the bank account and travelled to Biarritz. It was all possible.

"I expect that man will smash what's left in your flat," said Marie-Pierre, "but I'll tell you everything that happens after you've gone."

Sarah thanked her profusely. As she ended the telephone call, she found she was physically shaking and breathing heavily with the enormity of what she intended to do.

She was still finding it difficult to behave normally when James arrived. "You look worse than when you came," he said dismissively. "I told you all this Chinese rubbish would be a waste of time. You're just too much of an idiot to see it."

His words hit a nerve. *He's very fond of calling me an idiot,* thought Sarah, *but I've successfully managed vital infrastructure projects for international companies while he couldn't even hold down a simple job. If I'm an idiot, it's because I let him insult me while he lives on my money. That will stop.* She hung her head and walked haltingly to the car, but her heart and her mind had hardened. After serving dinner from the usual packets, to the usual criticism, she stacked the dishwasher and retired to bed.

***

On Friday the bridge club's first meeting was due in the evening. Sarah spent the morning in bed alternately practising yoga and refining the details of her plan. She still felt some compunction at leaving James in the lurch, but as far as she could see her money was the only reason they were together. James didn't enjoy her company. When they were together in the flat, he ignored her unless he was criticising her cooking or insulting her. He should have money in England, because both their state pensions were paid into the English bank, and he had a credit card on that account. He could surely afford a ferry ticket and he could take that ostentatious car with her blessing.

As soon as James left for the bridge club, Sarah quickly piled all her family photographs, family birth and marriage certificates, the legal documents for her properties, her old work contracts and tax receipts, all her jewellery and her most expensive clothes, shoes and handbags into three suitcases. Elodie arrived and stacked the cases in her car. She drove along the waterfront to Marie-Pierre's house, where a young nephew had been called in to carry the cases up to the attic. There Sarah emptied them into the boxes which Marie-Pierre had put ready.

Meanwhile, Marie-Pierre printed out the rental contract and a receipt for two months' rent. The nephew took the empty cases back to the ground floor. Sarah put the contract and receipt in her pocket and Elodie drove the empty cases back to the penthouse. It had been simple. Sarah decided to give up her Qi Gong class on Monday afternoon, and instead open an account at the bank next to the leisure centre.

When James returned from the bridge club, he was so late that Sarah was fast asleep, and he had to shake her awake to tell her how many people he'd beaten and what a success he was.

5

Saturday was the day of the social club mushroom-picking. Sarah was ready to leave at ten-thirty, but James didn't register her speedy recovery. He'd looked up cepes on the laptop and discovered the high shop price, so was enthusiastically looking forward to getting them free.

He drove to the forest and parked among the other cars of the group. As everyone gathered together, Marie-Pierre pointed out the direction to the first spot where cepes could be found. James immediately raced off into the trees at a fast pace. He spotted a huge specimen, charged at it and grabbed it like a trophy, waving it in the air.

Shouts from the others went un-regarded, but two angry men moved on either side of James and started to berate him in French, forcing Sarah to translate. Firstly, the prize mushroom should, in all courtesy, have been offered to Marie-Pierre, and secondly, in rushing to grab that one James had crushed into the soil dozens of middle-sized cepes which would have made fine eating for everyone else.

"Finders keepers," James said ungracefully. "Don't tell me off because you bloody French are too slow to take the opportunity offered." Sarah didn't attempt to translate. The gist was obvious from James' tone of voice.

But meanwhile, Marie-Pierre had identified a second patch and then a third one. For half an hour everyone moved around carefully picking cepes until they each had enough for a good supper omelette. The surplus cepes donated to Marie-Pierre were enough for her daughter and son-in-law as well as herself.

Satisfied with their harvest, the group walked on to the inn L'Orée de la Forêt. They pulled the tables together in the bar to create a one communal table, and ordered their lunches. Most of them asked for a glass of wine and a salad. The inn was famous for its wide choice of combinations of cheeses, cold meats, sausages, eggs and seafood served with mixed leaves and salad vegetables.

Sarah sat next to Elodie and chose a salad including prawns, avocado and smoked mackerel. James sat next to Sarah at the end of the table and ordered hamburger and chips, and a beer. As before, when the beer was served he downed it in one and handed the empty glass back to the barman while asking for another, saying neither please nor thank you. None of the facial expressions of the rest of the group registered this incident. Sarah realised they'd decided to ignore James completely.

Two waitresses delivered a succession of beautifully displayed salads and glasses of wine. The barman delivered James' burger. James immediately complained that it wasn't big enough considering the price. The barman probably understood James' English, but before he could answer, Sarah smiled charmingly at him and asked him to make James a second burger. The man was somewhat surprised, but returned a few minutes later with a second offering and more chips.

James then ordered a glass of red wine, having finished his second beer, and while waiting for it, he drank Sarah's. He took no part in the lunchtime conversation, but concentrated on his food. The rest of the group intended to stroll around the lake in the afternoon. Four of the men agreed a rota for pushing the wheelchairs of Marie-Christine and Laure, rather than leave them negotiating the gravel path entirely on their own. At the end of the meal, everyone ordered coffee or tea, except James who drank a double whisky instead.

As the party rose to continue their afternoon, James stomped off down the path to his car carrying the bag holding the cepes he'd picked and without saying goodbye to anyone. Sarah settled their bill as usual. She had no choice but to join James, so said her goodbyes. Her friends carefully wished her a safe journey; it was obvious to everyone that James must be over the alcohol limit.

Luckily there was little traffic on the main road home, and in the narrow streets of Saint-Edern other drivers instinctively deferred to the aggressively driven SUV. In the flat, James put the cepes on the kitchen counter and belligerently told Sarah to make sure she bloody cooked them this time. She suggested a mushroom risotto accompanied by grilled ham and peas, with an apple tart for dessert.

James grunted "Oh, do what you bloody like, just make damn well sure you cook those mushrooms." He slammed into the lounge, turning on the television before slumping in his chair, where he shortly went to sleep.

At six o'clock James woke and demanded to know where dinner was. Sarah had finished the apple tart and just started on the risotto. She put out a quick starter for James, hard-boiled eggs with anchovies.

James helped himself to a pre-dinner whisky. Fifteen minutes later the mushroom risotto was ready, and Sarah served it over a grilled ham slice, with a sprinkling of grated cheese and a decorative spoonful of peas alongside.

James poured a glass of wine each and then ate his plateful at his usual fast pace. Sarah had barely finished her smaller portion when he wanted his dessert. She served him a large portion with cream, and he finished it in seconds. He promptly left the table for his armchair and put on a DVD. Sarah stacked the dishwasher. By the time she'd finished, James was again asleep.

James woke suddenly at the end of the film, saying, "That's odd, I feel awful."

"You did get through a lot of alcohol today," Sarah ventured, hoping not to provoke a reaction.

"Then a hair of the dog will cure it," James said confidently. He refilled his whisky glass and downed it in one. "There's nothing like a good scotch," he said. "But it was a thoroughly tiring day. I think I'll go to bed." He was soon asleep.

Sarah couldn't calm down enough to sleep. She couldn't stop reviewing James' boorish behaviour in the forest, and she fiercely resented the fact that everyone had felt sorry for her. She finally succumbed at two o'clock, only to wake at five to find the light on and James missing. He was in the lavatory being sick.

"It's only a hangover," he said belligerently, "and don't you give me that holier-than-thou face. I bet you've never been drunk in your life. You're too damned cautious to know what living's all about."

Sarah didn't comment. She returned to bed and slept until the alarm at eight. James had returned to bed, and was snoring beside her, but for once the alarm didn't wake him.

***

Sarah decided to start the day at the usual time, but, not having had her usual ration of sleep, she wasn't fully in command of her actions. Automatically following the standard routine of thirty years' living in hotels, she filled a kettle, boiled water, spooned coffee granules into a mug, and took the coffee into the bathroom while she showered and dressed. Only when she returned to the kitchen did she realise that she'd drunk a full mug of coffee for the first time in a fortnight.

Aghast at her own stupidity, she waited for the onset of the headache. But the clock moved on past nine o'clock, quarter-past, half-past, and nothing happened. Obviously coffee made from granules was safe to drink. So only filtered ground coffee caused headaches. A puzzling and completely irrational conclusion.

At ten o'clock James got out of bed, showered, dressed, and left the house, moving clumsily because he was still hung over. He returned with a round loaf, a bag of filled croissants for his lunch, an apple tart, an English news magazine, and a bottle of whisky. He ignored the break in routine. He ate his lunch croissants in the kitchen while reading his magazine. Then he took the magazine to his armchair, but was soon asleep again. Sarah wondered exactly how much alcohol he'd imbibed in the last forty-eight hours. He'd certainly have drunk two or three glasses at the bridge club on Friday, probably all of them whisky, probably all of them doubles. She thought it likely that the hangover could last all day, and certainly the next two or three hours.

She moved into the bathroom, plugged in the tablet to charge it, caught up with the UK and French news headlines, and worked through her emails. James' sister Deborah had emailed asking jokingly if Sarah and James were still living together. Apparently James had sent her yet another email saying Sarah was extremely ill. Sarah started to type a reply laughing this off, but then she remembered very clearly how practical Deborah was, and how friendly and welcoming she'd been whenever they'd met. She realised that when she walked out on James she'd want Deborah to know why. She sent a factual reply detailing her problems with James' behaviour, his bullying tactics, his boorishness at the mushroom picking, his heavy drinking and the fact that he was in a drunken stupor at this very moment.

Deborah replied immediately:

'This is serious. You don't know it, but when he lost his job in Sheffield he was sacked for being drunk in the presence of a client. It wasn't the first time that had happened. His employers paid a subscription to Alcoholics Anonymous in his severance package. James did go to the meetings and did dry out, but he should then have given up alcohol forever. He gave my name as next-of kin because he said he was ashamed of what he'd done and didn't want you to know. That's why I haven't said anything to you before, but now I wish I had. Is there any organisation in France which could help? If he's drinking heavily again, he's endangering his own health as well as upsetting you and the entire population of Saint-Edern. I really don't like the sound of what you're putting up with.'

Sarah reflected that it would have been easy for James to conceal alcoholism while she only met him at weekends. He'd also concealed the reason for dismissal. He'd said the company had suffered financial problems and were saving money by sacking all the higher-paid staff. She now wondered whether he'd ever been one of the higher-paid staff. Unfortunately, dismissal had meant a problem with the purchase of his new Porsche, but Sarah had happily made the payments for him, glad there was something she could do for him after leaving him alone for weeks on end. She knew now that there was no way that she would ever have bought such a car for him, or any car, if she'd known he was habitually drunk.

She emailed Deb:

'Thank you for telling me. You're right, I didn't know about the dismissal or Alcoholics Anonymous. That does explain James' current behaviour. There's a similar French organisation which provides English-speaking help. I'll look into it.'

James woke just after four demanding something to eat. Thinking that the amount of alcohol he'd consumed ought to be balanced by a full meal, Sarah produced an early dinner by heating tinned soup, defrosting a meat pie, microwaving frozen beans, opening a jar of plums and making custard. But as she looked at what she'd done, she thought of the beautifully arranged and intriguingly tasty salad of the day before, and felt a sudden longing to cook something from fresh ingredients freshly bought instead of from tins and packets ordered monthly.

However, James wolfed down everything as usual, criticising whenever his mouth was empty. After eating he put on another film, and went to sleep in front of it for nearly two hours. He woke suddenly, stood up, and staggered to the lavatory. Then Sarah heard a strangled cry from the bathroom. She found James on the floor, almost unable to speak. "Pain, terrible, can't stand, get a doctor."

She dialled the ambulance service. In eight minutes a vehicle arrived with two paramedics on board. They agreed it was serious. They stretchered James down the stairs and into the ambulance, and rigged up a drip. One of them started treatment before the other had even started the engine, and the driver telephoned the hospital so that emergency services would be ready for their arrival.

Sarah had already packed her handbag with tablet, phone, keys, purse and James's wallet with both their medical cards and his insurance details. She grabbed a coat, locked the flat and sat next to James in the ambulance for the journey to hospital, where he was whisked into an emergency treatment room.

Sarah sat in a waiting room. A triage nurse arrived, and Sarah confirmed James' name and address, and medical card and insurance policy number. An intern arrived. He said the problem was kidney failure and asked if James had had kidney problems before. Sarah didn't think so, but mentioned that he was a recovering alcoholic who'd recently started drinking again. The intern noted carefully what James had eaten and – especially – drunk over the last two days, and his sickness during the night, and returned to the emergency room.

Eventually the team stabilised James enough to move him to an intensive care ward, but it was nine o'clock and they recommended that Sarah go home and get some sleep. She could visit after ten next morning. Sarah called a taxi and went home, put her tablet and phone on charge quite openly, set the alarm for half-past nine and fell asleep as soon as she got into bed.

***

She was woken by the telephone. It was eleven-fifteen; she'd slept through the alarm. The caller from the hospital first checked that she was speaking to the wife of James Pullen, and then said, "I'm very sorry to have to tell you, but your husband had a severe crisis this morning. We're not sure that he'll pull through. Perhaps you would wish to be here?"

"Of course," Sarah said, "I'll come immediately."

She dressed hurriedly, grabbed her handbag, and called a taxi. At reception, a nurse came to escort her to intensive care. Sarah took one look at James' swollen discoloured face, his complete unconsciousness among the winking LEDs of the equipment surrounding him, and burst into tears. The nurse settled her on a chair at his bedside and talked to her gently until she recovered a little.

Sarah then sat on her own with James. Unconscious, he looked younger, and she remembered how she'd first met him at university, when she was a just a quiet history student intending to teach, and he was the most charismatic student in the economics department, surely heading for the far horizons of international consultancy. When they were first married she'd enjoyed meeting his entertaining and energetic colleagues who made the world of business sound dynamically interesting. But two years later had come the trauma of James being let go.

Ironically his move from London, where Sarah taught in a well-known comprehensive, to Sheffield, where there was no opening for a history teacher, had triggered Sarah's successful and highly paid pan- European career. Without the marriage to James, and without James' failure to secure his future as a financial adviser, Sarah's life would have been far more ordinary. She'd always thought it was James' career pattern that she had to thank for her business success and her personal growth, but it was a tragedy that the charming and charismatic young man she'd fallen in love with had become damaged beyond recognition by those same career events.

She sat there in peace for an hour or so, remembering the time of falling in love. Then quite suddenly there was a change in James' expression, a soft sounding of alarms, a flurry of nurses, an emergency doctor, and in the middle of it all James passed away without regaining consciousness.

A nurse led her gently into a small waiting room. After a short interval she was joined by the emergency doctor, who apologised for not being able to do more. He said that James' kidneys and liver were in a very poor state, and the accumulated damage to them had prevented him responding positively to treatment. "I'm afraid that he had very little chance of recovery from any form of crisis. I can only offer my condolences on your bereavement."

"Thank you," said Sarah stoutly. "I'm sure you did everything possible. I'm ashamed to say that I didn't realise until recently how much he was drinking. I think he'd put himself beyond all help, but I do want to thank you very much for trying to save him."

The hospital's bereavement counsellor took Sarah to her office, where she carefully explained the formalities relating to a death in hospital. She offered

Sarah formal counselling, but Sarah found that after suffering the intrusiveness of James for so long, she preferred to be on her own, and she emphatically said so. The counsellor gave her a leaflet with all the emergency telephone numbers Sarah might want, and warmly asked her not to be shy of coming back if she felt the need to talk later on, but then let her go as she wished.

Sarah spent an hour alone in her flat, looking out at the view of the estuary. James had only been a background fixture for forty-seven years, but he'd always been there, always needing to be taken into account. It would take her some time to come to terms with the end of his influence. But the way she'd always stopped thinking of James was to go to work, and there was now plenty of work to be done. She emailed Marie-Pierre, thanking her but advising that there wouldn't now be any need for their rental arrangement, and that she would collect her property from the attic in due course. She then sent a general email to her more distant contacts.

Then she faced the call she most dreaded and telephoned Deborah. Deb was as shocked as expected, and immediately asked for details, when, where, why? But as she answered the questions, Sarah could hear the tone of Deb's voice changing as she adjusted to the news, and sure enough her first reaction was characteristic. "This must be a terrible shock to you, Sarah, how are you coping? Do you have anyone in France close enough to lean on? Would it help if I came over or would I be in the way?"

Sarah said that she could call on Elodie and Marie-Pierre, but added that she'd like Deb to come over for the funeral if that was possible.

"Of course it will be," Deb said. "Can I bring my husband with me? It will make more family there for you. Just email me when you have a date and time, and we'll be there. Now, would you like me to tell Charles? He's very difficult to get hold of, and I could save you a lot of bother."

"Oh, thank you," Sarah said, "that would be very kind of you." She'd wondered how to get the news to James' younger brother, for whom she only had a postal address, and was relieved not to have to tell yet another person of the death of close family.

Emails full of sympathy were starting to arrive from social club members. Marie-Pierre swiftly offered her condolences for the shock, but added a blunt recommendation that Sarah should take it as a gift from heaven. She offered her spare room if Sarah wanted to get away from the penthouse, and a chair in her kitchen any time Sarah needed company. There was no pressing need to clear her attic.

Sarah replied, thanking each sender, but hoping they'd understand that she wanted to be by herself for a little to get used to the situation.

6

On Tuesday, the bereavement counsellor phoned to confirm that the death certificate had been signed by two doctors, and suggested she could contact a funeral director on Sarah's behalf. Shortly after Sarah agreed to this, the counsellor emailed the details of the funeral company, so that Sarah could contact them when she wished.

Glad to have something to do, Sarah arranged an appointment that afternoon. The senior funeral director proved to be sympathetic, and the two of them worked through all the decisions which had to be made. The only sticking point was co-ordinating with the minister chosen to hold the service.

Sarah and James hadn't joined any local church when moving to France, and religion had played very little part in their lives, but when thinking about a funeral Sarah felt that Deborah would be more comfortable with a service, and one which resembled one from an English church. When she said as much, the funeral director said that there was an Anglican church just across the river in Dinard, with a largely English congregation and a bilingual vicar, and he offered to make contact with him. The three of them settled on a ceremony at the crematorium on Thursday morning at eleven o'clock, which would give Deborah time to come over from Sussex the evening before. The funeral director suggested a car to transport Deb and Clark from and to whichever hotel they booked, and another to transport Sarah to and from the ceremony.

When she arrived home, Sarah emailed Deborah with the time and place of the funeral, and received a reply saying that Deb and Clark had booked a hotel in Saint-Malo for Wednesday night. Deb suggested that after the event they should all three eat lunch in the hotel. Sarah wrote back agreeing, and contacted the funeral director to say that only one car would be needed after the ceremony.

The vicar had asked Sarah for a short summary of James' life, and in particular of his stay in France, and Sarah took her time to create and email a presentable view of James. This made her realise she hadn't contacted the bridge club, so she looked up the number of the Rowleys' fixed line and dialled. The phone was answered by Janet, who was shocked but immediately sympathetic, and felt that she and Brian should attend the funeral as well as passing information to other bridge club members.

Looking for something else to do, Sarah decided to sell the car. She walked to the local garage and asked if it was possible to exchange the SUV for something she'd prefer to drive. The salesman arranged for one of his mechanics to collect the car immediately, and then named a respectable price for it, but he also suggested a profitable exchange with his smallest model, a town car with restricted luggage capacity but decent performance, and which could carry four people, turn on a sixpence, and park in a very small space. Sarah immediately accepted the change down to a more appropriate vehicle. She moved on to the insurance broker to organise its insurance, and then happily drove home in her delightfully responsive little blue car.

Back in the penthouse, she went through James' cupboards and drawers looking for papers, but found only his passport, his driving licence and his credit cards. She was surprised that there were no statements or chequebook for the English bank account. She thought she'd better look up that account on the internet. She hadn't actively used the English bank for years, but she had retained an up-to-date login ID and password, and the internet banking system promptly let her in.

The first thing she saw was that the two original accounts, the joint current account and the joint savings account, had been joined by a third one, a loan account in both their names. This astounded her. As she knew nothing about it, James must have forged her signature on the loan account application. There was one pound in the current account and one pound in the savings account, but the loan account was in debt by £4,213.68. The loan had been partly paid off by the two state pensions for Sarah and James whenever received, and by some receipts from O Maynard – a name Sarah didn't recognise – but these were not enough to prevent interest being continually been added to the debt.

Sarah couldn't think of any reason for James opening a loan account. When he'd wanted money for buying DVDs and streaming films and playing games, he took it from their joint French current account. He could and did spend a very large sum in this way every month. So why was there a debt in England and why hadn't he done more to pay it off?

Only the current year's transactions at the English bank were online, and the loan was older than that. Hoping to find an answer, Sarah methodically downloaded the annual statements of the last ten years. Half-an-hour later she opened the earliest. It related to the year in which she'd sold her London flat.

When she'd been based in London she'd bought a flat on a ten-year mortgage, paid from her very substantial salary, and when she'd moved to work in Paris, she'd let it. But it soon became obvious that she'd never work in London again, so she'd decided to sell the London flat and buy in Paris. London prices were very much higher than those in Paris, so there'd be enough profit to buy a second flat in Huntingdon, where James was working at that time.

Sarah had found it difficult to handle the sale and purchase in England while travelling around Europe, so she'd signed an authority for James to act for her. She'd been delighted when James advised that the London flat, bought for £45,000 originally, had sold for £90,000 above the solicitors' fee. The tiny property bought in then-unfashionable Huntingdon cost £20,000. The £70,000 balance was transferred to her French bank, and easily covered the purchase cost, fees and some furniture for the Paris flat.

Looking for these transactions on the statement, she clearly identified the purchase of the Huntingdon property and the transfer to her French bank, but the solicitor's remittance for the sale of the London flat was £112,000 instead of the £90,000 notified by James. James had moved the £22,000 difference into their joint savings account.

A similar story applied to the sale of the Huntingdon flat years later. Train services had improved so much that the town had become a sought-after location in the London commuter belt. Prices had soared, and James had sent Sarah a transfer of £50,000, but the money actually received from the sale was just over £62,000 and the £12,000 difference had once again been moved to the savings account. In total James had creamed off £34,000 from the profit on the two flats.

His out-payments had begun with £15,000 to Miller & Partners, whoever they were, and then a series of small regular sums paid monthly to P P Williams, whoever that was. A series of incoming payments from O Maynard varied between £250 and £470, but were always paid at the end of each month.

£20,000 was received from a Porsche garage. James had been involved in a crash, but he'd said the insurers wouldn't pay for repairs because the other driver hadn't stopped. Sarah now suspected James had been driving while drunk and no other car had been involved. By not reporting the accident, James hadn't been breathalysed and had kept his UK licence free of recorded offences. The £20,000 for the wrecked car – less than a quarter of its undamaged value – had promptly been passed to P P Williams, but a bank loan of £3,000 had been taken out at the same time. This loan had been paid off by James' second embezzlement, but the next payment to P P Williams was £15,000 and this had necessitated a second loan of £6,000. James hadn't succeeded in substantially reducing this last loan, currently standing at £4,213.68.

The loan account was in joint names. Sarah couldn't think how to conclusively prove James' fraudulent inclusion of her name; that would almost certainly involve costly legal representation. She'd always had access to the English bank and could have discovered the loan years ago; it would be difficult to argue her way out of responsibility for it.

Paying off the loan would be cheaper than engaging a lawyer. She contacted a foreign exchange broker, obtained a quotation in euros for transfer of £4,500 to the English loan account, accepted it, and paid from her savings account. It was no great sum in comparison to her net wealth and the money would arrive in England next day.

But James' out-payments totalled £57,000. What could he have bought? Her attempt to discover who Miller & Partners were failed utterly; internet searching found hundreds of possible partnerships, and Sarah had no address or indication of profession. P P Williams was a similar problem.

Sarah wondered if James' telephone or email contacts would hold a clue. The telephone – the password was his birth year – yielded only the numbers of his sister, his brother, the English bank, and the name Piper. So P P Williams could be Piper Williams? But no such person was recorded on the internet.

James' email – the password was his Porsche registration number – showed only emails from his younger brother, Charles. Sarah opened the last one: 'Bank agreed 6 month extension but say absolutely the last.'

The email before that one said, 'Oliver paid £378.50', and the one before that, 'Total £4,213.68 due 31 July.'

So Charles knew about the loan account and the incoming payments from O Maynard, presumably Oliver. Perhaps Charles knew what the rest of the money had bought?

Sarah knew that Charles was the younger of James' two siblings, the afterthought, born after her marriage to James. He was twenty-three years younger than James, and eighteen years younger than Deborah, who'd brought him up from babyhood. He'd lived with Deb and her husband until he went to university. He was an accountant like James, currently working as auditor for a corporate accounting service who moved him around the country. His only marriage had ended in divorce. Sarah had sent his Christmas card to an address at 2 Mulberry Mews, Chichester, Sussex. She now knew his phone number. But she hadn't seen him since he was a baby, and certainly didn't know him well enough to ring and ask what was going on. She put the problem aside for the time being.

***

On Wednesday, Sarah embarked on tidying the penthouse. First on the list was clearing out James' clothes for donating to charity. She took a roll of black plastic sacks into the dressing room and started folding the clean clothes into the sacks, putting aside items which needed cleaning first. James had a rail of jackets and pullovers above a rail of shirts and roll-necks, with a shelf in between the two rails. As she took the jackets down, Sarah found items at the back of the shelf, hidden by the garments, two unopened bottles of whisky, a collection of packets of high-strength ibuprofen, all the recent prescriptions for painkillers in her name, stamped by four different local pharmacies, and two screw-top cans of a liquid labelled in German.

The whisky was no surprise but the rest was odd. She switched on the laptop and googled the German name of the liquid, which led to a website wholly in German. She copied what looked like a product description into a translation app. It described a fuel additive for diesel vehicles, so she'd obviously typed something wrongly. James' SUV was petrol-driven; he'd never owned a diesel, and anything to do with a car would surely have been kept in the vehicle. She had plenty to do, so yet again she put her questions aside.

She drove three bags of clothes to the local charity collection point and dropped off another bagful in the cleaners'. She then bought flowers for the apartment and cakes and scones for tomorrow's tea. She looked out her clothes for the funeral next day, and settled on the black skirt suit she used for formal occasions at work, teaming it with a grey silk pleated blouse and a plain gold necklace. She found her black suede formal shoes and matching handbag and gave them a good brushing. There was just time for a refreshing walk around the cliffs in the summer breeze. She bought a light dinner in the bar-tabac before taking an early night.

***

The Thursday of the funeral dawned clear and bright. Sarah descended to meet the car from the funeral company. The director himself handed her ceremoniously into the back seat of the limousine, and then sat next to the driver speaking on his phone. As the car slowed, the hearse carrying the coffin pulled out of its parking place and took the lead. A few hundred yards later, the car carrying Deborah and Clark from their hotel pulled into third place in the procession. Sarah felt strangely comforted by being swept up in this little ritual.

At the chapel of the crematorium Sarah was surprised to see a small throng. Standing in front was a figure in clerical dress. The funeral director presented her to the vicar, the bearers moved the coffin out of the car and placed the family wreaths on it, and automatically all the other mourners lined each side of the path to the door, to bow heads as the coffin passed. It entered the chapel, followed by the vicar, then Sarah, then Deborah and Clark, and then everyone else. There were five members of the Qi Gong class, the secretary of the pensioners' centre, ten members of the social club, including Gérard Lemestre and Marie-Pierre and Elodie, and all four bridge club committee members with their wives. It wasn't the sparse turnout that Sarah had expected.

The English contingent stood out by wearing formal clothes, the men in black suits and black ties, the women in black coats. None of the Frenchmen wore a tie at all, and although no one was dressed in bright colours, the French simply wore everyday clothes. Sarah thought that James would have appreciated the English more; indeed, he would have relished being the centre of attraction. Her mind whipped back through the years to a charismatic twenty-year-old holding centre stage at one college event after another, and she had to wipe away a tear over something lost for ever.

On the seats of the chapel were small leaflets with the order of service of the Anglican Church alongside its French translation. The vicar conducted the Anglican service in English, but included a short oration in both languages which did some justice to James. Deborah wept quietly through parts of it, in the shelter of Clark's arm.

Very soon the ceremony was over, and the vicar took Sarah by the hand to lead her out of the chapel at the head of the procession. The two of them stood together at the doorway, and Sarah shook hands or exchanged kisses with all those present as they left. Many of her friends put in a quiet but heartfelt word of support, and Janet Rowley said, "My dear, we must meet again when you feel up to it." Sarah felt warmed and supported by these attentions.

Finally everyone had been greeted. Sarah had thanked the vicar very warmly and shaken hands with the funeral director. It was time to leave. The car which had brought Deborah and Clark was waiting, and the driver handed Sarah into the front seat before ushering the others into the back. He drove at a sedate pace through the narrow gateway in the walls of Saint-Malo to the hotel front door.

Clark led the way through the hotel reception towards the lift to the roof, and in no time at all they were established in the roof-top restaurant surrounded by the panoramic view, enjoying the aperitif which the waiter had suggested and the pre-lunch snacks provided by the chef. Deborah and Clark kept up an easy conversation on life in Saint-Malo, the astounding view from the windows, France in general, the good weather, the other people who'd come to the funeral, the surprising fact that there was an Anglican church nearby, and the number of local people who spoke English.

Sarah told them something of the history of Saint-Malo, making them laugh when she said that the first book in French which she'd bought locally had a title she translated as 'Saint-Malo versus the English, a small town takes on a whole nation'.

At the end of the delicious lunch, Sarah and Clark argued over the bill before finally agreeing to divide it down the middle, paying half each. The three then walked to the top of the famous ramparts. It was a glorious early summer day with a light refreshing breeze, and it was low tide, so all the granite rocks and sandy bottoms were exposed. The causeways to the two nearest islands, Fort National and the Grand Be, were above water and thronged with walkers. Sarah pointed out to Clark the channel which the ferry would take later that evening, related some stories of the history of the town, its walls and its shipping, and showed her guests the famous statue of Robert Surcouf, the corsair who'd been ennobled by Napoleon for his depredations of English merchant shipping.

When the little party had completed their circuit of the walls, Sarah invited the others to tea in her flat. Clark led the way to where he'd parked his car, and asked Sarah to sit in front to navigate through the one-way streets. When they reached the flat, Sarah opened the underground garage so that Clark could park there, and they took the lift to the penthouse.

Deborah was astounded, but charmed and delighted, by the property, the furnishings and the view. "This is absolutely splendid," she said with enthusiasm, "and so very much more spacious than I thought it would be. I can hardly believe that James told us how small it was!"

Sarah grinned widely. "He usually described it as 'a piddling little flat'," she said, seeing from Deb's embarrassment that those were the exact words he'd used to her. "He really wanted a picturesque old farmhouse with no modern conveniences, miles out in the country."

"Well, I think it's splendid, and I'm very sure it's bigger than the average farmhouse. You were so clever to find this."

Clark asked questions about the age of the block, French building methods, cost of maintenance and services, local taxes, local transport and even the type of neighbours, but he was also obviously impressed.

Sarah made tea and served a platter of miniature apple tarte tatins, with a light Genoese sponge cake filled with raspberry jelly and decorated with cream. They sat in the lounge, eating from the low tables in front of the sofa and armchairs, so that they could enjoy the view of the river with all the windows open from floor to ceiling.

Before leaving to catch the boat, Deborah said, "We must meet again. Please don't lose touch. I'd love an occasional email. But I wholeheartedly agree with you wanting to stay in such a lovely place."

After she'd closed the garage security gate behind Clark's departing car, Sarah picked up the post from her box in the hall and carried it up to the penthouse. Some of the bundle of mail was obviously sympathy cards, and she decided to arrange them on the shelves of the antique dresser.

Halfway down the pile was an envelope with an English stamp. The card it contained held a short letter.

'Dear Mrs Pullen,

I write to offer you my sincere condolences on the sad passing of your husband James, whom I have known for some long time. We met often when he was a boy, as well as in recent years.

This is not an appropriate time to bother you with questions, but I am interested to know if you intend to continue the existing arrangement for the garden. As I am sure you realise, it would take me a little time to withdraw from your plot, so if you do decide to make changes I would appreciate a few weeks' notice.

There is no need for a quick answer. Until I hear from you to the contrary I will continue to make payments at the end of each month.

Yours sincerely, Oliver Maynard.'

The revelation wasn't so much the letter as the sender's address, which was 1 Mulberry Mews, Chichester. Charles lived at 2 Mulberry Mews. So Charles had told Oliver that James had died. Although Oliver had known James for some long time, he hadn't described him as a good friend or said he would be missed. He made payments to James' bank every month, presumably connected to 'the existing arrangements for the garden'. What linked James to a garden? It seemed probable that the answers to all Sarah's questions were in Mulberry Mews. Between them, Oliver and Charles could surely tell her what was going on.

Sarah preferred doing to wondering. She looked up the ferry timetable on the internet; there was a boat to Portsmouth at eight next morning. She booked herself a car space with a return on Monday afternoon. She booked Friday to Sunday night in a hotel chosen at random in Chichester. She packed a small suitcase with black and navy clothing. She charged up her tablet, added the English bank statements to her USB key and scanned in James' passport and death certificate, before packing the tablet in her large handbag. She emailed Marie-Pierre, Elodie and Irene Ho to say that she had to go to England for the weekend to sort out a problem in James' affairs. She set the alarm and took an early night before driving her little car on to the ferry.

7

From Portsmouth harbour Sarah drove along the coast road to Chichester and reached the hotel well before noon. Her room wouldn't be ready until two o'clock, so she drank a mint tea in the bar while consulting a town plan on her tablet. Mulberry Mews was only a short walk away.

Her first sight of the mews was a delight. A narrow tarmac road between two buildings, only three feet wider than a car, opened out on to a wide cobbled courtyard with a mulberry tree in the middle and with two detached Georgian houses facing the entrance.

From the entrance road, only one of the houses had been in full view, its front door clearly marked '1'; to the right, the second house was hidden. But as number 2 came into sight Sarah could see that all its windows were boarded up. The roof looked new, and the front door looked solid, though otherwise it seemed to be a building site. But there was no doubt that it was Charles Pullen's address; a note covered with a plastic bag and pinned to the front door jamb read 'Please deliver all post for Pullen to 1 Mulberry Mews'. Sarah couldn't believe anyone was actually living in the place.

Between the two houses was a garage with a neat Grecian pediment above the up-and-over door. A brass figure '1' was screwed above the door handle. On the right of number 2 was a patch of muddy gravel with tyre marks. Sarah walked across the gravel to the back of the house. She was completely unprepared for what she saw.

Behind the two houses was a substantial plot fully planted with orderly rows of crops. There were runner beans, peas, lettuces under plastic, carrots, leeks, asparagus, spring onions, strawberries and raspberry canes. It looked very professional, and had been thoroughly hoed, with planks in use between the rows as walkways. The vegetables obviously covered the gardens of both the houses. This must be Oliver Maynard's 'arrangement for use of the garden'. But he'd paid James for that arrangement and intended to continue to pay Sarah in future. Why didn't he pay Charles?

The basement door of number 1 opened, and a grey-haired gentleman came up the steps into the garden. He stopped when he saw Sarah. "Can I help you?" he asked in a well-educated voice.

"I believe you may be able to," Sarah said. "I'm Sarah Pullen, and I was looking for Charles."

"Charles won't be here until after nine tonight, Mrs Pullen," the gentleman replied. "But I'm Oliver Maynard, and I'm very glad to meet you at last. Can I offer you a cup of tea?"

"That's very kind of you."

They both moved into Oliver's kitchen, in a half-basement with steps down from the garden, and while Oliver made tea, Sarah sat in a Windsor chair at a scrubbed table bearing a vase of blue irises. Despite its functional contents – it housed an Aga, a fridge-freezer, and a washer-dryer – the room was warm and welcoming, brightly lit through its large windows, its walls painted butter yellow and all curtains and cushions in lemon-and-white gingham check.

"The garden's doing beautifully," Sarah complimented.

"We're close to the peak season for market gardening," said Oliver. "I presume James told you he suggested me renting the garden until the house is finished? I sell the produce in the market, and I pay James, well, I pay you now, dear lady, one quarter of my profit. That's half the profit of your half of the gardens. I don't really work for profit, it's more of a retirement hobby, but when I took over both gardens I invested in a few mechanical tools to assist. Of course, James thought he'd be living in the house within a few years, but restoration cost him more than he expected. So far he's only managed to get the roof on, and to create a little kitchen in the basement which Charles uses. There are no upper floors and no staircase yet, but of course you know that."

"I don't know anything at all about the house," Sarah said bluntly, registering the fact that Oliver regarded the house and garden as owned by James, not by Charles, and as inherited by herself, not by Charles. "James kept the whole thing to himself. I'm not even sure when he bought it. I do know he didn't declare ownership to the French government as he should have done. There are no relevant papers at home in France. That's why I was looking for Charles. I need the record of purchase, and proof of James' ownership. I'd hoped that Charles would have the documents here, or would at least know the lawyer's address."

"Well," Oliver said slowly, "Charles does have a deed-box full of papers in his basement, and if the contents relate to the house they would now belong to you." He paused, frowning. "But the papers may belong to Charles. You see, James gave me a spare key. I needed it to let in the restoration crew for him. So I could let you in."

"Oh, but that would be marvellous," Sarah said, amazed at this stroke of luck.

"It's just that I'm reluctant to pry into Charles's affairs," Oliver added. "James told me he'd been in all sorts of trouble, but he's very polite and quiet, and he's never caused me any bother."

"He's my brother-in-law," Sarah said firmly, "and I have no intention of upsetting anyone in the family."

"And as the owner you do have more right to the house than he has," Oliver agreed, nodding. "If you know nothing about it, I think you must at least see the building. Let me show it to you."

Oliver opened the back door of number 2 to reveal a room obviously intended as a basement kitchen. It held a cheap sink, a small table, a metal deed-box, a plastic chair, a single camp-bed with a sleeping-bag, and a stack of four suitcases. In the walls of the room were three door frames, one simply boarded up, one with its door shut, and one with the door standing open revealing a toilet and a wash-hand basin. The kitchen was lit by one bare light bulb.

Oliver went to the door at the back of the room. "This should open on to stairs leading up to the front hall." He opened it to reveal an empty space with all four walls of the house shored up with internal scaffolding. "But I'm afraid there's a lot to be done."

Sarah was astounded to see right up to the roof beams four storeys above. The house was simply a shell. She took photographs on her phone. "It looks to be quite a challenge," she commented bravely.

Back in the kitchen, Sarah picked up the deed-box. Its key was in the lock, and inside the first thing she saw were the bank statements for the English joint accounts, and under them the bank loan agreement on stiff paper, with a signature nothing like hers following James' usual one. "At least some of these papers belong to James," she said.

She sorted the papers into two piles on the table, separating bank account documents from house ownership; she described each one as Oliver watched.

The last document was confirmation of purchase from Miller & Partners (Solicitors) stapled to an auction advertisement, and underneath were the old title deeds tied with red tape. The chequebook for the current account had the first cheque missing but all the others were already signed by James. No document named Charles.

Sarah refilled the box. "This is what I came for," she said. "Everything's here. Thank you so much for helping me, Oliver. I'll tell Charles I've taken these papers, but if you need to contact me, I'll be at the Butter Cross Hotel until Monday morning."

Oliver smiled. "Eat in the hotel restaurant; they'll serve you my runner beans."

Sarah tore a page off a notepad and wrote down her telephone number. "This is my French mobile phone in case you need it. Now I think I need photos of the outside. James didn't have a single one."

"He knew it too well to need a photograph," said Oliver. "He used to come here by bicycle when he was twelve. I'd often see him standing by the mulberry tree, staring at the house."

Oliver locked up, wished her a good afternoon, and returned home. Sarah carefully photographed the outside of the house from all angles using her phone, taking one last photo of both buildings across the cobbled front yard with its tree.

After a hotel lunch of roast lamb – with delicious runner beans – Sarah settled in her room to read the documents she'd found. The story proved simple. The house had suffered from dry rot. The owners hadn't noticed as it spread throughout. The exterior walls were brick with decorative stucco, but they weren't structural. The internal load-bearing structure was wooden: wooden posts, wooden beams, wooden floors, and wooden roof timbers. The owners had asked Peter Piper Restoration to replace some affected timbers, but the restorer had done a thorough survey and discovered the extent of the problem. His report was in the box, recommending removing all woodwork from roof beams to basement, and burning it along with any wooden furniture. He'd signed as Peter Pepper-Williams. Sarah wondered amusedly if 'Peter Piper' was his school nickname.

A cheaper company had been asked to strip out all the wood, leaving the house derelict and roofed with plastic sheeting. It was on the market for two years, then it was added to the books of an auctioneer who specialised in hard cases. From the advertisement in the deed box, the other auction properties were small houses in outlying villages, probably mortgage repossessions. The Mulberry Mews house could only have received one bid, because James bought it at the reserve price of £15,000, promptly paid to the auctioneers' solicitors, Miller & Partners.

Nothing in the deed box explained why Charles spent weekends in that bleak kitchen. He certainly didn't own it, but he did oblige his brother by handling the bank statements, which were always sent to 2 Mulberry Mews rather than to Saint-Edern, thus efficiently hiding all English bank data from Sarah.

Sarah telephoned the bank from the hotel, found they'd received the money transferred from France, and asked for the loan account to be closed. The clerk calculated the final charge on the loan, and closed the account while online. Sarah then asked for the remaining accounts to be put into her name only, as her husband had died; she agreed to email the scanned death certificate. She asked for the account address to be changed to Saint-Edern, and the clerk agreed to do that if Sarah sent proof of address. Sarah asked for a chequebook in her name to be sent to Saint-Edern. When the conversation finished she emailed the bank, re-stating her requests and attaching copies of the death certificate and the Saint-Edern purchase deed. She now had full control of the English bank accounts.

Sarah phoned the Pensions Office, advised them of James' death and asked them to stop his pension. They asked for a paper certificate sent by mail, and Sarah obliged immediately. Close to the post box from which she sent the certificate, she found a pleasant café serving a light dinner. By then it was nine o'clock and time to tackle Charles. She walked back to Mulberry Mews. A car was now parked on the gravel patch. She knocked loudly on the basement door.

Sarah had never met Charles as an adult. She was quite startled when the door was opened by a man who looked exactly like James aged twenty, if a little shorter and slighter. He looked equally startled to see her.

"You probably don't recognise me. I'm Sarah Pullen, your sister-in-law," she said, "and I'd like to know what's going on."

"I'm not sure what you mean."

Sarah walked past him, shutting the door behind her. "What are you doing here?" she asked.

"James let me stay here at weekends. I don't do any harm. Really. I've got nowhere else to go."

"Where do you live during the week?"

"In a hotel."

"Who pays for that?" "My employers."

"How much do they pay?"

There was a long silence.

"Charles, I'm waiting for an answer. When I worked away from home, my employers paid a lodging allowance which covered accommodation and food for the whole period I was away, weekends included. Do yours do the same?"

Charles had a far more expressive face than James; it suffused with guilt. "Yes."

Sarah walked to the table, turned the chair to face him and sat down. "So you're taking a lodging allowance for the whole week but staying here at the weekend to make a profit out of it?"

Charles sat down on the bed. "Yes."

Sarah deliberately hardened her voice. "Now, let me get this straight. You're forty-three, you're a qualified accountant with twenty years' experience, you're employed at senior rates of pay by a nationally known company, you get an expense allowance sufficient to cover your needs, and yet you're prepared to live every weekend in this comfortless basement to make a tiny additional sum."

She was unprepared for the reaction. Charles lowered his head into his hands and sobbed uncontrollably.

It was some minutes before he calmed down. Sarah said prosaically, "I think that's established that you have financial problems. How did that happen?"

"You know I had a divorce?" Charles asked.

"I heard."

"I didn't realise that marriage would be such a financial complication. I was pretty well-off. I could put down a large deposit and my salary meant I was offered a large mortgage. So I bought a four-bedroom flat in the best part of Brighton. But I hadn't costed in much furniture. Unfortunately Celia wanted to furnish the whole place completely. So I had to use hire-purchase to buy more sofas and armchairs than we needed, beds and dressing tables and wardrobes in all the spare bedrooms, carpets and curtains everywhere. The mortgage took a vast chunk of my salary every month, but now there were monthly repayments for hire purchase.

"Celia was on a fixed salary and she'd spent all her savings on her wedding dress. But my employers were short-handed; they'd always pay for extra work. So I worked longer daily hours and all Saturday. I was practically never at home. When Celia wanted to go out, I wanted to sleep. So she went out with her girlfriends as she'd done before we married, and while out with them she met a man who offered to take her out dancing every weekend, so she moved in with him. She applied for divorce because she wanted the furnishings she'd chosen transferred to his flat. They were the most important things in her life, the reason she'd married in the first place."

"Did you miss her?"

"I hardly noticed she'd gone. But in the divorce settlement she got the flat as well as the furniture, and so I was left having to work extra hours to pay off the mortgage and loans for a place I couldn't live in."

"That doesn't sound very equitable," Sarah said, frowning. "Celia had no children, she was earning herself, she had another man supporting her and was living with him."

"That's what I thought, but the court decided differently. I was losing money by attending the court instead of working, so I hadn't wanted to pay for an expensive lawyer as well."

"But Celia did?"

"Her new man's younger brother is a divorce lawyer. I didn't know that until I got to the court."

Sarah blinked. "That was bad luck."

"Celia's flat was the best of the two they had, so her bloke sold his and moved into ours, well, hers. I've paid off the loans now but I'm still paying their mortgage for them."

"So your major problem is paying off the mortgage?"

There was a long pause during which Charles's face clearly showed that he was gathering his resources to explain something else. "James told me how he'd bought this house. He'd had a cash payment on the side from a grateful client and he'd staked it in a poker game and won; so he kept playing until he'd built up enough to buy the house. Then he carried on gambling to pay for the new roof. He told me I could win enough in one night to pay off the mortgage. I didn't try it because I don't really like joining card games. I don't fit in with groups of hooray guys bent on having fun, and I'm not as good as regular players at calculating the odds."

Sarah had found it difficult not to interrupt, but Charles was looking at the floor and didn't notice.

"Then we got a new boss at work. The new-broom-sweeps-clean variety. He started investigating how each of us worked. He said he was estimating the worth of each of us to the company. It was obvious he was going to cut staff or salaries. I was terrified. I couldn't take a pay cut because of the mortgage. If dismissed, I'd have to file for bankruptcy; that's death to an accountant. The boss asked everyone to formally re-apply for their job. I didn't want the damned job. I've always hated the work, every bloody minute of it, and it'd got far worse with him in charge. I certainly couldn't have written the best application. The boss called two of us in, me and Tom, and said he was cutting the staff by two to save costs, and we were the two. I went back to the hotel and got drunk." He fell silent.

"What happened next?" Sarah prompted.

"I had an almighty hangover, so I got in late next morning, and I walked into a shouting match between the new boss and one of the other team leaders. Our guy had found a new job, and didn't see any reason to stay and work his notice. He said he was leaving there and then. He told the boss in great detail and in public exactly what he thought of him, and walked out. In the afternoon, the boss called me into his office. He said there was now a vacancy, so in view of the long hours I worked, he'd keep me on. Only Tom was let go. That's been the problem ever since. I don't like the boss and he doesn't like me, but he's stuck with me because I work long hours. I hate the job. I don't know how much longer I can stand it."

"But that didn't cause any more money problems," Sarah ventured.

"It did in a way," Charles said. "I kept thinking that if I'd paid off that bloody mortgage, I could have walked out too. When I finished my work for the day, I used to read the internet news sites while I wound down, and one site carried an advert for a poker game. I remembered that James had won all that money. So I put up a stake and started to play. Only I lost. I kept playing but I kept on losing. It was unbelievable how often I lost. In the end I got fed up and went back to the hotel. Next night at work I looked up the site to see what I owed. It was frightening. So that night I played as seriously as I could to try and win it all back, but I rarely won, and in the end the debt just increased. I've never played again.

"They had my telephone number and email; they ask you for those when you sign on. They rang me at work. I was terrified someone would hear me talking to them. They sent me emails at work. I was terrified the boss could read them. So I said I really couldn't pay, and they mailed some legal papers to sign, to turn the debt into a loan with interest.

"I asked James for help but he said everything he had was laid out in property because he'd just bought a flat in Saint-Edern. He said he could probably help in a year or so when his big French client paid half a million at the end of their joint project, but meanwhile he suggested I could stay here at weekends and make money out of the allowance. So I only stay four nights a week at the hotel, I only eat four breakfasts and never eat dinner. It's paid off a lot of the poker debt. There's less than £3,000 of it left now. Another year and I'll have done it."

Sarah was horrified. "If you don't eat dinner, how do you manage?"

"I eat lunch. It's cheaper. It's in the canteen where I'm working so it's usually subsidised. I buy the cheapest option and I put the free bread roll in my pocket to eat in the evening."

"What do you eat between Friday lunch and Monday lunch?"

"Nothing at all. I just drink water." Charles looked quite proud of it. "You can see, can't you, that I have to be able to stay here?"

"No," said Sarah definitively. "Not at all. You're ruining your health and endangering your sanity. I wouldn't let a dog live the way you're doing, and I don't want it to continue. But I do see I'll need to think of an alternative for you. It's very late, so I suggest we meet tomorrow. If you come into the hotel at nine- thirty I'll buy you breakfast."

"But you will help?" Charles looked both devastated and confused.

"I may," Sarah said, not committing herself, "but there's more going on than you know about."

8

Being used to European time, Sarah woke well before breakfast next morning. She made herself a lemon tea in her room and then she checked through the deed box. The paper statements covered only fifteen months and didn't cover the sale of either of the two English flats. Charles would have had no reason to doubt anything James had told him.

Charles might superficially resemble James, but Sarah couldn't imagine James providing the naïve description of being sucked into gambling online, as supplied by Charles the night before. It was also an absolute certainty that James wouldn't have worked extra hours and missed two years of dinners to whittle down a debt. When circumstances had hit him hard, Charles had displayed a streak of practicality and self-reliance which reminded Sarah a little of Deborah. If he could get past this long episode of bad luck, he might well be able to make something of himself. She realised she wanted to do something to help that, though she acknowledged to herself this was probably based on Charles' resemblance to the young James she'd fallen in love with.

She went down to breakfast, carrying her coat, with the tablet in her handbag. She told the receptionist that she was expecting her brother-in-law to arrive. "There's been a death in the family," she said, knowing that would stop any questions, "so there are loose ends to be tied up. Please charge me for two breakfasts this morning, then I can talk to my brother-in-law in comfort."

Sarah took an orange juice and sat at a table for two facing the door. Just before half-past nine a nervous- looking Charles appeared in the doorway, and she waved to him. He smiled in obvious relief.

"Good to see you," Sarah said warmly. "Let's get something to eat." She helped herself to scrambled eggs in the hope that this would encourage Charles to take a decent breakfast, and was relieved to see him covering a plate with ham, eggs, tomatoes, mushrooms and fried bread, and filling another plate with muffins.

They returned to their table. "This does look good," he said, "Thank you very much." He attacked it with all the enthusiasm of a man who'd eaten nothing since yesterday's minimal lunch.

"I don't know very much about you," Sarah said. "You were born after I married James, and I stopped visiting Bognor while you were still a baby. I'm quite sure that I haven't seen you since, because I didn't know how much you look like James. I do remember being told you were doing well at school, and then that you'd got very good A Levels and a place at Sussex University. What degree did you take?"

The pleased expression was suddenly wiped off Charles's face. "Business management and economics," he said.

"Like your brother?" Sarah asked lightly.

"Exactly. Everyone expected me to follow James. My mother adored him. She told me about him all the time, what he was like, what he was good at, where he was going in the future." His expression changed subtly. "She was never interested in me. I was just the nuisance who'd made her give up her job in a gossipy agency full of friends to look after a baby.

"Deborah was the one who really brought me up. She'd joined the agency at the bottom and was intent on getting to the top, but when she wasn't at work she always found time to play with me. Evenings with Deb were the best thing in my life. She taught me to count and to read before I went to school. She took me to school every morning, and in the evening when we had tea together she always asked me what I'd done that day. When she married Clark, I was eight, and she took me with her. I'll never cease to be grateful to her, and to Clark, for that. I spent all my school holidays in the agency, helping Deb. I was so proud of being able to pay her back even in a small way.

"But Deborah meant nothing to my parents. For them it was James, James, James all the way. So I modelled myself on James. I did everything he'd done. I went to the same school. I did the same sports. I did better than he'd done at everything. I know that, because people said so. But it was no good. James had something else. People who'd met him once remembered him. People who saw me every day didn't notice I was there." He fell silent.

Sarah sensed the profound loneliness of an intelligent boy with no real home. Charles looked very much younger than his years, and still had some of the edginess of an adolescent, and she wondered if this was due to the insecurity of his upbringing as well as to the amount of bad luck he'd accumulated through no great fault of his own.

"You qualified for university, and for a course which is very well-regarded," Sarah said encouragingly. "That's no mean achievement."

"That was due to the school. They told me where to apply and for what. When I got the place, it was a four-year degree including work experience. The school was delighted. My parents were happy. Deborah said it was a real achievement. I was proud of having met everyone's expectations. But, when I started the course, I realised that I didn't really want to do it."

"Didn't you think of changing to a different course?" Sarah asked "What A levels do you have?"

There was another long silence.

"Pure maths, applied maths, history and French. If I think about it as I am now, I can see that I could have changed subject. But I was me as I was then, so it was impossible. I'd spent all my life following James. That set the goal. I had to get through four years of university and work experience, I had to get a degree in economics, I had to get my accountancy qualifications and then I had to work as an accountant. It was set in stone. I didn't know what other life there was." A pause. "I still don't really."

"People do change career after they graduate," Sarah said encouragingly. "After all, I did. I started out as a teacher."

Charles frowned. "But you didn't change career. I know you couldn't find a permanent job. James explained that you were working on supply, filling in for teachers going sick, and that was why you were working in London. And later you got those part-time jobs in Europe teaching English."

Sarah reined in her temper. "James could have made a career writing fairy stories! When he moved to Sheffield, there was no job for me as a history teacher, but there was a company offering jobs in computer programming to people with A level maths, which I have. I applied, passed their aptitude test, and they took me on. The first task they gave me was to install one of their systems in a local company, and somehow I stayed in implementation management and high-level system design from then on. After a year, I qualified for a government grant to take a master's degree in business administration, and when I passed the degree I was offered a job in London managing the implementation of financial trading systems for banks and stockbrokers. From there I was head-hunted by another company to manage implementations in financial organisations all over Europe. I did three years' teaching when I left college, but I never returned to the profession after that."

Charles was staring at her wide-eyed. "But whenever James mentioned you, he said you were away teaching."

Sarah looked straight at him. "James told people what he wanted them to believe, and what he himself wished was true. Unfortunately, it wasn't often correct." She rose and started to put her coat on. "I have lots of information I ought to pass on to you. Will you come with me?"

Charles hesitated, and then put on his coat, saying, "Of course. I've nothing else to do today."

Sarah had already decided on a venue for talking. She headed for the cathedral, and sat in a pew at the back far from the altar. "They usually let people talk very quietly in church," she said, as Charles hesitantly took the seat next to her, "and they'll probably think I'm showing you a guide to the building." She pulled the tablet out of her bag, added its keyboard, mouse and USB key and switched it on.

"You told me last night that James bought the house using his winnings at poker. Now I'll tell you the real story. This screen shows our joint current account, ten years ago. I owned a flat in London, which I'd paid for out of my own earnings, but I'd moved to Paris. So I wanted to sell the London flat, buy a flat in Paris, and buy another flat in Huntingdon for James.

"'The problem was that the French company sent me visiting their offices all over Europe. I changed hotel every few days, and switched off my mobile phone while in meetings. Neither my solicitor nor the selling agency used email, so they couldn't contact me. So I signed an authorisation for James to manage the sale and purchase in England on my behalf. I'd paid a deposit on the Huntingdon flat, and when the sale of the London flat completed, James paid the balance on the Huntingdon flat and transferred everything left over to my French bank account. Or so I thought.

"But if you look at this bank statement, there is the net amount received from the sale of the London flat, and there are the deposit and the balance paid for the Huntingdon flat, and there is the amount James transferred to my account in Paris. You don't need a calculator to see that the figures don't add up until you include this transfer of £22,000 which James had moved to the savings account. I didn't know about that transfer. James didn't tell me and I didn't use the English accounts at all.

"Here's the next year's statement, where there is a transfer of £15,000 out of savings, promptly paid out to Miller & Partners, solicitors. That was the purchase of 2 Mulberry Mews. There was no poker game involved. James simply bought the property at auction using the money he'd stolen from me."

Charles was staring in the direction of the tablet but no longer focussing his eyes on it. He said slowly, "The London flat. James said he'd bought a London flat because in London prices were always rising, and rose more steeply than anywhere else. He said if he'd bought in Sheffield, the price would rise very slowly, and chances were that the selling price would only be the buying price plus solicitor's costs, so when he sold up he wouldn't make any gain at all. He said the capital gain from the London flat would more than pay for the fact that he was renting in Sheffield, and as you were working in London, it saved him having to pay an astronomical rent for you."

"James could explain anything to his own advantage," Sarah said, keeping her voice down with an effort. "Here's the purchase deed for the London flat; the purchaser is Sarah Alicia Pullen, nee Cavendish. This is the deed for the Huntingdon flat; also purchased by Sarah Alicia Pullen, nee Cavendish. Just to complete the picture, here's the purchase document for the flat in Saint-Edern. The purchaser is Sarah Alicia Cavendish, otherwise Pullen. James doesn't appear on any of these documents because he contributed nothing to the purchase cost, and when he told you he bought these flats he was lying. I bought all of them myself with my own money.

"I won't bore you with the details, but James stole from me again when the Huntingdon flat was sold. That's how he built Mulberry Mews' basement kitchen. Unfortunately it cost more than he'd embezzled, and I've just had to pay over four thousand pounds to clear the outstanding loan."

Charles made no effort to move or to speak for several minutes. Sarah closed the tablet and put it in her bag. Eventually Charles said, "I'm finding it difficult to come to terms with this. For the whole of my life, James was the pride of the family. Everyone looked up to him. We all knew how successful he was, because he told us whenever we saw him. He was always well-dressed and driving an expensive car. And now you tell me that he had to steal money from you to buy that house? From his own wife? What happened to the money he earned? On his salary, he should have had a sizeable house of his own already. He told me he was making a mint from the Sheffield company, and he moved to Leeds and to Huntingdon to get even more. And that Porsche he drove didn't come cheap."

"I know it didn't," Sarah said wryly. "I paid for it. I had to, because just after he signed up to buy it, the Sheffield company sacked him for being drunk in the presence of a client." Charles looked startled. "I'm not surprised that's news to you. Only Deborah knew, as James had given her name as his next of kin.

"The severance terms included a subscription to Alcoholics Anonymous, because James had been found drunk in working hours before. After he dried out, James set up a company of his own, and everything he did from then on was on short-term contract. He told me it wasn't a type of work which paid well, but I now wonder how often he actively looked for work, and why no one ever kept him on for a longer term. I subsidised him considerably. I paid the loan and the insurance and the annual service on his car, the rent on his flats in Sheffield and Leeds, a new suit and new shirts every so often. Sometimes I just cleared a debt at the bank for him.

"There was no insurance pay-out when he crashed the Porsche. He told me this was because he'd swerved to avoid another car, which had driven away without stopping. I now think that he was driving while drunk, and didn't report the accident to the police or to the insurance company so that he didn't lose his licence. I paid for the lease of replacement cars for him, and then I bought him a new car in Brittany. Despite his qualifications and his many opportunities to earn a decent salary and to save money, when James retired he had only the basic state pension, no savings at all, no property apart from Mulberry Mews, and a bank debt which you know about."

There was another long silence. Charles stared into space with his eyes unfocussed. Then he said, "You've shown me the evidence, so what you say must be true. I do believe you, but it makes me feel like a complete idiot. I've spent my whole life idolising someone you've just revealed as a charlatan and a confidence trickster. I've tried to do everything he said he did, in the way he said he did it, but he didn't even do that himself. I've continually measured myself against what he said he was, and he's turned out to be smoke and mirrors." He took a deep breath and his eyes widened. "This makes a mockery of my whole life. I feel completely worthless."

"No," Sarah said forcefully. "Never that. You're stronger than James ever was. When James ran into a problem, he only knew three methods of coping with it: ignoring it, getting drunk or telling lies. When you hit problems, you face up to them. You've made mistakes, but who hasn't? You've had some rotten luck and some bad advice, but what matters is how you deal with what life throws at you. I'm impressed with how well you've managed to hold your own.

"I'm sure you have the potential to do better for yourself in the future, and I can do something to help you. As I don't now need to subsidise James for the rest of his life, I have more spare cash than I need. Your poker debt is less than the profit I made by exchanging James' flashy car for something more practical. If you can tell me the sum you need and give me the details of your bank account, the money will reach you next week, and you need never spend another weekend in Mulberry Mews."

For an appreciable time, Charles stared blindly at the faraway altar, his body tense and his face showing a visible effort to keep a blank expression. Eventually he said very quietly, "I wish very much that I could turn down that offer, but it would make an immense difference to my life."

"That's what I hoped it would do," Sarah said practically. "Now, do you have details of your account?"

"Yes." Charles pulled his chequebook from an inside pocket and detached a paying-in slip. "But I don't have the exact amount of the debt. It's on the computer at work."

"You don't have a computer of your own?"

"I sold it to raise money."

"You shouldn't be keeping personal details on a machine you don't own, and I certainly don't want any details of the emails you were sending to James held on your employer's database. I'd better give you enough to buy a decent laptop so that you can transfer all your data to it. You mentioned that the debt was less than £3,000, so if I send you £4,000 would that be enough to pay it off and buy a standard laptop with the usual office software on it?"

There was another silence, and then, "Sarah, I just don't know how to say thank you. This is all so much more than I ever expected."

"You can say thank you," said Sarah firmly, "by entertaining me over lunch. It's practically noon. I'm told they do a good table in the Red Pheasant and it's not far from here." She stood briskly and smiled warmly at Charles, who surprised himself by smiling warmly back. There was an offertory box near the exit and Sarah slipped a large note into it as she passed, in deep gratitude for the loan of the pew.

Over lunch in the busy dining room of the pub, Charles relaxed. When Sarah asked about Reading, Charles proved to know an astonishing amount about the city where he'd worked so often. He had its whole economic history at his fingertips. He could describe the changing pattern of local industries, from the farming and river trade controlled by the medieval abbey to the eighteenth century when the city was a stage-coach hub, to the nineteenth century when it was a railway interchange, to the present day 'silicon valley' enterprises.

Sarah found this a very unexpected side to Charles. He looked physically like James as she'd first met him, and when released from stress he was as charismatic as the James she'd fallen in love with, but beneath that he had an intellect capable of handling complexity, of rejoicing in the wealth of detail while staying firmly on the point. He had a grasp of business far superior to James' flawed understanding of it, and a love of history which she shared.

After lunch, Sarah paid for two copies to be made of Charles' key to the house. She asked Charles to take all his belongings back to Reading with him, and suggested that he drive back that afternoon, book into his hotel two days early, and take the rest of the weekend to relax.

"That would make sense," agreed Charles, carefully assimilating the change. "I want to start thinking the situation through. I'm sure you're right when you say there could be options open. Sarah, you've made such a difference to my life in just a few hours. I really want you to know how grateful I am."

"I'm glad to have helped." Sarah smiled. "Send me an email when you get your computer."

Back in her room, Sarah contacted the foreign exchange broker, who agreed a quotation in euros for £4,000 to be paid in England, but warned that Monday was the earliest date for moving the money. She arranged a transfer from her French savings account to reach the broker on Monday for onward transmission to Charles' account by Tuesday.

9

There was still the problem of the house, and who better to consult than the family estate agents? Sarah phoned Deborah to say she was in Chichester. Deb immediately invited her to dinner and said she'd send Clark to pick her up at six so that they could have a good evening together.

Clark drove Sarah to his comfortable home in a prosperous neighbourhood of Bognor. Deborah was warmly welcoming, and proposed sitting on the terrace while waiting for dinner to finish cooking.

"So why are you in England?" she asked.

Sarah said, "The short answer is that James was up to something, and I had to come here to find out what it was. And now I need an estate agent!"

She detailed the discovery that she owned a ruined Georgian house in Chichester. Clark was immediately interested, though he said bluntly he couldn't see an easy sale for such a place. Deborah was as puzzled as Sarah at what James would want with it. "What does it actually look like?" she asked.

Sarah showed the last picture taken on her mobile phone, and Deb visibly jumped. "Wait just a minute," she called as she rushed into the house. She returned with a box of old photographs. "Here you are," she said, having riffled through the collection. "This is Grandmother Isabel and Great-grandmother Harriet in front of their house."

The sepia-toned photograph showed a straight-backed lady with her hair in a bun, wearing a full-length dress with slanting lines of frilling on the bodice, and in front of her a young girl, greatly resembling Deborah, with long hair and a shorter dress with a lace collar. The two of them stood by a tree in the centre of a cobbled yard in front of two Georgian houses. Without the shadow of a doubt, they were standing in Mulberry Mews.

"I always thought this house had been somewhere in Bognor," said Deb, "and knocked down long ago. You've just uncovered our family history. Great-grandmother's eldest son died in the trenches in the First World War. After the war there was an influenza epidemic, which killed her husband and her younger son. She and her daughter recovered, but she had to sell up. She bought a small cottage in Bognor, and worked as a milliner, her original trade before marrying. She put her daughter Isabel through school and sent her to commercial college to learn shorthand-typing and bookkeeping. Isabel got a job in George Courtney's estate agents' and then married her boss."

"It's a family habit," Clark commented with a smile.

"Grandmother only had one child, my mother," said Deb. "When she was eighteen, Mother married Grandpa's junior partner, Edward Pullen."

"You see?" Clark interjected.

"Their children were James and me and Charles. Now if Great-grandmother hadn't sold up, Grandmother and then Mother would have inherited that house in turn, and Mother would have left it to James. He was her favourite. She spoiled him rotten. I'm sure I'm right. Great-grandmother was Mrs Alfred Murchison; she must be on the deeds."

"She is," Sarah confirmed. "Gregory Murchison built the house in the 1780s, and all the owners had that surname until 1920. That does make me feel sorry for James. He was trying to regain his lost inheritance."

"To be frank," Deborah said, "he was suffering delusions of grandeur. If he'd got that international partnership he was aiming for, he could have bought the house and run it in some style. But once he was relegated to being an ordinary person, he should have accepted things as they were. But there, I used to lose my patience with his grandiose ideas when we were younger, and here I am still doing it."

"Every family needs someone practical in it," Clark said, smiling at his wife.

"My big problem," Sarah said, "is that I don't want a house in Chichester. And I really don't want to spend money restoring this one. Is it possible to sell it as it is? Is there anyone who'd take on a roof and four walls? Would it be necessary to put some bare floors and a staircase inside to get a sale?"

"It would take some time to sell it as it is," said Clark carefully, "but it may be possible. I'll put it on our list if you like, and see what I can do. If no one's interested, perhaps I'd then suggest a partial renovation."

"I'd be grateful for any sort of help," Sarah said.

They went into the house for dinner and once the meal was over, withdrew to the lounge. Sarah took the opportunity to broach a new subject.

"Deborah, I do have something else to tell you. It's about Charles. I spent most of this morning talking to him, and I ought to pass on what I've learnt."

"I could do with knowing," Deborah said frankly. "I've been really worried about Charles these last few years. I'd welcome anything which would explain why he's so distant and so very unhappy."

"I can tell you that. I'll start with the divorce settlement. What do you know about it?"

"No details," Deborah said, considering. "When Charles said they'd separated, I didn't think he was much bothered about it, but the actual divorce hit him badly. He didn't want to talk about it, so I didn't push for information. But they hadn't been married long and there were no children. I've always assumed they sold off their flat, paid off the mortgage and divided the profit somehow. Am I right?"

"You couldn't be further from the truth, Deb. The court judgement strikes me as completely unjust. Celia got the flat and all contents, and Charles got the responsibility for paying the mortgage and the hire-purchase loans. He's paid the loans off by now, but he's still paying the mortgage."

"*What?*" Deborah shrieked. "He's doing what? That just can't happen. How did Celia engineer that?"

"Easily," Sarah said dryly. "Her new boyfriend's brother is a divorce lawyer, and represented her in court. Charles represented himself. He'd been working long hours and was too dog-tired to understand what he was up against. So now he's working all the hours he can to pay off the mortgage, but he'll never see any profit in it. He can't accumulate any savings; he can't buy or rent a home of his own; he takes no holidays. It's ruining his whole life."

"Dear God, that's totally unfair. Could a lawyer help?" Deborah asked. "I know a lot of solicitors. Maybe someone could recommend a divorce specialist. I'd really like to challenge that judgement."

"I'm not sure the original judgement can be changed," Sarah said cautiously, "but I've read enough newspaper reports where the amount to be paid has been amended at a later date. I'm sure it's worth a lawyer looking into it."

"I'll find one to do that. Thank you indeed for telling me, Sarah. I've been trying to find out what's bugging Charles for ages."

"It's not the only thing that's bugging him, Deb. Charles chose his career to emulate James, but when he got to university, he realised he didn't really want to study economics or accounting."

"But he got first class honours," Deb said, surprised.

Sarah's estimation of Charles rose another notch; he'd managed an admirable result in a subject he found uncongenial.

"Be that as it may," she said, "he's hated his job ever since he started work. Now the mortgage is forcing him to continue with it. He's working so many extra hours that he's too tired to think, and he keeps lapsing into despondency. I don't like the situation at all. I spent the last twenty years of my working life at the top of my profession enjoying every minute of my job. I don't want to see Charles remaining so unhappy for the rest of his working life. I'd rather he changed his job to something he could enjoy, but his sense of responsibility won't let him take any risks until that mortgage is paid off."

"I think you've explained more than you realise," Deborah said. "That's why he's so cagey when I ask how he's getting on. I've been feeling fairly hurt by the way he's cold-shouldered me. I practically brought him up, you know."

"I do know, and he remembers it very well indeed. He told me at very great length this morning just how much you'd done for him, and he's not just grateful, he has a very real affection for you. But he sees himself as a complete failure. He can't tell you that over the phone, Deb."

Clark had been carefully assessing what he heard. Now he said, "I've been annoyed with Charles these last few years; he seemed to be treating Deb very poorly after everything she's done for him. But now we know what's really going on, I think we should make an effort to help. He was a nice enough young lad when he lived with us, full of enthusiasm, and astoundingly intelligent. It's bad luck he's got trapped between a job he doesn't like and that iniquitous divorce settlement. There must be something we can do about those ill-advised financial obligations at least. I'd happily pay a lawyer to sort that out."

Clark drove Sarah back to her hotel, and as they said goodbye she gave him a key for 2 Mulberry Mews and arranged to meet him at the house on Sunday morning.

***

On Sunday she arrived to find Clark and Deb already in conversation with Oliver, who'd already agreed with them to withdraw from the garden by the end of July. Sarah immediately asked Oliver to keep any profit he made out of her garden from now on, and Oliver promptly suggested that he sow grass seed over her plot as he left it, to provide cosmetic assistance for a sale.

Oliver had already told Clark that Pepper-Williams had remodelled his own house, and Clark agreed with him that Peter Piper Restorations was probably the best renovation organisation in Sussex, so their construction of the roof of number 2 was a selling point.

As a qualified surveyor, Clark provided Sarah with a valuation for probate, and Deb took possession of the original title deeds and renovation receipts, promising to have them scanned and emailed to Sarah, but handed to a local solicitor for safe-keeping and passing to the eventual buyers.

Sarah could at last feel that the situation in England was under control. On Monday she took the ferry back to Saint-Malo and arrived home just as sunset coloured the sky and the river opposite the penthouse windows. After all the dark surprises lurking in Sussex, the peaceful beauty of Brittany felt like a true welcome home.

***

On Tuesday Sarah woke early, walked into the kitchen, reached for the coffee granules, and then stopped. Her headaches couldn't be blamed on the coffee machine. There could perhaps be something wrong with the packet of ground coffee, so she threw it away, broke the seals on a new one, and brewed a filter coffee. She deliberately drank the whole mugful. She showered and dressed and ate breakfast. There was no headache. There never would be.

In a determined mood, she went shopping. She bought magazines and the local newspaper. She bought bread, milk, cheese, fruit, vegetables, herbs and fish. She tried short conversations on the food in season, and found everyone happy to encourage her halting French. Passing the café Au Coin du Quai, she dropped in for a coffee. She recognised the brown-skinned proprietor immediately.

"Bonjour, Madame Pullen," he said cheerfully. "I'm Philippe Poisson. We've met at the social club. Can I suggest an almond pastry with your coffee?"

Agreeing to that, Sarah sat at the counter, but then asked, "Are you an immigrant like me?"

"Mon Dieu, non! The Poissons have lived in Saint-Edern for generations. But my mother's father was an immigrant." He paused for effect. "He was Irish." Philippe was obviously telling a well-practised joke, but Sarah was sure she could see some Irishness in his grin.

"You've inherited his sense of humour," she said. "So who was your mother's mother?"

"A Breton born," he said proudly. "Of course, her parents were Senegalese." His laugh was infectious. Sarah was still grinning when she returned home.

It took all afternoon to write carefully to the French tax authorities advising them that she was now a widow and had inherited a low-value English property. When she finished the irksome task, she followed a magazine recipe for white butter sauce, and served it with grilled fillet of sea bass. It made a superb dinner with asparagus and broad beans and fresh bread rolls.

Her laptop signalled an email from Charles with the subject 'Thank you!' Charles confirmed the receipt of the money she'd transferred, and his purchase of a laptop, to which he was transferring all his private emails and data and financial details.

'Thank you for your help and thank you even more for listening to me,' he wrote. 'I won't rush into anything, but I do want to do something better with my life now.'

It was satisfying to see another of James' victims starting to recover.

***

On Wednesday morning, Sarah walked the cliff path around the nearby peninsula of Alet. She'd intended simply to enjoy the view, but her brain insisted on working through what she'd recently learned about James, searching for a final understanding, for closure.

James had been born in Bognor, but always claimed he came from the grander cathedral city of Chichester. His great-grandmother's house must have been the key to his whole life. He'd cycled to it as a boy. He'd never lost touch with it. He didn't learn of the auction by accident, because he was then working in Leeds, and an auction of hard-to-sell houses in Sussex wouldn't have been publicised that far north.

The self-imposed pressure to repossess the house must have been intense. He'd deliberately chosen the only career open to him which would have generated enough money. He could have followed his father into the profitable estate agency, but that wouldn't have produced enough capital for the purchase, renovation and furnishing of the house or enough income for its maintenance. But a senior consultant – or better still, a junior partner – in an international financial advisor would certainly earn enough to take on a large Georgian house.

Because James had chosen his career for no reason other than maximum possible earnings, the work didn't suit him or even interest him. He'd passed his degree by learning the standard answers to the standard questions. He didn't progress into the career his degree should have opened for him, advising captains of industry, steering international companies, planning expansion into different markets, identifying good capital investments. He resented, and resisted, being taught. He didn't learn from experience. He didn't impress the clients or his employers. Partnership was a vain hope; he couldn't manage the work of the lower ranks.

Sarah realised that James had married her because her adoration stroked his ego. As she forged her career, James accepted her money but couldn't acknowledge her commercial achievements. While she attained recognition throughout Europe, James had described her as teaching English part-time. A successful Sarah wasn't the sort of wife he wanted.

Sarah's last job was in Brussels. If she'd retired to England, she'd have transferred her finances to their English bank, exposing James' duplicity. James' suggestion of retiring to France was a masterstroke. Sarah had transferred from a Belgian bank to a French bank, ignoring the English accounts completely. But James had had no intention of retiring to France. He intended to live in Mulberry Mews.

Neither Deborah nor Sarah knew about that house. Sarah could have been persuaded into restoration by that fictional character, her beloved James. But the real James hadn't asked her to. It was his home, and his alone.

So what did James plan to happen next? James had told Charles that 'his big French client would pay half a million at the end of their joint project'. There was no French client. But James knew Sarah's capital amounted to at least that, and James could have taken control of it by inheriting on her death, or acting for her because she'd become too incapacitated to manage her own finances.

If James had gained financial control, he could have liquidated her investments within days, sold the Paris flats within months, transferred the proceeds to England, rebuilt Mulberry Mews, moved the antique furniture there, and sold the Saint-Edern penthouse. He could then have used what remained of Sarah's capital to fund a useful annuity. Indeed, if she was still alive, he could continue spending her substantial pension.

For the first time in this affair Sarah felt vulnerable. She checked the fatal dose of the painkillers on her tablet. The amount in the dressing room was lethal, though the internet warned that in practice suicides were more likely to die from choking before swallowing the entire dose. But if she'd died, James would have had to obtain inheritance or control through the French courts, where the penniless husband of a wealthy woman who suddenly and inexplicably committed suicide would certainly be suspected of murder.

So James needed to ensure two things. Firstly, he needed to prove he'd done everything possible to save her, rushing her to hospital following the overdose; he would in fact have been safer and wealthier if she survived. Secondly, he had to establish a plausible scenario for the suicide attempt. He appeared to be intending to demonstrate that Sarah's apparently normal behaviour concealed underlying psychological problems.

Sarah's headaches had been recorded on her French medical record, but no cause had yet been found. Despite the MRI scan having found nothing wrong, James had insisted that she tell her Qi Gong tutor that she was seriously ill. A doctor in the bridge club was already spreading the rumour of psychosomatic syndrome. Once the French health service had proved there was no physical cause for the headaches, and indeed no proof they'd actually occurred, their specialists might well have reached the same conclusion. If

Sarah was then rushed to hospital after an overdose, that would confirm her psychological problems.

No wonder James was annoyed at waiting four weeks for more specialists to prove Sarah had nothing physically wrong. James needed money paid into the English bank within twenty-two weeks, or he'd lose the house. That was a tight timetable given the slow pace of the law, and James couldn't press for a decision without raising suspicions.

All this shone a different light on James' suggestion of moving to France. He'd intended to return to England as a wealthy man with an ancestral home. If still alive, Sarah would have been institutionalised and dumped in an asylum. The 'second honeymoon' was worse than illusion.

The cause of the headaches seemed obvious. Sarah walked home briskly and used a translation package on the fuel-additive maker's entire website. The additive had very few ingredients. Sarah then found an English website which warned that the principal component caused extremely painful headaches if accidentally swallowed. The bitterness of coffee would hide any taste. The additive wasn't lethal, but weeks of intense inexplicable pain, especially if it began recurring in the afternoons, would have left Sarah so confused that she'd probably have swallowed anything James insisted on. She'd escaped that scenario just in time.

Sarah sat at her desk for over an hour recovering from the shock of coming so close to oblivion caused by someone she'd trusted completely. Then, quite suddenly, she felt overwhelmingly sorry for James. He'd never got what he wanted. His work had proved one failure after another. He couldn't buy his house until it was ruined; then he couldn't afford to restore it. James could only cope with stress using alcohol. The strain of planning to eliminate Sarah, accompanied by enormous personal risk to himself, had required a fix more and more frequently. Eventually, he'd annihilated himself instead of her.

There was no one Sarah could confide in, but then, there never had been. She took the painkillers to the pharmacy for recycling, and the fuel-additive to the local repair garage, who knew how to jettison dangerous chemicals. In deliberately destroying the evidence she intended to forget the whole episode.

For lunch she experimented with a lamb chop marinaded in Moroccan spices, served on couscous with a sauce of cucumber and mint in sour cream. Dessert was a dish of fresh grapes. She ate at the picnic table on her terrace.

The sun was warm on her skin. The view was glorious. The meal looked attractive, smelt inviting and tasted superb. Contentment spread into her mind. This was how she'd expected to live in France.

In the beautiful May evening, Sarah took her place at the social club. Someone proposed visiting the Grottes de Saulges, a site of natural beauty just over the border in Mayenne, where the river has carved a gorge and caves through the limestone. It's one of the rare places where the cave-paintings and engravings of Stone Age man have been found in the north of France. So many people were attracted by the beauty and the pre-history that Pascal Rozko phoned down his list of coach drivers until he found one available to drive everyone there, and in serene anticipation, Sarah booked a seat among her friends.

10

For forty-four years Sarah's life had been planned around two fixed points: her work and James. She'd now lost both. She'd been busy all her life and had accepted retirement solely because it would allow her to devote herself to James, an objective now completely shattered. She needed not only to fill her time but to find a sense of purpose, and to set her own domestic lifestyle instead of blindly following James' requirements.

Starting to question previous decisions made under James' influence, Sarah decided to physically visit the supermarket whose goods she'd ordered over the internet, but which she had never seen. She located it on the map and drove there. It was part of a complex pedestrianised shopping mall with other boutiques and stores, a successful modern replacement for the old fashioned high street. The supermarket was deliberately sited at the end of the mall so that customers passed the small specialist shops on the way. It proved to occupy a huge space, and besides the usual shelves of produce in boxes, packets, tins and jars, it featured traditional counters for a baker, a pastry-cook, a greengrocer, a butcher and a fishmonger.

There was a splendid display on the fish counter, which promised the interesting meals of fresh food that Sarah had longed for, but she was disappointed to note that the names of the fish were unintelligible to an English-speaker apart from the turbots, all of which were far too large for one person. But as she watched, a customer asked the fishmonger for a filet of turbot and he extracted one small filet for her before putting the cut fish back on display. Now that she knew how to buy it, Sarah needed a recipe to tell her how to cook it.

She'd passed a bookshop in the mall, so she went back to it and discovered a whole shelf of cookbooks. She bought three: fish, shellfish and chicken. Returning to the supermarket, she bought turbot, prawns and chicken breast, gathered the fresh fruit, vegetables, herbs and spices required by her newly acquired recipes, the mills and graters required for handling fresh ingredients, and at the checkout added a magazine on Breton cookery for more inspiration. On returning home, she poached the turbot and made sauce hollandaise for it, enjoying the cooking experience, the taste of lunch and the feeling of achievement which went with them.

But she'd turned on the television as a background; it was tuned solely to English channels and streaming services via a satellite dish, representing one of James' major efforts to distance himself from Brittany. That needed to change. Sarah phoned Marie-Pierre to ask for the name of her service supplier. She visited their shop and bought a specialist box providing television and French-speaking streaming services via the telephone line.

It took half an hour to get the new system working, using the dictionary to translate the French installation instructions, but at last Sarah had all the French television channels. By teatime she'd discovered the subtitles for the hard-of-hearing, so that the French words of the slightly-too-fast dialogue were now printed along the bottom of the screen; a second chance to understand, an education course in themselves.

Sarah delightedly cancelled the satellite subscription. She spent the evening watching documentary programmes with subtitles while recording them, noting words she didn't understand, looking those up in a dictionary, and then re-running the programmes. She began to feel confident that she could master the language.

She made an appointment with the doctor on Friday morning, and then told him that she wanted to cancel the hospital visits and laboratory tests. When the doctor demurred, she said, "I'll try to explain. I don't think you know that my husband was an alcoholic. He'd been treated in England, but after we moved here he started drinking heavily again. He lost his temper continuously; he wouldn't listen to reason and he began to frighten me."

"Madame," the doctor said sympathetically, "that must have been a very great problem for you. I wish I'd seen it. Now that you've told me, I can see that he showed signs typical of an alcoholic, but I'm afraid I interpreted his behaviour instead as that of a man who was uncomfortable in an alien culture. So many foreigners behave in an exaggerated way when they first come to France."

"That was part of it, too," Sarah agreed. "James wasn't happy here. The stress at home was extreme. I'm quite sure that James was the cause of the headaches and the reason they didn't stop. James insisted on consulting you, and I was just a little worried that I could have a brain tumour. But the headaches have gone now and I don't believe they will return. I don't want to waste the time of hospital specialists for no reason."

"I'll cancel the appointments as you ask," the doctor responded, "but I must ask you to call me immediately if the headaches return. Now, how are you coping with the situation? I see that you're in contact with the bereavement counsellor at the hospital."

"She's very kind," Sarah said, "and I did appreciate her help in all the formalities, but I have good friends already in Saint-Edern, in the social club, and I'll manage very well with their help."

"That's good to hear," said the doctor. "I wish you a happy life in our little community."

By Sunday morning, waiting with the social club for the coach to the Grottes de Saulges, Sarah felt there was more of a point to her life. She would occupy herself in learning to cook and to speak better French.

The social club spent the morning learning about the formation of the cave system and what was known about its early occupation, and then explored the caves with a guide. They'd arranged lunch in the café on site, and Sarah sat between Marie-Pierre and Elodie to eat.

"I must thank you for recommending that television service," Sarah said to Marie-Pierre. "I now live in a wholly French-speaking environment."

"You can understand what is said?"

"Almost. I have the subtitles running under the image, and I record the programmes so that I can re-run and re-listen. It's the first time I've been glad to be retired, because I can spend the whole day working on my French."

"What was your job before retirement?" Elodie asked.

"Computer systems, in the financial and investment sector. I designed systems, controlled their development and managed their implementation."

"That sounds really high-powered. Have you stopped working entirely?"

"Unfortunately, yes. I do miss being at work, but at my age I don't want the pressure of ten-hour days and working at weekends."

"Couldn't you find different jobs or part-time ones?" Marie-Pierre asked.

"Not in my usual line," Sarah said, considering, "but you're right, there must be other jobs I could do, perhaps something locally."

"I wish I'd known about your skills earlier," Elodie said. "My cousin, Thais Bertrand, works for the prefecture. She runs a group controlling services provided to children who are suffering due to illness, handicap, poverty, family problems. They're a clearing house for what can be done. They've been logging everything on a spreadsheet for years, but the sheet is now very unwieldy, and it's insecure because data could be lost or amended by accident.

"The prefect said they needed a bespoke system with a secure database which could be analysed and reported on. A local developer agreed to create one, but it's just been delivered and it's unworkable. The staff are still using the spreadsheet, the developers are demanding payment and Thais doesn't know what to do. Would you be able to help her?"

"I can't guarantee it," Sarah said, "but I expect so. I like troubleshooting. I'd have to learn about Thais' office very quickly first, and then find out what the system developers have done. After that it depends how close their system is to what's needed. There's always hope that a few small changes might solve everything."

Elodie immediately phoned Thais, and it was agreed that Sarah would meet her on Monday.

After lunch the social club walked the footpaths exploring the area, and as Sarah had become interested in the local geology and the Stone Age, she bought books on them before boarding the coach home. *More words to learn*, she thought happily, unaware that the Stone Age would become a lasting passion.

***

On Monday Sarah spent the morning talking to Thais' staff about their work and their spreadsheet, and having the new system demonstrated as far as it could be run. She asked Thais for the design documents and was told there weren't any. A developer had taken a copy of the spreadsheet and said he would base a system on that. He hadn't talked to the staff so he didn't know how they used the spreadsheet, only what data was finally held on it.

Sarah asked Thais for the development contract. That did exist, and it stated that design documents would be produced for signing off before starting development. So the developers were technically in breach of contract.

Sarah called them and demanded a meeting that afternoon. They said they didn't have time, but Sarah had looked out her old guide to the legal side of buying a flat in France and unearthed some useful legal phrases, and eventually they agreed to come to the office at two o'clock. Sarah and Thais enjoyed a sociable lunch together.

At two, two developers arrived, bringing nothing with them. Sarah asked for the database schema, and they tapped a few keys to send it whizzing past on-screen. "If that's your standard of client service, I don't recommend it," Sarah said flatly. "Will you please deliver that as printout and in file format?"

"It doesn't do anything and you don't need it."

"It's system documentation, and I need it to check for errors. I've identified eight database design errors this morning and I'd like to know the full total before asking you to correct them all. I won't check the functionality until the database is correct, and you won't be paid until I've agreed that the functionality is correct. So you need to provide me with design information."

"That's not the way we work."

"It's the method of working described in the contract you signed. If you don't want to work as described in the contract, I'll consult the prefecture's legal department. You're currently in breach of contract, so they'll want the deposit returned; then they'll probably engage a company who will work correctly. I understand that you have two other projects for the local prefecture and another for the regional prefect, so publicising non-observance of contract conditions on this project will focus attention on contract conditions for those projects. You'll find that you'll have to provide design documents or face losing those contracts. I suggest that you deliver the schema."

The file arrived in Thais' mail within half an hour and the physical printout was delivered shortly afterwards. For Sarah it was a very small system; she'd listed all the design errors before five o'clock, and emailed them to the developers with a request for correction by noon next day, Tuesday. Thais was overjoyed when the developers agreed to that.

"They do seem more reasonable now," Sarah said, carefully optimistic. "Can I come in tomorrow morning and agree a functional specification with your staff?"

"We'll be delighted to see you," Thais said, warmly kissing her goodnight.

On Tuesday the database proved to have been corrected as required, so Sarah emailed the developers her functional specification, a set of test scenarios and some test data. The programmers must have worked late hours, because they delivered a replacement system mid-morning on Wednesday.

Sarah organised half the office as a test bed, and her team cheerfully logged half a dozen spelling mistakes on screen displays and one small calculation error, but the little system now ran smoothly and did everything required. The problems had all been in the reception and storage of input data, and the output reports were not only correct, but useful.

On Wednesday afternoon the developers made the system live by feeding the spreadsheet data into it, and Thais signed the instruction for payment. But she'd asked Sarah for a report of what she'd done and why she thought the problem had arisen, and she immediately passed Sarah's report up the chain of command; when it finally reached the prefect at the end of the afternoon, it was promptly broadcast down to other junior managers.

***

Sarah had found it very satisfying to work once again in a professional office. But she wasn't prepared for Wednesday evening, when she entered the social club to a rapturous welcome by Elodie, who described her success in glowing terms to the whole audience.

"You're embarrassing me," Sarah objected, "It was just a simple problem and no great effort."

"You can say that," Elodie said, "but no one else knew what to do."

"That was the prefect's fault," Sarah said. "He should give more guidance to his smaller offices and ensure that there's assistance available at the outset. He could have stopped this problem before it started."

"I think the prefect realises that now," said Gérard Lemestre. "Our prefect is female, by the way."

"Then she should have known better," Sarah said, unabashed.

Unsurprisingly, Sarah was quickly contacted by other prefecture departments enquiring what she would charge for assistance. She happily re-opened her old French consultancy company, and very soon amassed a trickle of earnings and, far more important, numerous short jobs making use of her well-honed talents while giving her a valuable insight into local business and local authority work in Brittany.

Naturally she was invited to the next social evening at the prefecture, where she met the local prefect, the regional prefect, a number of interesting, recently retired citizens who also assisted on a casual or part-time basis, and a number of managers and directors of local enterprises who worked for the prefects occasionally, many of them striking Sarah as potential sources of short projects.

One manager present was Jean-Jacques Keruan, a nationally known personality who worked very hard to give the impression of sailing effortlessly through life. He'd held many influential positions including member of Parliament for the area and anchorman of a national television news programme. He now had a comfortable retirement job as a magazine editor, but retained a reputation in the prefecture for his efficient chairmanship of meetings, and also for never missing a cocktail party.

Sarah had automatically worn her standard uniform for attending social evenings at international banks, a navy blue Dior cocktail suit, with shoes, handbag and delicate gold jewellery from the same designer. In less formal Brittany this had marked her out among the other women. Jean-Jacques, survivor of thousands of Parisian parties, had immediately noticed her, and became even more interested when others praised her organisational skills. He obtained her full details from the prefecture officials. Good organisers were few and far between, and well-dressed intelligent female organisers even more rare.

***

Next day Sarah answered the phone to a familiar voice. "Lemestre. We know each other from the social club, but this is a business call. The regional prefect has asked me to co-ordinate the work of a group of people and give some kind of overview of what's been achieved, at what cost, and where the problems lie. It seems obvious that if I'm to monitor work and costs and progress and problems, I'll need a computer system, but that's about as far as I can go without professional assistance. The prefecture suggested that you might agree to help."

"What kind of work is being monitored?"

"People, really. Unaccompanied child migrants. Hundreds have been found in refugee camps, and many have been allocated to Brittany to look after. They're mostly boys, mostly from Central African or North African countries, aged between thirteen and eighteen, sometimes non-French-speakers and usually poorly educated. They've been lodged in volunteer households throughout the region. There are small organised day-care groups in sizeable townships, but many instances of just two children in a small village.

"It's not easy for the children to assimilate into France, and it's not always easy for their caring families or teachers and supervisors to work with them. They've led demanding lives and coped with the worst too often. How do you instil citizenship in a fifteen-year-old who doesn't speak French but who knows how to live successfully by begging, threatening behaviour and petty theft? How does one discover his useful potential and persuade him to use that instead?

"Everyone's discovering best practice by trial and error. There are inspectors, but they're not experts in this field, either. The prefecture is always notified of difficulties and disasters, but good progress goes unremarked. There's no simple forum for carers to contact each other and discuss what's been tried with what result. You can see why the prefect wants a system?"

"I can indeed. But this is completely outside my experience. I come from securities trading and investment systems. I'm not immediately sure how to tackle this situation, and I could be the worst person to advise you."

"Thank you for putting that so clearly. But I'd value any contribution you could make, even if negative. You've covered in depth an area of which I know very little, the way electronic devices store, process and pass on data. I tend to concentrate on people, how and why they work together. I think a good outcome is possible if we can learn enough from each other to marry our two areas of expertise. Would you be prepared to try?"

"I think so. But I'd like a lot more information up front so that I can understand the situation before thinking about digitising it."

"I've arranged to meet an inspector and one of the day-care leaders tomorrow afternoon. I'm feeling my way myself, so I've picked the nearest to start with. I would very much like to have you with me on a watching brief, to understand what these people do in practice."

"I have the time free. But as I said, I'd prefer some overview information first. Do you have any?"

"I have too much. There are enough papers to fill a large suitcase. We'd need to meet somewhere where you could leaf through them physically. Could I perhaps offer you lunch today in the darts club room behind the bar-tabac?

The owner will let us stay there all afternoon, and there's a long table we can spread papers on."

"If there's an electric socket, I could bring my laptop and its portable scanner."

"Please do. Shall we meet there at noon? I'll order a buffet lunch for two, if that's acceptable."

"Thank you, it would be. I'll see you at noon."

Sarah started to think through what she knew about Monsieur Lemestre. There were sizeable gaps in her knowledge. All the social club members showed him a great deal of deference, though it wasn't obvious why. He'd just been given a complex brief by the regional prefect, so she must know him well, but he didn't sound like a civil servant. On impulse she looked up the online telephone directory. There was no personal entry for Lemestre in the local county, but there was a holding company, Participations Lemestre, with a box-office in Saint-Malo. But the internet held no indication of the type of business that company conducted, which, in these days of superabundant public information about everything, indicated deliberate concealment.

When Sarah arrived at the bar-tabac, the owner's wife bustled out from behind the counter and escorted her to the back room, apologising in advance that the buffet consisted solely of Monsieur Lemestre's preferences, but declaring herself ready to supply anything madame might wish for. Puzzled by all the attention, Sarah murmured, "I'm sure that Monsieur Lemestre has good taste."

The room was long and narrow, the floor marked in lengths from two electronic dartboards, but it did currently hold a large trestle table and two chairs. The food had been placed at one end of the table and Lemestre was sorting papers from a suitcase into piles at the other. He kissed a formal greeting, then said, "Perhaps you'd like to look at a few of these now, to give us a topic of conversation over lunch?"

Sarah selected the list of all the children with their current addresses, the map showing where they were, and one dossier on one child, full of loose notes. Over lunch she asked questions on the way the placements had been organised, how the initial medical examinations were conducted, and how the nationality and age of each child had been decided.

A chance remark led to Sarah learning for the first time the official aims of the widespread crèche system, which in French communes takes children from birth to five years old, and is intended to produce entry-level primary school classes consisting of children who speak French, are used to spending their whole day peaceably with their contemporaries, are prepared to eat a wide variety of food, have good manners, have respect for authority, and are eager to learn. The migrants were well behind the six-year-olds in many respects, and not finding it easy to learn what they'd missed.

But the single dossier Sarah held proved extremely useful in outlining the data required to be held in the system. There was a list of basic data about each child, but also a clearly defined need for correspondence back and forth between interested parties on specific topics. As an indication that the list of topics might not be predictable, this particular child had been attracted by a Breton bagpipe band, and had then quickly learnt to play a flute which had been donated, proving to have natural ability as a musician. Unfortunately he preferred playing his flute all day to taking French and maths and geography lessons, and his carers had asked if there were any other musicians among the migrants, hoping to compare problems and solutions.

Somewhere in the suitcase might be data on another musician, or maybe there was only this one. The need for immediate conversion of information into a searchable database catapulted Sarah into the project before she'd rationalised her commitment. At the very least she could get a database set up in the prefecture and give its staff the means to search and sort and count, and that would go some way towards monitoring the progress or behaviour of the migrants. She immediately jumped forward into connecting the database with the carers and inspectors, possibly via mobile phones, and providing a forum for correspondence. She spent an hour after lunch describing her thoughts to Lemestre and taking his comments into account.

He said, "Can I now take it that you intend to work on the project? To the extent of producing a system specification and identifying a computer professional to produce it?"

"More than one professional. There's a need for different specialists." Suddenly Sarah realised that she'd all but accepted the job without any negotiation. "We haven't discussed terms and conditions," she said warily.

Lemestre sat back in his chair taking her measure. "Do we need to?"

"I think the job needs to be defined."

"My own part in this project has yet to be defined, but I have asked you to help me. If you agree to do so, I'll keep you advised on my requirements as they develop and change, and I'd expect you to keep me in touch with what you do. I'll assist you wherever you think it necessary. If any part of what you do can be counted as a success, I'll see that you're acknowledged as the author of it."

It wasn't an answer Sarah was expecting. On impulse she asked, "How much are you being paid for this work?"

"Nothing. I used to work for the region, so they pay me a pension. I'd rather earn it." He paused, then asked, "Do you need to be paid?"

"Not as such," Sarah acknowledged, "but there might be expenses I'd want to claim, and the system will need to be paid for."

"Expenses I'd prefer to discuss in advance, but I'll accept in principle that you may need to claim some. For the system itself, if you estimate the costs and the payment timescales, the prefect will set a budget, regional administration will sign the contracts, regional treasury will pay when you agree they should."

Sarah was impressed. He'd seen that working on the project had caught her imagination, so he hadn't offered any sweetener from the region's public funding, only the possibility of a successful system. He'd said he concentrated on people, how and why they work together. He was obviously a master of that, and steel to the backbone. She would like to impress him in her turn.

Accepting the situation, she said, "I'd like to scan in as many of these pieces of paper which relate to people in the local county as I can. I intend to visit some of them to get a feel for the way access to the system will have to work. Can you sort the papers with .me?"

"Of course."

They worked in companionable silence for two hours before agreeing to meet and interview other parties next day.

11

Sarah's imagination didn't let go of the immigrant flautist. She waited a month until she and Monsieur Lemestre had interviewed all the inspectors and the day-care centre workers, and then, when it came to meeting the volunteer foster-parents, she suggested starting with the home of Gali, the musician. By this stage, Sarah had designed a database and had had it created. She'd organised a small team to scan the documents into an archive and a larger one to input document data to the new database. She was now interested in the way the data would be used, and also how those in the field wanted to read data and communicate with each other.

But Gali was a special case. Other migrant children were learning to play musical instruments, but for them music didn't have the intense compulsion that it appeared to have for Gali. The flute donated by a well-wisher in all good faith had caused real problems with Gali's education. His foster parents had all the usual Breton enthusiasm for music, but had found themselves out of their depth.

Once she'd collected enough details from Gali's fosterers for use in designing the system's front-end, Sarah surprised Lemestre by asking them, "Does this village hold a Fest Noz?"

No," the foster father replied, "it's too small. The nearest Fest Noz is held twice a year at Blaizec. They've got a big hall, they book four groups, and they attract everyone from the surrounding villages."

"Do you know the name of the organiser?"

It was on the foster-mother's phone. Within a few minutes, the Lemestre car was on its way to Blaizec, where the organiser was, of course, the wife of the mayor.

Sarah said she was looking for a musician who would have the time and inclination to help a young refugee who was showing musical promise; preferably someone with an instrument suitable for accompanying a flute-player, and able to teach the traditional Breton repertoire.

"Most of the players I know have a daytime job," the mayor's wife said, "but you could try Chouchen. He's retired and he's pretty good on the accordion. But he's Irish, so he plays mostly Irish music."

"Can you dance to it?"

"We do, every Fest Noz. Chouchen plays in between the main groups, and he can fill the floor."

Chouchen is the Breton for mead, the alcoholic drink from fermented honey. The accordionist's proper name was Padraic O'Shaughnessy, but he was happy with his local nickname. His imagination was caught by the problem, and he was willing to start helping immediately. He'd been a primary school teacher in Ireland before joining the music scene, and accurately assumed that the major part of his job would be to get Gali speaking and thinking in French, as he'd had to learn to do himself thirty years before. He drove behind the Lemestre car to Gali's home, and when Sarah explained what she intended, the foster father produced Gali's flute and asked him to play.

As Gali began his favourite tune, Chouchen's accordion softly picked out a harmony. They didn't quite mesh their two parts together, but using a combination of simple French and sign language they decided on a second try, and then a third effort where they managed to alternate phrases very successfully. They became so absorbed in working around the simple tune that neither of them noticed the others moving to the kitchen, where Sarah gave the foster parents O'Shaughnessy's address and telephone number. She suggested that Gali spend the morning attempting his lessons but as a reward spend the afternoons playing duets with Chouchen – and learning without knowing it. The foster parents were delighted to agree, provided Monsieur Lemestre could clear this with the inspectorate.

As he drove Sarah home, Lemestre observed, "You use a very strange method of creating computer systems."

Sarah laughed. "I'm just interested in producing a potential musician. I love dancing at village fetes. But Gali will need a day job as well, and he mustn't lose sight of that." The conversation moved on to the other cases they needed to investigate, and the good progress the database was already revealing.

***

Just after the beginning of Sarah's collaboration with Lemestre, Deborah had emailed to tell Sarah that she'd found a divorce lawyer to help Charles: Jeremy Prescott, son of a local solicitor. She wrote:

'Jeremy agrees with you that it's best not to challenge the court judgement; there are other ways of changing the situation. But he wanted exact details of the case, so I had to get all the references from Charles. Little brother was furious with you for telling me, but I got the details. Young Prescott can't give it priority, because he has cases under way and needs to earn his fees, but he'll look through it in his spare time. I've guaranteed that Clark and I will pay his costs.'

A few weeks later the next email arrived:

'Jeremy Prescott says the other side bent the truth right out of shape by not giving all the facts. No one mentioned that Celia was working full-time in a well-paid job and could support herself. No one stated that she'd left Charles' flat of her own accord and moved in with David Pickford. David Pickford wasn't even mentioned. The court just assumed Celia needed a home, so she got both flat and contents. Prescott knows Celia's lawyer, Roger Pickford (he would, of course) and reckons he can bring pressure to bear.'

In mid June Deb had better news:

'We've had a super slice of luck! David Pickford's been promoted to manage his company's Bristol office. He and Celia are moving there (they did marry) so the Brighton flat is being sold. The mortgage company gets first call on the proceeds, but the flat is up for sale at more than double what it cost, and Charles paid a large deposit and by now has paid almost half the mortgage, so there'll be a big profit.

The beauty of the situation is that, as there's a court order involved, the court has to be involved in the sale. If there's a full court hearing, Jeremy Prescott can highlight every fact that Roger Pickford omitted to mention. Roger will doubtless meet the same judge often in his career, and a reputation for slanting the truth might hinder his future success. So suddenly Roger wants to present to the court an agreement signed by everyone, to avoid a full hearing. Apparently David Pickford doesn't like the situation either. It was a good joke to get Charles to pay his mortgage, but a decent bloke can't let that run on for years. So both Pickfords are making concessions.'

A week later Deb emailed:

'Sarah, they've done it. Charles gets 93% of the cash profit (due to his deposit and total payments). Celia gets 7% but all the furnishings. Agreed by both of them, and the court took ten minutes to finalise the settlement. David Pickford hasn't lost out; he'd invested the cash from his old flat, and has banked his savings from living mortgage-free, so he agreed to pay Jeremy Prescott's entire fee – about time something got charged to him. I do hope Roger Pickford was working for nothing. The flat's already sold, so the solicitor will distribute the cash immediately. It's not just a question of stopping payments for the mortgage, because Charles will get more than double his money back! It's fantastic! I'm over the moon!'

Sarah replied:

'Brilliant! Absolutely brilliant! How's Charles taking it?'

'Good question,' Deb emailed. 'He shook hands with Jeremy, walked out of court, hasn't been seen or heard of since. If I didn't know him, I'd be worried, but he always needed time alone.'

'I can understand. It's an enormous change to his life,' Sarah replied. 'But I'm so happy with the news. I've been worried about Charles ever since he told me about the court judgement. You're a great sister to have, Deborah.'

'It's going to the right cocktail parties that gets you the contacts!' Deb boasted.

***

That proved true for Sarah as well, because Jean-Jacques Keruan phoned next day. He'd been appointed chairman of a committee which would meet for three days in the nearby town of Dinan to discuss a complex and pressing local issue involving twenty small communities. On the first evening the mayor was organising a tour of the historic town and a dinner for the committee representatives and accompanying guests. Jean-Jacques wanted to organise something for the second night, and asked her to be his guest for both nights.

Accustomed to hearing what hadn't been said, Sarah suspected he wanted the second night organised for him. She accepted his invitation and then suggested that he take the whole group out by coach to a restaurant in the forest of Brocéliande, for a gourmet dinner in a milieu known for its ancient abbey, its holy spring, King Arthur's knights, the wizard Merlin, the fairy

Vivian and magic galore. It was exactly the type of suggestion that Jean-Jacques needed someone to make, and he was delighted.

Sarah accompanied Jean-Jacques to the mayor's event. She stayed overnight in a hotel, enjoying a day exploring Dinan and its river, and on the second evening gracefully allowed Jean-Jacques to take charge of the party which travelled through the forest in the coaches she'd hired to the dinner she'd reserved. As a finishing touch she'd booked a local harpist to play Breton music during dinner, and everyone congratulated Jean-Jacques on the wonderful atmosphere this had produced.

Sarah was amused to see him accept the praise as his due. In her previous professional life, she was well used to the official plaudits going to the company chairman who'd commissioned her work. Her real reward had always been her private satisfaction of a job well done, and for this occasion that was enough.

**

She'd just reached home the next morning when her mobile rang, and unexpectedly the caller said, "This is Charles. Is it a good time to call?"

"It is. Can I help?"

"I hope you don't mind me begging a lift. I've booked a holiday cottage in Saint-Edern. I felt like sitting looking at the sea. I've booked as a foot-passenger on the overnight ferry. It arrives in Saint-Malo tomorrow at half-past seven."

"I'll be waiting for you. How do you pick up the key?"

"The owner said to give her a ring when I arrived. She's an Englishwoman, Mrs Rowley, and it's Anchor Cottage on the quay."

"Oh, I know Janet Rowley. Anchor Cottage is near my flat, and we can breakfast in the next door café while you wait for the key."

"Thanks, Sarah. That's very good of you."

Sarah put the phone down in a contemplative mood. This must be Charles's reaction to the court settlement. He was owed at least three years' allowance of holiday, and it was his first opportunity to take some. Sarah emailed Deborah:

'Charles has just phoned me to ask for a lift. He's booked a holiday cottage in Saint-Edern and is coming over tonight on the ferry. He said he wants to look at the sea. That's all I have so far, but I thought you'd want to know.'

Deb was online in the office and replied by return:

'Sarah, thanks a million. Not knowing was becoming worrying. Of course, Charles could look at the sea in Bognor, but I think the coast of Brittany is more interesting.'

Sarah replied:

'I think distance from work is the big attraction. Anything else I discover I will pass on.'

'Careful now!' Deb emailed back. 'Charles was very annoyed that you told me about the court judgement. He probably still is.'

'Then he can learn to put up with it!' Sarah responded.

After lunch, Sarah telephoned Janet Rowley. "I believe you've just let Anchor Cottage to my young brother-in-law," she said.

"I thought he'd be a relative," Janet replied. "The name Pullen was too much of a coincidence. He telephoned out of the blue this morning and booked four weeks. I'm ecstatic! That covers the fortnight's cancellation notified a week ago plus two weeks not let at all."

"So glad he's helping a friend. I'll pick him up at the ferry at crack of dawn tomorrow, and I wondered what time you want to hand over the key."

"Would nine o'clock be too late?" Janet asked tentatively, "I'm not a morning person and I need my breakfast."

"That's fine by me. We'll be breakfasting in the café Au Coin du Quai. You've no need to rush."

"See you there."

So Charles had booked four weeks. For relaxing? For exploring? Did he want a social life? Where and how was he going to eat? There was no future in asking questions until he arrived, and if he'd booked the holiday on impulse he wouldn't know the answers anyway.

***

Very early the next morning Sarah drove to the ferry terminal. She parked close to the exit just as the boat touched the dock and stood with the crowd waiting for other passengers. When Charles appeared he was unmistakeable among the jeans and shorts and colourful summer clothes. He was wearing the standard English businessman's navy woollen overcoat.

I bet he's wearing a suit and a collar and tie under that, she thought, *but why have any other clothes if he does nothing but work?* She waved, and was rewarded with a brilliant smile. "The car's just over there," she said as he approached. "Did you have a good trip?"

"Quite good," he agreed politely, not touching, while all around them Bretons were hugging and kissing friends and family.

Then suddenly his face lit up and his voice filled with enthusiasm. "I set the alarm so that I woke up in time to see the coast. I'm so glad I did. I'll never forget the sight of all those grand headlands and the little sandy coves between them, and the wicked rocks peppering the sea in a jumble until you start seeing patterns in their layout, and that strange high island out by the lighthouse, and all those dinky little forts sitting in blue water. And then, when the boat turned to come into dock, there was Saint-Malo silhouetted against the sun. That sight alone was worth the whole journey." He seemed excited, alert, on edge, and certainly looked much younger than his age.

"Saint-Malo is a view I never tire of," Sarah said, leading the way. "This is my car, a bit small, and a rather bright blue, but I think your case will go in the boot?"

"Easily," Charles said, hefting it in. "There's room for the backpack as well."

"Your laptop?" Sarah said, recognising the type of padded bag.

"It's another right hand, I couldn't leave it behind."

Sarah pulled out on to the road home. "Does the cottage have wifi?"

"Mrs Rowley says so," he replied cautiously.

"How did you find a holiday cottage?"

"A small ad in *The Spectator*. I sat in the library to work out what to do next. I picked the magazine at random, and when I reached the back pages I saw 'Saint-Edern'. So I phoned the number."

Sarah negotiated through the narrow roads, beamed opened the gate to her underground carpark and garaged the car in its usual space. "Bring your suitcase," she said. "Anchor Cottage is next door to the café Au Coin Du Quai, where we can have breakfast. Mrs Rowley won't be early."

The café was thronged, since it was one of the few open for the early morning breakfast trade. A crowd of workers were consuming coffee and croissants before starting their day, and Gérard Lemestre was sitting at the best window table with a newspaper, coffee and pain au chocolat.

"Bonjour, Madame Pullen," he said with a critical look at her companion. "Congratulations on finding a new boyfriend so soon."

"Bonjour, Monsieur Lemestre." Sarah added in French to Charles, "Monsieur Lemestre and I recently worked together on a project for the regional prefecture."

Charles replied promptly in French, "If he's usually that rude, I'm surprised they employ him."

Lemestre smiled his appreciation of both language and comment, and held out his hand.

"Pullen," Charles said, shaking it. "I'm Madame Pullen's brother-in-law. I'm staying in Anchor Cottage for a month on holiday."

"Then you'd best come to the social club and meet everyone. Better we talk to your face than behind your back." He nodded dismissal before returning to the business pages.

Sarah bought two fresh orange juices at the counter and they sat to read the menu. Charles decided on a substantial omelette and sausages while Sarah ordered croissants. The café slowly emptied, revealing newspapers piled everywhere.

"Are we allowed to read them?" Charles asked.

"Of course, but you can't take them away, because the café provides them for its customers."

Charles picked one up and skimmed through it. "Good coverage," he said. "I probably ought to buy this to know what's going on."

"There's a newsagent just up the hill, part of the bar-tabac."

"I'll walk around once I've moved in. What do you do with your time?"

"I have an exercise class on Monday afternoon, and Wednesday evening I go to the social club. The club organises outings for either Saturday or Sunday, and I go to most of them. I work freelance on small computer system jobs, but I recently took on something ongoing for the regional prefect. It will never finish: it needs tweaking whenever anyone gets a new idea. I'm also making an effort to learn how to cook the local produce. There are fish on sale here that I've never heard of before, and even the vegetables aren't the same varieties as English ones. I can spend hours with my head in a cookbook. I did think of taking formal French classes, as I struggle a bit with grammar, but there just isn't the time."

"So we should speak French together while I'm here?" Charles said in French.

"As long as you're prepared to be patient. You did at least pass A level; I only did O level."

"I haven't remembered it all yet," Charles said, reverting to English. "But there were crowds of French on the ferry, all talking nineteen to the dozen, and whole chunks of the language came back. I used to like the poetry best. French poets had a different view of life, and most of them were extremely cynical, which suited me as a teenager. I've only just realised how much I regret throwing away my schoolbooks. Is there a bookshop near here?"

"About a dozen in Saint-Edern and more than another dozen in Saint-Malo. I'm still astonished by the number of books the average French person buys. In summer you see people reading books on the beach and up on the cliff, and throughout the year there are readers in buses and cafés. This café only offers newspapers, but some stock a range of books in case customers haven't brought one with them."

"What a lovely idea," Charles remarked. "I knew I'd like it here."

They'd finished eating, but hadn't finished coffee, by the time Janet Rowley arrived. Charles stood to greet her. "Would you like to join us in a coffee?" he said.

"I don't mind if I do," Janet said. "It takes half a dozen to wake me up!"

When they left the café, Janet opened the cottage and showed them round. It was a tiny dwelling ranged over three storeys, but included one double bedroom, four bunk beds, a modern bathroom, and a well fitted kitchen-diner. Janet switched on the wifi equipment, the fridge and the hot water, and showed Charles the heating controls in case of need.

"That's very kind of you," Charles said. "Do you also own the cottage next door with the English name?"

"Tower View? Yes, they're both mine. They took the lump sum off my pension, and they bring in a decent income."

"They both face straight on to the quay. Does that mean they don't have parking spaces?"

"Ah, now you've hit the sore spot. There's free public parking a few yards away, but in season there are more visitors in Saint-Edern than there are parking spaces, and sometimes my tenants have to park ten minutes' walk away. I do get complaints."

"I can imagine. Are there many English-owned cottages in the area? I was surprised to find any at all."

"Oh, yes, at least two more owners on this side of the river and three on the other side. Now I really must go. But will you come with Sarah to the bridge club social on Sunday week?"

Charles smiled. "It's an English speaking bridge club?"

"Of course. We have twenty-eight playing members, and my husband's the chairman. This is our first social and we've opened it to the members' families. As James was a member we've invited Sarah. It's only finger food but it's an opportunity to natter to lots of people."

"It sounds very pleasant. Thank you for the invitation." Charles shook hands goodbye.

When Mrs Rowley had gone, Charles said, "I'd heard that the English in France live in little English speaking enclaves."

"I try not to," Sarah said. "I've made good friends among the local Bretons. But I joined the ex-patriates group to help James feel at home, and he joined the bridge club when it started. It's not part of my life at all."

"It doesn't sound very like you. But I'd better let you go while I unpack and work out what to do about lunch."

Sarah noted that Charles intended to eat alone and spend his time alone. She said, "I've brought you a town map so that you know where you are, and I'll leave you to it. If you need me, just ring my bell. But you might like to know that there's a social club outing tomorrow night, to the Fest Noz in Dol. That's the Breton version of a public dance, but traditional dances only. I'm definitely going. We have a coach booked and there are still a few seats free. Would you like to join in?"

"Who else is in the social club besides Monsieur Lemestre?"

"Local residents. About half are retired, but there are office managers and teachers and shopkeepers, and also the owner of the café Au Coin du Quai, Monsieur Poisson. I've made good friends in the club."

"It sounds as if I ought to come. Can you count me in?"

"I'll get it arranged. You have to be on the quay at seven o'clock prompt. You'll see the crowd waiting. Oh, just one thing, please don't wear a tie. Frenchmen don't usually wear one. In the social club no one ever does."

"I'm in favour of that," Charles grinned, pulling off the tie he'd put on automatically that morning, "I'm on holiday."

12

Charles unpacked and connected his laptop to the wifi. It worked immediately. The idea of buying French poetry books had remained in his mind. He'd recently banked an astounding amount of money, and he intended to use his holiday to decide what to do with it, but he could certainly afford to buy a few books. The internet indicated a bookshop a short distance away.

The shop had bookshelves extending into the depths of the long building. In the first aisle he was surrounded by books on Saint-Malo and its history, dozens of them. He returned to the counter to check that his English credit card would be accepted.

"Of course I'll take it," the bookseller said. "Do you need any help in choosing books?"

"I think I might. I want to read up on the history of this part of France."

The bookseller frowned. "If you're talking history, this isn't France. Until the Revolution, Brittany was a separate country, with its own laws, its own language and its own ruler. It's a difference we still cherish."

Charles was surprised. "I didn't know that. I definitely need a history of Brittany."

The bookseller pulled a number of books from his shelves, and Charles took a general history, a book with details of all the known rulers of Brittany, and half a dozen small books on specific events in the history of Saint-Malo. "Come back when you've finished them," said the bookseller, "I've always got more on the subject. We Bretons like reading about our roots."

"What about poetry?"

"I stock individual poets over there," the bookseller indicated, "and an anthology of modern poetry."

"I was hoping to find my old school textbook, poems from the Middle Ages to about 1920."

"I'm afraid I don't have that. You'd need a second-hand bookshop or one of the school textbook specialists. But if you like poetry, I can recommend this author, our best-seller. He's justly famous."

"All right," Charles said, "I'll take that one as well." As he paid, he asked where the nearest second-hand bookshop was.

"The nearest are in Saint-Malo, but they tend to stock antiquarian books and books on the sea. If you just want general second-hand books, fiction and non-fiction, there's an open-air book market in Rennes, in the Place Sainte-Anne, a stop on the metro. One never knows what's there, but the stallholders do take commissions to find specific editions."

Charles walked home with a carrier bag of books, but was now intrigued by the thought of a book market. On his laptop he looked up timetables, then caught a bus to Saint-Malo, and another to Rennes.

In Rennes, the bus station was near the pavement cafés facing the railway station. Charles picked a café describing itself as a crêperie, and opted for the special offer of 'a galette, a crêpe and a bol' without knowing what they were. The waitress described the galette as a savoury pancake made with sarrasin, the crêpe as a dessert pancake made from wheat flour, and the bol as a cup of cider. Whatever sarrasin was, the galette tasted delicious wrapped round cheese and ham; the dark, wafer thin pancake was more filling than it looked.

At Place Sainte-Anne the metro's up-escalator delivered Charles into the middle of the bookstalls. He swiftly amassed a collection of classic literature, but couldn't see the anthology of poetry he wanted. He asked a bouquiniste, who obligingly unearthed a couple of books from the back of his van. One was the exact edition Charles remembered.

"It's in a shocking state," the seller said sternly. "It's got coffee stains and finger marks, and there was even sand between the pages, would you believe? Some people just don't treat books with the proper respect."

But Charles immediately envisioned the last owner lying on a beach in the sun reading poetry, and hoped to do the same.

Drinking a coffee under a café umbrella, he realised he hadn't seen a map of Brittany or a guidebook. He asked the waiter, who recommended taking the metro to the big modern bookshop in a local commercial centre. Charles found the place easily. He bought a guide and some large-scale maps of the coast around Saint-Malo, but the shop also sold electronic gadgets of all descriptions, from computers to drones, and his eye was caught by a display of cameras. The salesman immediately homed in on a potential customer, and effortlessly sold him a high quality, multifunctional, palm-sized digital still camera.

Charles now carried half a dozen bags. He stopped in an ice-cream parlour for somewhere to sit. Watching the passers-by, he suddenly realised he was dressed differently to everyone else. He was wearing one of his two dark suits with one of his nine white shirts. Half the men passing wore jeans. There were smart jackets and trousers, but no suits, and no formal shirts. He must look like an alien.

There was a department store opposite; he started there. He talked to an assistant, discovered his French size, and acquired light olive chinos, lightweight jeans, a navy waterproof hooded anorak, a khaki multi-pocketed sleeveless jacket, and two checked shirts. It made a sizeable pile of clothes, so he asked for directions to the luggage department and bought a large wheeled bag. He changed into a checked shirt and then bagged his suit jacket, his white shirt and all his other purchases.

Having only one bag made it easy to explore other shops. He bought more interesting shirts, linen shorts, hiking boots, swimming trunks, a beach towel and beach sandals. A very trendy shoe shop sold him ankle-boots with light flexible soles and uppers made of soft supple tan calf leather which fitted like gloves. They felt perfect for dancing all night.

It had been far too many years since Charles had spent this much money in one month let alone one day, but he felt that he now had the ingredients for a new lifestyle. He made his way to the bus for Saint-Malo and spent his time on it reading the Brittany guidebook. On reaching home, he changed into jeans and sandals, put the sleeveless jacket over his checked shirt, and sat outside a bar on the riverside to order dinner. He blended in completely until he started taking photographs of the sunset.

***

On Saturday Charles decided to explore the local area. The guidebook said the hill above the cottage was called Alet. He found a path running along the edge of the cliff under pine trees. The water was a darker blue than the intensely blue sky. He sat on the first bench he found, and realised that the water wasn't the sea but a river estuary, with another town on the cliff opposite. His guidebook named that town as Dinard. As he watched, a small passenger ferry detached itself from the opposite quay and worked steadily across the water.

He could see a road across the estuary, maybe ten metres above the high tide. He consulted his guide and discovered that this barrage was an underwater electricity-generating station using both incoming and outgoing tide to create power. He was astounded to find that it dated from 1966 and was still producing enough current to power Saint-Malo, Dinard and Rennes. It seemed strange that it was so little known in this environmentally conscious age.

Charles left the cliff edge to walk through the gate of an old fortress, which at first sight was just a wall around a large empty cobbled square. He climbed the wall in the north corner. Through the trees he could see the dock entrance of Saint-Malo. The guidebook stated that by the seventeenth century, cannon had improved to the point where they could fire accurately from here to the town, so anyone stationed here could hold Saint-Malo to ransom. The town had constructed the fortress to ensure that the Alet peninsula was held by their own men. The enemy at that time was, to Charles' delight, les Anglais, the English. They'd never got close to war-ready and well defended Saint-Malo, so the fort wasn't used.

But in World War II the occupying forces saw this peninsula as the obvious strong point. Even better, it wasn't hard granite, but workable stone. Beneath the old fortress the Nazis excavated living quarters, kitchens, dormitories, recreational areas, a radio communications room, and a rabbit warren of tunnels leading to gun-turrets all over the hillside. They made Alet a bomb-proof redoubt. When the Americans arrived by sea, the strength of its armaments took everyone by. surprise. The state of the guns showed what a battle it had been to persuade the occupiers to leave.

Returning to the cliff edge, Charles rounded the headland. Suddenly he found himself standing next to one of the World War II bronze gun turrets, stunningly damaged by shell fire, and beyond it the walled town of Saint-Malo was spread out like a map.

He sat on a bench to drink in the view: the town, the islands, the forts, the rocks, the lighthouse further out, the yacht harbour, the ferry harbour, the inner docks beyond the sluice-gate, the relentless waves, the shifting breeze, the graceful pleasure yachts, the purposeful commercial ferry. Sarah was right, it was a view you couldn't get tired of. He pointed the camera at every photographable item in the panorama. It took several minutes to capture them all.

Charles continued his circuit round the headland. On the way he found a piece of damaged stonework, maybe a metre high, labelled as the last remaining part of the Roman wall around the city of Alet. He took the tarmac road leading down to Saint-Edern, and next to that road discovered the ruined cathedral of the city of Alet. The plaque claimed that Saint Malo himself had been its bishop. The city of Alet was part of the history of Brittany which he needed to learn.

In the bar-tabac he bought a newspaper and lunched on a salad combining pasta, smoked mackerel, bacon, mushrooms and watercress. He congratulated the owner's wife on the combination of flavours, and she said, "It was featured in that magazine there. It's full of good ideas." On impulse Charles bought a copy of the magazine and asked for directions to the nearest shops. He thought of learning to cook for himself.

In the baker's he bought a round crusty loaf and a pear and almond tart. The owner of the grocery sold him eggs, gave him detailed instructions on cooking an omelette, and sold him ham and tinned tuna and a jar of seafood as suggested fillings. Charles added four different cheeses and a bagful of staple foods for his fridge and his stock cupboards. In the greengrocers' he bought a wide range of vegetables and fruit. He had no idea what to do with anything in the fishmonger's, but the glorious display of sea denizens on crushed ice was so attractive that he photographed it.

He spent the afternoon reading the history of Alet, an ancient trading post in the middle Stone Age. It was the administrative centre of the Coriosolite tribe in the Bronze Age, and had prospered as a port under the Romans. Unfortunately it was a tempting target for Danish Viking raiders after the Romans left. When the Welsh monk Malo arrived and became bishop of Alet, he realised that the town needed to move from the indefensible land-based site. He moved it on to two large rocks out in the deep water.

Charles could hardly believe that this vast undertaking succeeded in the conditions prevailing around the year 600, but Malo was a statesman equal to his task. The two rocks were surrounded with massive defence walls, homes and warehouses were constructed inside, and the resulting town is still there. Malo's legacy – the security of monumental walls, the space for expansion within them, the sheltered deep-water quays alongside – ushered in a thousand years of prosperity, and the town is still the largest port on the Channel coast of Brittany.

Besides rebuilding the seat of his bishopric, Malo tramped up and down his diocese preaching the love of God and dispensing justice, a truly great man revered by everyone. Charles' book pointed out that Malo was ordained by the Celtic Church, and so he had never been recognised as a saint by the Catholic Church. But in the hearts of Bretons he can't be anything less, and his town still proudly bears the name ville de Saint-Malo.

***

That evening, Charles put on his new olive chinos, an olive and pale blue checked shirt, and his dancing boots. He attached the camera bag to his belt, and joined the crowd of social club members on the quay. He was immediately buttonholed by three women, who plied him with incessant and unconnected questions about himself, why he'd come to Brittany and what the cottage was like inside. When he saw Sarah he called, "Help!" with a big grin.

"Slowly now, mes amies," Sarah said in her best French. "My brother-in-law is here for four weeks, so you have time to ask him questions. We don't want him to think Breton women are nosey."

They laughed. "Wait until the men start, Monsieur Pullen!"

"Oh, please call me Charles."

"But of course," the leader of the group said. "I'm Elodie, this is Mauricette and this is Jeanne-Françoise." And all three gave him a kiss in welcome, while at the same time everyone present kissed Sarah good evening.

The coach slid to a halt alongside the crowd and everyone scrambled on board as fast as possible. Pascal Rozko counted heads, confirmed everyone was present, and the coach promptly moved off to cease blocking the road. In the seat behind the driver Jean-Yves Lagarde played his accordion to set the mood.

At eight they arrived outside the hall in Dol. The room was already half full. The walls had been lined with chairs and a bar set up alongside the stage, but the whole centre floor was clear. Around the edges of the room knots of people stood talking, while children played tag through the crowd. Jean-Yves Lagarde, the official warm-up artist, walked calmly to the stage, hitched on his accordion, sat on the edge of the platform, pulled a microphone down to the level of his instrument and began a lyrical ballad.

At the end of the tune, there was a smattering of applause. Jean-Yves immediately launched into a foot- tapping rhythm. A group on one side of the room promptly put their glasses down on a chair and started dancing in a ring, holding hands. The dance step was very simple. Charles watched intrigued as other people butted into the ring to join the dance; they just parted two joined hands and stepped into the gap. By the time the music ended the ring was rather oddly shaped. At the first chord of the next dance, the dancers split into groups of eight and began something resembling a square dance.

"How do they know what dance to do?" Charles asked Sarah.

"Jean-Yves announces it. But he doesn't speak loudly because this is the time of the evening when people are meeting their friends. Many people don't dance until the main group comes on stage; we all have lots of gossip to get through."

As if this was their cue, Mauricette and Jeanne-Françoise asked Charles what he did with his time in Saint-Edern.

"I take photographs of the fish on display in the fishmonger's," he said with a straight face.

"Is this the famous English sense of humour?" Mauricette asked flirtatiously.

"Not at all! There is nothing more worthy of being photographed than a brilliant purple lobster on a heap of crushed ice."

"It's better when it's pink and cooked," Jeanne-Françoise said, "and served with sauce Armoricaine."

The tune ended and Jean-Yves spoke three words before starting another. "Rond-Saint-Vincent," Mauricette said eagerly. "Come on!" She grabbed Charles' left hand as Jeanne-Françoise grabbed his right, and they dragged him into the ring of dancers. Sarah and Elodie watched with amusement as Charles worked out which foot to put where when, but he soon relaxed into the dance. By the time the main group was announced, he'd practised all the local dances more than once.

The hall had gradually filled to capacity, but as the group came on stage to great applause, the atmosphere changed. The chattering hushed. The floor cleared as everyone pressed back against the walls. This was serious.

At the first notes, a man walked out into the middle of the dance floor, put his left hand on his hip and held his right hand out to his right. Immediately four people formed a line holding hands on his right side, and they all moved into the dance in perfect unison, stepping to the left. More and more dancers added themselves to the end of the line. The dance leader followed a sinuous track around the floor with the lengthening line of followers treading precisely in his footsteps. On more than one occasion he led the line into a spiral and then out of it, so that dancers ended up moving back-to-back with each other.

By the end of the hypnotic, rhythmic tune, the floor was crowded with dancers moving faithfully along the complex path which had been set for them, and Charles was balancing on top of a stack of chairs holding his camera as high as he could in an attempt to record the pattern of the dance. The music ended with Mauricette in front of him. "It's good to see that you photograph something other than fish," she said with as a straight a face as she could.

By the end of the evening Charles had danced almost continuously. Dancing had been his main recreation as a young man, and he hadn't had as much fun as this for years. When the dancers had split into pairs for a polka or waltz or pavane, or into fours or eights for a set dance, he'd partnered all the women of Saint-Edern in turn and then women from places he didn't know. Here and there he took photographs of the musicians and the dancers, and during the changeover of the two groups he enjoyed the excellent cider so much that he photographed its name, Le Coudray, to remember it.

The crowd had retained its good humour to the end. The dance steps had been honed over the centuries to allow people to dance for five hours without becoming fatigued, and provided enough variation for individual dancers to enable all three generations of a family to dance together, whatever their energy levels and abilities.

There was an enveloping feeling of belonging, as warm and welcome to Charles as a glass of hot spiced wine in a chill winter. Sometime during the evening he fell in love with Brittany, with Bretons and above all with their musical heritage. At one in the morning, as everyone left, he discovered a woman selling the two bands' CDs out of a suitcase, and he bought one of every disc going in an attempt to hold on to the magic he'd just discovered.

He asked Sarah how often a Fest Noz was held. "Every commune with a suitable hall has at least one a year," she said. "On some Saturdays there are dozens of them. The musicians in Dol tonight are famous, and the quality of the music was exceptional. Local musicians in small villages don't reach these heights, but their enthusiasm is heart-warming, and they always produce a good dance. I go to as many Fest Noz as I can. I like the music, I like the dancing, I like the people."

"They were a good humoured crowd tonight and very well-behaved."

"I've never seen a troublemaker at a Fest Noz," Sarah said. "It's a family affair. You saw all the children on the dance floor. It doesn't appeal to rowdies and heavy drinkers, so it's a safe venue for the elderly and for single women. I intend to celebrate Fest Noz until I'm a hundred. Beyond, if possible."

13

Waking on his first Sunday in Brittany, Charles decided to go sight-seeing. He spent the morning in the Solidor Tower on his doorstep in Saint-Edern. The tower itself was constructed in the 1300s to control shipping in the river. Very tall, it provided a glorious view of the estuary from its roof-level walkway. The building housed a museum dedicated to the Cape Horners, the long-distance cargo vessels sailing to the other side of the world, giving a sailor's eye view of the ships and their trade.

Charles spent the afternoon in Saint-Malo, starting in the town museum, learning details of the lives of the people who lived there, and the boats they sailed. He walked the whole circuit of the magnificent town walls, taking numerous photographs on the way. He returned home to cook himself an omelette with ham, sweet peppers and mushrooms, with fresh strawberries for dessert.

On Monday he took the ferry to Dinard. He walked along the river esplanade, the Promenade au Clair de la Lune, a puzzling name which translated as Moonlight Walk. Suddenly the quay turned a corner and revealed the headland which was his first objective. He climbed the hill and found that he was directly opposite Alet, with a splendid view of both Alet and Saint-Malo. He sat down to enjoy that and to take photographs.

He walked on to the end of the headland, the Pointe du Moulinet, Windmill Point. The breeze didn't turn any mill-sails these days. The cliffs were covered with splendid mansions, some over a century old. At the point he descended to the path along the base of the cliff, and soon found himself facing a flat expanse of pale sand entirely filling a wide bay lined with hotels. July is the first month of the high season, so the beach was well-covered with deckchairs, beach-mats, sand-castle builders and energetic volley-ball games, the water being populated with swimmers and kayakers.

Charles followed the signs to the Tourist Information Office, where he collected all the leaflets he could see in the racks, and went up to the counter to ask for a free map. The tourist officer was a woman with a delightful smile and a warm welcome. As she gave him a map, she asked, "You're not French?"

"No, I'm afraid I'm English. I can see Dinard from where I'm staying, so I want to learn more about it. Do you have anything which describes its history?"

"The main guide book," she answered, picking up a copy and thumbing to the page. "There's a whole section on the foundation and evolution of the town, and it really is fascinating. There's a walk around the cliffs on both sides of the bay which is detailed in that leaflet you're holding. It's a very interesting shoreline."

"I think I've done part of that. I came over on the ferry and walked up the river to the end of the Pointe du Moulinet."

"That's where it all started, up there on Moulinet," said the officer, "so you might need to read about what you've passed already. I can certainly recommend the rest of the walk round the next headland. The houses here are unlike any others in Brittany, and the sea is impressive in its own right. But it's nearly lunchtime, so you'll need this map with the restaurants marked on it."

"That will certainly be useful. Do you also have information on buses?" She produced a bus timetable and marked the main bus stops on the restaurant map. "That's very kind of you. You couldn't have been more helpful," said Charles, "It's good to meet someone so enthusiastic. Do you come from Dinard?"

"I was born here. I'm a Breton," she said proudly. "My parents came from Réunion, in the Pacific, so they're French, and in school, I was told to say I was French, too, but I'm so much happier to be Breton."

"I'm glad to hear it," Charles said, "I'm sure it's the people who make Brittany what it is. It's a pleasure to meet you all."

"Thank you indeed, monsieur. Do enjoy Dinard, it's a town worth seeing."

Charles found a table on the pavement outside a crêperie, and ordered a galette filled with seafood and a bottle of cider, which he noted was from Le Coudray, a provably successful enterprise. He spread his collection of papers across the little table. It appeared that Dinard was a modern creation which hadn't existed before the mid-1800s, when villas were constructed on the

Pointe du Moulinet by a group of rich Americans and English interested in sea-bathing.

By 1880 it had become one of *the* places for fashionable Europe and America to spend summer promenading along the sands. More and more villas with improbable fairy tale architecture crowded the cliffs around the bay. Famous people came to stay, among them the composer Debussy. Charles realised that the Promenade au Clair de la Lune must commemorate the famous Debussy composition rather than the local moonlight.

Throughout its short history, no effort had been spared to attract people to Dinard. The English developed the yacht club so they could sail across the Channel in their own boats. A tennis club was formed. A golf course was constructed. A casino was built.

The two world wars must have had a devastating effect, but the town had survived both setbacks, and, while not relinquishing its top of the market hotels, it had now spread its net wider to embrace the middle classes, and in particular families, for whom the fine sand of the four beaches had proved irresistible. A regular festival of British films had proved so successful that other types of film festival had followed. In early July the town was already full; it had a prosperous feel to it which would surely continue throughout August, and into September for holidaymakers without young children. Dinard was nothing if not successful, and it showed.

Charles mentally paid his respects to the enormous amount of work involved on all fronts to create the town as an ideal place for relaxation, and to yet more work involved in maintaining it. There were five- star hotels, for example, which had been built to the highest standards of their day, but they'd certainly not been left as built. They must have been modernised and refitted over and over again to meet the ever increasing expectations of their clients. Even Mrs Rowley's cottages had to have wifi and microwave ovens. Nothing in the tourist industry could ever rest on its laurels. Everyone had to stay alert to all possibilities, ready for future requirements. It wasn't the boring type of employment where one worked up to manager status and then simply watched other people work. The constant challenge and the need for leadership must make a more lively profession.

Charles finished his seafood galette and ordered a crêpe with lemon and honey, without consciously realising that in less than a week he'd left his previous cautious, anxious, non-risk-taking, unconfident and thoroughly unhappy self far behind.

Reading the bus timetable, he discovered a bus from Dinard to Rennes which travelled down the western side of the river. The bus he'd used to go from Saint-Malo to Rennes had travelled on the eastern side of the water. The western bus from Dinard went through a town confusingly called Dinan. Charles looked that up on his mobile phone and found it was a historic city with a river port and a castle. It was certainly big enough to merit a whole day exploring it. So that settled where to go tomorrow.

After lunch he completed the walk round the second headland, the Pointe de la Malouine, at a leisurely pace, enjoying the sea and photographing the grand houses lining the cliffs. Then he returned through the town, investigating the shops, especially the one displaying 'non-iron shirts' in the window. He bought three hoping that the description was correct.

On returning home he downloaded his photographs into his laptop and looked through them. He quickly realised the need for photo-manipulation software. He searched the internet, found a suitable package and bought it. He initially learned how to make the horizon horizontal, which immediately improved a number of shots. Encouraged, he started working through the gamut of possible enhancements, and, with only a brief break for his magazine's recommended Provençal dish of tuna, anchovies, peppers, onions, tomatoes and rice, by midnight he'd succeeded in producing some images he could be proud of.

***

On Tuesday morning he started out very early, took the ferry across the river and caught an early bus going south. Dinan proved to be another spectacular walled town, perched very high on a bluff above the river. The centre of the old town consisted of medieval buildings in stone and in picturesque timber. There were historic buildings in all directions, and simply walking the streets was a joy. Charles bought the first tourist guidebook he saw and started to follow it, delighted that so much history had survived to the present day.

He managed to fit in the castle, poised high above the river and of course housing the town museum, to climb the clock tower and to explore the beautiful old basilica, but by then he was hungry. He not only needed a restaurant but something to read over lunch. In a newsagent's he bought a history of Dinan and a magazine called *La Charme de Bretagne*. He stopped in the first café with an interesting menu, La Cuisine d'Antoine.

Antoine was an adventurous cook. Charles ordered a starter of avocado, cucumber and grapefruit, followed by fillet of sea bass with prawns in a cream and ginger sauce on a bed of spinach. While waiting he flipped through the magazine, noting that it relied heavily on photographs. Slipping into audit mode out of habit, he counted the number of pages dedicated to articles – which attracted buyers – and those dedicated to advertising – which underwrote the publication costs. It was certainly a quality publication on heavy glossy paper, but it puzzled him slightly that all its adverts were placed by Breton firms, and its small-ads section was dominated by holiday lets in Brittany.

He looked up the editorial address. The magazine offices were here in Dinan. Why would Dinan residents rent holiday homes in Brittany? Then he thought that the magazine was probably sold in other regions of France, possibly even in other European countries. He wondered how to find out.

A well-dressed older gentleman on the next table had been interestedly watching him work forwards and backwards through the magazine. He leaned over and said, "You seem to be making a thorough investigation of that magazine. Can I ask what it is that interests you?"

"At the moment," Charles said, "I'm wondering whether Bretons buy a magazine on Brittany, and if so, why. And where else it's sold. In the rest of France, perhaps? Beyond the frontier?"

"The magazine is owned by a newspaper based on the north coast of France, so it appears in all the kiosks which sell the newspaper. People living in Brittany do buy it, in quantity. Possibly some just like to see pictures of their own country, but we've been told that the advertisements are particularly successful. People who want to take their families on holiday buy the magazine to see what pony treks or kayaking courses or fishing trips are on offer. Brittany is a big region, and even people who live in Dinan are quite likely to take hotel rooms or campsite places half a day's drive away in Finistère. And of course, all Bretons are interested in the photos and history of places they can visit."

Charles' first course arrived, and the waiter astutely pushed the two tables together so that his two clients could converse in more comfort.

"During the tourist season our sales treble, so we know the magazine is attractive to tourists. Some of them even subscribe to it, because new subscription sales peak in September. The magazine sells in great quantities on newsstands in Paris, and it does well in French speaking areas in other countries, Belgium, Luxembourg, Switzerland. Our subscribers cover the whole of France, including some strange places. There are twelve in Marseille, for example."

"That's not a town I'd have thought of."

"It's a seafaring port, and Bretons with skills in shipbuilding or navigation have been known to take jobs there. Perhaps the magazine keeps their families in touch with their roots? We have four Canadian subscribers in Montreal, and I expect they're descendants of Bretons, too."

"You're saying 'we'. Does that mean you're connected to the magazine?"

"I'm the editor," the gentleman extended his hand, "Jean-Jacques Keruan."

"Charles Pullen. Congratulations. It really is a quality product."

"Thank you for the compliment. Can I ask what is your interest in it?"

"Very casual, I'm afraid. I'm on holiday, this is my first day in Dinan and this is the first time I've seen the magazine. I was interested to see how it's made up and the balance between advertising and articles."

"So what do you do when you're not on holiday?" Monsieur Keruan asked.

"That's an awkward question," Charles said. "I graduated with a degree in business management and economics and became an accountant. I've worked at many of the major companies in England, so I now have a very strong grasp of the workings of British industry and commerce. But after twenty years, I decided it was time to move on, so I've taken a break while I decide what to do next."

"It's always good to change career direction," Monsieur Keruan observed, "I've done it frequently. It makes a more interesting and well-rounded life."

"That's encouraging. What did you do before you edited this magazine?"

"I graduated with a degree in literature, took a job in crime reporting, moved into political reporting, moved into public relations, moved into politics, held a seat in parliament for ten years, moved into television reporting, moved into television production, and then just as I was thinking of retiring I saw this job advertised, so I took it. I was born in Lanvallay, just the other side of the river, and it's good to come home after a lifetime in Paris."

"Heureux, qui comme Ulysse, a fait un beau voyage?" Charles commented immediately (happy the man who, like Ulysses, completes a long voyage).

Monsieur Keruan's eyebrows rose. "An English accountant quoting Joachim du Bellay? You must be unique!"

"I became addicted to French poetry when I was at school, and I've just started re-reading it."

"What else do you do? Have you met many local people?"

"I spent last Saturday night at a Fest Noz in Dol," Charles said, and launched into his impressions of the night, the crowd, the music and the dancing.

Monsieur Keruan looked at him with interest. "If you put that down in writing, I could pay you for the article," he said. "I do mean that seriously. You have a gift for a telling phrase and for highlighting interesting features."

Charles tried not to look completely taken aback. He said, "Then I'll certainly write it up for you. How many words do you need for an article?"

Monsieur Keruan produced a card with his email address on it, added the limit on words and the amount payable.

"We pay peanuts," he said, "because writing for us isn't a full-time job, and we pay less for words than for photographs, because pictures are what catches the buyer's eye. But you do have a different take on things. I could perhaps use other articles. Can you give me your name and telephone and email?" Charles obliged. "And now," Monsieur Keruan said, "I do have to go back to work. But I wish you luck for your future."

Charles felt curiously exhilarated. No one had ever commented on his powers of description before. It's not, after all, an aptitude required from accountants. He continued walking round town and then descended the precipitous slope between picturesque buildings to the medieval port down on the river. The two sides of the river were linked by a humpbacked bridge, but the port itself nestled in a gorge between vertical cliffs, and soaring high above was the eighteenth century viaduct bringing the major road into town from the heights opposite. Charles took so many photographs that he started to wonder when the camera would run out of storage space.

He ventured on a boat offering cruises up the river, which to his surprise turned into a canal heading for Rennes. On his return he found the small museum dedicated to both the local waterways. The seventeenth century canal had been important because it had provided a north-south route across Brittany, cutting out the need for sailing ships to round the dangerous point of Finistère in winter weather.

All too soon it was time to start the journey home. In the bus station Charles bought a pad of lined paper, and spent the journey writing the description of the Fest Noz which he remembered giving to Monsieur Keruan. It was about the right length for an article.

When he reached the cottage and switched on his PC, he found an email from Sarah. She reminded him that the social club would meet on Wednesday evening at eight, and invited him to dinner at half-past six beforehand. He immediately accepted.

14

Charles spent Wednesday morning working on his photographs. He very soon got the hang of improving street scenes and landscapes, and enhancing the light and the colours. He was particularly pleased with what the camera had produced at the Fest Noz. It obviously knew how to handle dim light and movement, and some of its pictures were excellent.

The pattern of the dance seen from above had come out well, but the perspective made it look odd. Charles spent an hour experimenting with possible changes of perspective, and finally improved the shot beyond recognition. His best three photos showed the pattern of the dance, a line of dancers moving in rhythm with obvious enjoyment, and two musicians of the main group, a flautist and an accordionist, facing each other intently as they wove their separate sounds into one complex thread of music.

Charles revised his article and then emailed it with the three photos to Jean-Jacques Keruan. He made himself a simple salad lunch before returning to his study of the history of Brittany.

Just before half-past six, Charles rang Sarah's bell and was buzzed in. "I'm glad you're early," Sarah said. "Tonight is a little experimental. I haven't had much practice in cooking a meal so that each course will be ready when we want to eat it."

"Do I just sit in the kitchen and watch?" Charles asked hopefully.

"Certainly not, you make yourself useful. Start by opening a bottle of red wine. The Saumur in the rack over there, unless you prefer one of the others."

"I'll follow your judgement, you've been here longer. Ah, found the corkscrew."

Sarah lifted two small meringues out of the oven and set them on a rack to cool. "Good, we have dessert. Now I can put this first course in the oven."

"What are they?" Charles asked, looking at the two small orange balls. "Miniature pumpkins, stuffed with duck, figs and sultanas. I do this for a light evening meal sometimes, but they're a bit fiddly. You have to cook the pumpkins first and then de-seed them, fill them and cook again."

"You've been to an enormous amount of trouble."

"Not really. I buy two cookery magazines every month, and as I live alone, I cook one of their recipes for each meal. But they're intended as part of three-course dinners, and I felt like trying that out."

"Always happy to oblige a cook!"

"Glad to hear it. Put that bunch of parsley through this herb mill into that bowl."

"What's the main course?"

"Grilled ham with Madeira sauce, served with rice and parsley. The sauce is ready, and the rice will go into the microwave while we eat the pumpkins."

"I see how your computer systems got installed on time. It's all in the planning?"

"Of course. How do you manage to eat in the cottage?"

"Mrs Rowley has supplied quite decent kitchen utensils and I'm learning fast. People who sell me food always seem to be happy to tell me how to cook it."

"Food is a major topic of conversation here; it's a serious subject." The oven timer rang. "The first course is ready, so take the wine through to the salon and I'll follow with the food."

They sat at the table in front of the windows overlooking the estuary. Charles poured the wine, and then started on his pumpkin. "I must congratulate you on your choice of cookery magazines," he said, "this is delicious."

"You can try the same thing yourself with a courgette. The round courgettes do well when stuffed, and they're quicker, they don't to be softened up first. You just scoop out the seeds from the inside and add butter and a little meat or fish, shreds of bacon, or tinned sardines, and after that anything goes. I use cheese, tomatoes, whatever's left in the fridge."

"I must have a go. But I've a question I need to ask someone. What's sarrasin? I ate it when I was in Rennes, and the internet just says it's 'buckwheat', which sounds American."

"It's a local crop. It was brought back from the east by the crusaders, and it grows happily on poor soil. Large tracts of Brittany aren't rich enough for wheat. Sarrasin is a close relative of quinoa, and its tiny seeds are ground into flour, which is very dark, almost black. Unfortunately medieval Bretons found it difficult to use sarrasin for traditional bread baking. So the regional dish of Brittany is a galette, a thin, flat, dark pancake."

"It's quite filling and it tastes superb," Charles said. "I suppose it's the equivalent of pastry, but it doesn't weigh on the stomach like the topping of a pub steak pie."

"The biggest advantage of the galette," Sarah said with a grin, "was that sarrasin wasn't considered by the French government to be a foodstuff, so it wasn't taxed. Wheat flour was taxed very highly. Nothing tastes better than a dish which hasn't paid any dues."

Charles laughed. "Now I really know why the Bretons adopted it!"

Sarah served two plates of grilled ham coated with thick sauce and accompanied with rice and plenty of parsley. "The sauce really includes Madeira?" Charles asked.

"Of course. I keep a half-bottle for cooking. I've a recipe for ham in Madeira flavoured jelly."

"I'll have to borrow your recipe collection. I've never been interested before, but suddenly food seems important."

"Same for me, I lived on canteen food and ready-to-cook packets for forty years, but now I could become a bore on the subject."

Sarah cleared the plates into the kitchen and returned with dessert. "Rhubarb meringue," she said.

Charles took a spoonful from his bowl and tasted it. "Goodness, what have you done with the rhubarb?"

"Well, under the meringue is a cake made from rhubarb, egg yolk, semolina, cream and vanilla."

"It's superb. I could eat three of these."

"Moderation in all things," Sarah said gravely. "In France people don't eat as much as they do in England."

"Taste instead of quantity? One can't argue. Can I wash up?"

"The dishwasher does that. But I'll be making coffee. Do you want an espresso?"

"Yes, please. If I can't help you in the kitchen, I'll have to raid your bookshelves."

"Look for the two cartoon books on Surcouf the pirate, and Jacques Cartier who discovered Canada. They're historically accurate and very well done."

When Sarah returned with the coffee she found Charles laughing over a book. "As far as I can see, when English history claims that Admiral Nelson and the British Navy commanded the high seas, Robert Surcouf was quietly making a fortune by capturing English merchantmen and selling both the vessels and their cargoes. And he managed it with little boats with only six guns and a dozen crew."

"Bretons had a certain reputation. If you were in charge of a twenty-gun, three-decker cargo carrier bound for England, and six Bretons came over the bulwarks with pistols in their belts and knives between their teeth, you and your whole crew would have surrendered immediately in fear of your lives."

"No wonder Surcouf didn't figure in my school history; the English don't want him remembered."

***

It was time to walk to the club. At the door to the restaurant they met Marie-Pierre, and as they entered the two women were called over by another group of women who had news to impart. Left on his own, Charles looked round the room. On the nearest table there was an empty seat next to Monsieur Lemestre.

Smiling delightedly, Charles asked, "Is this seat free?"

"Bonsoir, Monsieur Pullen, please join us," Monsieur Lemestre said gravely, and looking round his circle he added, "Allow me to present the younger brother of the late Monsieur Pullen. He's here on holiday and is staying in Anchor Cottage next to Philippe's café-bar." He then presented Monsieur Lagarde, Monsieur Lesur and Monsieur Laperriere. "Monsieur Poisson you already know."

"From the café," Charles acknowledged.

"Is your cottage one of those owned by that strange Englishwoman?" Monsieur Laperriere asked.

"An Englishwoman certainly, but I didn't find her strange."

"On the hottest morning in August when everyone is wearing shorts and sandals, she arrives wearing a skirt-suit and stockings and high heels and heavy jewellery," explained Monsieur Lesur.

"Ah, that's her English businesswoman's uniform," said Charles. "She only lets her cottages to English people. They can dress as if they're on holiday, because they are, but she feels the need to dress formally. If she didn't observe that dress code, she wouldn't feel in control."

"Madame Pullen wears the same style of clothes as other women of Saint-Edern, but I've heard that she's a businesswoman of some repute."

"That's true," Charles said, "but my sister-in-law worked in European capitals for twenty years and she adopted European ways. My brother worked in England all his life, so I expect he came to this club wearing a suit and a tie?"

"Always," said Monsieur Laperriere, "and he never spoke any French."

Monsieur Poisson added, "Madame Rowley is the same. I'm sure she understands French, but she speaks only English."

"It takes courage to speak a foreign language," said Charles. "Madame Rowley doesn't want to sound stupid in public."

"But you're speaking French."

"I don't speak it very well," said Charles. "I can read French very well, and write it fairly well, but speaking is quite different. At school, I learnt classical literature. There's a whole different vocabulary for everyday speech which I don't know. I also have problems with expressing opinions. For example, if you say something and I don't agree with you, I know how to say 'you're wrong', but that's impolite, isn't it? I also know 'that's a lie', which is worse than impolite, it's confrontational. I'm sure you say something else. In England, I know dozens of ways of saying something's not correct without starting a fight, but here I don't know a single one."

Monsieur Lemestre grinned mischievously. "Then we have a duty to help you. I suggest that every time you say something, one of us should tell you, politely, that you must be lying."

Charles laughed with sheer delight. "Monsieur Lemestre, I am so glad to have met you."

"Gérard," the older man said, holding out his hand.

"Charles," he replied, shaking it.

The others held out their hands.

"Philippe."

"Jean-Yves."

"Jean-Vincent."

"Yannick."

"And now we'd better call the meeting to order," Gérard said, "or we won't manage to organise the weekend." He signalled to Pascal Rozko, who walked into the middle of the room and clapped his hands.

"This Saturday I suggest we visit Fougères. There's a guide who can be available on Saturday at ten o'clock, and the café Fleurs des Marais would be happy to provide lunch, and there's a coach driver free from nine o'clock for the whole day." Pascal named the cost of coach and admission and lunch provided that thirty people joined the trip. Within minutes he had thirty-seven names and was sending confirmation emails to the guide, the restaurant and the coach driver.

After booking, Charles asked Gérard, "What is there at Fougères?"

Gérard raised his eyebrows. "You reserved a place without knowing where you were going?"

"This group doesn't go to uninteresting places."

"You may be right there. Fougères is on the border of Brittany. Its castle was the largest medieval fortress in Europe, and the outer walls survive intact. But its history is very complex. It regularly changed owners between Brittany and France. There was even a time when the English bribed their way into it and had to be thrown out," Gérard frowned threateningly.

"You'd better keep an eye on me on Saturday, then," Charles said, grinning, "You don't know what I might do." Yannick slapped him on the back as everyone laughed.

The barman placed a bottle labelled Le Coudray and six cups in the centre of the table. "You know our cider?" Jean-Vincent asked, pouring for everyone.

"I know this one," said Charles. "It was on sale at the Fest Noz."

"It's made by my cousin," Gérard said, paying the barman. "He has orchards along the river south of here. He's doing very well supplying bars and restaurants."

Charles agreed. "He certainly deserves to be successful. This is a fine wine made from apples."

***

Next day, Charles decided to buy his breakfast in the café Au Coin du Quai. He greeted Gérard, sitting in the best window seat as usual, bought coffee and fresh croissants at the counter and took a table at the back of the room, where he was soon engrossed in his book, oblivious to the morning rush.

When Gérard finished his study of the newspaper, he took a chair next to Charles and said, "What's in that book that makes you frown so much?"

"Poetry," Charles said. "I learned a lot of French poetry at school, but only poems written before 1900. This was recommended by the local bookshop, and I'm finding it fascinating, but difficult. I can translate the words, but somehow that doesn't tell me what they mean. They're so deliberately placed, with such elegance and precision, that I really want to understand."

Gérard lifted the cover to view the title and author. "Understanding might not be easy for a Frenchman. The author might well be the greatest poet France produced this last century, but his poetry is somewhat revolutionary, because he didn't follow the conventional route to literature. He initially studied mathematics."

Enlightenment spread across Charles' expressive face. "Elegance and precision. I should have guessed."

"You are also a mathematician?"

"Mon dieu, non, but mathematics was one of my favourite subjects at school, along with history and French literature. Unfortunately my university course was decided by the school and my parents, and they insisted I drop everything I loved to get a commercially viable qualification. I wish now that I hadn't given in."

"What qualification did you take?"

"Business management and economics."

Gérard showed surprise. "You didn't find that interesting?"

Charles frowned, thinking back. "I found all the wrong parts of it interesting. I've always been fascinated by patterns. Mathematics is patterns generalised from the real world. History is patterns of movement of people and ideas. There are speech patterns within languages. Economics showed me patterns of money and trade and international politics, and business management studied patterns of human behaviour and the design of working tasks." Charles' face had lit with enthusiasm. Then his face fell. "But to pass the exam we were told to learn by heart the standard answers to the standard questions, and all the jobs on offer after graduating were just routine."

"So what career did you follow?"

"Accountancy. Twenty-two years with no use for imagination."

"Surely you could have changed career?"

"There were reasons why I couldn't, but two weeks ago the last such reason disappeared. That's why I've taken this holiday. I'm forty-three. I'm trying to decide whether change is still possible. I'm not sure what's available. I'm not sure what I can do, and I certainly don't know what I would be allowed to do. But if I see an opportunity, I'm going to take it."

"And reading poetry will help you?"

"Yes," Charles said defiantly. "I want to rediscover what I enjoy, so that this time round, I won't give it up like before. I'm re-reading history as well."

"English history?"

"Actually, the history of Brittany. It's proving fascinating, especially when the Breton version contradicts the English."

"So which side do you believe?"

"I have to confess to becoming biased in favour of Bretons. I do like the way they've stayed true to themselves. They're so passionately attached to their history, and but they've never let that prevent creative new developments, or the adoption of new methods and materials, or radical changes to ways of life to allow them to succeed. I find their resilience and determination and inventiveness down the ages to be quite formidable."

Gérard smiled appreciatively. "I'm glad we've made such a good impression in so short a time. And I'm glad that you do use the business and economics you were taught."

Surprise briefly lit Charles' face.

Gérard stood and offered his hand. "I have to go, but I wish you good luck with your future."

Charles moved up to the empty counter to ask Philippe for another coffee. He'd always considered his degree result to be founded on rote learning, but he'd just remembered the interesting parts of the course, and Gérard seemed to think that he used then. And, of course, he did.

Following his years-long investigation into the economic history of Reading, which had sustained him through many a routine audit in that town, he'd now started investigating the economic history of Brittany. The books only recorded what the duke did and said, how the internal and external wars progressed, but Charles was working out the effect of all that on the local economy, and he'd started recording changes that happened in agriculture and fishing, in the lives of the people and in the growth of towns.

The patterns of managing people, learnt in theory, he'd certainly used when leading teams of younger staff through the stages of auditing, and when persuading client managers into a more productive or more effective method of working. Maybe he really could hold down some form of business management position? His degree might not be quite as useless as he'd always thought it.

Finding it easier to think while walking, Charles started out briskly on the cliff path, and reached the view over Saint-Malo in record time. He sat to enjoy it, but almost immediately his phone rang.

"Bonjour, Monsieur Pullen. Jean-Jacques Keruan here. Thank you for the email. I can certainly use the article and I think I'll use your photographs, though I'll add some others that I have in stock. I'll probably include it in the September edition. That means you won't get paid until then, but if you send me details of your bank sometime, I'll make the payment when it's due."

"Thank you indeed, monsieur."

"But that's not the reason I'm phoning. I mentioned you to someone who'd like to meet you. Would it be possible for you to go to Rennes tomorrow?"

"Certainly, where and at what time?"

"The restaurant La Fleur du Sel, at one p.m. It's in avenue Jean Janvier, the road leading north from the station. Ask for the table of Monsieur Le Quennac."

Charles wrote the details down in his notebook. "I'll be there. What can you tell me about Monsieur Le Quennac?"

"It's best that he introduces himself. But I'd advise you to wear a suit and a tie if you have them with you."

"Thank you," Charles said slowly, now aware that the meeting would be formal but that no explanation for it would be forthcoming.

He walked home replaying the conversation in his head. Jean-Jacques knew he wanted a new job, and might have found a suitable opening for him. Back at the cottage, Charles found a few internet mentions of the name Le Quennac in connection with the regional prefecture, but with no guarantee that this was the man he'd be meeting.

So he looked up the city of Rennes instead. It had a long and important history, but it intrigued him that it was the capital of Brittany despite being nowhere near the centre of the region. He discovered that it housed the offices of the regional prefecture of Brittany, and of the prefecture of Ille-et-Vilaine, the local county. There was a mayor of Rennes, but also a mayor of Rennes Metropole, which appeared to be a conglomeration of the city and the surrounding communes. How did all these people interact? Who was responsible for what? How were budgets and policies controlled in national and local government?

It was lunch time. On impulse he went into the fishmonger's. He came out with a jar of fish soup and a bag of mussels, cockles and prawns, with a recipe for making seafood gratin by boiling them until cooked then baking the extracted seafood in a cheese sauce. The gratin proved well worth the effort.

In the afternoon he researched the responsibilities of French local and national government until dinner time, when he heated the fish soup, served it with croutons of cheese on toast, followed it with a salad of green beans, pancetta and tomatoes, and for dessert half a ripe Camembert with grapes.

15

On Friday morning Charles dressed carefully in his dark grey suit, a new possibly-non-iron shirt in pale green and a dark grey tie with green diagonal lines on it. In reaction to this office uniform and the memories it produced, he put on his dancing boots. They made him feel more like an individual, an independent mind. The camera made a bulge in the pocket of his coat, but he couldn't leave it behind.

He caught the bus to Saint-Malo station and the train to Rennes. Inside Rennes station the arching glass roofs demanded several photographs. One of the shops beneath that glass sold luggage, and the small black leather satchel in its window would be ideal for carrying his camera, notebook and mobile phone. He bought it and sat in a café drinking a coffee while emptying his pockets into the bag. Then he walked up the avenue Jean Janvier to the restaurant. It was closed, but he felt better having located it. He walked on, found the museum and paid to go in. He thought a series of factual exhibits might calm him down.

Charles returned to La Fleur du Sel at precisely one minute to one o'clock, and asked for Monsieur Le Quennac's table. The waiter became markedly deferential, and led the way to a table for three in a side room. Two men were seated already, the younger one somehow familiar. Both were wearing suits and ties; as Keruan had indicated, this was a formal meeting.

"Bonjour, Messieurs," he said.

"Take a seat," said the older of the two men, and when Charles did so he extended his hand and said, "Le Quennac."

"Pullen."

The third man shook hands. "Guellou."

A waiter was hovering. Le Quennac said to Charles, "The chef's special today is beef bourguignon, is that all right for you?"

"Certainly."

"Three specials," Le Quennac ordered, "and three glasses of Château Lamartine." He continued to Charles, "I believe you're here on holiday."

"That's right," Charles replied. "I'm staying in Saint-Edern."

"How long have you been there?"

"Six days."

"And what do you find to do all day?"

"I've been trying to make sense of Brittany by investigating the history and economics of the nearest towns, Saint-Malo, Dinard, and Dinan."

"Have you succeeded?"

Charles gave a wry smile. "I think I can now estimate how much more I have to learn."

The waiter put plates of small snacks in front of each of them, and at a nod from Le Quennac, poured red wine into their glasses.

"What's been the best thing you've found so far?"

Charles hesitated. "Two things have impressed me a great deal. I don't know what order to put them in. One is the food. The sheer variety of it, the local traditions, the skills of cooks at all levels, the subtlety of the flavourings, and above all the stylish presentation of everything from the raw ingredients to the finished article. The other is the people, their warmth and their welcome, the way they live and work as a society, their pride in their history, their adaptability and their creativity and their practicality."

The waiter interrupted with a first course of scallops, celery and apple in a caramel sauce. After his first mouthful, Charles said, "What a splendid combination of tastes! But now I realise that I don't know where scallops come from. Are they fished off Saint-Malo?"

"These are very large, so they probably come from Finistère," said Le Quennac. "The Atlantic coast has the fewest, but the biggest. There are scallops all along the coast. They're very plentiful in the bays of Saint-Brieuc, Saint-Malo and Mont-Saint-Michel. Brittany produces at least half the tonnage consumed in France."

"What type of industry is it? Do they dredge them off the bottom or are they farmed like oysters and mussels?"

"Dredged. Little fishing vessels with special trawls go out between October and May. It's an industry tightly controlled with quotas and licences. Over-fishing would be a disaster. But Bretons bring in seven thousand tonnes a year, and there's a big festival at the end of the season to celebrate the year's catch."

"Let me guess," Charles said, grinning. "First, everyone eats as many scallops as they can manage, then there's hours of music and dancing."

The other two laughed.

"You've certainly picked up something about Brittany," Le Quennac said, "but you haven't mentioned the coast, which some of us think of as our biggest asset."

The waiter exchanged their plates for a sumptuous beef bourguignon.

"I'm afraid that I don't have a car here," Charles replied, "so I've only seen the estuary at Saint-Malo. But from the maps and the guidebook photos, I'll agree the coastline is a valuable asset, and not only for stretches of fine sand. The sheer number of different seascapes is astonishing; they must fascinate everyone who sees them. I've been told that there are hundreds of Dutch and Belgian tourists, and I wonder if the coast is what brings them here? All those cliffs and rocks and islands must make a strong contrast to their own flat sands."

"It would be good to know why so many Dutch come," Le Quennac mused. "We have some chance of discovering why some of the Belgians holiday here, those of them who speak French, but Dutch is a rare skill."

"But it's not the only language the Dutch use. The ones I've met have spoken excellent English. Maybe if someone asked them in English why they come, they would respond?"

"You have a good point there."

By now it seemed obvious to Charles that Le Quennac worked in tourism, with an interest possibly covering the whole region. Charles ventured, "Do you advertise Brittany to the Dutch? Or to other specific nations in Europe?"

"We do. Our website gives descriptions in French, English, Dutch, German, Spanish and Italian."

"But not Chinese? Or Arabic? Or Brazilian Portuguese?"

"It does cost money to translate," Le Quennac said, frowning. "One would need to be sure of getting a return. For instance, thousands of Chinese visit France every year, but they only ever want to see Paris."

"A few of them do come to Mont-Saint-Michel," Guellou interjected, "but the Mont is a special case, and it's officially in Normandy, which doesn't help us."

"So you'd have to charm the Chinese tour operators first?" Charles asked. "Perhaps you could tell them that a different tour would attract well-off Chinese who'd already done their Paris visit?"

The waiter replaced their plates, serving a feather-light pastry filled with spiced pineapple.

"It would take a lot of energy to crack the Chinese market," Le Quennac said, "and at the moment we don't have energy to spare. We're a little short-handed, and the situation is about to get worse, because Monsieur Guellou is leaving for a position in French national tourism."

Charles raised his eyebrows. "Good career move?" he asked.

"Very," Guellou said smugly, "but it's still a wrench to leave the region where I was born."

"Until the end of September," Le Quennac continued, "Monsieur Guellou oversees tourist information offices in the region and publicity for the region. He has two assistants, enthusiastic young workers and promising well, but they're new to the office and they need direction, not promotion to a position they couldn't possibly hold. My own administrator will retire next year, leaving me without another major assistant. So we have a thriving organisation, plenty of well-qualified, enthusiastic and hard-working personnel at the customer interface, but we're starting to lose management at the top."

Charles looked straight at Le Quennac with an open face.

Le Quennac said, "I've been told that you have a degree in business management, and some experience in how organisations work."

"I have absolutely no experience in tourism."

"At management level, that's something that can be learnt on the job."

"I'm not a Breton; indeed I'm not even French."

"My administrator is an Irishman born in Cork. It's not an obstacle. A feeling for Brittany is far more important than an accident of birth."

"Do you have any information on the terms and conditions of employment?"

Guellou produced a folder of papers from his briefcase just as the waiter appeared with coffees. There were a few minutes of silence. Charles leafed quickly through the papers. They included the business cards of Maximilien Le Quennac, regional director of tourism for Brittany, and Erwan Guellou, assistant director, tourism, both their addresses given as the Prefecture

Administration Centre in Rennes. The position offered was probationary manager, tourism, based at the regional prefecture, salary and allowable expenses stated.

"If I wished to apply, what would be the next step?"

"You'd need to make a formal application to the recruitment committee of the regional prefecture. I presume that you haven't formally applied for a job in France before?"

"I haven't. Is there a set procedure?"

"There is," Le Quennac confirmed.

Guellou intervened. "I believe you know Gérard Lemestre. He knows the procedure well and he's said he'd be willing to help you." Charles's surprise showed in his face. "He's my cousin," said Guellou, and Charles realised that he'd seen the facial resemblance.

"Don't tell me you make Le Coudray cider?"

Guellou grinned broadly. "No, my brother does that."

Charles had intended to spend the afternoon in Rennes exploring the city, but he found himself on the next available train home with the papers stowed in his bag. He read and re-read them on the way. They offered a position for one year. Was that because it would take a year to learn the job? Presumably he wouldn't be offered another contract unless he did learn. But this was a new career, full of interest, and close to his inclinations. He tried desperately to see the downside of it, the stark reality underneath, but his imagination was soaring above the clouds and his heart was singing.

***

He arrived at the cottage at four o'clock. He made coffee and started to think seriously. He didn't have enough data. Gross salary was all very well, but what was the cost of living here and how much tax was deducted? He switched on his laptop. He looked up the government tax rates. He looked up rents in Rennes, where there was plenty of one-person accommodation, being a university town. He found an advisory site for students giving minimum costs for food and heating, which he prudently trebled. He looked up insurance premiums and pension contributions. By four in the afternoon he'd conclusively proved that the probationary salary wouldn't make him rich, but it could provide a living for a single man.

It still seemed too good to be true. He wanted to talk to someone. Someone with feet firmly on the ground. Someone who knew him well enough to stop him being stupid, or encourage him to fly. He'd dialled the number before he realised.

Deborah Mitchell saw the name on her phone and answered immediately. "Charles! Good to hear from you. Are you still in France?"

"Brittany. There's a difference."

"Uh-huh?"

Charles sighed heavily. "I'm sorry. I should have thought what to say before I dialled."

"Has something gone wrong or has something gone right?"

"Deb, you're a mind reader."

"I'm someone's sister. Which of them is it?"

"I'm not sure. I've just been offered a job."

"In Brittany?"

"Yes."

"As an auditor?"

"No."

"Can you live on the salary?"

"Yes."

"Have you accepted it?"

"I don't know if I can do it."

"Someone must think you can. What is it exactly?"

"Managing tourist information offices in Brittany."

"Those little offices who give out leaflets to visitors? Book hotels and boat trips and pony-trekking? Sell souvenirs?"

"Yes."

"How many offices?"

"I didn't think to ask. There must be hundreds of them."

"Charles, I manage an estate agent's office in every town in Sussex and most towns in the surrounding counties. Is it a job like that?"

There was a surprised silence. "Thanks, Deb, it must be a job like that. So I do know how it works."

"You should, it's in the genes. We're the fifth generation providing a service to the public, and you worked in the agency often enough in the school holidays."

"I do need to learn something about tourism."

"Can you buy books on it?"

"Yes."

"Then buy them. You'll have learnt it all by next week."

"Deb, now I know why I telephoned. You've made it sound like a practical proposition. Thank you."

"So when do you start?"

"It's not quite that simple. Today I met the manager I'd work for, and the man I'd replace, but I have to write a formal application for the job and that goes to a committee. If all goes well, I suppose I'll start in the autumn."

"Then you'd better resign from your job in auditing."

There was a long silence.

"Aha!" Deb said. "You've already resigned, haven't you?"

"Yes."

"You're on paid holiday?"

"Yes, I had sixteen weeks owing. That covered more than my notice period. They've agreed to pay my salary to the middle of October for doing nothing."

"Charles," Deborah said in her best telling-off voice, "Don't ever do that again. You can't survive without taking a break."

"I do know that now, Deb, and I didn't exactly enjoy learning it. Things will be different from now on. That reminds me, I've never said thank you for everything you did. I know I wasn't comfortable with you interfering, but I couldn't have got that legal result without your contacts and your guarantee to meet the costs."

"I don't need a thank you; it's enough to know that you're free of the problem. But I do intend to charge for helping. From now on I want a phone call or an email at least once every month so that I know you're still alive. Otherwise I shall come over to Brittany and make you wish you were not."

Her phone echoed to the long unheard sound of Charles laughing. "You've forgotten something, big sister," he said. "I've grown up. You don't scare me any more."

When he ended the call, Charles thought through the information that he would normally provide when applying for a job in England. He found he had an old CV on his laptop, so he checked through it, updated it and tidied it up. He had a scanned image of his degree and his accountancy qualification, but he'd left the originals behind in England. He hadn't asked his last employers for a reference. Did any of this matter?

He really needed to get in touch with Gérard Lemestre. The internet confirmed that he wasn't in the phone book, so Charles went into the café and asked Philippe how to get in touch with Gérard.

"He'll be on the coach tomorrow," Philippe said cheerfully.

"It's a matter of business," said Charles.

Philippe's smile didn't change. "Not in the evening, it isn't. Gérard doesn't work in the evenings. Why are you trying to contact him?"

"Erwan Guellou told me to."

"Then Guellou's told Gérard already and Gérard will get in touch when he feels like seeing you."

Charles was intrigued. "You do know Gérard's telephone number?"

"Yes," Philippe said, grinning, "And I don't pass it on."

"Do you also know why I'm trying to contact him?"

"I didn't until you mentioned Guellou."

Charles laughed out loud. Of course, everyone would know that a replacement was needed for Guellou.

"I could suggest a glass of Luberon and a plate of smoked duck breast?"

"With salad," agreed Charles. He returned to the cottage for a book to read while eating.

***

Next morning the club members lined up on the esplanade at nine o'clock ready for the coach to Fougères, and Charles met Sarah for the first time in three days. As they found a seat in the coach he asked, "How far back does Fougères go?"

"One can only guess. The town's at the crossroad of two Roman roads, so there would have been a Roman settlement, probably replacing something Bronze Age or even Stone Age, but there's now no trace of its early beginnings. It stands on the hill above the castle, which was built on a rocky outcrop in the middle of a marsh. In the days before cannon, that was defensible. The first castle was built about the year 1000, but was razed to the ground in 1166 by Henry Plantagenet, Count of Anjou, who later became King

Henry II of England. But the Breton owner just rebuilt it even larger, and those walls are still there."

The castle appeared suddenly on the right of the coach, impressively high walls rearing up from the low ground and a wide moat, flags waving defiantly in the breeze. Pascal paid for group entry and introduced their guide. For an hour and a half the club members followed the guide through every part of the huge edifice, up and down towers and along parts of the wall walk, while the guide recounted the convoluted history of sieges, changes of ownership, changes of loyalty and Breton popular rebellions from the year 1000 to the present day. She even included the story of the local Colonel Armand who'd assisted the young United States of America to defeat the English colonial troops.

Having applauded the guide for a virtuoso performance, the group retreated to the nearby restaurant, Les Fleurs des Marais, for lunch. As they waited to be served, Jean-Yves Lagarde played old tunes on his accordion and the club sang along. The music ceased as the food arrived. The group tucked into asparagus in cheese sauce, followed by duck à l'orange and sauté potatoes, with apple tart to finish. Jean-Yves returned to playing while coffee was being served, and received a well-deserved round of applause.

As the group left the restaurant, Charles found Gérard alongside him. "I believe we need to meet?" Gérard said.

"I really do need your help," Charles replied.

"Then can I suggest ten o'clock tomorrow at my house?"

"That's very kind of you."

Gérard handed over a card with his address, email and telephone. "You'll need your computer, your passport, your work history and your qualifications."

"I don't have original documents with me, only scanned images."

"They'll be enough."

Charles and Sarah spent the afternoon in the upper town, admiring the houses, churches and monuments. Charles tried not to pay over-much attention to the tourist information office, but Sarah walked in to pick up a town map, and he automatically noted the opening hours, the number of staff, the working conditions, the pamphlets and books and souvenirs on offer. It was welcoming, well stocked and very well run.

They returned to Saint-Edern at sunset, the whole coach singing along to Jean-Yves' accordion. As they parted company Sarah reminded Charles of the bridge club social on Sunday evening at seven. "If you come over at half-past six, I can take you in my car. And do remember to wear a suit and tie. It's a British occasion so don't try to be comfortable."

"What are you wearing?"

"Little black dress, full make up, highest-heeled shoes and heaviest gold jewellery."

Charles sighed theatrically. "I don't think I'll be able to compete with any of that."

16

On Sunday morning, Charles discovered that Gérard's house was ingeniously built alongside a granite cliff. The ground floor on a narrow street housed only a large hall and a three-car garage, but the floor above was on top of the cliff and very much larger. On the second floor the front of the house was occupied by a room with one floor-to-ceiling sliding window along its whole length. At the far end of the room was a sturdy table burdened with computer equipment, but the body of the room was occupied by well used sofas and armchairs facing the panoramic view. The roof on the other side of the road was much lower, allowing a prospect of the estuary which could only be described as glorious. Charles said so.

"This was my grandfather's house," said Gérard, "so I grew up here watching the river, and I've never tired of it. There's no view like this for you in Rennes, I'm afraid. Now, if we both sit at the table, we can start drafting your CV."

"I do have a CV, but it's in English," Charles said.

"Plug your laptop in there and let me see it," Gérard said, and when he saw the document, "That's a good start. The general format will serve, but the headings must be translated. Save the file under a new name so that you keep the original," and then he dictated the changes and Charles typed them in.

"Now let's look at the content. You list your degree and your accounting qualification, but I think you have other examination results?"

"Advanced Levels?"

"Yes, that's the Baccalaureate, is it not?"

"I have pure maths, applied maths, French literature and history."

"Then you should include them. Do that now."

Charles obliged, but asked dubiously, "Do they help?"

"Of course they do. French literature is very important because knowledge of the French language and its cultural heritage cancels out the fact that you weren't born or educated in France. History is a strong thread running through tourism, and an understanding of our heritage is very necessary to the position. Your CV now shows you have a good foundation to build on."

"My school told me never to list French and history on my CV because they were non-commercial subjects."

"Then the school lacked imagination," Gérard stated decisively. "A well-rounded personality is a commercial asset."

Charles remembered Jean-Jacques Keruan saying much the same thing.

"As you've cited your degree, you'll need to provide a copy of it." Charles duly displayed the scan on his screen. Gérard raised his eyebrows and said, "First class honours. Did you tell Monsieur Le Quennac you have a first class?"

"No. He didn't ask."

"He'll be surprised. His diploma is second class."

"I don't know how to comment on that."

"I do. That degree will encourage the committee to employ you. But don't hide it. Write 'first class' after the degree on your CV."

Charles did so.

"Now, you list only two employers and you don't describe the work you did. How can you make the list longer?"

"I could list all the companies whose accounts I investigated, and the types of industry they operated in."

"That would be a good start. Did you ever take responsibility for a team of workers, or for training junior staff?"

"Both, all the time."

"Then state that. For each position, the size of team, the number of trainees. The committee needs to see you as an experienced team leader. Do you have enough information on your laptop to make a concise table of that information?"

"Yes, but it will take some time to type it all in."

"Then start now. I'll make us coffee."

Charles set to. He was halfway through when Gérard returned, and continued while the older man leaned back in an armchair enjoying the tide and the birds and the yachts moving through his line of vision. When Charles finished, Gérard paged through the document.

"This is much better. This gives a clearer picture of your skills and achievements, and where you fit the job on offer."

"Please change anything you wish."

"No, I won't do that. You want a document which is yours, not mine. This will do very well for the CV. Now we need the letter of application."

Charles frowned. "I'm not sure what that is."

"It's a very formal letter with three paragraphs. The first just names the position for which you are applying. The second says why you want to do it. The third says what you can contribute."

It took half an hour before Charles had a draft, and then he and Gérard discussed what he'd written and polished it up.

"That's all," said Gérard. "We need to print your documents so that you can post them. Send them by registered post on Monday. The committee meets on Thursday next week, so you won't have long to wait for an answer."

Charles connected his machine to Gérard's printer and printed the CV, the letter and copies of his qualifications. He asked, "Do I need a reference from my last employer?"

"That's not necessary. Your CV confirms your capabilities, and you have three good character references."

Charles was surprised. "I do?"

"Myself, Max Le Quennac and Jean-Jacques Keruan. We'll all write a letter in support of your application."

Charles stilled as he took this in. He knew the business status of Le Quennac and Keruan, and he now connected that to Gérard's enormous house and the amount of respect paid to him locally. He said, "I think perhaps I should apologise. I've been treating you like an ordinary fellow club member, but you obviously have an importance well beyond that. Is it impolite for me to ask who you are?"

Gérard smiled innocently. "I'm a Breton and I'm retired."

Charles smiled in appreciation. "You're a very private person. I do respect that. But I get the feeling there's something I ought to know."

"You'll discover it soon enough when you start work."

"When. Not if. Why?"

"You're the only candidate good enough. The post needs to be filled quickly."

Charles' mind went into audit mode. He said sharply, "If that was true there'd be no need to involve you, because any form of application would result in my getting the job. So how and why are you involved?"

The two men looked at each other for some seconds until Gérard said sternly, "I don't betray confidences."

Charles retreated. "I've taken this conversation beyond the bounds of politeness. I do apologise. Please ignore the question."

Gérard said carefully, "I can tell you part of the story. When France was organised into regions, I left my post in the local prefecture to start the Regional Office of Tourism, so you're about to join the office I created. After a few years I engaged Max Le Quennac as my second-in-command. We worked very closely together, and we achieved a great deal. Later on we employed my cousin, Erwan Guellou, as a junior. Two years ago I retired. Le Quennac took my job and Guellou took his. Since then I've taken care to distance myself from the office, to give Le Quennac the opportunity to make changes and the freedom to make his own decisions in his own way.

"But my cousin applied to join French National Tourism and asked me to support his candidature, since I'm well known in Paris. When Erwan succeeded and resigned his Breton post, Le Quennac knew that I'd have supported him. Unfortunately that resignation left Le Quennac needing a second-in-command urgently when there was no suitable candidate available within the regional or local prefectures; he resented my part in his problem. He telephoned his entire contact list seeking candidates, omitting to phone me, naturally. But he was lucky, because Keruan suggested you. Jean-Jacques had learned of your qualifications and experience, and knew you were looking for a job. Unfortunately, he also knew that you were staying in Saint-Edern.

"Saint-Edern is my ancestral home. Le Quennac never takes unnecessary risks, so he felt obliged to ask me if I'd met you. Your abilities have always been obvious to me, and after I'd spoken to you in the café I'd been considering how I could inform the prefecture that you existed, so I was delighted that Le Quennac had found you already. I confirmed Jean-Jacques' opinion of you, so Le Quennac invited you to interview in La Fleur du Sel.

"You must have handled that meeting well, because Le Quennac has very definitely chosen to employ you. But the position was advertised and there are already other applicants. So your application will be marked by the combined endorsement of Le Quennac, Keruan and myself. The recruitment committee will understand what that means.

"I will also advise you that every successful application is held permanently on record in the government personnel database. A poor quality application is never to be recommended even if it secures a job, because it will be re-read at every change of responsibility or title in the future. Your record will now commence in acceptable style."

Charles's face lit up with gratitude. "Thank you indeed, Gérard. I'll keep all that to myself. But I must say that you're taking an astonishing risk in using your position to support someone with no track record at all."

"You do have one," said Gérard. "It's just not in tourism. You have a proven intellect, above average intelligence, an understanding of business, the ability to work with people, the habit of team work, a willingness to learn and a strong bias in favour of Brittany. Go and prove me justified."

He offered his hand. Charles shook it. "You were the first Breton I met when I arrived here," he said. "I didn't realise then how lucky I was."

Gérard smiled in return. "Neither did I, Charles, neither did I."

Charles returned to the cottage, dropped off laptop and paperwork, and went up to the bar-tabac for a galette and crêpe lunch. He bought a newspaper and read it while letting the morning's events sink in. It was a very comfortable feeling to be so well supported and to have the position guaranteed, but there was a challenge in it. He was determined not to let anyone down.

***

At six-thirty, wearing his best black suit, a white shirt and a black tie – he was sure that the expat British would expect a formal display of mourning for his brother – he went up to Sarah's flat. He'd never seen Sarah in formal dress before, and the transformation was marked. Her 'little black dress' was a top designer creation. It had a strapless silk-satin bodice of tiny pleats at an angle to the centre seam, making a chevron pattern front and back. A wild silk, tulip-shaped overskirt opened front and back over a pencil slim silk jersey underskirt. Sarah wore black stockings, black stiletto heels, and a necklace of heavy gold orchids with matching earrings. With striking eye make-up and perfectly cut short silver hair, she looked formidable.

"However long did it take to get that eye stuff on?" Charles asked.

"Twelve long minutes. And years of practice," Sarah said.

Charles smiled. "Will you drive, or could I volunteer?"

"The car's insured for you to drive, if you want."

"This is my work suit and shoes. I'm used to driving in them so I'll be happy to oblige," said Charles. "Do you always dress up to this standard?"

"Not at all, but this is the bridge club, and every time your brother attended a meeting he spread rumours about me. This is my first real chance to hit back."

"What did he say precisely?"

"He hinted to everyone that I was eccentric, erratic and probably mentally ill. One of the club members is a medical consultant, and without ever having met me he diagnosed that I had a psychosomatic syndrome and was in need of psychiatric care. I was infuriated. I intend to be in businesswoman mode all evening."

"No," Charles said, "that isn't the way to go. By all means look as if you can run a business, but go out of your way to be warm-hearted and charming and considerate."

"How will that help?"

"It'll fit what I'll be telling everyone about James. I can talk about him in a way you can't. He was an alcoholic and a liar and I wish I wasn't related to him, but I think it was so very gallant of you to stick by him and subsidise him when he didn't deserve it." Sarah was speechless. "It'll work. The truth always does," Charles said confidently. "Just you wait and see."

Charles drove with Sarah giving directions, and entered the room with her on his arm. "Any friendly faces in sight?" he asked.

"Jane Porter-Hughes over there, red dress in a group of four women." He took her to meet the group. She introduced him as her brother-in-law.

"You do have a strong family resemblance," Mrs Porter-Hughes said.

"Only facially, thank goodness," Charles said. "I don't much like meeting people who knew James. Just because I look like him people tend to think I'm a bully and a liar like he was. Not to mention being a drunk. I really don't know how Sarah managed to put up with him."

"It's true, then, that he died of alcohol related complications?" Mrs Porter-Hughes asked, head on one side, avidly interested.

Charles recognised that he'd found a born gossip. "He died of drink, yes," he said bluntly. "His behaviour was beyond a joke, and by the end he couldn't even hold down a simple job. Without Sarah being so highly paid that she could subsidise him, he'd have gone under years ago. It was a shock when he died, of course, but I have to say it was something of a relief to the family."

The entire group of women was drinking in the information. A stately blonde, with a diamond comb in her chignon and a deceptively simple black silk shirtdress with diamond buttons, took Sarah by the arm and said, "You poor dear. I know a little of how you feel. My late husband, the colonel, was far too fond of his brandy, and developed into a stickler for having everything done his way. By the end I really couldn't think what I'd ever seen in him. I find life so much more comfortable as a widow. Can I introduce you to Paula Morton and Annie Chevening? I'm Beth Farley, and we were just thinking of checking out the food." The women moved in the direction of the buffet with Sarah in their midst.

Charles looked for the nearest available group, and smiled charmingly as he joined it. He introduced himself, and the name Pullen made someone see the facial resemblance to James. The same storyline worked a second time. And then a third. The function lasted for two hours, and Charles ensured he spoke to everyone in the room.

He certainly met the retired medical consultant, Paul Harrier, who made the mistake of warning Charles not to be taken in by someone as obviously mentally ill as Sarah. By the time Charles had described Sarah's business career, her successful investments and solid wealth, her current consultancy work for the prefecture, and her standing in the local community, and after Charles had compared that to James' abysmal record, the consultant was forced to recognise that relying on the word of a deceased habitual liar wouldn't absolve him from an action for defamation of character.

Doctor Harrier didn't quite apologise to Charles, but he must have said something to his wife, because when Charles met Mrs Harrier afterwards she profusely apologised for not having understood what poor Sarah was going through while married to that awful James.

At the end of the evening Charles met Brian and Janet Rowley. Brian was rather sore at the information about James which had travelled at speed around the gathering. He'd strongly supported James as treasurer of the club, and was still trying to find a replacement treasurer. He wasn't disposed to be polite, and openly expressed distaste for someone who arrived on a short holiday and belittled the club committee.

"It's not a short holiday, I'm afraid." Charles smiled like a practised swordsman duelling with a novice. "I came here to interview for a job, and

I've now been offered it. Once the details are finalised, I'll be living in Brittany permanently."

"What sort of job?" Janet asked.

"In the regional prefecture."

"But don't you need French qualifications for that?"

"Not at my level. My degree's in business management and economics, and it's recognised as equivalent to a French diploma. I'm in the same position as Sarah, except that of course her degree is a master's, so she's automatically known as Doctor Pullen in every European country she works in."

"Sarah has a master's degree?" Brian asked, surprised.

"Certainly she has. She has an international reputation. She's now undertaking work for both the regional and local prefectures; they're impressed with what she can do."

"Goodness," Janet exclaimed, "I hadn't realised how important she was."

"She doesn't go in for self-promotion," Charles said, "but just look at her. That dress is Yves Saint Laurent and the jewellery is solid gold Whitfield Jack from Florida. When she worked for international financial houses, her salary was enormous, well above the exorbitant cost of supporting poor James."

As they settled into the car to go home, Sarah said to Charles, "I'm not quite sure what you've done or how you've done it, but I'm now getting overt respect for being a business success and much commiseration for putting up with an alcoholic husband."

"Isn't that what you wanted?"

"No, I just wanted to kill the rumours."

"I've done that, too. Paul Harrier now realises it's actionable to pass around a diagnosis of someone he's never met. He's not used to being wrong, and he's not the type who apologises, but he won't repeat the story any longer or give it credence if anyone else does. Mrs Harrier is telling everyone her husband was completely misled by a habitual liar."

"I think I have to say thank you."

"Not at all. I have my own reasons for trying to establish a distance between myself and James. I have to live here, too, and I don't want anyone thinking that just because I look like him, I behave like him or approve of anything he did."

Sarah hadn't missed the throw-away line.

"You have to live here too?"

"I'm planning to stay in Brittany. I've applied for a job in Rennes, and I've passed the interview. There's some official processing to be done, but I've been assured that I'll get it."

"What sort of job?"

"Office of Regional Tourism. Part of the regional prefecture. I'd be involved in publicity for the region and overseeing the tourist information offices all over Brittany."

"It's a management position?"

"Yes."

"With a decent salary?"

"A probationary one to start with, because I haven't any previous tourism experience. But I've calculated there'll be more left over every month than I had when working extra hours auditing, and once I pick up the job, promotion is possible."

"Is it something you can put heart and soul into?"

"Oh, more than that. Heart and soul and mind and spirit. I've fallen in love with Brittany, and someone wants to pay me to persuade other people to do the same."

He turned the car into the underground garage and parked it. As they parted in front of the lift, Sarah said, "I can't tell you how happy I am. I do hope everything works out for you."

Charles grinned. "I can't tell you how happy I am, but 'ecstatic' would be a good word to start with." And he put his hands on her waist and waltzed her round in a circle. They were both laughing as they parted company.

17

On Monday morning Charles posted his application by guaranteed delivery to the prefecture, then took the train to Rennes and revisited the bookshop in the commercial centre. It was only weeks before the start of the college year, so the shop stocked two different sets of textbooks for the diploma course in tourism. Charles put both sets into a basket. He found a series of small books intended for citizenship classes, which covered central and local government institutions in succinct detail. He piled them into the basket as well, adding the local newspaper and two cookery magazines. On the journey home he started reading in earnest.

The textbooks on tourism were aimed at someone younger with no experience of business, but were packed with interesting detail. So were the books on the governance of France. By dinner time Charles was confident that he would very soon understand both subjects, so he relaxed with poetry while he ate.

Tuesday morning he spent on Saint-Edern beach. He prudently left his clothes and towel above the high tide mark and walked into the warm and welcoming water. It was the first time he'd been swimming for twenty years. It was exhilarating, and, after ten minutes, tiring. In his new life he would have to make an effort to get fit. He wondered if swimming and dancing would be enough exercise? Meanwhile, he lay on the beach reading all afternoon.

On Wednesday he tried out the beaches around Saint-Malo, and walked out to the islands connected by causeways at low tide. By the time he reached home, he just had time for a salad before the social club. He sat at a table including Sarah, Marie-Pierre and Pascal. There was no discussion on where to go, because the Fête des Remparts was taking place in Dinan the next weekend. This enormous biennial festival celebrates the city's mediaeval past, and as usual a full programme was planned, covering mediaeval crafts and music and sports, with stalls selling merchandise and food. The event is made more colourful by the number of attendees who come in medieval costume.

Pascal had already arranged a coach, and groups of club members started animated discussions on what to see and how to dress.

On her table, Sarah didn't join in. "You're very quiet," said Marie-Pierre.

"I'm in an awkward position," Sarah said. "Jean-Jacques Keruan has asked me to be his partner at the mayor's costume dinner on Saturday night in Dinan. I'll need to get back home after the dinner, so I'll have to drive there by car. I'd much rather be on the coach. I don't think Jean-Jacques wants to visit the stalls and craft areas and jousting. His invitation was just to meet him at seven-thirty, wearing costume. I've hired one to be picked up in the town hall at seven."

"When does the dinner end?" Charles asked.

"I'm not sure. The diners take part in a procession through the town first; we eat afterwards. Perhaps about eleven?"

"Then it's easy. You go by coach with all your friends, and you enjoy the festival. The coach returns at seven without you, and you change into your costume at the town hall and meet Jean-Jacques. I'll go to the festival on the coach and return on it, but then I'll drive your car over to Dinan and pick you up at the end of the dinner."

"Are you sure? It'll be a long day for you."

"Not at all, I'm never in bed before midnight."

"Well, thank you. That solves the whole problem."

Pascal laughed. "Not for me. There'll be a different number on the coach going and returning. You people have no consideration for us poor retired tour operators."

"Retired?" Charles queried meaningfully.

"Not poor either," Marie-Pierre stated with a grin.

***

Next day Charles woke early and tried not to think about the committee meeting. Presumably they'd write in answer to his written application, and he wouldn't get the letter until Monday. No sense in fretting about it. He bought croissants and a newspaper, and settled down in his own quiet kitchen, reading up on local events. At quarter past ten his phone rang. A voice he didn't recognise asked, "Can I speak to Charles Pullen?"

"You're speaking to him."

"Bonjour. This is Brendan O'Donnell. I'm administrator to the Regional Office of Tourism. The recruitment committee has just approved your application to work with us, so I've left the meeting to ask if you can come into the office today to sign a contract."

Charles just managed, "Yes, certainly," in a steady voice.

"That's good. Now, the one thing I don't have is a start date. When are you free to join us?"

Charles grinned from ear to ear. "Tomorrow?" he asked.

O'Donnell's voice also had a smile in it as he said, "That's just a little too soon to get everything organised. But it seems you don't have to give notice to your last employer?"

"I already have. I came here on terminal leave."

"Lucky for us that you did. The most convenient start date for me is the first of August. Would that suit you?"

"It would."

"Then I'll put that date on the contract. Shall we meet at two this afternoon? I can give you plenty of time once this meeting is over."

"I'll be there."

"Bring your passport and your driving licence," Brendan added, "and wear a tie for the security photograph."

Charles put the phone down, and let a wave of pure happiness wash over him for a few minutes. The mood vanished suddenly as he realised that he was very ill-prepared to start a job in Brittany in two weeks' time. He had nowhere to live, no bank account, no car, and what little he did own was on the other side of the Channel in Reading. Then he remembered that O'Donnell had come to Brittany to work some years back, and must know the problems and their solutions.

Charles changed into a suit, ensured that his bag held the required documents and a book of poetry, and travelled by bus and train to Rennes. He took a taxi to the prefecture administration centre. He arrived too early, but there was a café a few metres away, so he bought sandwiches, took a seat under some trees, and read poetry while eating lunch.

At two o'clock he asked the receptionist for Monsieur O'Donnell. "Are you Monsieur Pullen?" she asked, and when he agreed that he was, she whisked him into a small room to have a security photograph taken, giving him his copy enclosed in a badge on a neck ribbon.

She then called O'Donnell, who proved to be unmistakeably Irish in manner and accent despite thirty years' living and working in Brittany. He welcomed Charles into his office, and ignoring his desk, settled the pair of them in comfortable chairs on the same side of a coffee table, taking off his jacket and telling Charles to do the same and to remove his tie.

"We'll start with the formalities," he said. "Here's the letter offering the position, signed by the chairman of the committee. Put that somewhere safe."

Charles opened the envelope, read the brief letter, and filed it in his bag.

"Then we have the contract itself. This is a probationary position because you don't have any experience in the business, and the contract's for one year only. That's the formal side of it, and you ought to read the conditions, because that's what I'm asking you to sign. But I'll just say there's nothing to stop Monsieur Le Quennac replacing one contract with another at any time he wants to. Promotions don't go through the recruitment committee; they're agreed between Le Quennac and the prefect. I say that because you'll very soon realise that you're being asked to do Monsieur Guellou's job without being paid his salary."

"I do have a lot to learn," said Charles, "and it seems reasonable to have to demonstrate I can do it. I'm a single man with no dependants, so a temporary dip in revenue is no great hardship."

"It's a good attitude. Do you think you can sign that contract?"

"Certainly," Charles said, doing so.

"Thank you," O'Donnell said, giving Charles one copy and reserving the other two. "Now we can get to practicalities. In this office, management tends to wear something with a jacket, though not necessarily a suit, and as you can see, jackets spend most of their lives on backs of chairs. Similarly, all the men have a tie in a desk drawer in case anyone calls a formal meeting, but that's mercifully rare.

"The office opens at nine o'clock, but on the first day I'd like you to arrive at half-past nine. By that time everyone else will be settled down and working, and if you ask for me at the desk, I'll take you round and introduce you to everyone. Then at ten o'clock Monsieur Guellou can start passing on the details of the job."

"That sounds very practical, thank you."

"Just to give you a head start, this is the hierarchy chart of all the people who work here and in associated parts of the prefecture. When I first arrived, it was the pronunciation and spelling of names that caused me the biggest problem."

"I can imagine," Charles said, reading a list of names originating in numerous European countries and most of the French-speaking world.

"You'll have the use of a car, for your private use as well as for driving around the offices. Can I photocopy your passport and your driving licence so that I can pass them to our insurers?"

Charles handed over the documents, and O'Donnell passed them through his scanner. "You'll need to get this licence converted to a French one within a few months now that you're staying here permanently. It's a simple process. You just hand it in to the office downstairs and they post you your French licence within the week. Unfortunately, I can't let you have the car before you report for work. That's the insurance policy rule."

"It's not a problem."

"Now," said O'Donnell, "do you need any help with the practical problems of leaving England and moving to Rennes?"

"I'd certainly like to ask a few questions. The first one is, how easy is it to get a bank account?"

"That's the second question," O'Donnell corrected, "because no bank will give you an account without knowing your address. So the first thing you need is somewhere to stay. Do you have any ideas on that yet?"

"Not really. Do I just look up hotels on the internet?"

"You can, but what you might find more congenial are the apart-hotels. They give you a little studio flat with its own kitchen and bathroom, all fully equipped, plus use of the washing machines and the luggage store in the basement. They don't do meals apart from breakfast, and they don't run a bar, but they do clean the apartment, wash the dishes and change the bedlinen for you. They're very popular with professionals who are only here for a short time or are looking for something permanent. If you tell the hotel you'll stay for a month or two, they offer better rates. There are two apart-hotels within walking distance," O'Donnell handed over two brochures, "but there are others in town. Wherever you decide to stay, book at least a month in advance and ask for a receipt. That receipt is proof of address for the bank.

"You just take proof of address and your passport and your contract to any bank you choose, and they'll open an account within minutes.

Alternatively you can do it over the internet; there are banks which only operate over the internet these days."

"That sounds very simple."

"It is if you have a contract of employment from the regional prefecture; the bank doesn't have to run checks on you, because I've done them already. Your bank will give you a debit card within days. Getting a credit card is a little more difficult, because the bank wants money in the account first. But if you can make a deposit, you can apply for a credit card as soon as the bank receives the money.

"The third thing you need is health insurance. You must register with the government health authority for the basic service, and then you need to buy a decent top-up policy from one of the big insurance companies. I've collected a few brochures to help you decide. And that's all until you start work."

"Thank you. That was very efficient," Charles said, rising, "I look forward to working with you. I'll see you on the first."

"Until then," O'Donnell said, smiling broadly as they shook hands.

When he arrived home, Charles sent an email to Deborah and Sarah saying simply: 'Will be starting work 1st August.'

He went to bed early and was relaxed enough to fall asleep immediately.

He spent Friday sorting out the details of his new life. He booked into an apart-hotel, opened a bank account, moved money from his English bank to his new French one, and arranged medical cover. He hired a small van for a week from Sunday. He booked the early ferry from Saint-Malo to Poole on Monday and the overnight ferry back, so that he could drive to Reading and pick up his belongings. By Friday evening he was happily swimming off the beach next to the yacht club in Saint-Edern.

***

On Saturday morning Sarah and Charles arrived in Dinan on the club coach and joined the Fête des Remparts. It was a lively experience, with sideshows featuring everything from fire-eating to sword fights to whirling dervishes to lute music to mediaeval jokes. There were stalls selling all kinds of food and merchandise, educational displays explaining different crafts belonging to different ages, musicians of all historical types, a jousting tournament, and a colourful crowd with large numbers dressed in costume.

The coach returned to Saint-Edern without Sarah, who walked to the Town Hall instead. She collected her costume and headed for the ladies' changing room. Her high-waisted and full-skirted dark green robe was worn over an underdress of mid-blue which showed under the cross-over bodice. The edges of the green material were heavily embroidered in gold-coloured thread, and the huge wide sleeves revealed the narrower blue sleeves of the underdress. Her own gold chain filled the neckline. On her head was a small hat like a heavily embroidered green fez, with huge wings of starched and folded gauze rising vertically above it. As she'd chosen the outfit to match Jean-Jacques' it was more striking than she would have selected for herself, but it was splendid, and she did enjoy seeing her medieval self in the mirror.

As she left the changing room, Jean-Jacques swooped on her. "You look absolutely magnificent," he said.

"So do you," Sarah said truthfully. "What a fantastic hat you've chosen!"

Jean-Jacques' ankle-length robe was a matching green, with a fur-edged slash neckline, and with long sleeves which had a short slit in the front so that his arms, in the sleeves of his blue undershirt, appeared through the slit and left the gold embroidered over-sleeves trailing to the floor. He wore an elaborately fake-jewelled metal belt. His headdress had been made by rolling an ornamental fringed and padded green tube around the head three times before letting the long tasselled end hang over one shoulder. He had the bearing to carry this off and looked positively regal.

The diners were to progress around the town before returning to the town hall for their meal. The mayor took his time to get the procession into order. It was led by people dressed as men-at-arms, followed by musicians and then by the mayor and his guests, with six knights on horseback in the rear. Jean-Jacques was very put-out to be last in line of the mayoral guests, but Sarah said, "Surely the most important person is always last in the procession?" and Jean-Jacques, surprised, agreed with a genuine smile. Of course, the king is always the last to arrive.

Charles, concealed behind the trunk of a street tree, took photographs of Sarah and Jean-Jacques and the procession before finding his dinner in La Cuisine d'Antoine.

Sarah worked very hard to keep Jean-Jacques in a good mood throughout the stately progress and during the ensuing dinner. She kept up a conversation on different topics with their dinner companions but always including Jean-

Jacques and deferring to his opinions. Jean-Jacques had originally accepted his invitation simply to ensure his continuing status in the town, but during the evening he unexpectedly found himself enjoying it. He knew why. As Sarah said goodnight in the lobby of the town hall, Jean-Jacques pulled her to him, knocking her headdress sideways, and kissed her full on the lips.

"I've been wanting to kiss you all night," he said so loudly that people turned to look at them, "but I didn't want to ruin your headdress. It's been wonderful to have you as a partner," and he kissed her again.

Sarah's company manners sustained her in a brilliant smile, although inwardly she was fuming at such a public exhibition. She made him a very grand and deep curtsey, and said, "Thank you for the invitation, Monsieur Keruan," before leaving to find her own comfortable clothes.

Charles had been waiting in the lobby and had seen both the public embrace and Sarah's annoyance. In the car on the way back he and Sarah chatted about Dinan and the festival, but when they reached Sarah's garage and Charles opened the car door for her, he said seriously, "I think I should have a word with Jean-Jacques?"

"He's not worth making a fuss about," Sarah said. "Just let it go."

***

On Sunday Charles took his hired van on a short trip to get used to the large vehicle, driving up-river to the yacht basin at Port Lyvet. He sat on a sunny bench to do some more studying, but he'd quickly realised from the numberplates of parked cars that many of the yachts must be owned or hired by people from other regions of France.

He wondered how many tourists of what nationalities visited Brittany by boat, how many boats were available to hire and where they were based, what facilities yachting and motor-boating tourists needed, where they were publicised. The perceived limits of his job expanded rapidly.

On Monday he easily accomplished the cross-channel trip to Reading, loaded up the van with his suitcases from the storage facility, and returned to Poole well in time for the overnight boat to Saint-Malo. He managed more reading on board, but didn't forget to get up in time to make a permanent photographic record of the early-morning landfall at Saint-Malo in all its glory.

He drove from the ferry to the cottage, picked up everything he wouldn't need in the next few days, drove to the apart-hotel and spent the day re-arranging his belongings between his studio and the luggage store. He'd decided to move out of the cottage on Thursday morning, so that he could spend one last Wednesday evening with the social club.

But on that Wednesday evening Charles wasn't prepared for the welcome he got when he arrived. Everyone knew about his new job, and he had to endure multiple congratulations on the appointment, and many frank expressions of delight that he'd chosen to stay in Brittany, which the club members rightly took as a compliment. Charles looked suspiciously at Gérard, who smiled but shook his head.

Then Charles saw the knowing grin on Marie-Pierre's face. He sat down at her table and said with exaggerated respect, "I can't think how you found me out, Madame. Are you perhaps the sister of the regional prefect?"

Marie-Pierre was greatly amused. "I'm not so highly placed," she said comfortably, "but my brother's granddaughter is the receptionist who took your security photo. So not only do I know where you're going to work, I'll know everything you get up to when you do." She laughed infectiously, and so did Charles, finding himself so delighted to be caught up in the web of friendship that he kissed Marie-Pierre warmly on both cheeks.

18

On Thursday morning Charles left the cottage some days early. He'd phoned Mrs Rowley and told her to keep the money for the next week's rental because he'd been so grateful to find the cottage. He didn't mention that he probably owed his job to taking it. He arranged to leave the key with Sarah.

Naturally Sarah thought that she should check that he'd left the place in a good order. She opened the cottage, but found everything left tidily with no trace of Charles' presence except the used sheets and towels neatly folded into Janet's laundry bag. But as she left, Sarah ran into a family row taking place in front of Tower View cottage next door.

The family consisted of a husband and wife, a fractious toddler and two very small twin babies in a carrier. The language was English. The wife was berating the husband for something, trying to stop the babies crying and at the same time keep the adventurous little boy under control. Sarah didn't hesitate. "Can I do anything to help?" she asked.

"I'm not sure anyone can help," sighed the husband, "The problem is we've got all the baby stuff in our car, but it's parked up on top of that hill. That's too far for Elaine to walk in this heat carrying the twins, but I can't identify what she wants."

Sarah immediately thought of her own garage; besides her unused spaces, the management company owned two parking spots but their cleaners only ever used one. "Would it help if you brought the car nearer? I can find you a space for the week under that building over there."

"You can?" the man tried hard to believe the impossibility.

"Certainly, I live there and I know which spaces are free. If you fetch the car now, I'll show you how to get in and out of the carpark." She turned to Elaine and said, "Perhaps I can look after your little boy while we wait?"

Elaine didn't hesitate for a second. "We'd be so grateful. Jeff, you go and move the car. This lady will help me."

"The name's Sarah. Now, what colour and make of car so that I recognise it?"

"Toyota, mid-blue, GB plates."

"OK, Jeff, I'll watch for it." Sarah scooped up the toddler and put him on her shoulder, bouncing him up and down until he became so interested in what he could see from up there that he stopped fighting to get down.

The blue Toyota duly arrived. Sarah beamed open the security gate and walked to the space at the back of the garage with the child still clinging to her shoulders. She gave her passkey to Jeff once he was out of the car; she had five more available up in the penthouse. She asked him to give the passkey back when he left, or, if she wasn't in, to leave it in the café-bar Au Coin Du Quai. Elaine had followed her into the garage, and had already found what she wanted in the boot. Sarah helped them take the children and their packages to Tower View.

It had been an exhausting ten minutes on a hot day. Sarah called into the café-bar for a mint tea and an ice-cream, and sat at the counter to tell Monsieur Poisson what she'd done, so that he wouldn't be surprised to be given a garage passkey.

"That's very kind of you," he said. "Do you know the owner of the two cottages?"

"Madame Rowley? Yes, I do."

"I believe Charles has left Anchor Cottage and moved to Rennes?"

"That's right."

"So Anchor Cottage is free at the moment?"

"It's possible. I don't know if Mrs Rowley has already relet."

"Well, if she hasn't, the four people over there are Belgian and they want a place to stay for a week." Sarah quickly dialled Janet on her mobile phone.

Janet hadn't relet the cottage. She told Sarah her usual tariff, which was in pounds. Sarah turned over one of the newspapers on the counter, found the exchange rate and converted the sum to euros using her phone's calculator. She then approached the four Belgians.

They immediately asked to see inside the cottage, so Sarah let them in. They were delighted. They'd fallen in love with Saint-Edern, but all the small hotels in the area were full. The cottage would do splendidly. They could treat it as a hotel by eating and drinking in the café next door. But they wanted to pay by credit card. Sarah was only at a loss for a few seconds, then she asked Monsieur Poisson if he would take the card payment, and he agreed. He asked the Belgians for a name and address and telephone number to accompany the payment, and the cardholder cheerfully wrote his details on Philippe's order pad, producing his Belgian identity card which Sarah promptly photographed front and back with her mobile phone.

Once the Belgians had taken over the cottage and its key, Sarah went back to the café. She phoned Janet and told her that the Belgians had paid by credit card in euros, and asked Janet where she wanted the money sent. Janet had a French business account and gave Sarah the details, and while she was still online, Sarah asked Philippe if he was able to move the money directly to Janet's account. He agreed to do that once he received the money in two or three days' time. Janet agreed to all this, and said she would drive over that afternoon with the clean sheets.

When Sarah ended her phone call, she found another mint tea in front of her. "It's a hot day. You need to drink a lot," said Philippe, "and I'm celebrating having learnt a new skill. I'm sure that I'm now involved in international money-laundering."

"Monsieur Poisson…" Sarah started to refute the idiocy, but she was laughing too much to do it.

"Philippe, please. Are we not partners in business?"

"Sarah," she said shaking his hand. "You're a good friend."

"No, no, no, I'm very commercial. There are now four Belgians who will eat breakfast here, and buy packed lunches, and sometimes dinner, every day for a week. And when I tell them about the fifteen different Breton beers that I stock, they will each have to try each beer once, and then they will have to take crates of them home to show their friends."

***

Sarah went home to a simple lunch of chicken in Caesar salad and a bowl of cherries, but she couldn't rid her mind of the impression she'd gained of the system Janet used to rent out cottages. Janet advertised in one English magazine, and expected payment by an English cheque to an English bank. In this day and age, when the first thought of a party of Belgians attracted by Saint-Edern was to use their mobile phone to see what lodgings were available, Janet's paper-based UK-limited system was too primitive to survive.

After lunch, however, Sarah started work on Janet's primary problem, parking spaces. She telephoned her building's management company and suggested that they could sell one of the two spaces marked 'Reserved', as it was never used. She was passed up the hierarchy until she reached senior management, who agreed that it would be possible, and indicated a price. Sarah strongly suspected that the man had no idea what parking was like in Saint-Edern in the summer, as the price was far lower than she'd expected.

She then phoned Janet and relayed what she'd done for the family in Tower View, and the fact that the space their car was now sitting in was available to buy. Janet jumped at the chance of buying the space, but not for the cottage: she wanted it for herself. She had to park in Saint-Edern every weekend during the summer, to deal with the changeover of tenants. Sarah thought to herself that a half-mile walk to and from the hill-top car park while wearing a formal suit, tights and high heels must be absolute torture in August. She agreed to arrange the purchase and to accompany Janet to a meeting to sign the intention to buy.

"Are there any other parking spaces free in your building?" asked Janet. "Would it be possible to rent from their owners?" Sarah knew there was a bunch of spaces always empty. She said she'd investigate.

Acting on intuition, she knocked on the doors of the four small studios on the first and second floors. She found one tenant at home, and he knew the other three, since they were all students at the same institution. He confirmed that all four studios were rented from a local agency specialising in one-person lodgings.

He knew that each studio owned a car space, because the agency offered to rent them out separately, but none of the current four students had a car.

Sarah took details of the agency address and contact, and went back to the penthouse to phone Janet. Janet was in favour of renting two spaces rather than buying them, and told Sarah what she thought they were worth to her. Sarah contacted the agency and the suggested rental charge was promptly agreed; to the saleswoman on the phone it was unexpected profit at no cost whatsoever. Janet decided to rent two spaces until the end of September, and Sarah arranged this.

There was still the problem of Janet's primitive cottage booking system. On impulse Sarah looked up Jane Porter-Hughes in the telephone directory, and phoned to ask how she obtained clients. As expected, Jane used the same paper-based English cheque system, but advertised in *The Times* instead of *The Spectator*. She and Janet had agreed that if a client wanted to book a week already taken, that client would be given the telephone number of the other owner, but this didn't always result in a booking for the other one. She was quite happy to name other English owners in the area. She knew of eight, with twenty-two properties between them.

"That's probably enough to create a viable computer system for booking by internet," Sarah said.

"Wowee!" Jane reacted. "That's a big jump. I'm not sure I could handle that."

"Do you buy anything from the internet?" Sarah asked.

"Of course. My hands are too large for any gloves stocked locally so I searched the net and found a super made-to-measure leather shop in Burgundy. I buy handbags from them now, too. And the first pack of gloves was accompanied by an advert from a company in Strasbourg selling those beautiful candied fruits and marzipan sweets, so I buy them to send to England as Christmas presents. Actually, when I order from paper catalogues, I always input the order on the internet, because the items are delivered sooner."

"You're sounding like an expert in how the internet works," Sarah said encouragingly. "All you'd have to do is walk round the other side of the shop counter and sell instead of buying."

"Goodness me, is it that simple?"

"If you've got a decent system, yes. Do you think any of the others would join in if we started one?"

"I could put a feeler out in the British expats' newsletter. Beth Farley organises that and it's emailed to people I've never met."

"Ask them to get in touch with you to express an interest, and ask them to say how many properties they're renting out. If the numbers warrant it, we can organise a meeting and I'll describe the system I could produce."

***

The idea went better than Sarah had expected. For a start, there were fifteen English owners with forty-one properties in the general area of Saint-Malo and Dinard, and all of them had experienced far too often the annoyance of one or more high-season weeks without tenants. Sarah didn't even have to organise a meeting, because Janet Rowley was not going to be upstaged by

Jane Porter-Hughes and Beth Farley, and immediately offered to host a get-together at her home on a day in the next week.

Sarah quickly started on an outline system design. She began by checking what was possible. She contacted the database and functional developers she now knew well, and they gave her the names of two local organisations who provided web-hosting services. The developers had never created a booking system but they knew someone who had. This front-end designer proved to be two local young women with good references from local companies, and they were happy to send a demo to Sarah showing their hotel-room booking system, which allowed multiple photos of the hotel and of the selected room, and selection by date, place, price or size of party.

Basing her design on the demo, Sarah mapped out a front end from the client's point of view, allowing the client to pick properties by location on a map or by town, type, number of beds or date range, and for each property providing multiple photographs, plans, a list of contents, directions for finding it and a list of attractions in the local area.

Then she mapped out an underlying booking system which she restricted to full weeks, Saturday to Saturday, in the high season, while allowing booking by the day outside July and August. She incorporated the published rules of one of the international payment systems for putting the money received by credit card or bank transfer into the bank account of the owner of the property rented. She listed the reports required by an owner, including an on-screen calendar showing what dates were still free in case an existing telephone client got in touch.

She drafted out the design of the database underlying the system, with a list of all the functionality required, and obtained estimated costs from the website host, the database and function developer and the front-end creator. It was a small system and most of the functionality had already been developed by the technicians for other clients, so the cost wasn't astronomical, especially when divided by fifteen owners.

On the day, Sarah drove to Mrs Rowley's up-market, fully restored and enlarged eight-bedroom farmhouse. It was a long single-storey building parallel to the road, complete with lawn and rock garden in front, swimming pool, sundeck and barbecue terrace in the rear, and a square-cut solid cypress hedge three metres high along its entire field boundary. The property sat next to the road, surrounded by wide flat fields which had just been ploughed after the harvest. It looked as alien in the landscape as a spaceship just landed, and there were gnomes on the rockery. Janet certainly deserved full credit for Keeping Up Proper English Standards in Foreign Parts. Sarah slid her little car alongside the seven SUVs already parked on the brick-paved apron, and Janet enthusiastically shepherded her into the grand salon, where fourteen more English ladies were waiting.

Sarah set up her easel holding a large pad of paper, and readied her collection of felt-tip pens. She then said good morning to the audience and introduced herself, ensuring that everyone had her name, address, email and telephone. "If you think of a question after I've gone, don't hesitate to get into contact," she said.

She then described how the client would see the system. She drew diagrams on the easel, handled questions, and every so often noted a point raised by the audience. Some of the ladies had come well prepared with notepads and were writing busily throughout.

After an hour Janet organised a coffee beak. When the audience returned Sarah followed a different tack by asking who had a computer at home already. As expected there was one person who didn't, and only two who had a machine which was their own, not used by other members of the family. Sarah started to talk about security. She pointed out the problems of having only one computer in the family and one shared login identity, and recommended at least a separate identity for each user.

She then pulled her tablet from her handbag. "This is all you need for the system I'm proposing. It connects to the internet and has an internet browser. You don't need a full size computer for this system." She quoted the price range for suitable tablets and offered to help anyone who wanted advice on buying one or setting it up.

Sarah then started on the underlying process of booking, and found that she was ahead of the audience on the problem of bookings which were not Saturday to Saturday. Their advertisements were only placed for whole weeks in the high season. The idea of renting for a few days at Easter and the autumn half-term took root, and Sarah's initial suggestion of a day rate outside the high season was enthusiastically received.

They broke for lunch, the audience having all contributed snacks and salads to the buffet, and afterwards Sarah moved into reporting and tax returns.

She also explained how the owner could input a booking for a phone client who didn't have internet access.

Sarah revealed her provisional estimate of the total cost of development and the annual running cost. She then asked Janet to take over, so that the audience could decide how to go forward. All the owners decided to join the project provisionally, but naturally wanted exact figures for the cost, and one asked for urgent lessons in using a tablet, which Sarah agreed to provide.

It was decided that Jane Porter-Hughes would co-ordinate information on advertising, and at the next meeting they would vote on where to advertise and when, but the crucial point of all advertisements quoting the website address was fully agreed. The ladies simply wanted to have every cottage and flat booked as often as possible, without quibbling about which advertisement had secured which booking. Mrs Porter-Hughes herself could envisage that they would eventually advertise in common.

Sarah agreed to provide a demonstration system which they could try out at the next meeting. She already knew the developers were happy to work through August, as they preferred to take their long holidays in the skiing season, and the front-end designers didn't have a lot to do to change their demo. As Janet served tea and cakes, the whole audience showed their enthusiasm.

When Sarah left, she took care to thank Janet very warmly for hosting the meeting, but Janet returned the thanks. "I think you've just revolutionised all our lives," she said. "It's so good that we have a real professional in our midst." Whatever Brian Rowley's opinion of the Pullen family, his wife was obviously intent on retaining a link.

***

It was a good thing Sarah had prepared so well that there was little left for her to do, because next day, Jean-Jacques Keruan rang.

"I must apologise for calling you, my dear, but I really don't know who else to ask for help. You see, I'd stupidly forgotten that now I'm no longer in television I don't have the staff I used to have, and when my friends reminded me it was my turn to hold a party this year I just gave them the date without realising I had no-one to organise it. I don't want to let everyone down. You did such a magnificent job with that dinner in Brocéliande. Would it be possible for you to help me out again?"

Sarah hesitated. Working with Jean-Jacques wasn't what she'd have chosen, but he did sounde in need of help and she was too polite to say no outright. She prevaricated by asking "What sort of party?" thinking that the dinner in Brocéliande hadn't been much trouble.

"At my house in Lanvallay. A marquee on the lawn with a bar and a buffet. The guests are all in television. You'll recognise their names. Photos get into all the magazines. There are three of us who organise the annual get-together and this year it's my turn, so I just picked the first Sunday in October as usual and issued the invitations without thinking." He paused. "Two hundred of them. People will have booked their hotels already. I don't know how to organise it myself. There are things like portaloos that I know nothing about. I'll need a hostess in charge on the day as well. I think you're my only hope."

The thought of Jean-Jacques ordering portaloos made Sarah laugh. It wasn't something could do. She'd attended enough corporate garden parties to know how they were organised: it seemed a straightforward task. Jean-Jacques was a nuisance but somehow she couldn't leave him standing on his own lawn apologising to two hundred guests for nothing being ready. She provisionally agreed to help, subject to seeing the house and garden.

"My dear, that's simple," said Jean-Jacques, his charming voice sounding deeply grateful, "I'll send you a set of keys by taxi. You can come over any time. I'm out all day every day, of course."

Sarah remembered the mayor's wife from the costume dinner, and felt she could telephone and ask for assistance. As she'd hoped, that lady happily passed on a long list of her local contacts for marquee supplies, caterers, wine-merchants, sound-system providers, florists, photographers, and cleaning firms.

The house proved to be a large eight-bedroomed mansion, architecturally heavy, faced in granite blocks with columns and pediments, and looking as fake as a film set. The spacious salon on the ground floor had full-length windows giving on to a huge back lawn with a spectacularly ugly baroque fountain in the middle of it. The kitchen was small, and apparently unused. The interior of the house was gothic, dark and designed for dozens of servants to maintain. It was definitely a challenge.

Sarah met the marquee supplier's representative at the house and agreed on a tent covering the lawn and the fountain, plus a tent for caterer's stock and a tent of portaloos, all with wooden floors. There would be a buffet table in the salon, a bar in the tent, and a scattering of tables and chairs around both. Sarah agreed three changes of buffet with the caterers, plus serving staff. She agreed wines, fruit juice, whisky and bar staff with a local wine merchant. She arranged for a covered walkway from gate to front door, a secure cloakroom and a security check on invitations.

She asked Jean-Jacques where everyone parked their cars.

"My dear! Everyone comes by taxi. No one will be fit to drive home. I'll book a taxi for you as well. Just say when you want to come and go." He hadn't given any form of budget but the total so far didn't seem to bother him at all.

Sarah engaged a photographer, who whistled in appreciation at the guest list and the chance of selling pictures to the gossip magazines. He recommended his cousin as the florist, because she'd done the flowers for a party there three years before.

"You need quantities of pale flowers in that dark hall," the florist told Sarah, "especially a huge display in the middle of the stairs to stop people going up and using the bedrooms. Those television types have no morals." Sarah felt quite naïve, as that problem hadn't occurred to her. She agreed to a rose arch over the entrance, flowers and ferns filling the fountain, and scented standard roses in pots along the walls of salon and tent. It was all as over-the-top as Jean-Jacques himself; he'd certainly love it.

She arranged for light melodic background sound, harp, flute, guitar and soft piano, and for the wine merchant's staff to control the volume. She arranged for a company to clean before and afterwards. That was as much as could be done in advance.

19

Back on the last Friday in July, the manager of Courtney & Mitchell Estate Agents' branch in Chichester, Corinne Wetherall, had been sitting at the reception desk while her assistant typed details of properties into the computer. She could see a grey-haired couple looking at the photographs in the window and discussing something with each other. They decided to come in.

"Good morning," the gentleman said, in an accent something like American. "We'd like to discuss what types of houses are available round here. We're thinking of buying within the next two years or so."

"What sort of price range are you thinking of?"

"That's one of the things we want to find out. At the moment we're more interested in the type of house. We want a family house which is manageable by the two of us, but with space for the family to visit, and we would like something with a bit of history to it rather than outright modern. You have a photograph of a very attractive building in the window, but unfortunately it's marked 'sold'. What we'd like is to discuss what it might be possible to find, and to arrange that when something we would like comes on the market, we could be told immediately."

"I get the picture," Corinne said, "but it's not me that you want to talk to. You want the owner of the agency, Mr Mitchell. He's been in the business in this district for forty years, he has agencies all over Sussex, and he knows the area better than anyone. Would you mind if I telephone him, and find out when he can come in?"

"That sounds good, go ahead."

Corinne phoned Clark, outlined the customer requirements and asked if he could come in and meet them. Clark was on a nearby new estate, just finishing his discussions, and he could be at the office in half an hour. The two clients agreed to return in thirty minutes, and did so just as the boss's car slid into the agency parking space.

Clark extended a hand. "Clark Mitchell. Pleased to meet you."

"Robert Henry," the client said, "and this is my wife Marguerite."

Clark was intrigued. "I can't quite place your accent,'" he said.

"We're Canadian."

"Ah, now you've said it, I can hear it." Clark led the way into the inner office and asked, "What makes you want to buy on this side of the Atlantic?"

"Well, I'm coming up to retirement. I teach European history at the University of Vancouver, and the idea of retiring to Europe took hold a few years back. I don't speak any language other than English, so this is the obvious country to settle in, and one of my ancestors came from Chichester, so this seemed a good place to start. I must say it's a very attractive town. It looks exactly how Canadians think historic English towns should look, but it has all the necessary modern facilities as well."

"Are you looking for a place for just the two of you, or do you have family?"

"We have two daughters. One of them lives in France, and the other lives in Edinburgh where she's married to a Scot and has two young children. We need the sort of place which can provide a home for just the two of us, but allows the family to stay on infrequent occasions."

"We're dyed-in-the-wool city folk," Marguerite added. "I'd like to be near the centre of town because we want to join in the social scene, and it's easier to join in if social events are within walking distance. And of course we'll grow old, and will eventually need the sort of services you can only find in built-up areas."

"I'm beginning to get the idea," Clark said, "but I have to warn you that good quality historic town houses in Chichester come on the market rarely."

"We thought that would be the case, so we decided to come over and start prospecting. Then if something good comes up, you could let us know?"

"It's part of our service," Clark agreed.

"What made us come in here was the picture in the window," Marguerite said. "I know that one is sold, but if you ever get any others like it, we'd like to know."

"Then it might be worth looking at the details of that one. I've got them here on the computer. You can see the price it went for a few months back. Is that within your range?"

"It's the sort of price I was expecting to pay."

"Here's where it is on the map of Chichester, it's very central, but it's on a very busy road. The last owners fitted some unobtrusive double-glazing to deaden the sound, and that did work well. The front of the house is right on the street, and is very Georgian. The front door is the original. The back of the house has been extended over part of the garden and modernised, as you can see from these photos, and this plan. It still leaves a garden in the rear, as in this photo. It gives you the best of both worlds, I think, the beautiful old frontage married to a modern kitchen and bathroom. I don't think anyone now wants to live exactly as the Georgians did."

"I'm sure it's impossible to get their servants," Robert agreed.

"Now, if we start with this house, what is it that appeals to you most? And least?"

"I like the style of the house," Robert said.

"I do like the front door and those windows, they look so English," Marguerite said, "and it has four bedrooms, that's probably our minimum."

"And two modern bathrooms," Robert added.

"It's nice that all the back windows are so big. That's what we're used to," Marguerite said. "I find our hotel a bit dark."

"And what don't you like about it?" Clark asked.

"Being next to the road," Robert said promptly. "The front door opens straight on to the pavement. And it's a solid wooden door; you wouldn't know who was there when you opened it and walked into them. And it doesn't have a garage."

"It does," Clark advised, "but further along the street in a converted stable block. So, to sum up, your ideal purchase would be a Georgian frontage, set back from the road, fully modernised interior, small garden, large modern windows at the back, somewhere to put a car, four or five bedrooms, two bathrooms, and right in the centre of town. But you don't want to move in for two years."

"That sounds about right," Robert agreed.

Clark hesitated for less than a second. He hadn't got to be a successful estate agent by passing up on opportunities. "Well, now," he said, "I could leave it like that and say, yes, there's always a chance that something like that will turn up and if it does, I'll let you know. But it's just possible that you'd be interested in a very unusual property we currently have on our books.

"It's the shell of a Georgian house, quite literally, four walls and a roof and nothing inside. It's right in the middle of town but in a tiny cul-de-sac, very quiet. It's going for a song, because there's everything to be done. We have some suggested designs for refurbishing it which have been drawn by a specialist renovator, but I'll admit that it will take courage and imagination and money to turn it into a home. If you'd like to have a look at it, I'll happily take you there, but I'd quite understand if you don't want to take on that sort of project."

"Whereabouts is it?" Robert asked.

"About ten minutes' walk away in Mulberry Mews."

There was a prolonged silence as the two clients looked at each other. Marguerite spoke first. "Can you tell us where Mulberry Mews is? I couldn't find it on the map we bought." She produced a small map book from her handbag.

Clark deliberately didn't ask why they'd been looking for that address. He thumbed to the correct page, and said, "Mulberry Mews is that little cul-de-sac there. It's so small, there's no room to print the name. There are only two houses in it."

The clients looked at each other. "Robert," Marguerite said, "we have to go and see it."

"I agree," Robert said. "Can you show us how to get there?"

"I can take you there," said Clark. "My car's outside. And if you do find you're interested, I can show you the book of designs for renovating it. I keep that in the house."

As the three left the office, Clark said to Corinne. "You have Pepper-Williams' number?" She nodded. "Send him round to Mulberry Mews if he's free."

"Sure thing, Mr Mitchell."

As his car pulled into the narrow entrance road of the mews, Clark said, "If I stop here, you can see the possibilities. That's number one Mulberry Mews, and it's in a very fine state. Inside it's been fully modernised, but from the front it looks just as it did in the 1780s. And then if I pull into the mews, you can see the difference in number two. The possibilities are still there, there's a good new roof, but there's a lot missing." He put the car on the gravel patch. "This could be the site for a single garage, or you could put a double garage at the end of the garden."

Clark continued. "You can see that the house was originally three storeys high at the front and four at the back with the attics. That makes it a good size inside, but it's more vertical that the average home, so the owner next door had a lift put in. If you're not too shocked, I can let you in via the back door."

But Robert Henry was staring at the front of the house, lost in contemplation. After a few minutes his wife said, "I would certainly like to see inside. Come on, Robert!"

Just as they started towards the back door, a small van drew up behind the Clark's car and Pepper-Williams stepped out of it.

"Mr and Mrs Henry, may I present Peter Pepper-Williams? He's the best of our local restorers, and he's produced some designs for renovating this place. He's also done some sterling work on the house next door, so he knows this mews better than anyone." Everyone shook hands and Clark led the way to the back door.

As soon as they were inside, Pepper-Williams took centre stage and described the basement they could see, and the basement that would have been there when the house was built, with doors to the cellars for wine and dry goods such as the all important tea, and a door to the cook-housekeeper's parlour. All these were in the area between the basement kitchen and the front of the house. He described the two sets of staircases, the gracious sweep of the main stairs for the owners, and the hidden, narrow, steep servants' stairs from attic to kitchen. He pointed out the archaic arrangement of rooms in the original house. On a level with the front door, on either side of the stairs, would have been the study of the owner of the house, where clients and tradesmen could be received, and a billiard room for the sons of the house, which could double as a cloakroom when the family was entertaining. The first floor was wholly dedicated to entertaining, usually as a separate dining room and withdrawing room, with a wall between them which could be folded away to produce a room where ten couples could dance. All the family bedrooms, and the dressing rooms of husband and wife, were squashed into the second floor, and by modern standards they were very tiny. The attic with its single window in the gable was where the indoor servants slept. There would have been a carriage house in the garden and the outside men would have slept above the horses.

Pepper-Williams then took the Henrys through into the ruin to see for themselves the possibilities. The original building had been built of wood internally, but he favoured using modern techniques with steel beams and light-weight sound-proof blocks for the internal walls and floors, though he recommended covering the floors with oak planking to reproduce the original feel of the house. He showed the clients some of his designs for a more modern use of the interior, with a family dining room in the basement, a lounge/diner for entertaining at front door level, good sized bedrooms and a modern bathroom on the first floor, and more bedrooms and another bathroom on the second.

"If you look at next-door," he said, "you'll see clearly that there are four floors at the back, because I've put dormer windows in that roof. You can't see the new windows from the front, so they don't spoil the first impression. The furthest dormer is actually the cover for the head mechanism of the lift housing. I flatter myself I've hidden that lift very well."

In the back of the portfolio were some sketches and plans which obviously related to the original house before the wood was removed. These interested Robert Henry far more than Clark would have thought, and he said, "If those interest you, you can take them with you. Peter has all his drawings scanned into his computer, so he can always print another copy."

"Thank you, I would very much like to have them," Mr Henry said, and turned to Pepper-Williams. "Do you have any estimates for the cost of turning this into the modern home you were describing?"

"I do, although it depends on details, what type of basic structure, exactly how many bedrooms and bathrooms, what type of wood finish, that sort of thing," and Pepper-Williams named a range which neatly bracketed the price of the house the Henrys had seen in Courtney-Mitchell's window.

"And how long would it take to finish the reconstruction?"

"Minimum sixteen months, more likely two years. It's always better to wait for the right craftspeople to become available. If you become serious about it, I'll ask around and give you a true figure. There are lots of good local specialists who'd prefer to work on a job like this."

"I certainly want to think about it. It's very good of you to give us your time like this."

"Well, if you are seriously thinking about it, would you like to take a look at next door? I know Oliver Maynard very well and I'm sure that he'd let you see how he's adapted his house to modern times."

"If it's not too much of an imposition."

"I'll go and ask him. He can always say no," and Pepper-Williams let himself out of the basement to knock on Oliver Maynard's door.

A few minutes later he returned with Oliver himself, who shook hands all round and said he would be happy to conduct them round his house, as long as they didn't object to the untidiness of the premises. "I'm a widower," he said, "and like all bachelor pads, the house is full of piles of things which haven't been put away. But I have altered the original design of the house, or rather I've persuaded Peter here to alter it for me, and that will give you some idea of what can be done."

The Henrys spent a very enjoyable half-hour touring Oliver's home, exchanging comments with Oliver and Peter. Clark silently brought up the rear, not quite daring to believe what was happening. The tour ended in Oliver's welcoming basement kitchen. "Have I shown you enough?" he said.

"Indeed you have," said Robert Henry, "You've been very kind."

"Then can I indulge my curiosity? Your accent is Canadian?"

"It is."

"British Columbia?"

"Spot on! How did you guess?"

"My son went to university in Vancouver, and your voice reminds me of the people I met there."

Robert looked at Oliver. "I teach in the University of Vancouver. European history."

"I'm afraid that my boy took engineering, so I doubt that you met. But he got a darn good education there, found himself a good wife as well. The two of them now work all over the world, Australia, Brazil, China. They come here between contracts, so I get to see them occasionally. One has to let the young go free."

"We let our daughters go, and they both came to Europe," Marguerite said, "so to some extent we're following them. But of course a huge number of Canadians have origins somewhere in Europe."

"Have you looked up your ancestry?"

"Well, in a way that's why we're here," Robert Henry said . "You see, my mother's great-great-grandfather came from here. I think in fact that he was born next door."

"He was a Murchison?" Oliver asked.

Robert was startled. "You know the Murchison family?"

"I know they built number two at the same time as the Maynards built number one. If it hadn't been for the First World War they'd have still been here, but the eldest son was killed in the trenches, and his father and brother died in the 1919 influenza epidemic. That left a widow with a small daughter. She had to sell up and move out.

"But the Murchisons have definitely had an effect on my family. My great-grandfather knew that one of our neighbours had gone to British Columbia. He did very well in school one year and won a prize book, and when the school asked him what he wanted, he said 'a book on British Columbia'. I still have the book, which has become a piece of family history, and so my son was brought up knowing about it. One day when he had to give a talk in class at school, he chose British Columbia as a subject. After a few weeks researching the province in the library, he became so enthusiastic about the region that some years later his first choice university was Vancouver. So without anyone intending it, our families have become a little interwoven. I shouldn't influence you, but I'd find it appropriate to have a Murchison next door."

"I'm beginning to agree." Robert Henry turned to face Pepper-Williams and Clark. "Now, this is quite definitely not what I was looking for when I came to England, so I need to check things over very carefully. It might yet prove to be impossible. Can I ask you to let me keep the design portfolio for a few days?"

"Take it with you," Clark said. "This is my card, and this is Peter's. I think I speak for both of us when I say we would be happy to answer any questions at any time." Pepper-William nodded assent. "And there's no hurry at all. You have first refusal on the house. Can I take you back to your hotel?"

As he drove home, Clark thought of telling Deborah, but decided against it. No sense in two people being disappointed if the deal didn't come off. But for the whole weekend he was distracted, his thoughts continually drifting to Robert Henry's ancestry, the tenuous connection with Oliver Maynard, and the amazingly coincidental connection with those other descendants of the Murchisons, James, Deborah and Charles.

20

At a few minutes past nine o'clock on Monday morning, Clark's telephone rang. "Robert Henry," the transatlantic voice said. "I'm dotting i's and crossing t's. Exactly how much is the house shell on sale for?"

"Sixty thousand pounds," Clark said.

"Thank you. Now I need to pin Peter Piper down to more exact figures. I'll get back to you."

It was Wednesday before Clark heard again. "We've decided to go ahead," said Robert Henry, "so I guess the first thing I have to do is buy the house."

"I'm delighted to hear it," Clark said. "Do you have an English solicitor?"

"That's a lawyer? I'm afraid I don't. Can you recommend one?"

"Certainly. There's a good one right opposite your hotel, John Stanley of Josiah Stanley and Partners. I'll get the paperwork sorted out here and passed on to him today, and I'll persuade him to give you an early appointment. Can he phone you at the hotel?"

"He'd be better off with my mobile phone, I bought one here to get a British number," and Robert dictated the telephone number.

"It should be a straightforward purchase," Clark said, "although I have to tell you that the seller is a widow who now lives in France. She's using an English solicitor, so there shouldn't be a problem, but if she has to, she can come over on the ferry from Saint-Malo at short notice."

"Oh, not another coincidence," Mr Henry exclaimed. "My youngest daughter is in Saint-Malo."

"Then you'll have no trouble keeping in touch. From my experience, there's a good service across the Channel."

"It adds to the attraction of the house. Thank you for everything. I think things are going to work out better than any of us imagined."

Once he'd put the phone down, Clark went into autopilot mode. He drafted out the terms and conditions of sale, and the details which would be required by the Henrys' solicitor. Sarah was using Jeremy Prescott's father, Michael Prescott, as her solicitor, and he already held the documents of the previous sale, so that side of things was complete.

Clark decided to drive into Chichester and see John Stanley, feeling that this was especially necessary considering that the Henrys were buying a very unusual property which wouldn't fit the usual pattern of solicitor's questions. He was lucky enough to get ten minutes of John's time, during which John phoned Robert Henry and made an appointment for the next day.

As he was only five minutes from the Chichester office of Courtney-Mitchell, Clark called in to thank Corinne Wetherall in person, as it was her prompt referral to Clark that had started things in motion, and her call to Pepper-Williams which had sent the designer to the house.

"I'm putting the sale through the books of this agency," Clark said. "It's not a big one, only sixty thousand, but it will add some useful extra pennies to your commission."

"But you did all the work!"

"Actually, I think Pepper-Williams and the next door neighbour did all the work. I just stood there and watched the client warm to the project. I wish it was always as easy."

Clark returned to his main office in Bognor. It was time to tell Sarah. Clark dialled her mobile number, and when it connected he said, "It's Clark Mitchell. Is this a good time to call?"

"OK by me. I hope there's nothing wrong?"

"Exactly the opposite. There's a Canadian professor on holiday in Chichester who wants to buy your house."

There was an audible indrawn breath. "You mean the ruin? He wants to buy it? As it is?"

"He's agreed to buy it as it is, and he's going to use Peter Pepper-Williams to reconstruct it. He has no illusions about how much it will cost or how long it will take, but he wants it and he appears to be able to afford it. He's briefing a solicitor tomorrow."

"I can't believe it. Clark, you must have worked a miracle to get a sale on that place."

"Actually I did nothing. The place sold itself as soon as I mentioned its address. I still find this difficult to believe, but the buyer had come to England to find his roots. His mother was called Jane Murchison, and her great-great-grandfather was born in that house."

"But this is incredible! Another Murchison has turned up? Of course, no other family would want that wreck."

"I could agree with that. But you're being very un-commercial," said Clark. "You haven't yet asked what it sold for."

"As long as they take it off my hands, they can have it for nothing."

"How does fifty-eight thousand and two hundred pounds grab you?"

"Say that again."

"Fifty-eight thousand and two hundred pounds, which is net of my commission, but there'll be a solicitor's fee from Michael Prescott."

"Clark, that's daylight robbery. You valued the house at six thousand and seven hundred and fifty pounds."

"That was the value for some land hosting a useless building which would cost money to be demolished. Now, if you value the place as the basis of a reconstruction, using the fact that it has four strong walls, a new roof, historical value, and a good location, you get a very different figure."

"When you retire from being an estate agent, Clark, I recommend that you become a politician! But thank you for getting rid of the place. You've just solved the last big problem in my life."

The next person who needed to know was Deborah. Clark phoned home but got no answer, and Deb's mobile was obviously switched off. He let it go. He would see Deb in the evening, and meanwhile he had to prepare for a client appointment in half an hour.

Deborah was in fact in Chichester. She regularly visited the agency branches to give the staff an opportunity to talk to their management, and that morning she'd driven as far west as Havant before turning in her home direction. She called on Corinne Wetherall practically at lunchtime, so she suggested the two of them have a light lunch together in the Red Pheasant. They found a table and ordered. That gave them the leisure to look round the restaurant at the other customers. Corinne's face lit up, and in answer to her smile a grey-haired man left his table and came across with his hand held out to her.

"It occurs to me that we've never said thank you," he said. "Putting us in touch with your boss was exactly the right thing to do, and now we've seen Mulberry Mews, we're hooked."

Deborah carefully expunged all expression from her face.

"Mr Mitchell told me you were going to buy it," Corinne said happily, "and I'd like to wish you all the best with the restoration. This is a lovely town to live in, and that house will be really handsome when it's finished."

"I'll second that," said Deb. "You can see from the house next door that it'll be worth it."

"I should introduce you," said Corinne. "This is Mr Mitchell's wife, who's a partner in the agency. Deborah, this is Professor Henry, from Vancouver University."

Deb raised her eyebrows. "That's quite a journey you've made, to buy a place in Chichester," she said.

"I came over to see where my ancestors came from," said Mr Henry, "and I struck lucky. My mother's great-great-grandfather was born in the house I'm going to have restored."

Deborah stilled completely. "Your mother was a Murchison?" she asked.

"Good heavens, does the whole town know about the Murchison family?"

"No, but those of us who belong to it do. My grandmother was the last Murchison born in Mulberry Mews, and I've always been told that I look like her."

"But you must do! I can see a resemblance to the photos in our family album." He beckoned his wife over. "Marguerite, this is Clark Mitchell's wife, but I've just found out that she's another descendant of the Murchison family."

"Oh, this is beyond anything great! So glad to meet you, Mrs Mitchell," Marguerite said, shaking Deb's hand. "Why, we'll have family here in Chichester."

The waiter arrived with food for Corinne and Deborah.

"We must leave you to your lunch," Robert said. Deborah quickly produced her business card and wrote on the back her private email address and telephone number, and Robert did the same with his, saying, "We must keep in touch."

As they exchanged the cards, Deb gave him a broad smile and said, "Welcome home, Cousin Robert. I look forward to meeting you often."

When lunch was over and Corinne's work had been discussed and suggestions noted, Deborah returned to her car. She sat in the driving seat and sent an SMS to Clark. 'Just met long-lost Canadian cousin.' Her mobile rang immediately.

"Trust you to find out all my secrets before I have a chance to pass them on!"

"But it's splendid news. He really has bought the place?"

"He's signing up with the solicitor tomorrow."

"Is that what had you on tenterhooks all weekend?"

Clark groaned. "I can never keep anything from you, can I? It was all too good to be true. I expected to be told at any minute that it was cancelled."

"It is a sort of miracle. Does Sarah know?"

"Oh, yes. She's just told me off for selling it for too high a price!" The phone echoed to their shared laughter.

Given the unusual circumstance of a transatlantic visitor buying a historic ruin, the two solicitors were inspired to work as fast as they could to complete the sale, so that work could start before winter. They completed in three weeks. Sarah promptly closed her English account after arranging for the UK government to pay her state pension in France. She could now concentrate solely on life in Brittany, as she had always intended.

21

By mid-August, the database, the functionality and the front-end of a system for holiday letting had all been delivered and Sarah had spent some time checking that it was correct according to her specifications. Once she found that it passed her testing, she paid the developers in advance, but warned them that that there would be changes to come.

She made an effort to put meaningful data into the system for the forthcoming demonstration. She took photographs of her own rooms and terrace, her garage, the beaches of Saint-Edern, Marie-Pierre's house and every room in it, a number of local houses to stand in for holiday cottages, Philippe Poisson's back yard with his deckchair, the fort and the ruined cathedral on Alet, and a view of Saint-Malo. She invented fictitious cottages and flats to let, used her photographs to show what they looked like and listed what local attractions were nearby. She invented routes to find the premises from cross-channel ferry points and made inventories of rooms and furniture, and kitchen contents. She thought stoically that she was doing more work than any of the computer technicians, but the presentation was always what sold the system to the potential buyers.

On the last Tuesday in August, Sarah drove once more to the Rowley farmhouse. She put up a projection screen to show everyone the demonstration system operating on her laptop but she also connected to the demo database all the tablets of those who'd brought them, and downloaded the system on to their machines. She got a few ladies to input bookings in sequence from the client's view, showing clearly that bookings, once paid, prevented anyone else booking that week at that cottage. This was a considerable surprise to all those who never left their houses without taking their list of bookings with them in case a client phoned.

Sarah then moved into the functions available for property owners and showed the ladies how to create a cottage to let and how to add descriptions and photographs. She then ran the report-printing functions, displaying the reports on-screen but also handing round printed copies she'd prepared beforehand.

In all this she insisted that the input be done by all the ladies with access to a machine. Many of them were quite surprised that they could work the system at all, but, as Sarah pointed out, they were all running a very complex paper chase to cope with the organisation of letting, so they should expect to understand the simple computer system. Emboldened by this encouragement, a few of them started to criticise the screens, functionality and reports. Sarah happily logged all their criticisms. At last, she was discovering what they really wanted. And so were they.

They briefly discussed the problem of access to the system: who would count as an owner of a cottage to let, and who would control that status? A committee of three, inevitably Janet Rowley, Jane Porter-Hughes and Beth Farley, was appointed to oversee security and access.

But a surprising vision of the future surfaced when the ladies discussed advertising. Everyone still wanted to advertise in English quality news media, but in the middle of discussing when and where, at what cost, Paula Morton said, "If the site is on the internet, do we need to advertise at all?"

Jane Porter-Hughes immediately understood. "You mean people could find us by searching for cottages to let in Brittany?"

They all looked at Sarah.

"Certainly, if someone searches using the keywords we've set to describe the website, our site will appear on their list of search results," she confirmed. "But to start with, your current clients won't know you have a website, so you need to repeat your old adverts at least once. You might still pick up new clients for the website by advertising in magazines, though I think the social media page I've proposed will be more successful in the long run. I've put a 'How did you hear about us?' question on the internet booking form, so that you'll know how people found the site. If you find that new people do come via a specific newspaper, then obviously you'll want to continue advertising in it. But if a journal hasn't produced any new clients for a year, maybe those adverts could stop."

Paula Morton was obviously very astute. She said, "Can anyone find us on the internet? I mean, not just English, but French?"

"Oh, yes," Sarah confirmed.

"My goodness, how can I possibly cope with the French?" Annie Chevening gasped, panic in her voice.

"It's simple," Sarah said. "You meet them at the cottage, give a welcoming smile and hand over the key. It's all they need. They've already paid. If they'd had questions, they'd have emailed you, and you'd have put their email through a translation package, written a reply in English, put your reply through the translation package and sent it to them. You might need to translate the cottage inventory, but the translation package will do that too. Remember that every European under forty learned English at school, so they may even understand your English, as long as you speak slowly and clearly in simple sentences."

Janet Rowley suddenly came to life. "Would this system cope with those Belgians who took Anchor Cottage?"

"Of course," said Sarah. "Philippe Poisson would have made the booking on his bar computer and the card payment would have gone straight to your bank. You'd have had to drive over with the key and sheets, that's all. It's in Philippe's interest to have your two cottages full for as long as possible, because everyone in them eats breakfast in his café, buys his packed lunches and canned drinks, and often eats there at night as well. So he'll monitor this site to see when he needs to find a tenant for you."

From the astonishment on her face, Janet was clearly re-thinking her relationship with Philippe Poisson. Sarah couldn't resist adding wickedly, "If you let to the French or the Belgians or the Dutch, you don't need to wear high heels and a suit to hand over the key."

Janet's eyes lit up. "Thank you!"

By the end of a day's hard work on the part of the ladies, Sarah could at last provide all the developers with final specifications, and most of the ladies had gained enough confidence to ensure that the system would be used as intended. It would be ready well before the December-January peak of holiday bookings, and it would make a tiny difference in the area of Saint-Malo to have all forty-one properties occupied as often as possible with people who would spend locally, grow to love Brittany, and maybe return for years afterwards.

22

By the first week of September, Charles had been working in the Regional Office of Tourism for a month. He'd started by working closely with Erwan Guellou, but had already progressed to dealing with the greater part of the job on his own. Guellou was content to take things easy, and found his replacement's boyish enthusiasm extremely amusing.

Charles now controlled the two trainee managers, Jeanne Thanh and Giorgio Coccini. They spent nine hours in college every Tuesday, studying tourism. Charles had always kept close to his English trainees, so continued his usual practice. He set aside time on Wednesday morning to discuss with Jeanne and Giorgio what they'd learnt the day before.

The trainees welcomed this attention. Their principal classes were lectures to eighty students by speakers who didn't expect or answer questions, and didn't provide written notes. With large classes and a crowded syllabus, the college couldn't attempt individual support. The lectures were very good, but Jeanne and Giorgio were new to the profession and needed firmer reinforcement. They especially needed assistance to relate what they'd learnt to real life in their own jobs. Charles could lend them textbooks that they couldn't afford, he had work experience they hadn't acquired, and he knew how to push them into discovering answers for themselves. He managed this educational support without impacting his own work, which he took home if he ran out of time in the office.

The office hierarchy before Charles' arrival had been simple. Max Le Quennac, as regional director, had a secretary and two assistant directors, Erwan Guellou and Brendan O'Donnell, reporting to him. The two trainee managers and five telephone support staff all reported to Guellou. But Charles now worked for Guellou while officially reporting to Le Quennac. Rather than interfere with Guellou's handover, Le Quennac had asked O'Donnell to keep him informed on Charles' progress. It was a simple brief for O'Donnell who could, and habitually did, go everywhere and talk to everyone.

O'Donnell had noted the trainees' enthusiasm for Charles' assistance. He knew that Guellou hadn't offered them help, although when Guellou had been a trainee his directors had overseen his studies. O'Donnell checked on Charles' work quality and quantity when next speaking to Guellou. He casually timed his coffee break so that he could ask Charles what he was working on and how.

In his next meeting with Le Quennac, O'Donnell reported that Charles had visited all the tourist information offices in two of the four Breton counties, and had taken over all Guellou's work with them. This effort didn't take him as long as it had Guellou. In the time he had spare, Charles devised and oversaw tasks for the trainees to provide practical experience of the theory they were learning.

Out of hours, Charles was teaching himself about Brittany in an unusual fashion. He drove to a different town each weekend, stayed over Saturday night, explored all the nearby tourist venues and bought guidebooks to read during the next week. Charles hadn't broadcast the fact that his old office was still paying him, or that their contribution was used to fund his personal study of tourist Brittany. All O'Donnell knew was that he didn't charge the hotel, petrol, literature or entry fees to his office credit card.

This behaviour wasn't what anyone had expected. Charles wasn't operating within the straitjacket of a promoted civil servant – which both Guellou and Le Quennac had been – and his approach struck O'Donnell as showing potential advantages for the office. But there was a drawback to employing a foreigner, and Le Quennac was profoundly irritated by Charles' non-observance of the correct etiquette.

So O'Donnell invited Charles to lunch. He began by asking about Charles' previous work. In Charles' last audit, he'd been one of three team leaders of equal rank with a disliked absentee boss. Charles had formed a good enough relationship with the client's managers to instigate changes in working practices to produce lower costs and a better environment for the staff.

"That's surely not an auditor's job?" O'Donnell queried in surprise.

"Not exactly, but it costs nothing, and makes the client more likely to use the same auditors next year."

"Did other team leaders do this?"

"They had no management training, so didn't usually see the problem. But once you see it, you have to do something."

O'Donnell found this disconcerting. "If anything needed changing here, what would you do?"

Charles grinned. "Tell the administrator." But for some reason O'Donnell wasn't reassured.

He moved on to the major problem. "What did you call the other team leaders?"

Charles was puzzled. "Brian and John."

"If you had to mention them to one of your team, what would you call them?"

Charles couldn't see the point. "Brian and John."

"If you were talking to Brian about the boss, what would you call the boss?"

"William."

"And if William was present, what would you call him?"

Charles' face showed complete confusion. "William, of course."

"When would you use his surname?"

Charles hesitated. "He was introduced to us as William Broughton, but no one ever called him Mr Broughton."

"You've explained a lot," said O'Donnell. "We're more formal here. For instance, if you wanted to attract my attention across the office, what name would you call?"

Charles looked wary. "Brendan?" he asked cautiously.

"Certainly not. I outrank you, so you call me Monsieur O'Donnell on all occasions until I give you permission to say otherwise. Which I haven't yet done."

Charles frowned. "But you call me Charles."

"I'm senior to you. I can call you Charles if I wish. But if I spoke to you in the presence of your Trainees, I'd call you Monsieur Pullen. If I talked to the trainees in your absence I'd name you Monsieur Pullen. If I call you Charles to your staff, I'm putting you on the same level as Jeanne and Giorgio."

Charles closed his eyes briefly as he took in what hadn't been said. "I think I've been annoying people."

"You have."

"Thank you for telling me, Monsieur O'Donnell. I apologise for appearing impolite. The people I've annoyed must include Monsieur Guellou and Monsieur Le Quennac as well as yourself?"

"Monsieur Le Quennac certainly. He asked me to talk to you about it."

"Should I apologise to him?"

"No, it will be enough to observe the rules from now on."

"Thank you. Did you leave out Monsieur Guellou deliberately?"

O'Donnell suddenly recognised the source of his unease. He was dealing with someone who saw things as clearly and as quickly as Gérard Lemestre used to do.

He said, "I think you could usefully learn more about the office. Can you give me half an hour when we return?"

"Certainly, Monsieur O'Donnell. I'd be interested in what you have to say. Now, what happens to the bill for this lunch?"

"We each pay our own."

"At last, something I'm used to," Charles said happily.

Back in his office, O'Donnell seated them both in his armchairs. He looked seriously at Charles. "I'm sorry I had to put you through the hoop. From now on, while we're alone as we are now, but only while we're alone, you can call me Brendan. I hope we're going to be close colleagues for the year I have left.

"Now, about the office. France was divided into administrative regions in 1982, and tourism was made a concern of the regional prefect. This office was started by Gérard Lemestre. He had a first class diploma in finance and administration; he'd been a director for the local prefecture. Four years later he made me administrative assistant, my first job on leaving Ireland. I got the job because I had a sense of humour. It was my only defence against that brain of his. I think you know him?"

"I can confirm the brain and his sense of humour, but there's also a habit of pulling strings behind the scenes."

"That's the man. He made a significant contribution to tourism in the region without looking as if he'd lifted a finger, and at the same time he took the tourism diploma, and passed it first class, of course. When he needed a tourism manager, he chose Max Le Quennac out of the prefecture's administration. Le Quennac was a good choice, but he's no Lemestre. He held Lemestre in awe, still does. He has finance and administration at second class.

Lemestre wanted him to take the tourism diploma, but he was married with a family, and didn't want to study in the evenings, so he's never qualified.

"Lemestre and Le Quennac made a remarkably successful partnership. But eventually they needed assistance, and Erwan Guellou was brought in as trainee manager. He's Lemestre's second cousin and I'm certain Lemestre paid for his tourism course. When Guellou qualified he was promoted to manager, but he'd only passed at second-class, and Lemestre had expected better from his own family. We took on another trainee who proved unequal to the job; he left in May, so we've just taken on two trainees instead of one, to make up for the shortage in numbers.

"Two years ago Lemestre retired. Le Quennac became regional director. As Guellou was second-in-command, he was promoted to assistant director. He'd only spent one year as manager, and that promotion took me six years, the usual interval. Guellou will be an assistant director in National Tourism in Paris, and they won't know he doesn't have six years managerial experience, so he'll get promotion to director sooner than if he stayed here. Paris salaries are higher, of course, though so are Paris living costs.

"Guellou openly thought he'd be replaced with another trainee manager. He can't see that's impossible; the office must have a second-in-command. But, if a trainee had been engaged, then in eight years' time when Le Quennac retires, there would be three junior management staff, none with the seniority and standing to become regional director, so that post would be advertised. If Guellou applied, he'd be the favoured candidate: Breton born, known to the region, full director by then."

Charles looked thoughtful. "Have I ruined things for him? He hasn't made me feel unwelcome."

O'Donnell was dismissive. "Guellou has Lemestre's face but not his brain. He's never even asked to see your CV. He has no idea of your age, experience or qualifications. He has a simple mind. He's a Breton, you're a foreigner. He's got the tourism diploma, you haven't. He's sure you're younger than him, and you do look it. You're on probation, so you're a trainee, n'est-ce pas? He's happy with all that. But you were taken on with the intention that you'd become Le Quennac's second-in-command and eventual successor. And your problem in that matter," O'Donnell paused for effect, "isn't Guellou."

Charles frowned. "I hope I don't understand you."

"Charles, your contract says you report to Le Quennac. You've been here a month, and he hasn't called you in yet. He relies on what he learns from me and from Guellou, and he doesn't entirely like what he hears. He sometimes felt uncomfortable working with Lemestre, and he feels you're a Lemestre clone. You do remind me strongly of my old boss. You see things so quickly, you see possibilities other people don't see, and when you think something needs doing, you just do it.

"Can you please look at that from Le Quennac's point of view? He's not the absentee boss you're used to. This is his office, not yours. It should run under his control. If you want to make changes, you need his permission, so you ask him, and you give him time to think through the idea. He's no fool, but his brain doesn't naturally hop from problem to all possible solutions at the speed yours does, and he's been well trained never to change anything which has previously proved successful. Le Quennac needs to be very confident that a change will benefit the region. He won't risk reporting failure to the prefect, or a budget overrun.

"It's an awkward situation that you're working for Guellou while you're learning his job, because Le Quennac naturally refrains from interfering with Guellou's staff management. He's somewhat at fault there, because he could have found a way to talk to you. But he's heard you name him as Max to the trainees, and he knows you've re-arranged their work without consulting him. The results of what you're doing there look good to me, but in Le Quennac's view you're bypassing his control of his office. It's a bad sign that he asked me to stop you misusing his name. He should have told you off himself. You've a problem to solve, Charles, and it's not one where I can help you."

Charles' face blanked free of all expression. He said, "Can I ask a favour? Can I just sit here to think through what you've just said?"

O'Donnell rose to his feet. "Take all the time you need. I've got reports to run." He moved to his desk and switched on his connection to the office computer system.

Charles reviewed the two versions of office history he'd been given. O'Donnell had subtly criticised Le Quennac, but had still established a working relationship with him. Gérard hadn't criticised Le Quennac at all, and was acknowledged to have had a good partnership with him. Charles had no relationship whatsoever.

He realised that the fault was his. He'd jumped eagerly into the job as if auditing a new type of company and needing to find out how it worked. He'd dismissed Guellou as a source of information, since Guellou was patently a junior manager promoted beyond his capability. But in that situation during an audit, Charles would have tried to make contact with Guellou's boss. He needed to do that here. A proven method of making contact was to find common ground and ask for help. Charles carefully selected the appropriate subject before returning to his desk.

23

Regional tourism was concerned with overall publicity for Brittany and so had a presence at tourist exhibitions. The annual Holiday Exhibition in Brussels was due in late December and Guellou had already asked Charles to check the Brittany stand well in advance. The photographs on the stand, chosen by Lemestre many years before, were reprinted for every exhibition, no matter which, always showing the same view of tourist Brittany: coast, lighthouses, historic buildings, lace bonnets, bagpipes, cornfields, cider and biscuits. Charles didn't entirely agree with that presentation so had deliberately chosen it for a discussion with Le Quennac.

Next morning, he knocked on the door of Le Quennac's office, smiled respectfully and said deferentially, "Bonjour, Monsieur Le Quennac. May I ask you for some advice about the December exhibition in Brussels?"

"Have you asked Monsieur Guellou?"

"I'm not sure that he's concerned, monsieur. He leaves us next month, but you'll be representing Brittany at the exhibition, so I'd prefer your opinion on the stand to his."

Le Quennac had his elbows on his desk. He rested his chin on a fist and asked, "Why do you need an opinion? We have a well-designed stand which always works efficiently. The posters and leaflets need reprinting. It's a simple job."

"That's true, monsieur, if we continue to use the same posters and leaflets as for the last twenty years."

Le Quennac frowned. "You see something wrong with that?"

"Not if it's what you want, monsieur. But I did wonder if, after twenty years, it could be time to make a change?"

"What change do you have in mind?"

"I'd like to remove the big poster of the cornfield and replace it with a poster of bottles of Breton beer."

Le Quennac was visibly surprised. "That's not a simple change, that's a drastic revision. Why would you propose such a thing?"

"I have two reasons, monsieur. The first is that a photograph of our countryside is not enough to encourage a Belgian to drive for a whole day just to get to Brittany. There are scenes very similar in southern Belgium and in north-eastern France. Both those areas are nearer to Brussels and both have stands in the exhibition. Our coast is unique, but our cornfields aren't.

"My second reason is that food and drink are a very great interest in Belgium. They brew lots of different beers, and they're very proud of them. But Brittany has lots of little independent breweries, too. I think publicising the number of beers on offer would make Brittany more attractive to a Belgian. I think Breton food like a seafood galette and a Far Breton plum flan would add to the interest as well."

"It would cost more than reprinting the current photographs."

Charles was careful to remain deferential. "Not necessarily, Monsieur Le Quennac. I'd expect to get photos of beer bottles for nothing, since it's good publicity for the brewers. I thought of associating each bottle with a photograph of the place where it's produced, but we already own the appropriate photos. Once I've got the montage worked out, printing it would cost exactly the same as reprinting the cornfield photograph."

Le Quennac was still frowning.

"I don't need an immediate answer, monsieur. I really came to ask if you were interested. If you are, I thought I could create the poster online and sketch the stand to show you how it would look."

"Do you have the time to do that?"

"I believe I do, monsieur."

"Then I'd like to see it. But I'd want some accurate costings with it."

"I could list those too, Monsieur Le Quennac. Could I show them to you tomorrow?"

Le Quennac looked up his online diary. "I'm free at ten o'clock."

Charles smiled gratefully. "I'll bring everything to you then, monsieur. Thank you."

After he'd gone, Le Quennac sat for some minutes without moving.

Next morning at ten, Charles produced his draft of the big poster. It was composed of fifteen pictures of different beer bottles alternating in chequer-board fashion with photos of cliffs, beaches, rocks, rivers, islands, lighthouses and ports. He had a sketch of the stand with the poster-montage in place, and also details of slightly changed posters on the side-wings, where the two lighthouses and two historic buildings were now seen behind different plates of food on a table top in the foreground. He'd produced a draft leaflet detailing two hundred different beers with a map for locating the breweries, and another with recipes for cooking seafood galette, gingered scallops, salt-caramel apple tart and the plum flan known as Far Breton. He'd included a detailed list of costs, marking which had been agreed and which were still estimates.

Le Quennac solemnly accepted the documents and said briskly, "Thank you, Charles. I'll look through these and give you my opinion when I've read them."

"Mais bien sur, Monsieur Le Quennac," Charles said, deferentially accepting dismissal.

After four minutes, Le Quennac phoned O'Donnell to come in, and was relieved to see that Brendan was just as startled as he'd been, and then just as enthusiastic.

"Max," Brendan exclaimed, "this is brilliant. Now I've seen it, I can't think why no one has ever thought of using beer and food to attract Belgian tourists. That's their national stereotype, after all."

"I didn't know we had so many little breweries. I'm certainly going to use this. But how do I handle someone who thinks up ideas like this?"

"Same as you do with me and the accounts. Institute a weekly meeting at which Charles tells you what he's doing or wants to do, and why. You'll find he takes criticism without arguing. He's nothing like Erwan; he wants to work for you. If you'll let an old friend overstep the line, I'd say he's been hurt by being ignored."

Le Quennac narrowed his eyes but didn't comment.

That afternoon Le Quennac called Charles into his office, and for the first time asked him to sit. He said, "To start with, I want you to go ahead with your plan for the Brussels exhibition, as long as you keep within the costs you've given me."

Charles smiled gratefully. "Thank you, Monsieur Le Quennac."

"Then I'd like you to start reporting to me formally every week, on your own work and the work of the trainees. I suggest at ten o'clock on Thursday mornings, since I have a meeting with the prefect on alternate Thursday afternoons."

Charles' face lit up with delight. "Thank you, Monsieur Le Quennac. I'd like to do that."

Le Quennac registered the truth of O'Donnell's remark. He also remembered that when they'd first met, he'd found Charles' enthusiasm, energy and ideas attractive. For the first time it hit him that Charles was twenty years his junior, had never worked in France before, and, despite his intelligence, ability and creativity, he needed Le Quennac's help to make a success of his job.

Le Quennac thought back to yesterday's meeting with the prefect. "When you report, Charles, can you include anything you do outside the office which might become connected to the office?"

"I'm not sure I understand you, Monsieur Le Quennac."

"Your newspaper article on the *Economic Impact of Summer Music Festivals in Brittany*."

Charles looked startled. "But they didn't print my name, and I didn't tell them where I worked."

"Any internet search on the name Charles Pullen currently places your regional employment at the top of the resulting list. The regional prefect was so interested in the article that she asked the newspaper for the name of their source, and as they knew exactly where you worked, their answer embarrassed her."

Charles screwed his eyes closed. "I really do apologise, monsieur."

"No need," Le Quennac said, smiling reminiscently. "It does no harm for the prefect to be impressed with the quality of my staff."

Charles registered surprise. "Thank you for the compliment, Monsieur Le Quennac."

"Max," Le Quennac said, making a sudden decision, "but only in private."

Charles smiled brilliantly in his relief. "Thank you, Max. I'm so sorry I got that wrong. Please, will you tell me immediately when I go wrong in future? I do know I've got a lot to learn."

24

In their inaugural meeting the next Thursday, Le Quennac asked Charles to think about the region's slot for advertising in the Paris Metro stations in mid-November. There were four reserved slots each year, always using the same photograph: blue sky, bluer sea, interesting rocks, sandy beach.

Charles immediately thought of using four different seasonal photographs, as incentives for visiting Brittany at four different times of the year. Searching for a unifying theme, he'd hit on the slogan 'Earth, Air, Fire and Water'. Brittany was famous for rocks, wind and water. Fire would be the spark, the surprise.

Surely the aim of the November posters should be the New Year break? Charles found an independent photographer's record of a firework display on the harbour jetty of a little port on the Gulf of Morbihan, with an enthusiastic crowd thronging the quayside and all available balconies, faces lit and eyes shining. In a top corner he'd splashed the words 'Earth Air FIRE Water', and across the bottom of the image 'Celebrate the season in Brittany!'

From the same photographer, he'd selected for February an inspiring impression of the spring flower island paradise of Bréhat with a flame-coloured azalea in the foreground; for May an impassioned rock group firing up a sun-bronzed audience on a beach stage-set near Pléréhel; and for August the autumn red-gold colours of trees on the far side of a foaming weir at Saint-Nicholas-des-Eaux.

Max enthusiastically used his remaining annual budget to pay for the November and February photographs, promising to buy the other two next year. He showed the regional prefect screen versions of the proposed posters, and the photos were promptly used on the regional website at their appropriate time of year. The November poster of New Year fireworks caught everyone's imagination, so no one was surprised when hotel associations reported a sudden surge in New Year bookings from the Paris region.

In mid-November, with his poster being featured and praised in the Breton press, Charles suggested to the marketing manager of a bank that he could use the same photo to attract Breton clients. He did. He kept 'Earth Air FIRE Water', but changed the subtitle to 'We understand life's essentials'. He added 'Port Navalho, Morbihan, Brittany' clearly at the base of the photo, and then used the publicity countrywide, subtly publicising Brittany at no cost to the prefecture.

The prefect, almost taken aback by this extension of the reach of her tourism office, recognised once again Charles' insight into local and national business.

The Brussels exhibition and the Metro posters initiated a strong and enduring partnership between Charles and Max. To no one's surprise, Le Quennac marked Guellou's departure for Paris in October by asking the regional prefect to promote Charles to assistant director at Guellou's salary. The prefect was only too glad that Le Quennac had found a second-in-command of the right calibre, and readily complied.

***

It wasn't the only unexpected bonus reaped by Charles that autumn. Some months earlier, Sarah had received the sale proceeds from Mulberry Mews. She was already finding that money was accumulating in her bank account due to not having to support James' lifestyle, and this extra capital was an almost unwanted addition to her finances. She had a place to live in and enough to live on, and adding to her already-substantial investments seemed pointless. Her mind kept returning to the one recipient she knew for whom the money would make a substantial difference, and she decided to follow through on that idea.

At the end of September she'd spent a day in Rennes looking at the type of accommodation for sale in the centre of town. Her requirement was for a modern building. Historic homes were likely to involve additional maintenance, and for this purchase she wanted low running costs and no bother. She didn't want a new building without its functional areas complete. She wanted something which already had a high quality kitchen and bathroom, ready for moving in immediately.

But, having got used to the grand vista from the penthouse, she was convinced of the necessity of a wide view. It was too late in the season to find small flats at low prices because the students and young professionals were already in residence, but for someone with a different ambition, a taste for quality and an appreciation of comfort, there were opportunities enough. She made a short list of accommodation which fitted her stringent criteria.

In the evening she rang the bell of Charles' apart-hotel. Charles was surprised to see her, but courteously invited her up to his studio. Sarah looked round the little apartment with approval. "They've fitted this out very well," she said. "It's tiny, but you've got everything you need."

"I'm finding it very convenient," Charles agreed, "except that it's a bit small for all my books and CDs. I've probably got too many. I keep most of them down in the luggage store, and cycle them round between this studio and my suitcases."

"Well, I'm proposing to do something about that," Sarah said. "As you've covered the table with your books, I'll have to spread these out on the bed," and she pulled three sheaves of paper from her handbag and started to lay them out in three lines on top of the duvet.

Charles watched her in disbelief. The papers obviously related to three apartments, with numerous photos as well as the estate agent's description and a purchase price in large bold figures in full view. "This is my favourite," she said, pointing to the top row. "It's got a view over all the roofs in town including the cathedral's and you can see quite a bit of both rivers. But the other two have wide and interesting views as well, and they're all two-bedroom flats with large balconies suitable for breakfast, large enough lounges to take a sizeable collection of books and music, well-fitted kitchens and bathrooms, and secure covered car-parking. I think any of the three would suit you."

Charles' dismay showed all over his expressive face. "Sarah, they're completely out of my reach. I won't take on a mortgage I can't afford."

"I wouldn't expect you to do so after your experience with the last one. But your brother's house has just been sold, and that's landed me with a wad of extra capital I don't need. I think it's about time you got some benefit out of being James's brother, and if I add that capital to the amount still left over from your divorce settlement, there's more than enough to buy one of these flats. You'd need furniture, of course, but not much to start with, and if you stop paying rent you'll soon afford more. These are all good propositions. They're well-built properties in sought-after central locations, and will certainly increase in value over time."

"Sarah, I don't like this."

"Well, I do. Now, is it possible for you to go to an estate agent tomorrow and sign an intention to buy?"

"No."

"Why not?"

"Please understand, Sarah, I can't take any more money off you."

"It's James' money. It's a bit late, but you did once ask him for some, if I remember correctly."

"Sarah, he stole this money from you. If I take it, I'll be doing the same. I can't."

Sarah stood in silence for a minute and then said, "Very well. I'll accept that. That leaves me with an amount of capital which I need to invest. I usually invest in property, and I prefer properties likely to retain their value, such as one of these flats. Unfortunately, I can only afford half of one. As you have enough capital to buy the other half, it makes sense to purchase a flat together. Will you join me in that?"

The two of them stared at each other for some time before Charles said, "I still don't like it."

"Charles, I'm older than you, so I expect I'll die before you. I own three flats in Paris, the penthouse in Saint-Edern and a sizeable chunk of investments. I have no family whatsoever, so when I made my will, I simply left everything to you. I'm only asking you to enjoy a very small proportion of what's coming to you while I'm still alive to see it."

Charles sank down at the table with his eyes closed and his head in his hands. After a while he said, "Sarah, please listen. I'm very conscious of what you did for me that weekend we first met. You gave me what you described as a small amount of money, but to me it was a significant sum. The way you listened to me and the way you reacted to what I said were even more significant. It was the first time I'd ever been able to talk to anyone about the problems in my life. You made me realise that I was in a trap of my own devising, and that I had enough intelligence to find a way out. I did think it would be a slow haul to get out of the financial grip of the divorce settlement, but you intervened there as well. I know it was Deb who solved the problem, but only because you'd told her about it.

"When I realised that the opportunity had arrived, I came to Brittany; I'll be honest, out of pure superstition that if I got closer to you maybe more luck would brush off on to me. I was right about that, because it did. You introduced me to Lemestre and he was a key to getting my job. The work I'm doing is more interesting and far more satisfying than anything I've done before. It's a solid career, it promises me a future and it's opening out my mind in unexpected ways. In a very short time you've wiped out all my past mistakes and given me a life worth having. I'm happy to acknowledge all that, but I can't keep taking from you. I need to achieve something on my own."

"Charles, you've already achieved a very great deal on your own. You won your current job on merit; it wasn't luck. I'm glad to hear that you're doing well in it, but that's not due to anyone other than yourself. You've made influential friends in Brittany with no help from me. And another of your achievements is that final divorce settlement. That was money you'd earned in the first place, increased by the capital gain from investing it in a well chosen property. You should re-invest that capital quickly and wisely in order to retain and increase its value.

"Now, what I'm offering is a partnership. We'll own the flat together, in the proportions of our contributions. If it's ever sold, we'll split the capital gain between us on those proportions. If you sell in order to trade up, I'll keep my part but you'll increase yours. I'll leave you my part in my will, and you should do the same for me. You can accept my offer on those terms with no loss of dignity. It won't belittle what you've already achieved on your own, or what you'll achieve in the future, but having the good sense to buy the right type of home makes your future achievements more likely, because you'll have a better environment to live in and relax in. You just need to plan the move now because the final purchase is always subject to three months' delay."

Charles ruefully assessed the determination he was fighting, the practised professional success. "Sarah, has anyone ever succeed in stopping you doing what you wanted?"

Sarah smiled triumphantly. "Not in the end."

Charles sighed. "You'll be on my conscience for the rest of my life. But what you've said makes sense, and I'll agree as long as you really do retain a share in the property. What time tomorrow and which agent?"

"Well, I'd say the best of the flats is this one, and that agency opens at ten. Can you meet me there then?"

"I'll be there. Sarah, I really am grateful. I'm sorry if I've not been very gracious at accepting it. I do know a decent home will make a difference."

"It's no more than you deserve," Sarah said, kissing a formal goodnight without revealing how much joy she felt at the outcome.

25

The first Saturday in October was the day before the garden party at Jean-Jacques' mansion. Sarah supervised the initial cleaning, the marquee erectors, the portaloo installation and the stationing of the caterer's fridges and ovens. She tested the sound system, and then drove home for a good night's sleep.

At half-past eight on Sunday morning she dressed in her working clothes and carried her party outfit in a small suitcase down to the taxi which Jean-Jacques had sent. On arrival at the house she put her case in a spare bedroom ready for changing later, and went down to deal with the florist, the security team, the wine delivery, the food, the baristas and the caterers. At quarter past three Jean-Jacques sailed in, obviously from a good lunch, and was full of praise for everything except the way Sarah was dressed. She took the hint and went upstairs to don her pale green silk cocktail suit, her delicate jade and gold filigree jewellery, and gold high-heeled sandals, remembering to return via the back stairs because the florist had now finished blocking the main staircase.

She was just in time to stand with Jean-Jacques as the first guests arrived. She didn't know any of them, and Jean-Jacques greeted everyone by their first name, so that didn't help much, but she thought she probably wouldn't know who they were with full name and address. Her concentration on television documentaries didn't help her recognise these faces.

As Jean-Jacques moved into the marquee, she stayed to keep an eye on the front gate, dealing with the inevitable guests who'd forgotten their invitation cards, ensuring that everyone entering was offered a drink, and generally keeping the line moving through to the marquee. As Jean-Jacques' only job was to stand in the marquee and talk to as many old friends as he could, he proved a genial and surprisingly capable host.

Sarah avoided the marquee. It was full of people she didn't know and couldn't talk to. Instead she busied herself keeping an eye on the provision of wine and food and the changeover of music, and welcoming the photographer. So she knew to the minute when the last guest arrived.

At half past eight, wearing a dark charcoal Gucci suit over a pale gold silk shirt with heavy platinum cufflinks, altogether more fashionable that she'd ever seen him before, Gérard Lemestre strolled casually up the covered walk. In the salon he accepted a drink from the tray, saluted her gravely with it, and moved into the marquee.

At this point in the evening Sarah knew precisely two of the people present, but as the crowd moved around the space available, they were drawn into the salon to sample the food, and inevitably came across to talk to her. She was interesting to all the guests because she was a complete novelty. The inevitable topics of conversation were who she was, and where she'd met Jean-Jacques. She confined herself to the description of a widow living in Saint-Edern, and that she'd met Jean-Jacques at a party in the local prefecture.

Neither Saint-Edern nor the prefecture were of interest to any of the enquirers, who immediately turned the conversation in the direction of television programmes or national politics, and proved to be solely interested in studios, production, producers, who was about to get which job, who should have been given the latest series, what chance one had of becoming the next anchorman of a popular news magazine, how to get on a government committee, how to get a seat in the Senate, which political party offered the best prospects of such employment, and other topics well beyond Sarah's conversational ability.

Towards eleven the salon emptied somewhat and Sarah was breathing more easily when one of the guests, a voluptuous bleached blonde at least thirty years younger, walked into the room and said, "There you are! I suppose you think you're pretty clever to have got yourself into this position?"

"I'm sorry," Sarah said, "I don't understand you."

"Oh, yes, you do! He's out there telling everyone how clever and capable you are, so it's pretty obvious you're warming his bed for him. Well, I can tell you it won't last for you any more than it lasted for any of the others."

"I think you misunderstand the position completely."

"I never misunderstand him. He made my mother's life a misery and I hope he makes yours the same."

She turned on her heel and returned to the marquee with a plateful of canapés, leaving Sarah taken aback. The blonde must have been Jean-Jacques' daughter. She knew that he'd been married four times and had two children. Sarah hadn't realised that his daughter was on the guest list, but of course her current surname was probably not Keruan. Sarah was slightly perturbed that people were getting the wrong impression about her relationship with Jean-Jacques. She made the fatal error of moving into the marquee.

Jean-Jacques saw her the minute she entered the tent. "Sarah, my dear," he called. "Come over here." When she reached him, he was talking to a couple she didn't know, and he reached his arm around her shoulder while he continued to talk. There wasn't a graceful way to wriggle out of the embrace in public. Jean-Jacques greeted other old friends and moved, with her locked under his arm, to talk to them.

When the friends finally moved away, Sarah said to Jean-Jacques, "I need to be going soon. I believe I asked for a taxi at half-past eleven?"

"You won't need that," her host said. "You can stay here for the night."

"No, I do need to get home."

"You'll be better off with me. I didn't book a taxi because I can hardly wait any longer for you. You aren't going to let me down are you?" And he kissed her full on the mouth for a long time, right in the centre of the party under the eyes of all the guests.

Sarah thought very quickly. "I think," she said jokingly, with a flirting upward glance and a giggle, "that you're just trying to prevent me having another glass of champagne," and she twisted out of his arms and made for the bar. She picked up a glass and saluted him with it, laughing. He laughed back at her delightedly.

She then pretended to hear a request from the salon, raised her eyes to the ceiling in resignation, and went to 'answer the call'. Once inside the house, she ran through the kitchen and up the back stairs. In the spare bedroom she swiftly changed into working trousers, folding her cocktail dress into the suitcase with her sandals. She assumed she'd have to walk through the town and across the viaduct into Dinan to get a taxi, as there was no taxi-rank in Lanvallay. She put her coat on, ran down the back stairs and through the kitchen, meeting no one on the way, and then walked out of the kitchen door into the dark hall hoping her exit was clear.

A voice said, "If you want a lift to Saint-Edern, my car's outside, and I could take you there."

"Monsieur Lemestre!"

"Would you like a lift home?"

"Yes."

"Come on, then." He took her case, held her hand and walked to the gate, nodding acknowledgement to the staff as he passed them. He opened the back door to his car and put the case on the back seat. "Sit in the back," he said, "and treat this as a taxi. There's no need to talk." He drove competently on fast roads and at some speed back to Saint-Edern.

At her building he stopped, opened the door for her to get out, handed her the case and waited while she found her passkey. "Everything's all right, now that you're home?" he asked.

"Yes, thank you."

"Then I'll return to Lanvallay and tell Jean-Jacques you got home safely." Sarah was visibly startled.

"It's just a matter of courtesy. Can you give me your keys to his house? I'll find someone else to supervise the clearing up tomorrow: you'll have no need to return." With that, Lemestre drove off into the night.

***

Sarah hardly slept on Sunday night, and took the whole of Monday to fully recover her equanimity. Even in the Qi Gong class her usual serenity felt fragile. On Tuesday and Wednesday she carefully filled her day with work.

On Wednesday evening, Sarah took care to arrive at the social club at the last minute to reduce the amount of talking she would need to do. There was only time for a brief reply to her friends' questions about Jean-Jacques' party, confirming that the marquee and catering and music had all gone well, that it was an event little short of brilliant – photos had appeared on social media already – and that she was still exhausted.

Elodie sensed that Sarah was holding something back, and she had her own way of getting news. "Jean-Jacques must be very proud of you," she said, "When are you seeing him again?" But at that point Pascal called the meeting to order, to discuss the next weekend's outing. Sarah's reply was necessarily limited to a shrug of the shoulders, which suited her fine.

After some discussion on a number of possible outings, the club unanimously decided to attend a charity garden party being held on Sunday in the garden of Château Le Bras. This building was a malouinière, one of the houses built in the eighteenth century by successful sea captains operating out of Saint-Malo. The château was apparently almost unaltered inside, and beside the stalls selling refreshments and craft items, and the Breton traditional games which would be set up on the lawn, the owners would be selling tickets for tours round the house, a rare opportunity.

When the meeting broke up Sarah kissed Marie-Pierre and Elodie goodnight and turned for home. She was surprised when Monsieur Lemestre approached. "May I walk you home?" he asked courteously, offering his arm.

Sarah's thoughts flew back to Sunday night. As they started walking together she said, "I hope you aren't about to tell me there's bad news from the weekend."

"No, not at all. Everything ended very smoothly. The next time you meet Jean-Jacques he will kiss you heartily, and tell you what a wonderful organiser you are."

Sarah demurred. "I'm not sure that I want to meet him again."

"He's impossible to avoid entirely. And he does still want to marry you."

"Well, I don't want to marry him," Sarah said forcibly.

"I'm glad to hear that," Lemestre returned. "I can't imagine you enjoying being married to someone so like your first husband."

Sarah stopped dead as that comment hit home. "Mon dieu! You're so right," she said. "I can't think why I didn't see it." Jean-Jacques had assumed she would jump to his bidding in the same way that James had done. He'd been very hard work to entertain, just like James. He showed no sign of really caring for her, but used her for his own ends as James had.

Lemestre had stopped when she did. He said reflectively, "I assume that you freely chose to marry James Pullen, and because I thought he was the type of husband you preferred, I've done nothing to interfere with what looked like your inclination to marry Jean-Jacques."

Sarah was suddenly aware of standing in the open street discussing a personal matter with a comparative stranger. "It's not your business, Monsieur Lemestre, but, for your information, James was a complete and utter mistake, and I don't intend to marry anyone ever again."

"That's a very great pity," Lemestre said evenly, tucking her hand back into his arm as they both walked on, "because I'd hoped I could eventually persuade you to marry me."

Sarah was suddenly and completely lost for words, and unexpectedly emotionally at sea. "Monsieur Lemestre…" she began, but couldn't think what to say next.

"Sarah," he said calmly, "you must surely know my name's Gérard. We've reached your building, so this is where we say goodnight. But I intended that as a serious proposal. If you should wish to accept, you'll find a way to tell me. We'll continue to meet as usual, but I won't raise the subject without your permission." He made a formal double kiss, and then turned in the direction of his home. Bewildered by this development, Sarah stood watching him walk away before pulling herself together and letting herself into the hall.

***

Next Sunday the weather produced an Indian summer. Elodie drove Sarah, Marie-Pierre and Mauricette to Château Le Bras for the garden party. Sarah had told Charles of the visit, since he'd formally joined the social club, but he'd laughed at the idea of accompanying the members. "Château Le Bras is where my boss lives, so I've been forcibly roped in to help out."

"Monsieur Le Quennac lives in a château?" Sarah asked, awed.

"His wife does," Charles clarified. "Her grandmother was a Le Bras. It sounds like the usual complicated French inheritance: the building has twenty-two owners, but Madame Le Quennac is the only one with the right to live in it. You'll like her; she's a practising dentist under her maiden name, Doctor Hélène Beaumont, professional to her fingertips, decisive, and very practical."

"I think she needs to be to run a château," Sarah agreed.

Externally the house was elegant. In the gardens, the old-fashioned roses were in their second bloom, heavily scenting the air. Stalls in tents edged the lawn. Charles was busily wheeling provisions to the food and drink sellers, and numerous old-fashioned games were underway on the grass, under the supervision of the teenage Le Quennac sons, Malo and Péran.

Gérard and Philippe were playing palets, a Breton game in the same general family as bowls and petanque, involving tossing small heavy metal discs on to a wooden floor to land as near to the marker disc as possible, or to knock another competitor's disc further from the marker. Philippe was an acknowledged master, and predictably Gérard lost. Immediately Yannick paid Malo a stake to take his turn against Philippe.

Gérard smiled at Sarah. "There's lemonade on sale over there," he said. "May I buy you a glass?"

She hadn't realised how delighted she'd be to see him. "That would be pleasant, thank you."

They collected lemonades at the stall, and then moved away to the nearest rose-bed to admire the flowers. Searching for a topic of conversation, Sarah said, "I've only just realised that this is the home of Charles' boss. It must be splendid to have such a place in the family."

"Not necessarily," Gérard said realistically. "There are usually drawbacks with historic properties. Monsieur Le Quennac has often complained about the inconveniences, but he can't make any changes without the agreement of all the owners, and it isn't easy to persuade the entire Le Bras family to agree to anything. You should go on a tour of the house. It's certainly worth it for historic detail, but you might well decide you couldn't live in it."

"You've seen it before?"

"Often. Has Charles not told you of the relationship between me and Le Quennac?"

"No."

"It's good to know Charles kept my confidence. Le Quennac and I used to work together in the Regional Office of Tourism."

"What rank did you hold?"

"Regional director. I retired two years ago, but as you've noticed, I still do odd jobs for the region."

"I wouldn't describe them as odd jobs," Sarah said indignantly. "The way you got care for the unaccompanied child migrants organised considerately and efficiently made me proud to be associated with the project."

Gérard looked at her without speaking and with a closed expression for twenty seconds. Then he smiled. "I'll take your glass for Charles to wash up," he said. "I can recommend the tour of the house."

"I'm definitely interested in that," Sarah said, taking the hint to cross the lawn to the queue.

The tour guide was Doctor Hélène Beaumont, who gave an informative and amusing commentary on eighteenth century life in the malouinière. Despite the size of the house, its grand sweeping staircase and huge formal reception room, there was very little personal space for the people who lived and worked in it. Thirty tiny cupboard-sized rooms in the attic were set aside for the house servants, who included the cleaning, kitchen and dairy staff, and the maids and valets who also served at table. The butler and cook had rooms a little larger, but not by much, and lived on the ground floor alongside the kitchen, the scullery, the storerooms for food and fuel, the dairy and the milking parlour.

The audience was astounded to discover that the cows came right into the house. Behind the deceptive facade copying the latest Paris fashion for elegant Grecian styling, the building was nothing more than a fully functioning farmhouse with some extra facilities added for impressive entertaining.

On the wall above the sweeping staircase hung an oil painting of the first owner, Rémi Le Bras, dressed for the evening. He wore a beautifully cut jacket in fine-spun wool, an embroidered silk waistcoat over a shirt of finest Breton linen trimmed with elaborate Breton linen lace, knitted silk knee-breeches, embroidered silk stockings, and buckled high-heeled shoes. But there was no hiding the man underneath all that. No one knew how tall Rémi was, since the portrait was larger than life-size, but he was very well-muscled, and Sarah thought he was probably short and stocky. The artist had depicted a hint of stubbornness. Rémi seemed determined and equal to anything. He was a practised seafarer and a commercial success, and he looked both of those roles.

For some reason Sarah found herself comparing him to Gérard. Gérard was taller and more urbane, but the two men had the same air of being in total control. In Gérard the determination wasn't as obvious as in Remi. He could, and did, conceal his intentions in a way a ship's captain couldn't. But there was no mistaking the underlying steel in both men.

As Sarah walked back into the sunlit garden, she remembered once again Gérard's oblique proposal, and the fact that he had carefully let her make up her own mind about Jean-Jacques, and about himself. It was an approach which appealed to her. As she was sure he knew.

When the event closed, Sarah found Gérard standing next to her. He said, "It wasn't possible to talk with you here as I would have liked. If I invited you to lunch on Tuesday, would you talk to me?"

"Would you talk to me?"

"Yes."

"Then yes."

"I thought to drive to Rennes. Have you seen anything of our capital?"

"Some of it. Charles needed a flat, so I inspected some properties for sale, and of course I've seen his hotel. But that's all, I'm afraid."

"Then I'd be delighted to introduce you to the more picturesque aspects of it. If I call for you at ten-thirty, we could follow one of the tourist trails before lunch. It's a city which repays strolling around, but make sure you wear shoes that suit cobbled streets and gravel walks in the park." He smiled.

Sarah smiled in return. "Until Tuesday," she said.

26

On Tuesday Sarah put some thought into what to wear. If anyone else had invited her to lunch in the regional capital she'd have opted for something Parisian in style, but that didn't fit Gérard's mention of following tourist trails in comfortable shoes. She decided on weekend-casual instead, wearing her favourite turquoise knitted pullover with fine horizontal stripes of navy and white, with navy trousers, navy flat-soled ankle-boots and a navy loose jacket.

Gérard arrived wearing the well-worn black leather blouson Sarah had seen often on club weekends, so she'd guessed right. It gave her confidence. As Gérard kissed good morning, he said, "I do like that bright turquoise. It looks well on you."

"Do you find that line works on most women you meet?" asked Sarah.

A half-smile curled the edges of Gérard's mouth. "Only when it's true."

They walked to Gérard's garage, and then Gérard manoeuvred his car through the narrow streets. When he reached the main road, he said, "I thought of taking you to Rennes because no one there will know you. That's a type of privacy we won't find in Saint-Edern. I used to live there, and I still find it interesting. It's a lively town. The centre's full of cafés, ranging from cheap student eats to serious four-star chefs. I'll confess I was thinking of my favourite crêperie, but I could easily find lunch in a different style if you wish it."

"I like galette-and-crêpe," said Sarah. "It's not something I can easily cook for myself. The official recipe uses one egg for six galettes for six people, so I'd have to make six and throw five away."

"You should buy ready-cooked," said Gérard. "Crêperie Claudette will sell you one galette and one crêpe to take home and finish by yourself."

Sarah stared at him in delight. "Gérard, you've just made my day. I've collected dozens of recipes for fillings, and now I can use them. Does Monsieur Poisson sell ready-cooked as well?"

Gérard demurred. "He does, but I'd advise buying Claudette's. No one knows what she does to the batter, but hers is different."

Gérard manoeuvred past an awkward bunch of lorries at an illegal speed, and then settled into a smoothly relaxed journey. "What would you like as a topic of conversation?" he asked. "We're half an hour from the city."

"The history of Rennes," Sarah said promptly, "if you know it in any detail."

"I have my own view of it. But the early history of the city has been revised over and over again in the last thirty years, and not everyone would agree with me."

"That explains why the internet information is so muddled. But I do have to start somewhere. It's my first reaction to a new town, to try to work out why it started and why it's still there."

"That's a tall order. But I believe I can cover the beginning. The last ice age covered Europe down to the Mediterranean. No one could live in it. Spain was ice-free behind the Pyrenees and so was the area in Greece south of the Balkan Mountains. The people penned up in Spain excelled in boats. The North Atlantic had frozen over, and they fished all along the edge of the ice-sheet, and got to America before anyone else did. As the ice retreated in Europe, these people moved north, always in boats. They eventually reached Scotland after settling on all the coasts on the way, the Basque country, Brittany, Cornwall, Wales, Ireland. They also settled the banks of major rivers, and they certainly sailed up the Vilaine, a highway leading them to Rennes. By the time tribes of Gauls arrived on foot from the Balkans, the western area of France was already full.

"Each tribal group had two main centres, the chief's house, where the chief controlled the administration and dispensed justice, and the temple, a place of worship and healing, with a hospital. I believe the chief of our local tribe lived at Rennes and the temple was downriver in present-day Redon, becoming the abbey of Saint-Pierre. There's nothing in writing about this, but when the Romans took over they usually retained the existing social structure. The Romans recognised Rennes as the tribal administrative centre, so it must have been the chief's home. That would indicate that the chief had lived in Rennes since the Stone Age."

"Is there any archaeology to back up your idea?"

"No, and there won't be any. A thriving town would have been a collection of thatched wooden buildings with a big hall for the chief's official business. The Romans built over it; the Vikings burnt any trace left above ground; cellars have been dug through all remaining evidence since mediaeval times. Roman stonework has been found, a few pre-Roman hearths have been identified, but there's no chance of finding anything from as far back as the Stone Age.

"A big problem for Rennes, and all of Brittany, is the lack of good building stone. There's only granite. It's strong, but slow and costly to work. Rennes old town is built of wood. Even houses with stone facades have wooden internal structures. The result is extremely picturesque, but hasn't been easy to maintain over the centuries, and it perpetually worries the fire brigade. The city has a programme for improving the central housing stock without destroying its character and attractiveness. I often get involved in that."

Sarah frowned. "As regional director of tourism?"

"No, as managing director of Participations Lemestre. That's my grandfather's construction company."

Sarah blinked. "You've been running two jobs at once?"

"Yes," Gérard said simply.

"That's impossible."

"Not really. I've been involved in building since I was a boy. The secret is to train the staff, support them, pay them well, and trust them. They need direction, but not me continually breathing down their necks."

"What do you build?"

"Places to live in. Places to work in. I renovate as well as build."

"Do you let the properties?"

"A few of them."

"I bought properties which I rent out."

"Do they pay well?"

"Yes."

"So they're in a good area."

"Three flats in Paris."

"Whyever Paris?"

"I worked there, so I bought a flat there. I moved to Frankfurt, so I let it. It proved a good investment, so eventually I bought two more flats in the same street. When I retired, I bought the penthouse from capital and I use the Paris flats for income."

"Couldn't you sell them and buy in Brittany?"

"Yes, but capital gains tax would reduce my investment, and returns from Paris are much higher for the money invested."

"Sadly undeniable. You earned a good salary, to be able to buy in Paris."

"True."

"So your job was important."

"In a way."

"Where was James?"

"In England."

"He didn't object to you working in Europe?"

"He found the money very useful."

They'd come through the outskirts of Rennes into the central one-way-street system. Gérard turned the car into the narrow entrance to an underground carpark and stopped to take a ticket at the barrier. "How many years did you live apart from James?"

"None. I went back home as often as possible at weekends."

"How many years did you work in a different town to James?"

Sarah took a deep breath. "Thirty-eight."

Gérard couldn't stop himself. "So why on earth did you re-join him when you retired?"

Sarah didn't reply. Gérard parked the car, and then turned to look at her. She was upset, and trying not to let it show. "Sarah," he said apologetically, "that was one question too many. I'm really sorry. Can I call a truce?" He held out his hand. Sarah hesitated, but then gave him her hand. He held it between both of his for over a minute, willing her to calm down. Then he said, "Come and see Rennes." He helped her out of his car and held her hand in the lift to the street.

They walked through the town with Gérard giving a short history of the buildings they passed: the modern law faculty, the eighteenth century conservatoire teaching music, the seventeenth century parlement building still used for hearing court cases, the gracious stone frontages around the Place du Parlement concealing the wooden structures behind them. They turned into a street of crooked timber-fronted buildings which brought Sarah's camera out of her backpack. Gérard was interested to see that she recorded only the sculptured figures and small details of the wooden frontages, because he was used to tourists attempting to get a whole building, or even the whole street, into a photo, and failing utterly.

They moved downhill to Saint-Germain church, unfortunately severely damaged by bombs at the end of the war, but still housing its magnificent organ. They threaded through narrow streets and more timber buildings into the shopping area, with its elegant boutiques behind carved and polished wooden frontages. They passed the cathedral and walked through a gatehouse of the medieval wall, strolled through the huge space occupied on Saturdays by one of the largest food markets in France, and into a narrow alley where another medieval gatehouse, once the prison, now housed a collection of bars and restaurants. A little further on they found the crêperie Gérard had been aiming for.

But as they arrived, the waiter met them at the door and shook hands with Gérard like a personal friend. They'd hardly seated themselves at a table on the secluded terrace behind the building when the proprietor – who was the cook – rushed out in his apron to shake hands briefly with Gérard.

Sarah and Gérard discussed the menu at length. Sarah finally decided on a galette of black pudding and apples, followed by a crêpe Grand Marnier. Gérard picked the galette with Camembert, Roquefort and goat's cheese, followed by a crêpe filled with cinnamon-flavoured banana. Gérard ordered a bottle of Le Coudray cider, explaining to Sarah that it was made by his cousin, and they sampled it while nibbling the plate of snacks supplied by the cook.

"As everyone here knows you so well, you must come here often?" Sarah asked.

"I did when I was working in Rennes. But the welcome is probably due to the repairs I did to the building. The four floors above the restaurant are all let to tenants. The cook rents the restaurant and also the first floor flat. The second and third floors are on long lets to families who take good care of them, but the fourth floor used to be a problem. It had low attic ceilings and was divided into three tiny studios with very few amenities. The rents were too low to keep it in good repair. Inevitably the studios attracted poorly paid workers doing long hours, and one night one of them dropped his cigarette on the bedclothes. The ensuing fire put a hole in the roof. The fire service threw everyone out of the building and wouldn't let them back in. I managed to persuade them to let my men do a structural survey, and we proved the problem was solely confined to the roof and that it would be quite safe to allow the restaurant to operate and the other tenants back into the building. That made a big difference to all of them."

"What happened in the end?"

"I leaned heavily on the owner of the fourth floor, persuaded him to allow me to raise the roof, enlarge the studios and fit modern shower rooms, good lighting and heating, built-in furniture, and better fire protection. It took me six months, but when I'd finished the studios could be let for higher rents to better tenants. The owner recouped his costs within two years, and the whole building is now much safer. Meanwhile the restaurant only lost two days' income and its insurance covered that."

Sarah had seen a gap in the information. "How did the fourth-floor owner raise the money for extensive renovation of three tatty flatlets?"

Gérard smiled. "The first thing I noticed about you was your intelligence. I lent him the money because I could see that he'd be able to pay me back eventually. The banks were as unhelpful as usual."

"But if you had money available, shouldn't you have put it where it would earn the best commercial return?"

"You mean to get more money, so I'd then have to think of something to do with that? Is that how you treat yours?"

Sarah thought back to the sale proceeds from Mulberry Mews, passed on to Charles. "Actually, no. But it's the accepted wisdom."

"Always question what people tell you. If they can't give you a succinct reason, disregard what they say." There was a glint of steel in his eyes.

Sarah smiled at finding something fundamental they both held in common. "That's why my computer systems succeed," she said.

After lunch Gérard suggested they continue their walk. They were crossing Place Sainte-Anne near the children's carousel when a boy on a scooter came down the ramp at full speed, swerved at the last minute to avoid a toddler who'd wandered into his path, and collided with Gérard. Gérard grabbed him, said "Stand there!" in a stern voice and went to pick up the toddler, who'd fallen over his own feet once his concentration was wrecked by the incident. The little face screwed up ready to scream, but Gérard calmly tapped his nose and said, "Aren't you a brave boy?" The child looked bewilderedly back at the stranger. He clung hard to his mother when she rushed over, but he didn't cry.

Gérard waved away the mother's thanks and turned to the scooterist. "If you can't control that thing, it'll be taken away from you. You must never go at that speed in town, do you understand?"

The boy hung his head and said, "I'm sorry, monsieur. It's new and I didn't know how fast it would go down the slope. I really am sorry I hit you."

"Accepted. Carry on, but take more care when the path slopes."

"I will, monsieur. Thank you, monsieur."

Sarah had watched, fascinated. "Do you have children of your own?" she asked as they walked on.

"No, I've never married. But I have a younger brother and sister I looked after, and they married. They each have two children, and so far there are seven in the next generation. And I have two cousins close by, both married with children. I've always been used to having children around."

"I'm afraid I've never really met any."

"You didn't have brothers and sisters?" Gérard asked.

"I'm an only child. I think my parents were, too. I don't know of any cousins."

"You didn't have a family with James?"

"We decided not to start a family immediately. Then work took over."

"Do you miss having children?"

"No. I'm not used to having any family at all."

"Except Charles."

Sarah looked almost startled. "Charles isn't family. We're not even related."

"You're related by marriage; that counts. You care about each other in a way I've seen often, like aunt and nephew, like godmother and godson. It's reciprocal, and it enriches both your lives. Don't discount it."

They'd reached the park. They walked hand in hand to the aviary. As they stopped to watch the antics of the budgerigars, Gérard said, "Sooner or later, we'll have to mention James."

"What do you want to know about him?"

"Where did you meet?"

"First year of university."

"When did you marry?"

"When we both graduated."

"And when you married, you were happy?"

Sarah hesitated. "No," she admitted. "It was always difficult. I thought it was my fault. I tried very hard to make James happy. But I was happier at work, and I spent as much time there as I could."

She swallowed hard and took her hand out of Gérard's.

"You asked me why I re-joined James when we retired. I had a picture of him in my mind from the day I first met him, the man I fell in love with. It was total illusion, but I didn't realise that. I didn't know what he was really like. When we retired here I discovered that he didn't care for me at all, and was solely interested on getting his hands on my money. I still haven't come to terms with being stupid enough to be taken in by him, but I was planning to leave him when he died."

"How were you going to manage that?"

"I'd rented a room from Marie-Pierre to get proof of a different address so that I could open accounts at a new bank. I planned to move my rents, my pension, and my investment income into my new account instead of having them paid into our joint account. For the last bridge club meeting in the month, James would have been away for two hours. My friends volunteered to move my personal possessions and laptop into Marie-Pierre's attic, and I would have withdrawn all the cash out of the joint account, and travelled to a cottage near Biarritz. I'd have been untraceable for weeks even if the police were notified. James' credit card and mobile phone would have been stopped when they weren't paid up. Marie-Pierre would have told me what he did next. I thought he'd go back to England."

"Good planning. Practical and comprehensive. So you weren't sorry when he died?"

"I was very shocked because it happened so suddenly, but in the end it's been a relief."

They followed the path into the park and sat on a bench. Gérard said, "You have a pension, but that will die with you. You own properties and investments, and I'll guess you've left them to Charles?"

"Yes."

"So if you married again, you'd want to retain your rights over the wealth you brought to the marriage, and to eventually leave it to Charles?"

"That's more than one question."

"So it is. I just need to point out that in this country anything to do with money and property becomes complicated by marriage. Under French law if

I die childless my wife will inherit all my property. For example, my house was my grandfather's and I want it to stay in my family. If I die first, I don't want the ownership to pass to you and then to Charles. But I would want you to have the right to live there for your lifetime. That entails a legal change.

"I've invested in numerous small businesses where my shareholding should go to the business owners. But I also hold investments in quoted securities, and I own Participations Lemestre. For both those I would welcome you as an equal partner, as a second opinion in life, and as a beneficiary on my death. So before we could marry, we would have to make precise decisions between ourselves on every item of our joint wealth, and then ask a notary to make any necessary changes to shareholdings and ownership of wealth and rights to usage, before drawing up a suitable marriage contract. The town hall will need the contract to register the marriage."

Sarah was astonished. Gérard seemed prepared to discuss his entire financial situation. She suspected he was far richer than she was, but he was offering joint management of his wealth. He'd mentioned marriage but hadn't asked her to marry him. For the first time, she wondered what he would be like as a husband. Remembering James, she drew in her breath sharply.

"That wasn't a pleasant thought?" asked Gérard.

Sarah said the first thing that came into her head. "Why have you never married?"

"I always expected to, but somehow it didn't happen. My family was controlled by my grandfather. Once my career was established, he suggested suitable brides. I met them all and I chose Mireille. Grandfather talked to her parents, who agreed, so I proposed to Mireille and she accepted. Things had been done like that for hundreds of years. That was how Grandfather had married. He'd been very happy.

"We intended to be engaged for two years, to get to know each other. But eight months later we went to a reception in Dinan, and Mireille fell head over heels for Jean-Jacques Keruan, down on holiday from Paris. She asked her parents to break the engagement. They refused; they wanted an alliance with Grandfather. So Mireille eloped and married Jean-Jacques in Paris. I never saw her again. I know she had a son, but that a year later she divorced Jean-Jacques for adultery. Her parents refused to receive her, a jilt and a divorcee! So she never returned."

"But you see a lot of Jean-Jacques. How do you stay on terms with him?"

"I've known him forever. We were in the same class at the same schools. He's never been a friend, but we know each other well. In business and public life he deserves respect. He was our member of Parliament for ten years and he excelled at representing Breton points of view in Paris and ironing out problems with central government.

"His journalism was of a very high order, truthful and insightful and readable, and his television programmes were superb. Unfortunately his private life consists of falling in and out of love too easily, too quickly and too publicly, so he doesn't fit the role model of a good citizen."

"Did you love Mireille?"

"Not exactly, but I'd imagined a lasting relationship and I'd become fond of her. She didn't deserve what happened. Her parents bear some of the blame, but I think it's obvious I do, too."

"Why didn't you find someone else?"

"Well, I was rather hurt. But it wasn't up to me to find another fiancée. I waited for Grandfather to make further suggestions, but circumstances turned his attention elsewhere.

"My brother Mathieu wanted to marry a girl he'd met at university. Grandfather was not happy with that. He considered love-matches to be disastrous. He always cited my parents as a typical example. He'd had to allow their marriage because my mother was expecting me, but once married they contributed nothing to the family or the business, and they completely ignored their children. Grandfather was my only real parent.

"Agreeing Mathieu's marriage took a year. Agnes' parents lived far away in the Auvergne. They were suspicious of people from a different region, and they too distrusted love-matches. But Mathieu and Agnes opened my eyes. They were, and are, a good partnership, good parents, and quite simply happy.

"They had a two-year engagement, and then at their wedding our sister Severine became interested in one of the Auvergnat guests and Grandfather's attention switched to her. Then Mathieu's first child, Richard, was born. I had a flat in Rennes out of Grandfather's sight, and I settled into a comfortable bachelor existence."

"With no women in it?" Sarah asked.

Gérard smiled reminiscently. "I couldn't claim that. But I didn't meet anyone I wanted to spend the rest of my life with," he paused, "until recently."

Sarah turned to look at him. He was regarding her very seriously. As she watched, his mouth broadened into a smile and automatically she smiled back at him. The kiss was inevitable.

Sarah had never experienced anything which overwhelmed her so completely. When the world stopped spinning round her, she struggled to return to her normal practical stance, but couldn't think what to say or how to behave. Gérard was regarding her with a very satisfied expression. He said, "Tomorrow, perhaps we could make a start on our contract? It might take all day, and there's the social club meeting in the evening."

"Are you going to say anything to the club?"

"Do you want me to?"

"There's nothing to say. You haven't asked me yet."

"I don't have to. If we produce a contract, it's the mayor's job to ask if you agree to marry me on those terms." He was laughing. It was catching. The second kiss was as mind-bending as the first.

Gérard whispered, "This has to stop. Obviously we could spend all day in each other's arms. That promises well for our future, but it's a little inappropriate for a public park. I'm going to take you home, because you'll have to spend hours searching out the paperwork or computer data you'll need for tomorrow. But I'll tell you now, you're everything I've been waiting for." He pulled her to her feet, gave her a quick hug and led the way through the park to the car, and the road home.

27

That evening after dinner, Charles was reading in his hotel room in Finistère, when his mobile rang. "Bonsoir, Charles, this is Gérard Lemestre. Do you have a few minutes?"

"Of course, Gérard. Why are you calling?"

"To let you know that Sarah and I have decided to marry, and to invite you to act as the witness for the bride."

For half a minute Charles couldn't think of a reply.

Gérard said, "I've surprised you."

"You have. Sarah hasn't mentioned you." Charles hesitated. "I'd have expected her to tell me before you did."

"Stop being polite, Charles. Just say straight out what you think."

"I think I don't like it."

"Why not?"

"Because Sarah can be pushed into something she doesn't want. My brother was a complete bully, and Jean-Jacques isn't much better. I've never thought of you like that before, Gérard, but you're very used to getting your own way."

Gérard smiled. "That's true. But you've underestimated Sarah. It is easy to push her into something she doesn't want, but once she realises that's happened, she always engineers a way out. For most of her marriage she didn't live with your brother at all, and when it proved a mistake to have joined him on retirement, she evolved a very practical plan to dump him; he was lucky he died when he did. She escaped from Jean-Jacques without my help; all I did was drive her home. You don't need my assurance that she wants to marry me, because if she doesn't, she simply won't come to the town hall on the day."

"Gérard, Sarah's very special to me, and I'm trying to tell you that I don't want her to be hurt."

"We agree on that, Charles. I've seen her hurt, by your brother, and I'll do anything to prevent that happening to her again."

"I'd still rather talk to Sarah than you."

"That's beginning to worry me. Listen, Charles, if you ask questions, Sarah will give you answers. You'll ask the questions you think are important, and she'll give you the answers she senses you want. By the end of the conversation you'll have pushed her into stating a position she hadn't previously planned to hold. If it's a position she doesn't like, she'll get out of it, but to do so she might have to sever all connection with you. If she loses you, she'll have no family at all. Please don't spoil your relationship. I phoned this evening out of courtesy, because the news will be all over Saint-Edern tomorrow night, but I'm asking you now to wait until Sarah contacts you, in her own way and in her own time. She will, you know that."

There was a long silence before Charles said carefully, "I have to trust you're right. I'll agree not to phone her. But please note that I am expecting you to take proper care of her."

***

Next day, Sarah picked up a briefcase of papers and her laptop and arrived at Gérard's house at nine. She was intrigued by the building's construction. The ground floor on the narrow street consisted of a three-car garage and a good-sized hall with the stairs. The main base of the house was built into the hillside at first floor level, and was four times the size of the ground floor. The second and third floors were the same size as the first.

Seen from the street, there was a line of seven high dormer windows at third floor level, and originally beneath them had been two rows of seven full-length windows on the first and second floors, but on the second floor the original windows had been combined into a single panoramic expanse of glass, which could be slid back in summer to open the room completely to the river view visible over the roof of the building opposite. The house bore a street number, but no name. It was discreetly faced with polished pale grey granite, but all the window frames, shutters and external doors were bright Breton blue.

On the way up the stairs, Sarah passed a dining area on the first floor. She found that the panoramic widows on the second floor lit a viewing lounge which also housed Gérard's computer and printer. There were obviously other rooms at the back on each floor. But despite being clean and tidy, the house looked neglected. The furniture and decorations hadn't changed for fifty years.

Sarah and Gérard discussed their joint finances in the lounge for the whole working day, apart from coffee breaks in the kitchen, and lunch in Philippe's café-bar. Gerald explained the way French law differentiates between ownership of property and the right to use it. He then recommended some legal changes to the company managing Sarah's properties and more changes to her investments, to provide a more tax-efficient way of eventually leaving them to Charles.

They then started working through Gérard's investments and business. Besides earning a good salary, Gérard had inherited family money, and hadn't let it lie dormant. He'd made loans to individual Breton entrepreneurs and taken shareholdings in local companies. He held internationally quoted shares and investment funds. But primarily he owned Participations Lemestre, which built and renovated local housing and commercial projects, and rented out industrial properties. Sarah was overwhelmed to think that Gérard was offering her an equal shareholding in this complex organisation, and she was indeed very interested in the way it was administered.

The list of required changes to ownership was long and involved, but after that the marriage contract and their new wills would be relatively simple. They finished in time to share an early dinner in a small restaurant, until it was time for the social club.

At the club, Gérard normally sat with a group of unattached men. Sarah normally sat with Marie-Pierre and Elodie, and insisted they keep to this arrangement. Gérard agreed, and they parted at Sarah's door. He went on to the club and she returned her documents and laptop to their home.

Sarah entered the club room at the last minute to find that Marie-Pierre had saved her seat. After discussion about watching a carriage-horse competition or a kite-surfing championship, the clement weather led the members to vote for a scenic walk through a forest to an ancient alignment of menhirs with a small museum and a good café, and then on around the shores of a lake.

As the members began to decide who would travel in whose car, Gérard rose to his feet, moved into the middle of the room and clapped his hands loudly until he gained everyone's attention. Sarah surprised her friends by blushing rosily. Gérard walked over to her chair, took her hand and invited her to stand next to him. He turned to the audience with a triumphant smile and said simply, "Mesdames, messieurs, I have the honour to present to you my future wife."

The club members erupted into a round of applause. Beneath her smile, Sarah said to Gérard, "I think you're trying to ensure I can't back down."

"But of course I am. Has it worked?" he asked, smiling back.

When they were walking home she thought of someone else. "I'll need to tell Charles," she said. "I can't let him hear gossip from the club."

"He knows already," her escort replied. "I phoned him last night. It was an interesting conversation. A man twenty years younger than myself told me to look after you properly." Gérard sounded amused at the irony. "But he will act as the witness for the bride."

Sarah tensed, suddenly realising that she might face questions from Charles, and that she hadn't yet rationalised her feelings enough to reply.

"I telephoned Jean-Jacques last night as well, to put a stop to him escorting you around in public. And I phoned my brother Mathieu and my sister Severine, who are now both intent on finding ways to meet you."

Sarah hadn't thought of Gérard's family at all. "I would like to meet them," she said tentatively, "but could you tell me a little about them first?" Her hand on Gérard's arm betrayed her increasing tenseness.

As they reached her building, Gérard said, "Please let me into the hall. I don't want to speak to you in the open street." They walked in together.

"What did you want to say?" Sarah asked.

Gérard put his hands on her shoulders. "That Charles and my family have to be told as a matter of courtesy, but that I don't care what they think or how they react. My life now centres around you. And at this moment you aren't happy." He bent his head to kiss her gently on her cheek and said, "My dear, I love you with all my heart."

Tears streamed down Sarah's face as the tension dissolved. It was some minutes before she could be persuaded to let Gérard leave.

***

On Thursday morning, Gérard rang to say he'd arranged a meeting with a notary that afternoon. He drove Sarah to the lawyer's office at two o'clock, and at the end of a long afternoon they had the printed confirmations of changes to property ownership and usage rights, two new wills and their signed copies of the marriage contract.

On Friday morning they went to the town hall in Saint-Malo and applied for registration of their marriage, booking 27th December for the official ceremony. That was far enough ahead for Sarah to meet Gérard's family beforehand, and for Gérard to book a honeymoon over New Year.

That evening Gérard hosted a dinner in a prestigious restaurant in Saint-Malo so that Sarah could meet his younger brother, Mathieu – who would act as the bridegroom's witness – and Mathieu's wife, Agnes.

Mathieu bore no resemblance at all to Gérard except in height, but the brothers were only five years apart and obviously very close. Mathieu was a qualified veterinary surgeon who'd progressed to running a large agricultural practice in Corseul, and had now, approaching retirement, become a consultant for the Ministry of Agriculture. There wasn't a useful animal species from cattle to chickens for which he couldn't tell a good story or reel off statistics. He was warmly welcoming and entertaining company.

Mathieu's wife Agnes was also a qualified vet, but she'd become interested in Breton wool embroidery, and in recent years her hobby had taken over from her job. She owned an atelier which made uniforms for Breton bands and dancers, and spectacular embroidered dresses and jackets for popular singers. Agnes wore one of her own creations to the dinner, a dark brown wild silk jacket embroidered in fine wool with hydrangeas in shades of blue and green on one shoulder and down the sleeve, with one flower head on the opposite cuff. Sarah was immediately interested, and the two women easily made friends.

As the coffee was served, Mathieu leaned back in his chair and said, "I presume you two are going to live in Grandfather's house?"

"You're a bit in advance of us," Gérard replied, "We haven't discussed that yet."

"Mon dieu, what do you talk about all day?" Mathieu said, grinning at his elder brother.

"We have found other topics of conversation," Gérard said evenly. "Do you have a reason for asking?"

"I do. Between you, you have one property too many. My son, Richard, has taken a surgical consultancy at Saint-Malo Hospital from January, so he needs to buy something suitable for his family and for entertaining his new colleagues."

"Well," Gérard began, as if considering, "I live in the largest private house in Saint-Edern, and Sarah has a magnificently large penthouse which is unique in the town. Richard couldn't do better than purchasing one of them. Of course, both properties would be very expensive due to their size and their panoramic views over the river, and also due to the ten per cent surcharge for selling within the family."

"After the twenty per cent discount for Richard being your godson."

The two men managed this exchange with straight faces, but Agnes and Sarah collapsed into laughter.

Gérard looked at Sarah and said, "Are you prepared to give in to this blackmail?"

"You aren't going to move out of your house, are you, Gérard?"

"I'm afraid not."

"So we could sell mine."

"If you really mean that."

"I do. It makes more sense than hanging on to it, and you'd like your family living nearby."

Gérard picked up her hand and kissed it. "Mathieu, you'd better tell Richard to bring his wife to see Sarah's penthouse before any of Severine's family decide to bid for it."

Gérard drove Sarah back to Saint-Edern, parked in his garage and started to accompany her home. "Are you really willing to give up your flat?" he asked. "I'm relying on gossip, but I've been told your lounge is more spectacular than mine and that you have some very large pieces of good furniture which might not fit into my house."

"I'm very proud of the penthouse, because I put a lot of work into it, but I bought it for James. I wouldn't have chosen it for myself. James chose the furniture as well. I'd have preferred modern, so I won't miss it. But I haven't seen much of your house yet."

"Do you like what you have seen?"

"The general design is fascinating, but it badly needs renovating. Especially that 1950s kitchen."

"You cook?"

"It's my favourite hobby. I like trying out recipes."

They'd reached Sarah's building. Gérard said, "Would you mind if I came up and looked round? I think I'll soon be discussing an equitable price with my nephew."

"Of course. It's probably not very tidy."

Sarah gave him an estate agent's tour of the property, but identifying where she'd moved walls to create the huge master bedroom and the vast lounge-diner. She said, "If this flat is now intended to house a family, those walls should be replaced."

"I'd agree with that, but I won't like destroying your work. This is a superb achievement. I really hope you have a similar effect on Grandfather's house. I've never really known what to do with it. We'll certainly have to replace the entire kitchen to the standard of this one."

Sarah was suddenly hit by a total loss of confidence. "I'm not a real cook. I'm only self-taught from magazines. It's just a hobby. I can't possibly compete with a trained chef."

Gérard put his arms around her and kissed her gently. "Tonight was a special occasion. I don't want five-star food and waiter service every day. I eat very often in Philippe Poisson's café, as you well know. He's not a trained chef either, but he produces a decent lunch. Is your cooking equal to his?"

"I think so."

"Then if you want to cook lunch, I'll be happy to eat it. And if you don't, we'll take what Philippe offers, or go to the bar-tabac or one of the little restaurants in town. I'd like my wife to have the best equipment available to use, but I don't want her tied to the kitchen when she doesn't want to be, and I don't want her pushed into doing something she doesn't enjoy."

In his arms Sarah turned and buried her face in his shoulder.

"Whatever have I said?"

"I'm sorry," she sobbed in English, "I'm not used to anyone being so nice to me."

For half-an-hour Gérard had been remembering James, and now his temper rose with a force he wasn't expecting. He replied in English, "I'm not being nice. I love you," then kissed Sarah hard and passionately, attempting to tell her beyond language how much she meant to him. Sarah surprised him by responding with equal passion. They were standing next to the large leather sofa, and it was simply instinctive to collapse on to the cushions. What followed next was everything Gérard had ever dreamed of.

***

Afterwards, while balancing overwhelming joy against feeling slightly ashamed of himself, Gérard became extremely worried about Sarah. He was sure that he'd carried her with him, but now she was tense, and she wouldn't look at him. He tried feathering adoring kisses along her cheeks. He turned her face towards him and kissed her warmly on her mouth. Her eyes slid away. Something was badly wrong. He gently withdrew from the kiss.

As his lips left hers, she buried her head in his shoulder and said, "I'm sorry, I'm not very good at it."

For several heartbeats he was lost for words. Then he said softly, "Sarah, that's the first time you've ever lied to me." He felt the change in her as she registered his meaning. He kissed the top of her head and whispered, "My dear heart, I love you. I love being with you. I love the feel of you in my arms like this. And I loved making love to you."

The tenseness was still there, but it had changed. "Gérard," she started, but couldn't find words to continue.

"Sarah," Gérard said with a smile in his voice, "I know I shouldn't have allowed that to happen, but for me, it was like discovering paradise. And I think you enjoyed it a little?" He felt her nod. "So, we love each other, and we make love beautifully, and we have all the rest of our lives to enjoy being together." He felt the last of the tension go, and he lifted her head to face him. Her eyes were full of tears. She blinked hard to clear them. They looked at each other seriously for half a minute, and then Gérard smiled, and miraculously Sarah smiled back.

Delighted, he said, "Now, suppose we move to a comfortable bed, and do that all over again?" To his surprise she giggled. He laughed, and kissed her for minutes before he found the strength of mind to move to a proper mattress.

***

Over an early-morning coffee in the kitchen on Saturday, Gérard said, in his most business-like voice, "We need to agree what happens next. If you want to live here until the wedding, I can't object. If you want me to keep my distance in future, I'll ensure that I do that. But what I really want is to take you with me when I go home this morning."

"I'd prefer to come with you," Sarah said in her most practical voice. "There's a lot of work that needs to be done in your house."

"That too," Gérard grinned at her and she laughed back, delighting him.

Sarah packed essentials quickly, took her cases to her car, and drove it up the street to Gérard's garage. Gérard then took Sarah on a tour of her new home. It was idiosyncratically arranged. On the first floor, alongside the dining area which was open to the stairs, were the kitchen, the laundry room, a wine cellar, and a library which Gérard said had been his parent's bedroom. There was a paved terrace alongside the library, accessible through tall windows, exposed to the afternoon sun, but completely empty of plants or furniture. On the second floor, behind the lounge with the panoramic view, was a huge master bedroom with a large en-suite bathroom and a sizeable dressing room. The east-facing back windows overlooked the flowering bushes clinging to someone else's hillside. On the third floor was a motley collection of spare bedrooms and one bathroom.

They spent the morning measuring and re-planning the kitchen, and the afternoon searching for a new one. They finally found a specialist prepared to start work the next Tuesday, for a steep price, but Gérard was prepared to pay it. Sarah happily commenced measuring the rest of the rooms, drawing plans, and planning renovation of the entire house. It would be a sizeable project just to re-decorate, and she'd already decided to insert a lift into the stairwell.

On Sunday they joined the social club walking through the woods. Sarah quietly enjoyed the felicitations of her friends, and Gérard was amused by her criticism of the noticeboards at the megalithic site. She took their small defects seriously enough to take photographs and make notes for contacting the relevant authority.

On Monday morning Sarah went shopping before cooking her first lunch in her new home. She deliberately kept it simple: a first course of pineapple, apple, cheese and broccoli in a vinaigrette followed by fillets of John Dory in orange butter sauce, but despite wrestling with the seventy-year-old kitchen equipment she was as confident and competent as she'd only previously been when at work, and Gérard's appreciation made her day.

That afternoon she thought of getting in touch with Charles. She emailed:

'I believe Gérard has told you that we intend to marry, and has asked you to be my witness. We've arranged the registration at Saint-Malo Town Hall on 27th December with a few family present: Gérard's brother Mathieu and his wife Agnes, Gérard's sister Severine and her husband Nicolas, you and Deborah and Clark. There'll be a huge party afterwards at the Hotel Château Malouine with half Saint-Malo present. I do hope to see you there.'

It looked stilted, but she couldn't think how else to put it.

Ten minutes later Charles rang her phone. "Sarah, thanks for getting in touch. I've only got one question. Are you happy?"

"Yes," she said prosaically without thinking, and then with a smile in her voice, "Yes, yes, yes and yes."

"That sounds as if you're in love."

"I believe I am."

"Sarah, I'm so happy for you. I'll be proud to witness for you, and I wish you all the joy you deserve."

"Thank you."

"Is Gérard going to move into that fantastic penthouse of yours?"

"No, I'm selling it to his nephew. I'm going to renovate his house instead."

"Ciel! That'll keep you busy. I saw it a few months ago; very interesting layout, but everything was astonishingly old-fashioned."

"Especially the kitchen. It should be in a museum. I can't wait to see it being ripped out tomorrow. It was quite tricky today just cooking a simple lunch."

Charles said tentatively, "That sounds as if you've moved in?"

Sarah used her flattest voice. "There's no way to get a house into shape except by living on the premises." They both burst out laughing at the same moment.

28

On Tuesday the kitchen fitters arrived early to commence dismantling the kitchen. Sarah had already stacked the kitchen contents in the library, and instructed the fitters to move the old kitchen table there and put the microwave oven, coffee-maker and kettle on it. A rudimentary lunch would have been possible, but Gérard insisted that they eat in the bar-tabac.

As they left, new hardwood flooring was being laid, and the lorry parked in front of the house was using its integral crane to winch the old kitchen out through the dining-room windows. When they returned a second lorry had just finished hoisting in the new equipment. The basic kitchen was complete by nightfall. Lighting and tiling were scheduled for the next day, but the cupboards and worktops were all in place and the fridge, freezer, sinks, dishwasher, ovens, microwaves and hotplates were in working order. Sarah triumphantly produced a ham and courgette risotto and a cherry clafoutis to prove it.

On Wednesday the tiler and lighting technician arrived, and Sarah left for the furniture warehouses. She regarded ergonomic furniture as absolutely necessary for using a computer, and intended to replace the table and dining chair Gérard used for his computer work. She ordered two matching desks, two top-of-the-range adjustable chairs, a printer table and filing drawers, and then asked for the quickest delivery.

"I regret that Saturday is the earliest I can arrange," said the salesman. Accepting that, Sarah gave the number and street of the address in Saint-Edern. "Any special instructions for finding it?" the seller asked.

"Everyone calls it the Lemestre house," said Sarah.

The salesman's expression changed instantly. "Excuse me a minute, madame," he said, disappearing into an office before returning to say, "We can deliver in two hours, madame." Sarah was almost shocked at the effect of Gérard's name.

By noon, the kitchen was complete. Since Gérard was lunching with his building manager, Sarah ate a quick snack in Philippe Poisson's café before spending the afternoon installing the two computers on their new desks. She produced a light supper of haddock and mushroom galette followed by a pear, cucumber and mint dessert, before she and Gérard attended the social club.

With the essential changes out of the way, Sarah started on detailed planning for the rest of the house. She couldn't see the need to move walls on the first and second floors, but the third floor layout didn't appeal at all. If she wanted to invite guests, they would have to be housed up there. Thinking she'd rather pay for Deborah and Clark to stay in a good hotel, she thought of creating hotel-style suites on the third floor.

Shamelessly copying all the best ideas she'd seen while living in hotels herself, she used up half a pad of paper finalising the design of three palatial suites, each with two bedrooms, a sitting room and a bathroom, two with river views, one facing east.

It was obvious to her that the third floor was the place to start renovating the house. Once it was finished she and Gérard could move there while the second floor lounge and bedroom underwent rewiring, repainting, recarpeting and refurnishing, and while the master bathroom was replaced entirely. But the third floor renovation would complete more efficiently if the planned lift was installed beforehand. She explained all this to Gérard over dinner. He spent the meal enjoying her enthusiasm and her ideas, but he was impressed by her planning. When she asked him how long it would take to get a lift installed, he laughed. "Ten weeks minimum," he said. "But I'll see what I can do."

Next day, Gérard asked his usual elevator sub-contractor to install a four-storey lift in the house within a week. Once the installer was convinced that his normally rational client was serious, he agreed to use the parts of a four-storey lift which had been delivered, but not yet assembled, at one of Participations Lemestre's new warehouse complexes. He switched his best crew from their current task and sent them to the house accompanied by enough extra hands to speed the work. They completed in four days. The resulting lift had industrial-style doors, but more elegant replacements were on order, as was the replacement warehouse lift. The head mechanism protruded slightly above the old roof level, but Gérard had already drafted in a team to change the roofline.

Inside the house during that week, Sarah oversaw the demolition of all the third floor walls, and then the rewiring and re-plumbing required. The first materials carried in the new lift were for building the suite walls, followed by the bathroom fittings and new double-glazing units for all the dormer windows. After another week painters, tilers and paper hangers were hard at work, and in the fourth week the guest-room furniture arrived ready for assembly.

Walking round the three guest suites at the end of an action filled month, Gérard was hard put to recall the jumble of little rooms they'd replaced. Sarah's choice of paint and wallpaper was striking but not obtrusive, and the furniture was the most modern in the house. Gérard and Sarah moved into a guest suite as work began on the second floor.

That paid off. The third floor had become luxurious, but over the next four weeks the second floor lounge became utterly magnificent. Its panoramic river view was balanced by dark green walls displaying Sarah's paintings from the penthouse and newly cleaned canvasses of Gérard's inheritance. The old armchairs were replaced with an extensive collection of modern, pastel coloured, leather units which could be re-arranged to suit the gathering. An efficient office was tucked into a back corner, but with the desk chairs facing the view. Out of site behind the lounge, the renovated master-bedroom suite was sumptuous and the replacement bathroom palatial.

But Gérard was impressed by more than the renovations. The workmen were his direct employees and sub-contractors, but Sarah had directed their work personally. They must have known that the marriage hadn't yet taken place, but even when talking among themselves without realising he could hear, they always referred to Sarah as Madame Lemestre, and with respect.

Once the renovations were underway, Sarah had turned her attention to the office systems of Participations Lemestre, but although she immediately outlined improvements, for these she intended to pace the changes slowly so that the office staff had time to assimilate each one before the next was installed.

Sarah's energy, and her habit of making systems and workers perform at their best, were as welcome in Gérard's professional life as the warmth she'd brought into his personal life. He'd seen the marriage as a second chance for both of them to find a mutual domestic happiness, but now he realised the welcome change would extend into both their working lives.

***

In the middle of the second floor renovations Gérard's sister phoned with an invitation to spend a weekend with her in the Auvergne. Severine and her husband, Nicolas Gaultier, lived in a large farmhouse, but they had two children and five grandchildren, who would be with them at the half-term weekend. Gérard decided that it would be a little crowded and uncoordinated, and not quite the right setting for Sarah's first meeting with Severine.

Instead he suggested staying in a hotel in Clermont-Ferrand, inviting Severine and Nicholas to dinner there on Saturday, and then visiting the farmhouse for the Gaultier family's Sunday lunch. Sarah wanted to meet Gérard's sister and brother-in-law, but also welcomed the opportunity of seeing the whole Auvergne family and Severine's home. When Severine agreed to his plan, Gérard told Sarah that they would drive to the Auvergne on Friday afternoon and spend Saturday showing her the area.

Sarah found the trip fascinating. The Auvergne countryside is unique, since it was once, many thousands of years ago, covered in volcanoes. The grander eruptions resulted in huge spectacular hills, and smaller ones produced collections of extinct volcanoes of a domestic size, many less than knee high, scattered in the corners of fields or in gardens among the autumn daisies. Many local buildings were built in black volcanic stone. Gérard took Sarah for a scenic drive on Saturday morning, and in the afternoon they enjoyed the spectacular museum dedicated to volcanology.

On Saturday evening they hosted Severine and Nicolas to dinner in the hotel. The Gaultiers were an entirely different couple to Mathieu and Agnes. Both were qualified lawyers. Nicholas was an advocate in court and Severine, who looked very like Gérard, was senior legal advisor for the regional prefecture. They both had razor-sharp minds. For a few minutes Sarah found Severine very difficult to deal with, until Gérard bluntly told his sister, "Stop cross-questioning. Sarah isn't in court." Severine burst out laughing and apologised gracefully, but she didn't entirely stop firing questions.

On Sunday, Severine displayed a completely different side to her character, serving a good country dinner cooked by herself and her daughter-in-law, in the chaos of a farmhouse full to bursting with adults and children. She took part good-naturedly with Gérard in her grandchildren's games on the lawn while Sarah talked to Nicolas, who'd undertaken to introduce her to all the family one by one, giving a potted history of each of them first. Sarah left for home feeling, not so much that she'd successfully coped with Gérard's family, but that she'd joined it. She could certainly now see the point of the big French family wedding which re-affirms the ties uniting everyone who attends it.

***

But one outstanding family matter had been bothering Gérard for some weeks. The next Monday, he telephoned Brendan O'Donnell and asked if Charles was in the office. "He is indeed," O'Donnell confirmed, "but there's a little matter of finance for publicity being finalised this morning. It's the Paris-Metro posters, and it'll be worth buying a ticket to Paris just to see them. So if it's talking to him you intend, I'd recommend the end of the afternoon when everything's signed off."

"I'll take your advice," Gérard said, and went on to discuss his company's partial renovation of the old house in Morlaix to which Brendan intended to retire next year.

At five o'clock, Charles' mobile rang and the name Lemestre showed on screen. He answered it while immediately moving into a discussion room in search of privacy. He sat in an armchair just as they finished the usual round of polite greetings, and then heard Gérard say, "I'm phoning to invite you to dine with me this evening."

Taken aback, Charles said, as smoothly as he could, "I'm not sure that's possible."

"I'm sure you can make it possible."

Mentally chastising himself for not preparing for this conversation despite deliberately avoiding Gérard for over a month, Charles tried the weak argument, "I'm not really hungry enough for dinner, I'm afraid. I've only just finished a late lunch, and it was a bit of a celebration."

"That's good news for me as it happens. Sarah served a rather splendid curry for lunch today, so I feel the same. I thought we could have a light supper at Valery's, the fish restaurant next to the Opera. At seven-thirty?"

Gérard was obviously determined, and if he was going to be a problem it would be best to face him. "Thank you for the invitation," Charles said politely. "I'll be there."

When Charles arrived, Gérard was already ensconced in the back corner behind the screen of plants. He was sitting with his back to the wall and the only other chair had its back to the other wall of the corner, the table being laid for two people almost side by side. Gérard had already ordered one of the fixed menus for both of them, so almost as soon as Charles was seated a waiter discreetly delivered the starter, rolls of crab, quinoa, spices and herbs wrapped in smoked salmon.

When the waiter left, Gérard said, "It's nearly two months since we had any sort of conversation, Charles, or even a casual meeting at the social club. I believe that to be deliberate on your part?"

Charles didn't attempt to contest the truth.

"It's a personal disappointment to me, because I like your company, but what worries me far more is that you've also distanced yourself from Sarah. She's been too busy ripping my house apart to realise it yet, but very soon she'll notice, and she'll be hurt. I don't want to see that."

Charles was deeply uneasy, and looked it. He picked his words carefully. "You and Sarah have been very good to me. I'm grateful to you both. But there are other considerations." Gérard looked a query. "The major one is Monsieur Le Quennac. He's extraordinarily sensitive where you're concerned, and he is my regional director."

"Are you enjoying working for Max?"

"Yes. Very much."

Gérard smiled approval. "Max is very astute. He always runs a good office, and he's obviously discovered how to harness your creative talent. This afternoon the regional prefect described the Paris-Metro poster campaign as a splendid collaborative effort by the pair of you."

Charles hesitated. "I don't think we should be discussing that. Le Quennac wouldn't like it."

"You're reading him wrong, Charles. Max would be delighted that I know how well his office is performing. When we worked together, he saw himself very much as the second-in-command, and that's why I've tried to keep out of his way since my retirement, to hand over control. It was unfortunate that Erwan had other ideas. He kept involving me, and always on the assumption that I'd support him against Max. I couldn't persuade Erwan to see reason, so I ensured that he moved to Paris, where they'll soon teach him how to work and how to behave. I'll admit he's soured relations between me and Max on occasion, but now I've kicked him out that won't happen again."

Charles was shaken to realise that what O'Donnell had seen as a promotion ploy by Erwan had been engineered by Gérard without Erwan being aware of it.

Gérard continued, "For me, your appearance on scene was sheer luck. I thought you looked as if you had the potential to work with Max. I could see your management skills, and your gift for handling people, but I'm afraid I simply didn't notice your creativity. When O'Donnell told me about the poster of beer bottles, I was taken aback to realise how far your imagination outclasses mine. Obviously Max is happy to use that skill. I've never quite lost my affection for the Tourism Office, and you've done far better for it than I could have wished, and sooner than I expected. You deserve your promotion."

"Thank you."

"Max won't object to you lunching with me occasionally, or meeting me at social events."

Charles frowned, but he could now contrast O'Donnell's views with Gérard's real regard for Max and his careful distancing himself from tourism despite continuing involvement with the prefecture. "I think you may be right in that. But that's not my only problem." He looked directly at Gérard. "The fact is, Gérard, you're way out of my league, and so is Sarah."

"You mean we have more money?"

"It's more than that. I've only recently realised how much Sarah is worth, but to me, the fortune she's earned is a measure of the person she is. When I asked who you were, you quoted your old prefecture rank, but you have influence well beyond that, and although you were given a fortune you've practically trebled it. I don't live in the same universe as you two."

The waiter replaced their plates with gingered scallops accompanied by asparagus and artichoke puree.

"When I first met you," Gérard said, "you were confident and adventurous."

"I was on holiday, Gérard. I had no responsibilities and I wasn't taking anything seriously."

"Why should you now? You're hardly halfway through your working life. Don't measure yourself against anyone who's had more time to accumulate wealth and standing, or who started with more than you did."

Charles hesitated. "You do know what Sarah's doing for me?"

"Sarah doesn't hide anything, Charles. She's paying half the cost of your flat, and you're the residual heir under her will. Those are her own decisions, even if I do support her in them. But they mean you owe something to Sarah, Charles, and you should acknowledge it, openly. When Sarah joins my family, you'll join it with her."

"It's not so simple."

"It is, Charles. You didn't come to Brittany by accident, did you? You came because Sarah was here and because you feel a strong connection between the two of you. It's a connection Sarah values and wants to continue. I believe your official godmother died years ago, but Sarah attended your christening and she's decided to take on the role. She's told the whole of my family that you're her godson, because that's a connection all of them understand, a responsibility creating a type of kinship, an explanation for her treating you as if you were part of her family. It isn't a lie; that's how she sees you, and that's the role she wants you to accept.

"Godparent is something I know well; I'm Richard's godfather. Even in Richard's privileged upbringing that's proved useful to him, and it's given us a relationship we both value. I want you to accept Sarah as your godmother, Charles. Be honest with yourself; acknowledge the link between you."

Charles' mind flew back to a Saturday in Chichester, to Sarah listening, to Sarah suggesting he could forge a better future. "It's been there since the day we met. But I owe her so much, and there's no way to repay her."

"Charles, she has no family and you're young enough to be her son. There'd be a yawning gap in her life if you didn't exist. She's interested in you. She's helped to establish you. She needs to know how you're doing, what you're doing, what interests you're pursuing. Simply talking to her will enrich her life. That's the repayment I'm asking for. It will be easy to do; you can just come to the social club every so often. You won't be able to attend every Wednesday and every weekend, but you can do so often enough to keep Sarah happy."

Charles hesitated. "You're quite sure I wouldn't be pushing myself into Sarah's life?"

"I'd say it was the other way about, that Sarah pushed herself into your life whether you wanted that or not." Gérard was grinning widely.

Charles laughed in response. "She rocked my life to its foundations, Gérard. It was shattering."

"You should see my house these days," said Gérard. "It's suffering the same treatment. But when Sarah decides to put something right, the result is beyond imagination, n'est-ce pas?"

Charles relaxed suddenly. Over the raspberry mousse he described his vision for changing Gérard's standard publicity to focus on the exact result required from each poster campaign or exhibition, and was even encouraged to float ideas for using tourism to finance rejuvenation of small fishing ports.

But over coffee, Gérard said seriously, "There is something else I'd like to say, Charles. You're still very new to Brittany. You're living in a foreign culture with a different language and different social nuances. You need someone you can talk to about anything whatsoever, and I do mean anything; someone to tell you how life works here. Things that your father or your godfather would have told you if you'd been born Breton. Sarah's been good to you, and she'll continue to be, but a woman and a foreigner can't help you in the way I can. I'm offering to act as if I was your godfather."

Taken completely by surprise, Charles closed his eyes while mentally reviewing the number of dilemmas that might solve. He said tentatively, "I believe I'd welcome that, Gérard."

"I certainly would. What's your best day of the week to meet for lunch?"

"At the moment, Friday."

"Then we'll meet at noon next Friday. But if you need to talk before that, phone or email, don't hesitate."

As Gérard shook hands with Charles outside the restaurant he felt satisfied that he could now pass on to him the benefits which Sarah had brought to him.

29

Sarah had arranged to put the penthouse back into its original condition by using some of Gérard's employees to re-erect the walls. She'd already re-used her dressing room fittings in the third floor suites of the Lemestre house, returning the dressing-room to bedroom status. She'd moved two sideboards and all her artworks to Gérard's house. But there was still a quantity of antique furniture in place, as well as the curtains, carpets, lighting fixtures, bathroom and kitchen equipment.

Gérard's nephew, Richard, spent the autumn half-term weekend with his father, Mathieu, and arranged to view the penthouse with his wife, Solin, on the Saturday. When he arrived, he immediately headed for the lounge windows and said, "Aunt Sarah, this is magnificent. I'll hardly need a television with this to look at."

Sarah looked at Gérard. "Is this the point at which I double the price," she asked innocently, "or should I wait until they've seen the kitchen?"

Richard grinned delightedly. "It's going to be good living near your sense of humour, Aunt Sarah," he said. "Now what's this about the kitchen?" Sarah showed it off, detailing the equipment, which had been installed to suit the use of caterers for parties, and advised that she could recommend a local caterer.

They moved on to the enormous bathroom. That didn't find favour with Solin at all. "For a family of four, this is wasted space," she said. "Is there any way it could be divided up?"

"I hadn't thought of that," Sarah said apologetically. "To start with, I know there's plumbing, under the floor and currently unused, for an en-suite shower-room and toilet inside the main bedroom. I can also see how to divide this room into a bathroom and a shower-room and at least two separate toilets. Is that enough?"

"That would be pure heaven," said Solin. "In Paris we have one shower and one toilet and four people who get up at the same time every morning."

Sarah made notes of the requirement. "Do you need any other changes?" she asked.

Solin had never rearranged a flat before, but she was learning fast. "Yes, the dining room. It's too large for family meals. Is it possible to divide it into two so that the boys could have a room of their own?"

Sarah agreed immediately and made another note. Gérard sighed theatrically.

"Are we causing you a problem, Uncle Gérard?" said Richard.

"Not at all. I like my entire workforce working for nothing just to please my family."

"Glad to hear it!" Richard responded disrespectfully.

But the penthouse was very much larger than Richard and Solin's Paris flat, and Richard clearly saw its status and entertainment possibilities, besides its domestic comfort. Sarah was sure that she could organise the work to finish before Christmas; she would engage a house-clearance company to remove the furniture no longer required, but agreed to leave behind three antique cabinets which Richard very much admired.

Gérard and Richard went out on to the terrace for a last look at the view. Sarah knew that Solin worked in a Paris pharmacy, and she took the opportunity to ask, "Will you be looking for a job here?"

Solin hesitated. She said, "I originally qualified as a dentist. But it's been difficult to find a permanent place in a dental clinic, so I changed to working as a pharmaceutical assistant."

Sarah could sense more than Solin was saying. She said, "There are plenty of dentists here already, but it takes far too long to get an appointment, so obviously we need more. I'm sure that you could find a dental position in Saint-Malo."

Solin was blinking away tears. "People don't always want to employ a foreigner," she said.

Sarah suddenly realised the significance of Solin's shining black hair, suntanned skin and dark eyes. "You weren't born in France?" she asked.

"I was," said Solin, "and I'm French by birth, but my parents aren't. They came from Iran. We're Yazidi. My parents fled persecution and ended with nothing. They sacrificed so much to get me to medical school in Paris, but I keep meeting people who don't want me around."

"Well, I'm a real foreigner," said Sarah stoutly, "I wasn't even born in France. I have to say I didn't get on all that well with Parisians, but I've had no trouble here. Don't give up your profession. I do know one local dentist, and I'll start looking for vacancies if you'd like me to."

Out on the terrace, Gérard, who'd been puzzled by Richard moving to Saint-Malo instead of following through his successful career start in Paris, had prised the same story out of him. Solin had given up her job as a dental surgeon when a newcomer to the large practice didn't want to work with her, and previously suppressed prejudices had then surfaced among other surgeons and technicians. The pharmacy who then employed her had also treated her with less consideration than their other staff, and Richard was now so sensitive to the issue that he thought he could see problems starting at his sons' school, because the boys had combined the Lemestre face with their mother's eyes, hair and skin.

"The capital isn't always a comfortable place to live," Gérard agreed. "But I wouldn't expect to see that attitude here. You won't have any trouble with the boys if you're sending them to College Philippe Keiffer. I know the headmaster well, and he employs his staff for their excellence at teaching rather than their ancestry, so you'll find they're an interesting mix in themselves. His pupils have roots in every place Bretons ever sailed to. And in this area the name Lemestre counts."

***

On Tuesday Sarah telephoned Doctor Beaumont and asked if it was possible to meet her for lunch. When the two women were comfortably ensconced in a small café enjoying their salads, Sarah explained that Gérard's nephew was joining the hospital as a surgeon in January, and that his wife was a qualified dentist looking for a job in Saint-Malo.

"I'd heard a Lemestre had taken that post," Hélène said, immediately interested, "but I didn't know his wife was a dentist. Do you have any details on her?"

"I have an old CV," Sarah said, unearthing from her handbag the one she'd printed from an internet recruitment site.

"Well, that looks perfectly normal," Hélène said. "Why hasn't she just replied to my adverts? I've run one every three months for the last year in our professional journal."

"Because there's a history of racial discrimination. She lost her last dental job because of it," said Sarah. "She's French, born here, educated here, but her parents came from Iran, and she does look Middle Eastern."

"Long thick black hair and beautiful big dark eyes?" Hélène sighed.

"Exactly."

"I'm jealous already," Hélène smiled, her fine mouse-brown hair pulled into a tiny bun and her grey eyes twinkling behind glasses. "But in the practice we judge colleagues by their work, and if she can do the work, we can take her on. We have an empty surgery, and we're turning patients away because there's no one to treat them."

"So how do I get her to interview with you?"

Hélène produced her business card and said, "Tell her to send me an up-to-date CV. Tell her to be completely honest and tell me what she's doing now and why, exactly how long it is since she practised dentistry and what type of work she did then. I'll arrange for her to be interviewed by at least two of us in the practice, preferably all three. We'd all be prepared to help the right candidate get back into the profession. It would be worth the effort because someone with a husband and children fixed in Saint-Malo could well be working with us for years. It's just a question of fitting in. We're a pretty mixed bunch already. I'm Breton born with one Canadian parent and went to medical school in Lyon; one colleague is Spanish, educated in Toulouse in France, but trained in Florida USA; and the other is Belgian but trained in Berlin. We're not exactly narrow-minded Paris-establishment types, and nor are our patients."

Sarah emailed Solin with everything she'd learnt, and two weeks later Solin was interviewed by all three dentists in Hélène's practice, and was taken on for a start in the second week of January.

Meanwhile an architect had drawn up plans for the extra work on the penthouse, and Gérard had put a senior foreman in charge of the work, which finished only one day later than hoped, probably due to Sarah visiting every four hours to solve problems.

Sarah hadn't ceased work on the Lemestre house. By mid-December she'd had the dining area completely re-organised, new lighting installed, wallpaper and carpeting renewed, and all the dining chairs replaced. She'd kept the useful old expanding table but had it professionally re-polished, and she'd installed the two antique sideboards from the penthouse to hold her collection of small modern sculptures.

She invited Richard, Solin and their sons, Armel and Cornély, for a weekend to get to know Saint-Edern. For dinner on the Saturday night she invited the whole Le Quennac family: Max, Hélène and their sons, Malo and Péran. Within a few minutes it was discovered that Armel was about to join Péran's class at school. Max and Hélène promptly invited Richard and his family to the Le Bras family New Year celebration in Château Le Bras, and when Hélène discovered that would leave Solin's parents alone on New Year's Eve, she invited them as well. Far from despising foreigners, she assured Solin that the Le Bras, a family of merchants and explorers, had always been interested in meeting different people with different points of view.

On his return to Paris, Richard sent a very flippant email to Gérard congratulating him on his choice of wife, and hoping Sarah would transform his life as she'd just done Richard's.

She already has, Gérard thought to himself. *I can remember life before Sarah, alone in the bleakness of Grandfather's house, no family except my brother, no aim other than work, no likelihood of any change in future. Sarah's a catalyst; I suspect she always has been. She's even exorcised Grandfather. She's settled my nephew in this commune where his family will be happier and where I can watch his children grow. She's given me Charles as the intelligent protégé I couldn't make of Erwan. She's breathing new life into my company administration and prospects, and I don't think it's hubris to notice how happy she is in herself. The death of that salaud James Pullen has given all of us a second chance in life.*

***

Charles' thoughts were similar to Gérard's. In mid-December the deed of sale for his flat had been formally signed by Charles, Sarah and the vendor in front of the notary, and Charles took over the keys. He'd found it difficult to decide on the initial furniture he needed to buy, so Sarah had taken him to the warehouses, told him what to order, and arranged for delivery on the day of purchase of the flat. On that day Charles took two journeys to transport all his belongings from the apart-hotel in the office car, and a third to stock the kitchen with essential food.

But he didn't immediately start unpacking. He felt the need to stand quite still on his balcony, drinking in the wide view and the feeling of freedom which came with it, coming to terms with the change in his circumstances, and quietly acknowledging what he owed to Sarah and to Gérard. Because in this flat, in this city, in his work and in the Brittany he'd loved as soon as he'd seen it, he'd found for the first time in his life somewhere where he belonged.

30

The Lemestre wedding had been booked for the twenty-seventh of December. Sarah woke to find Gérard watching her in smiling adoration. "This is our day for celebration," he said, "and I'm rejoicing with my whole heart. You're the most wonderful gift I've ever been given."

"Gérard," Sarah sighed happily, "I do love you."

"That's the first time you've actually said it."

"I think it all the time. But I can't talk poetry in the way you do."

"You just stick to the facts? If that's one, you've made my heart sing."

They ate a lazy breakfast before dressing. Gérard chose a silver-grey suit with a turquoise silk shirt. Sarah had taken her turquoise outfit to a silk embroidery specialist recommended by Agnes, whose Breton wool embroidery wouldn't suit such fine material. For the first time Gérard saw that the back of the loose coat had been delicately stitched with two over-life-size swallows flying towards each other, beautifully detailed with wing and back feathers in shades of dark blue, white rumps, red foreheads, pale beaks and long, long trailing tail feathers. On the sleeveless dress two smaller swallows had been embroidered in silhouette on the right shoulder, flying upwards.

Gérard recognised the harbingers of spring, the symbols of new beginnings, the flight which lifts the hearts of its beholders, and realised that there was more poetry in his prosaic Sarah than she knew.

The town hall of Saint Malo is in the citadel inside the old walled town. Gérard had ordered a limousine, and they passed through the massive arch of the town gates with five minutes to spare. The car stopped opposite the Citadel entrance. Gérard alighted and opened the door for Sarah. As soon as the bride set foot on the path, the music began. The traditional group of musicians which Bretons call a 'fanfare', naturally headed by Jean-Yves Lagarde playing accordion, led the way playing Breton wedding anthems. There were two accordionists, three flautists and two violinists, including both Chouchen and Gali.

The procession filed into the wedding room, followed by the family guests, and the musicians stood against the back wall. But instead of taking her seat, the bride broke all protocol by crossing the room to embrace Gali. "I'm so glad to see you again," she said. "You're playing beautifully."

"I work very hard," Gali said firmly. "I know Breton dances. I know Irish jigs. I know French and geography and mathematics as well." Next to him Chouchen rolled his eyes to the ceiling. Laughing, Gérard shook hands with all the musicians, reminded Sarah that they had a wedding scheduled, and led her to her seat so that it could begin.

Once everyone had signed the official forms, the mayor made a speech which ended in wishing the bridal couple a long life together filled with every happiness, and everyone applauded.

The whole party, including the mayor and his wife, then drove on to the Hotel Château Malouine, where the guests already assembled gave the wedding party a round of applause as they entered, preceded by the joyful noise of the fanfare. Taking their places on the top table were Gérard and Sarah, Mathieu and Agnes, Severine and Nicolas, Charles, Deborah and Clark. The rest of the huge room was covered in round eight-seater tables, and it was full.

Most of Gérard's wide-spread family had come, as had the social club, the managers of Gérard's local business interests, some of his other business acquaintances, the mayor, two prefects, the whole of the Tourism Office with their families, the administrators of the pensioners' centre and Sarah's Qi Gong class. Realising that Deborah and Clark would be lonely English speakers marooned in a sea of French, Sarah had invited the English holiday lets group as well.

Over the first course Sarah said to Gérard, "I didn't ask why you chose this hotel. It's not on our list of joint investments, but you must have some interest in it?"

"I'm the guarantor for the owner's bank loan. I funded him when he started from nothing, but this is his third venture after two successes, and this time the banks were happy to lend."

"So we're making it less likely that you pay the guarantee?"

"That's highly unlikely. The hotel's fully booked for the next conference season. But it's hardly good business to publicise his rivals, is it?"

"Is the manager one of his own guests?"

"No, he insisted on overseeing the event himself. He's the one in the uniform coat who welcomed you in. But his wife and her sister and his children are somewhere in the room. I'll take you round and introduce you to everyone this afternoon, at least until we run out of stamina."

Following the mercifully short speeches, the tables on the dance floor were moved out of the room, and a group of musicians took up residence on the platform in one corner. The first tune they played was the traditional waltz, and Gérard took Sarah on one turn of the floor before the rest of the guests joined in. The event turned into a social gathering as guests began to move around, talking to or dancing with the others. Business managers commenced talking shop with their fellows, especially those they were meeting for the first time. Small children began to play with children they'd never met before, and younger members of the Lemestre clan cautiously embarked on relationships with the cousins who would figure largely in their lives.

There was a pause in the music as the small band of musicians playing conventional dances were succeeded by two accordionists, two violinists and a clarinettist playing Breton Fest Noz dances. The Saint-Edern Social Club immediately formed a ring. Charles walked up to the contingent of English ex-pats and invited Annie Chevening to join in. She picked up the dance easily. They made a pair for the next set dance. When the next ring formed, Paula Morton and Beth Farley joined in of their own accord, and for the next pair dance Philippe Poisson daringly asked Janet Rowley to be his partner. The major function of a wedding celebration is to blur boundaries and establish ties among all present. At the end of the dance, Janet said, "Merci, Monsieur Poisson, c'était très agréable," surprising herself as much as him.

For the rest of the afternoon and evening, Gérard worked his way round the room deliberately ensuring that Sarah met everyone connected to their list of joint investments, and every partner of Participations Lemestre. Very often an introduction was followed by an animated discussion between a business manager and Sarah, which Gérard watched with a proud smile. His new partner had a gift for asking pertinent questions and going straight to the heart of the subject under discussion. She didn't always share the conventional viewpoint, but her common sense and determination were unmissable.

As they moved round the room, she gained respect in her own right, not just as Gérard's wife. At intervals Gérard took her on to the dance floor to take the opportunity to tell her how she filled his heart and how much he valued her in his life.

For their honeymoon, Gérard had booked into a New Year party at a château in Finistère. The old defensive building had been mellowly converted into a splendid private residence in the nineteenth century and recently re-converted into a small luxury hotel. It boasted a celebrity chef for this occasion and had attracted an interesting mix of guests from different walks of life and different parts of France.

The château was well-placed for exploring the tourist venues in southern Finistère. Encouraged by the mild sunshine, Gérard and Sarah lunched in Pont l'Abbé, in Concarneau, in Pont-Aven and in Quimper, enjoying museums and galleries and churches and lighthouses and ports, and in the evening they found pleasant company among their fellow guests. On the midnight before the New Year, after a six-course virtuoso dinner, the fireworks, shooting brilliant colour into the clear air, delighted everyone.

But on the first morning of January the legendary Breton mist arrived; at last the right day for visiting the Pointe du Raz. Gérard drove westward, and parked on the shore of the little bay between the Raz and the Pointe du Van. They stood together above the beach, looking westward directly into the saturated breeze, Sarah snugly held in Gérard's encircling arms.

It wasn't exactly raining, but the air was thick and wet. The forbidding headland of the Pointe du Raz was only just visible at the southern end of the bay. But good high surf had built up, and to ensure that this precious gift wasn't wasted, two young men in wetsuits were spending New Year's Day zipping in and out of the waves, balancing upright on their surfboards with the lazy ease of long practice.

"I always come here whenever I'm within reach of it," Gérard said, "because I find this place fascinating. The Pointe du Raz isn't in truth the westernmost headland in Brittany, but it's far more spectacular than the one which is. That powerful dark water rolls straight in from the Atlantic Ocean. We're facing due west, and at the end of a fine day the sunset on the opposite horizon is unforgettable.

"But on days like this it's the old legends that come to mind. This is the Bay of the Dead, the beach where all Breton souls come when they die. It's said that at midnight, on nights when there is no moon, a black ship with black sails enters the bay. It has no visible crew and its presence is identifiable only by its wake glittering in the starlight. It comes to offer the souls a passage to Heaven, the Isle of the Blessed, far out to the west on the other side of the ocean."

"But the other side of the Atlantic is America," Sarah said flatly. "I wouldn't consider Manhattan to be the Isle of the Blessed."

Gérard was delighted with the prosaic response. "It depends where the ship makes its landfall. There's a story told about Saint Brendan, who sailed around the coast of Ireland in an ocean-going coracle with his monks as crew. One day the boat was blown off course and swept westwards for days, but eventually it beached on a marvellous island. When the boat was re-stocked with fruit, fish and water, Brendan sailed east back home, where the scribes recorded his detailed description of the wonders of Paradise, the Isle of the Blessed. Unfortunately, Brendan hadn't seen Heaven; he'd just washed up on Jamaica."

Sarah laughed. "I couldn't imagine you believing all that."

Gérard swung her round to face him, delighting in the droplets of water clinging to silver tendrils of her hair. Like Brittany itself, she was beautiful in the rain, and he rejoiced at the way that her total lack of romance hid her passionate nature. "I almost wish I did believe the legends," he said, "because then I'd know that if I waited here until you joined me, we'd enter Heaven together and stay together for eternity. But why should I bother about the next life, dear heart, when you've given me Paradise in this one?"